CW01645417

Raine, Raine, RUN AWAY

INDIA TUNGATE

Raine, Raine, Run Away

The Covewood Series
Book I

India Tungate

ISBN:

Ebook - 979-8-9901699-0-6

Paperback - 979-8-9901699-1-3

Cover Design by Ink and Laurel

Copy and Proofread Editing by Jenn Lockwood Editing

Instagram: @Indiatungateauthor

Created with Vellum

To Nana,
You're the person who inspired me to become a writer and always encouraged me to chase my dreams no matter what they were. I wish that I could've had your guidance with this book, just like you used to do with my (super cringy) stories in the past. Unfortunately, your death is a huge part of what inspired this book. There's pieces of you weaved within these pages and because of that, this book is my love letter to you. Raine and Ryland's story helped me to heal parts of my grief from losing you, creating beauty from ashes., and I know you'd be proud of that.
I miss you and will love you forever.

May the God of hope fill you with all joy and peace as you trust in him, so that you may overflow with hope by the power of the Holy Spirit.

— Romans 15:13

Contents

Raine, Raine, Run Away Playlist

I am the type of writer who enjoys listening to music as I write. Music is my biggest inspiration for writing and it's fun to have songs that remind me of my characters. For those who enjoy listening to playlists that go along with a book, this is for you. I hope you enjoy listening to these songs.

1 Lost Without You - Daniel Robinson

2 Landslide - Robyn Sherwell

3 Sweet Heat Lightning - Gregory Alan Isakov

4 All That Really Matters (stripped version) - Illenium, Teddy Swims

5 Come Back To Me - David Cook

6 Visiting Hours - Ed Sheeran

7 Heal - Amadeus

8 I Knew I Loved You - Savage Garden

9 The Way It Was - Backstreet Boys

10 Dancing In The Sky - Liv Harland

11 Return To Me - Radio Company
12 Its Always Been You - Phil Wickham
13 Pieces (hushed) - Andrew Belle
14 Goodbye To You - Michelle Branch
15 Dare You To Move - Switchfoot
16 You And Me - Lifehouse
17 Heartbreak Warfare - John Mayer
18 Glitter - Nicolina
19 Peace (acoustic) - Anna Golden
20 Like The Raine - Clint Black
21 Up In Fire - McKenna Breinholt
22 Nobody Knows - Rayne Johnson
23 Forget Me (acoustic) - Bailey Rushlow
24 Biblical (acoustic) - Calum Scott
25 The House That Built Me - Miranda Lambert
26 Paradise (feat. *NSYNC) - Justin Timberlake
27 Whole Heart - Jervis Campbell
28 Be Slow - Harrison Storm
29 Oceans (Spirit Lead Me) - Liv Harland
30 Love Story - Taylor Swift

The full playlist is on Spotify.

Raine, Raine, Run Away Playlist

Author's Note

Dear Reader,

First of all, thank you for picking up this book and giving it a chance. It truly means the world to me. This book helped me with the healing of my own grief after I lost my grandmother. A lot of what I personally experienced after her loss is weaved within these pages. I hope that this story can bring healing, comfort, and a warm hug to my readers.

While this story is a lighthearted romance, it also deals with some heavier topics. I wanted to give you a warning before you chose to read further. I pray that I have portrayed these topics with sensitivity and care for the characters and for each of you. I want to take care of your heart and it's important to me that you know the general content so you can respect your boundaries.

Content Warning:

- Mentions of parental abandonment and physical abuse
- Alcohol abuse
- Grief of family members (heart attack on page)
- Mentions of postpartum depression

Chapter One

Now

Raine

H*onk.*

Honk.

Splash.

I close my eyes and twist, feeling my entire backside get hit with cold water. I inhale sharply as a chill seeps through my clothes and onto my skin. *And my heart.*

"Are you kidding me?" I throw my hands into the air and shout toward the yellow taxi that ran through a puddle, ruining the expensive dress I have on. Luckily, I was able to turn just in time and protect the camera in my hands from getting wet.

"As if today could get any worse!" I add, not caring about the side-eyes I'm receiving from a few people who speed-walk past me. No one stops to see if I'm okay or offers to help. It always seems like the people here in the city only care about what is going on in their own lives. I'm just the background noise.

Back in my hometown, there are no rude taxi drivers, and if there were, I could guarantee more than just one person would have stopped what they were doing to make sure I was okay.

The people of Covewood go out of their way to provide a warm comfort that clearly the people of Rockdale know nothing about.

But I've chosen not to live in Covewood, I remind myself. Lately, I've caught myself comparing my small hometown to the overly populated city of Rockdale, where I have lived for the last ten years. I chose to make this city into my new home because, at the time, I needed to hide away in a place that was the complete opposite of where I grew up, no matter how much it hurt leaving behind the people I love.

Covewood, Kentucky is full of rolling green hills, stretches of farmlands, and a giant lake. Rockdale, Virginia, however, is covered in tall buildings, metallic and salt-scented air, and beaches littered with people and trash. Side by side, these places are obverse, and that used to appeal to me.

But not anymore. Somewhere along the way, something has changed. *I* have changed. And admitting that truth is terrifying. Because the last thing I want is to return home and confront my past. I'd rather escape among the sea of constant moving feet, bottle up my feelings, and bury them with the rest of my skeletons.

I shake away my spiraling thoughts and instead focus on wiping away the small rocks and smudges from my backside.

"Ew," a blonde woman snarls as she jumps away from me. She lifts her hands, the expression on her face studying me as if I have a contagious disease. "You just flung some of that ick onto my brand-new Prada heels!"

"Boo hoo, lady! I'm the one who had my favorite Max Mara dress ruined by some—"

"Whatever!" she hisses and stomps down the street.

I squint my eyes and watch her, mentally wishing she would roll her ankle or break her ugly heels and fall down. The dark thought is enough to snap me out of my angry bubble, and I realize how hypocritical I am being. I quickly ask God to forgive me for thinking of harm happening to someone.

This isn't like me. How in the world have I gotten to this place in my life?

Unhappy.

Unsatisfied.

And apparently, a total grouch.

Here I am, blaming the people around me when I know not all people who live in the city are self-absorbed. I have met some kind people since moving here. I, personally, seem to have lost the humbleness I had grown up with. If only I could go back in time and change my choices from ten years ago. Would life be better? But the thing is, it wasn't *just* my choices that brought me here.

I weave my way through the crowd of people on the sidewalk. The noise of the city fades back into existence, becoming louder the farther I walk amongst these strangers. My ears are overwhelmed by blaring horns, clicking heels against concrete, and everyday chatter. It causes me to feel overstimulated and crave a breath of fresh air.

Unfortunately, there is no fresh air in the middle of the city. Smothering smoke and body odor cling to the atmosphere instead. The tall buildings block any breeze that could possibly swoop in and whisk away the stench. I miss the smell of freshly cut grass, blooming flowers, and murky lake water.

I miss Covewood.

Relief washes over me as I spot my white Honda Accord and quickly escape inside. Thankfully, I have a spare beach towel in the backseat that I use to protect the driver's seat from my soaked dress. Once I shut the car door, the busy sounds of the city outside set my teeth on edge. I need to go somewhere quiet, somewhere I can gather my composure instead of returning to the office like I had originally planned.

As I reach for my keys, I notice the tremble in my hands. Inhaling a deep breath, I squeeze my fingers together in an attempt to stop the shaking. This is how I know the *old* Raine is starting to seep through. *The shaking.* Always with the unsteadiness of my hands. The quivers give me away.

I look into my rearview mirror and use a makeup remover cloth to wipe away the splash of dirt from the side of my face and the smudge of mascara under my eyes. Taking the clip out of my hair, I run my fingers through my long dirty-blonde strands before replacing the clip. As I stare at my reflection, I give myself a pep talk.

"You're okay. It's not the end of the world. No need to have an anxiety episode today. You've come so far. You're not that weak little girl anymore. You're a strong, capable—"

Honk.

Honk.

Honk.

I jump in my seat as a nearby car blares its horn, and I'm close to losing it. I swallow the acid that is rising in my throat, tuck my camera into its padded bag, and turn my key. I cannot get out of this city fast enough. As I drive down the street, I watch as the sun drops slowly, casting sunbeams in every direction while illuminating the city before me.

The buildings start to dwindle and become smaller the closer I get to the beach. I roll down the windows. The air is slightly chilly in late March, and I welcome the refreshing salty scent. Instantly, I feel my anxiety begin to dissipate. Twenty minutes later, I park my car and walk to the small bridge that leads to my favorite spot on the beach. As soon as my feet touch the sand, I take off my heels and wiggle my toes into its gripping sensation.

I exhale the pent-up air in my lungs and embrace the feeling of earth beads massaging the soles of my feet. The sand wedges itself into my toenails, dusts my skin, and coats the bottom of my feet like butter on toast. My stress begins to melt away with just a simple touch from the earth.

I walk along the beach for a moment, saying a thankful prayer that only a few people have gathered here this evening.

The wind tugs at the clip in my hair, so I reach up and free my waves. The briny scent grows stronger as I march my way toward the water and enjoy the coldness of the ocean as it rolls upon the shore and onto my feet and legs.

Seagulls chirp above me, and it catches my attention. I watch as one swoops down and snags something, a French fry I suspect, and takes off toward the sky again. A few others follow him closely, squawking in protest, and shove against him. The French fry falls to the ground only for another to dive and clamp its beak against it.

Lately, I have felt like that French fry, certain people in my life swooping in like the birds, nipping pieces of me for their own pleasure, until there is nothing left of me to devour.

It was good for a while, being here. I didn't have anyone who could hurt me anymore, nor did I give anyone the chance to. But as time goes on, it's like I can hear myself from far away, begging for permission to come back. I'm beginning to feel incomplete. Restless. As if something very essential is lacking in my life, and I am in a perpetual state of searching for it, even though I don't know what or *who* it is that I am looking for.

Acting on instinct, I reach for my cell phone and open up Facebook. I type in the name *Ryland Quinn* and click on his profile. He has it set to private, but I'm able to see his profile photos. I scroll through them for a while until I come upon a few photographs of the two of us together. I pause on an image of him and I sitting on the porch of my grandparents' home, both of us laughing, his arm around my shoulders as I lean into him. I'm looking toward the camera, but his eyes are glued on me.

My mind always seems to find a way back to *him*, especially whenever I am near water. Many of my summers as a teenager were spent with Ryland. Whenever we weren't at my grandparents' farm, we were swimming in the lake by his house, jumping off the little wooden dock built by his grandfather, taking rides side by side in a pedal boat, and witnessing breathtaking sunsets together in each other's arms. The ocean may be bigger, sandier, and smell of salt, but the second I hear the crashing waves and feel the water touch my skin, Ryland takes over my thoughts.

Maybe that's why I love coming here. I have made sure to surround myself with things and people that are the opposite of him in hopes of trying to forget about how he broke my heart all those years ago. The water is the only thing that connects me to him now.

A ping on my phone grabs my attention, and I welcome the distraction, especially when I see it's a message from my best friend, Olivia.

LIV

Good evening. Don't forget to FaceTime me later for our annual Bridesmaids rewatch. I'm making a homemade pizza and—ouch, my toe. Why did I have to drop my favorite mug onto my toe? Son of a biscuit that hurts. I forgot I was voice texting this, so enjoy this hot mess of a message because I am too lazy to go back and type this out myself. Love you.

I laugh out loud as I walk over to a spot that is far enough from the loud sound of crashing waves so I can call her. I take a seat, not caring that I'm still wet and the sand will stick to me, and hit the green icon to FaceTime her. A wave of relief washes over me as Olivia's beautiful face appears on the screen.

"My toe is fine, I promise!" She giggles.

Our connection isn't very clear. She freezes for a few seconds, and I hear the sound of clinking dishes, an opening door, and her feet shuffling. Finally, her face becomes clearer as she makes her way inside her house.

"Wow, you look like crap. Is everything okay?"

She is always one to be honest. "Yeah, I had a crappy day at work, and then some jerk taxi driver gave me an unwanted shower, which sent me spiraling into the darkness of my thoughts and debating all my life decisions. You know, a typical Monday," I say and cross my legs to get more comfortable.

"I'm sorry, honey," she says with a sympathetic smile. "What happened at work? Did Mr. Brown-Noser do something today?"

I work for a local magazine company as one of the head marketers in their digital content department. *The Rockdale Journal* has grown since I joined years ago. My team and I now have to manage the website, Instagram pages, and a newly developed podcast. Magazines aren't what they used to be. Everything is slowly becoming digital, and the job keeps me busy.

What drew me to this career was my love for photography. It often feels like that is the only piece of my old self that I decided to keep. Photography has always been my escape, a chance at self-expression, my way of being understood.

Thomas, aka Mr. Brown-Noser, a nickname Olivia chose, wants nothing more than to steal my job. His purpose in life has been to try and outdo me each day, and today, he won.

"My bosses picked his proposal over mine." I roll my eyes at the reminder.

"What happened with yours?" she asks before lifting a mug to her lips, a tea bag string hanging off the side. I notice it is the mug I sent her as a Christmas gift last year that reads *"Distance is just a test to see how far love can travel"* and has a picture of Kentucky and Virginia with hearts connecting the two states.

I exhale. "They didn't understand my idea, I guess. Or didn't care to. I'm tired of focusing on the corporate businesses in the city. By doing this, we're hurting the smaller businesses, and I suggested we start highlighting them instead. It feels like —" The rest of my words lodge in my throat.

"Like what?" Olivia asks, bringing the phone closer to her face. I can see the tan freckles across her nose, the flecks of gold within her green eyes, the light scar just below the right side of her jaw where she tripped on the playground in fifth grade and a wood chip stabbed her there.

She's the one person, besides my grandparents, that I can trust with my whole heart. But saying these words out loud makes it become more real. I swallow against the discomfort before I continue, "Like I'm wasting my time here. My bosses use me for everything *they* need, but when it comes to what I want to offer the company, they keep turning me down and going with Thomas' ideas. When will my work mean something again?"

She tsks and sets her mug down. "Your work has always been too great for them. Why don't you quit already? You've been miserable for the past two years."

I give her a knowing look, but she ignores it as she always does. "I'm just saying."

"I know." I revert my eyes to the beach ahead, watching the waves crash, wishing my best friend was sitting beside me instead of being on a phone screen. "Enough about me. How was your day?"

"Oh, you know...same ol', same ol'. I managed to catch up on all my orders and baked a new scone recipe, which did not turn out as delicious as I had hoped, but I'll get it there. Luke stopped by for lunch. And later I have a date!" She practically squeals the last part.

"Who is the newest victim?" I grin with the tease.

She squints in disapproval before continuing. "Some guy that my neighbor Edna swore to me, and I quote, '*is a hottie with a body*.' It's untelling with that woman. The last two dates she's set me up on turned out to be a disaster, but maybe the third time's the charm."

She shrugs, and I release a laugh. "Please keep Luke on speed-dial just in case."

"Of course! It's one of the perks of having a bestie who's a cop." She eyes me for a moment before adding, "Speaking of dating, are things still weird between you and Samuel?"

I exhale a second time. The longest relationship I have had since leaving Covewood was with a wonderful guy named

Samuel. We first met at a local coffee shop three years ago. He was standing in front of me in line and paid for my drink. He then asked if he could sit down with me, and we ended up spending most of our Saturday morning getting to know each other. Before we said our goodbyes, he asked if he could take me out on a date sometime. I said yes, mainly out of loneliness.

His company became comforting, especially since he was the complete opposite of Ryland in many ways. I liked the way Samuel looked at me with admiration and how he took my mind away from everything else. He helped me feel like I could become whomever I needed to be. And the first few years with him were blissful. I was swept away by how light life felt with him around.

It was easy to become someone who was spontaneous and flirty, someone who cared more about her looks and spent way too much money on clothes than I'd like to admit, all to keep him impressed—maybe myself too.

My favorite thing about Samuel is that he never pushed me to talk about my past, and I did the same for him. Our past never needed to be a part of our relationship. He cared for me as I was, and that was what I needed in my life at the time—until it started to feel fake. We somehow lost our spark.

"Yeah. I haven't heard from him since the breakup," I say.

On our three-year anniversary, Samuel asked me to move in with him, and I turned him down. Afterward, he became more reserved. For weeks, he didn't bring it up again, and neither did I. We were both ignoring the issue, and as badly as I wanted to run away from it, after a while, it finally got to him, and he broke up with me.

Running away from problems has always been what I do best. And it has always resulted in some sort of destruction in my life.

"It was probably for the best," I add, and her expression turns into pity.

"You were with Samuel for three years. Don't you think

moving in together should have been the next step for you both? I hate that you've always lived alone in Rockdale."

"I had roommates before," I snap, feeling defensive all of a sudden.

She lifts one brow, disapproving of my tone, and says, "Don't look at me like that. Besides the two roommates you had in college, you've been *alone*. You never dated a guy longer than a year until Samuel came along. I kind of thought he was the one."

The one is exaggerating a bit, but I understand where she is coming from. The reason why I didn't date anyone for a long time was because I wasn't willing to chance getting attached. I keep sturdy walls around my heart, and the moment things shift into something more serious, I run.

Samuel was the first man to take his time with me and keep the past where I wanted it to be—*nonexistent*. It was a relief being with someone who seemed just as guarded as I was, which was why I was so shocked when he asked me to move in with him. I panicked, basically shouting the word *no* inside the fancy restaurant, earning a few scolding and wide-eyed looks. I was mortified. And so was Samuel.

"You're one to talk. You basically have the same dating history as me and have been living alone since college too," I reply, earning an eye roll from my best friend.

"Okay, you got me on the dating part, but in my defense, the guys around here just aren't marriage material, but I've been willing to open my heart to them, unlike you. You need to stop being so protective of yourself, Raine. You're never going to find someone until you let go of the past and move on. You deserve to be in love and to be happy." Her face softens, a knowing look crossing her face, and it stings.

I've been in love before, and I have no intentions of going through a heartbreak again. I'm not sure I *can* love again. It's as if my heart broke ten years ago and didn't heal properly.

Olivia walks through her living room into her brightly decorated kitchen and sets her phone on the windowsill above her sink. The sounds of running water and her clanking mug echo from the phone's speaker. She studies the mug for a second and holds it up to the camera.

"This love should travel back home soon," she proclaims, and a sinking feeling grows in the pit of my stomach. "I miss you."

"I miss you more," I admit with a huff.

"I whipped up a homemade detoxing soup and took it over to the farm this morning. I hope it helps your Mamaw get her strength back. I also took a basket of chocolate chip muffins. However, your Papaw doesn't know that I made them with organic ingredients and no sugar. I hope he can't tell the difference." She grins as she starts gathering ingredients. The woman never stops baking.

"Oh, he will." I laugh, and she does the same. I called my grandparents this morning, like I always do, but Papaw said that Mamaw wasn't feeling like herself, that she was possibly getting over a cold caused by the seasons changing. I hate not being there to help them out, but it brings me comfort knowing I have friends who care for them.

"Thank you for checking on them often and for sneaking in some healthy foods. I don't know what I would do without you, Liv."

"I mean, your life would definitely be boring and less colorful." She chuckles with a flip of her bright-red hair. I laugh as flour flies into the air and sticks to her freckled cheeks.

"I love you," I say softly and blow a kiss to the screen.

"I love you too. I better get ready for my date. I'll let you know when I'm headed home after so we can watch *Bridesmaids*!" she adds, and I'm already looking forward to it.

"Okay. Have a good time," I assure her before we end our conversation.

Once her face is off the screen, I can feel the trembling in my hands return and the sting of tears in my eyes. I lock my phone and see my reflection within the glass. I do look like crap. My hair is a mess from the breeze. I grab the clip I slipped into my pocket and pull my hair back and put it back into place. I wipe away the few tears that slip down my cheeks and inhale a deep breath of the salty air.

When I ran away from home, I had no guilt about my choice. I truly believed that leaving was for the best for everyone, including my grandparents. But today, I'm not so sure. If I was there with them, I would be able to help take care of them.

A few times a year, I travel to Covewood to visit them. I make sure to avoid going into town, thankful that my grandparents' farmhouse sits on the very edge of town and close to the interstate exit. It's easy to slip in and slip out without certain people knowing I'm there. I still haven't seen Olivia's home in person or stopped downtown to visit my other childhood best friend, Luke, while he's working. I most definitely stay away from the familiar cabins on the lake and the old house I used to live in, where my mother still resides.

I ask my two best friends to visit me at the farm when I'm there, making them promise not to tell anyone when I visit. Sometimes, my grandparents, Olivia, and Luke will travel to Rockdale to spend time with me here. However, my grandparents' visits have grown less frequent as the years gone by. And because of this, my guilt has grown, even more as I notice my grandparents' aging increasing with each visit.

I'm missing out on so much with them, and I know they won't be with me forever. I will be devastated if something happens to either of them. And if something does, I will be miles away. I didn't think about this when I ran.

I'm left feeling more unnerved than I was hours before. The roar of the ocean does nothing to comfort me. Something feels off, the tightening deep in my core agreeing with my thoughts.

I look around and see an older couple walking along the shoreline, a young child tossing sand into the air as his mother lies on a beach towel, and a man reading a book several feet from me. I take a deep breath, bring my hands together, bow my head, and close my eyes.

God, I know it's been a while since I last prayed to you, and I'm sorry for that. I promise to make a better habit of it. I'm begging you to please watch over my grandparents, especially my Mamaw, who isn't feeling well. I want to ask you to please heal her. And please let them forgive me for not being there. Amen.

I sit in the sand for a few moments, trying my best to envision my Mamaw healthy and vibrant. Once I open my eyes, I stare toward the ocean for a long moment, lost in thought. I sense movement and blink to clear my vision. Time passes, and the movement reappears. I watch as a dolphin bops up for a breath, a puff of water and air shoots into the sky, and then it sinks back into the curtain of water. I watch as the dolphin does this several times, and a wave of peace washes over me. A peace that I know only God can bring to my heart.

The trembling in my hands stops. The guilt within my heart evaporates. And a calm takes over my body like a warm hug.

Mamaw is going to be okay.

Chapter Two

Fourteen Years Before

Ryland

I've spent a total of sixteen hours in this tiny car. Outside of the car window, I've watched as the land has changed multiple times from tall buildings, dusty flatlands, rolling mountains, bright-green farmlands, to endless rows of trees passing by. I would have enjoyed the change of scenery if I didn't have to also endure Mom's horrible taste in music or my little brother's constant fidgeting and humming. I'm about to lose my mind.

"Zane!" I mutter under my breath, making sure to scold him quietly without Mom hearing. "Stop."

He sticks his tongue out at me like a toddler instead of the eleven-year-old that he is. He stops humming, and for a blissful five seconds, I enjoy the calm. *Tap, tap, tap.* Zane is now drumming on the book that's sitting in his lap, and I bite the inside of my lip to keep from yelling at him again. Instead, I shove his shoulder and give him a look that says, *I will break your fingers if you do not stop.*

He seems to take the hint and turns his face toward the window. I let out an exhale and peek toward the rearview mirror. I was about to ask Mom if we are there yet, but I shut my mouth the moment I notice silent tears streaming down her face.

It's not just Zane and me leaving behind the only home we've ever known, our friends, and our father. She is leaving things behind as well. I often forget that she is hurting too, but even so, I'm still annoyed with her decision.

She wipes away the tears before letting out a loud exhale and looks at me through the rearview mirror. I quickly dodge her sight because I'm upset with her for making us move multiple states away. However, there's also a part of me that understands why she chose this for us. I'm just too stubborn to admit that she is *somewhat* right.

She announces, "We're almost there, boys."

Thank you, Jesus!

I keep my eyes on the trees passing by. We turn onto a dirt road that cuts through the dense forest. Beams of light peek through the leaves and dance against the ground as we move by. I watch as squirrels chase one another up trees, as birds swoop from branch to branch, and I spot a deer jumping over a log. I'd find it beautiful if I wasn't so torn up about being here.

"Listen, I want you both to be on your best behavior. Promise me that you will be?" Mom asks after she turns the radio down.

"I promise," Zane says in a small voice, and I manage a *humph* in reply.

"I know this is a lot to take in, but I promise this is going to be such a wonderful fresh start. You'll get to spend your summers swimming in the lake and winters in a cozy cabin. Your Nan can bake like no other, and your Pops can teach you so much, like fishing, hunting, even building something on your own. He will be good for you boys. You both need a positive male influence in your life." It sounds like she is trying to convince herself of these things, which only deepens my anger.

"The last thing I want is another male to try to influence me. I'm fine on my own," I snap and cross my arms.

Guilt finds the pits of my stomach, turning it sour for being snippy toward her, but I can't help it. I have always spoken my feelings out loud. It became a big issue between my father and me, my mouth landing me a few yellings and punishments. It's always been a challenge for me to bite my tongue.

"I know you think you're a grown man, Ryland, but you're only fifteen years old. You've hardly had any experiences that can help build you into a man. You'll thank me one day for moving us to Covewood. Trust me."

I huff and squeeze my arms tighter around myself. My gut tries to tell me that she is probably right, but my heart is too upset at being taken away from my home. She's making us live in the middle of nowhere. All we will be learning is how to survive in the wild, and this is not what I signed up for. Couldn't we have just moved houses instead of across the country?

"Mom, did you like going to school here?" Zane asks beside me, his fingers drumming on his book again. I grind my teeth together in an attempt to not slap at his hands.

"I did. Everyone here has always been kind. You'll be making new friends before you know it."

"I don't want any new friends. The friends that I have are just fine," I add.

Mom's shoulders sag, and she gives me a warning look through the mirror. "Ryland, you were hanging out with the wrong crowd and headed down a bad path. We've had this discussion already. You will make some really good friends here if you give them a chance. The people here are—"

"Hillbillies?" I offer and instantly regret my choice of words. I wince at the look Mom gives me. She stomps on the brakes, sending Zane and me bumping our heads against the back of the seats. I rub my forehead and dare to look up at

Mom's heated gaze. She twists in her seat until she is facing us both.

"If I hear you call anyone that name or any cruel names at all, I will take your phone away and probably some other things I'll figure out to punish you with. Do you hear me?"

"You're already punishing me by bringing me to the middle of nowhere."

"This isn't nowhere. This is where *I* grew up. This is where Pops and Nan live. And if you could just give it a chance—"

She closes her eyes and pinches the bridge of her nose. Beside me, Zane crinkles his nose and shakes his head. *Such a mama's boy.* He always takes her side. What happened to having each other's backs in this? I know he didn't want to move away just as much as I didn't. *Traitor.*

Mom exhales, and I glance up at her. Her tears have returned. The sight punches me right in the gut. She has always tried her best to hide her emotions. I always thought it was so she could appear strong for us. But after we left my father and lived in a hotel for three weeks, I saw her cry more than I ever have in my fifteen years of life.

I want to tell her that I'm sorry, but my pride gets in the way, so I don't.

"This move isn't easy for me either. You're not the only one leaving behind a life. But what you don't understand—because *you're* the teenager and *I'm* the mother—is that this move is worth you being mad at me because I am protecting my boys by removing us from the awful situation we were in. What kind of mother would I be had I let us stay any longer? I regret staying with your father for as long as I did. Would you prefer that we had continued to allow your father to treat us the way that he did?"

No.

"Would you want to end up in juvenile detention like the boys you were hanging out with?"

No.

"Don't you want to live a peaceful life? For the three of us to be happier?"

Yes.

"Just..." she continues with a shaky voice. "Just give this a try, okay? That's all I ask."

I nod and look back out toward the forest, unable to stomach the tears on her face. I see out of the corner of my eye that she watches me for a moment and pats my brother on the leg before turning forward in her seat and continuing down the gravel road.

After a few minutes, I see some cabins up ahead. There is a set of three. The smallest cabin is closer to the edge of the woods and overlooks the lake. The middle cabin, the one my Mom points to and says we will be living in, is nestled back in the woods. The larger cabin sits up on the top of the hill, which is where my grandparents live.

As Mom pulls the car into the driveway of our new home, an elderly couple, who I quickly recognize as Pops and Nan, is sitting on the front porch. They wave to us with bright smiles on their faces. Once or twice a year, we spent time with our grandparents either making the trip here or them coming to us. They always made sure to call us multiple times during the week. But for the last year, my father's drinking issues increased, and so did his need to control us, which included him not wanting my grandparents involved in our lives.

As soon as the engine is off, I shuffle out of my seat as quickly as I can, and without a glance toward the cabin or at my grandparents, I stomp my way toward the lake. I take a deep breath, already feeling a bit better with the distance between myself and them.

I can taste the freshness of the crisp air. I faintly hear a small rustle in the surrounding greenery and the roar of a motor from a nearby boat. Once I find a dock at the edge of the trees, I walk across its creaky wood and take a seat at the edge. I welcome loneliness like an old friend.

A few minutes tick by before I sense that I am no longer alone. I turn and see Pops walking across the dock, and he takes a seat next to me. We keep our attention toward the lake and our words to ourselves. It's awkward sitting here in silence—for a moment, that is—and then it becomes somewhat comforting. *Finally*, someone in my family who understands the importance of being quiet.

Pops looks over at me, and the left side of his lips slightly turn into a grin, raising the edge of his thick white mustache. "I've never taken you fishing, have I?"

I contemplate this for a second, thrown off by the random question. I shrug my shoulders, which has his grin growing into a full smile revealing bright white teeth. "No," I admit.

He pats my knee, which causes me to jerk. The touch is affectionate—something I'm not used to from my father. Pops seems to notice as he removes his hand quickly and gives me an apologetic smile. "I'd like to take you tomorrow, if that'd be okay with you."

I ponder for a moment, and since I have nothing better to do in a small town I know nothing about, I agree.

"Alright. I have to swing by my buddy Earl's house in the morning and get some of my gear I lent to him. He has a granddaughter about your age. I have a feeling you and she could become good friends."

I shrug my shoulders, not willing to tell him that I don't want new friends, and keep my eyes on the lake in front of us. He makes an approving sound, pushes himself up, and begins walking back toward the cabins. He says over his shoulder, "I'm glad to have you all here."

Chapter Three

Now

Ryland

My anxiety always spikes as I step foot onto the cemetery grounds. It feels like a shallow place for the living to be. Each puff of breath that escapes my dry lips seems to be inhaled by death as it lurks in the shadows, watching closely and waiting for my clock to finally stop ticking. I'm being dramatic, but it has always felt like this for me.

The rows of withering tombstones have witnessed the tears of many pained souls, mine included. I try to visit my grandparents' graves at least once a week. Some days, I weep because I miss them so much. Some days, I sob thinking of life without them. And other days, I shed happy tears over stories that I share with them of my daughter, Annabelle.

My grandmother passed away before Annabelle was born. I wish they could have met and wonder often what type of bond they would have created together. She was blessed to have my Pops around for her first five years of life. He completely spoiled her, snuck her candy when I asked him not to, and from day one was smitten with her. We all are.

Life without them has been a lot harder than I could've ever imagined. I often wonder what kind of man I would have become if I hadn't spent so many years being angry with my father and had more of a childhood that included my grandparents.

I know that God always has a plan for everything, and I'm thankful that he brought my little brother, my mother, and me to Covewood, Kentucky, where we were blessed to spend some amazing years with Nan and Pops. I smile at the memory and look toward Pops' grave.

"I've said this before, Pops, but I was such a little punk when I showed up on your doorstep all those years ago." I close my eyes and can see the smile on his face, the twinkle in his light-brown eyes, and feel a ghost of a pat on my shoulder with his callused hands. "Thank God I had you to help shape me into a better man. I don't think I ever told you that enough."

Pops and I had our fair share of arguments, but he always showed me patience. He loved Zane and me in a way we never experienced before. It wasn't long before I started to look forward to our bi-weekly fishing trips so we could have more time to bond. He was the greatest man I have ever known.

I check my watch and see that I'm a few minutes late and give my grandparents' tombstone a pat goodbye before making my way over to the truck that I inherited from my Pops. The dark-orange Ford truck with its white pinstripping brings my heart joy. She's got some life left in her as I turn the key, and she roars, still as loud as the first time I sat in her.

I drive through town and feel a sense of contentment as I pass the small place in Kentucky that quickly became my home. I watch as the small businesses turn into rolling green farmlands through my windshield as I make my way toward the Wiley Farm. As I turn right, the road becomes gravel, leading through a large green gate that's always open.

Up ahead, I watch as the old farmhouse comes into view. Its

once pearly white exterior has turned into a dusty yellow over the years, but I'm here to change that. The two-story home was built in the late '40s and is still standing firm. My favorite part of the home is the front porch, which also needs some work done to it, but when I'm finished, it will look brand new.

The Wiley Farm became my second home during my teenage years. After Earl's granddaughter, Raine, and I became close friends, we were inseparable. On the weekends, I was either visiting her at the farm, or she came to the cabins, and we'd swim in the lake from sun-up until sun-down.

Anytime I'm here, something always reminds me of Raine, which then causes me to miss her. Even after I let her walk away ten years ago, my heart still carries a piece of her with me. It's cheesy, I know, but the heart does what the heart wants—or however that saying goes.

Back in the fall, Johanna and Earl Wiley made the decision to renovate their house and requested that I personally help them with the process. After Pops passed away almost three years ago, I took over his construction company. We work mostly on renovating the older homes around the county as well as buildings and businesses. We do a little bit of everything, really, and business has been going really well.

Monday, Wednesday, and Friday, I've been working on the old farmhouse, and we have another month or two left until she is completed. I know Johanna has been more than ready for things to be done so she can have her home back to normal—or so she's expressed a time or two. Although, for the past week, she hasn't seemed like her normal, chipper self. Mom sent me with a new herbal tea she swears helps knock out any sickness to give to Johanna, and I pray it does the trick for her.

I put the truck in park and make my way toward the house. I see Earl leaning against the porch railing and hum in approval as I sniff the air. The scents of fresh grass, brewed coffee, and the slightest hint of hazelnut touch my nose. It's a heavenly aroma.

"Is that hazelnut I smell today?"

"Yeah, I think that new fancy coffee maker is rubbing off on me." Earl shrugs as he reaches down and grabs his mug, taking a sip to finish what's left.

He hands me a mug, and I nod a thanks. I lift the mug to my lips, the liquid feeling lukewarm as it hits my tongue, reminding me that I'm late. "I'm sorry for running behind. I was visiting my grandparents."

Earl waves me off. "Oh, that's okay."

I watch him closely. For as long as I have been working on the renovations, if I was even just a few minutes late, Earl always made a comment. He appreciates punctuality, whereas my Pops was always late to everything. Somehow, they always made it work with their friendship. I secretly think they enjoyed having a reason to pick on one another.

I notice the way Earl's brows are pulled together in concern, his lips are in a tight line, and his shoulders are tense. Something is bothering him. I take a sip of the semi-warm coffee, allowing the flavor to perk me up for the hard work ahead, and ask, "Everything okay this morning?"

Earl huffs and shakes his head. "Sorry," he says and blinks away the thought he was trapped in. "Johanna is still feeling bad. I finally talked her into letting me take her to the doctor this morning."

"The soup didn't help?" I asked, remembering Olivia saying that she was bringing her famous bone broth concoction that she, too, swears fights illnesses away. Johanna Wiley has me convinced that she is superwoman. Anytime she is sick, she can be found up before dawn, prepping her animals and garden or painting away with a cup of coffee in her free hand. Nothing stands in her way, except whatever is going on with her now.

"Nah, she said it was good but couldn't even stomach it after a few sips. Nothing keeps her down, so we need to get some answers," he states, determined. I nod in agreement.

"I can call Luke in," I add as a smile plays on my lips. Luke is my best friend and just so happens to be a cop.

Earl chuckles and shakes his head. "Now, that would be a sight to see. She'd manage to put up a fight."

"Eh, Luke can handle her."

"I'm going to make a quick breakfast. Would you like something to eat?"

I shake my head and point toward the barn. "No thanks. Have you messed with the animals this morning?"

"No, I haven't yet, but you don't have to do that."

"Nonsense. I'm here to help. Afterward, I'll finish up this railing," I reply and place my hand on the wooden railing, giving it a shake. There are a few places that need a replacement, and then I'll work on getting it stained. Earl gives me a wave and retreats inside the house.

I say a silent prayer over Johanna as I walk toward the gate where the animals are kept. The wind sweeps against my body, a slight embrace that feels like a hug. The mornings still hold a slight chill as a reminder of the cold months we had to endure. I swing open the gate and am greeted by a bark.

"Hey, ol' girl!" I reach down and pat Daisy, the Wileys' Great Pyrenees, on the head. She gives my hand a lick, her white fur sticking to me. She barks with eagerness. Even with her old age, she's always ready to work in the mornings.

"Alright, alright, give me a second," I add and grab one of the wicker baskets that hangs inside the opening of the chicken coop. I gather the colorful eggs and am instantly swept away with the memory of meeting Raine for the first time.

I chuckle, remembering the look on her face as she ran smack into me, crushing several eggs all over my sweatshirt. She was horrified. I, however, had never been happier to be covered in egg yolk.

I pull myself out of the memory and return to filling the feed and water containers, and then I leave the coop door open to allow the chickens to roam the farm. I make my way toward the barn and whistle, signaling Daisy to go in before me. I open the gate, and Daisy does her job of herding the sheep into the field.

This farm used to contain so much life—sheep, goats, pigs, chickens, and even a few ducks at one point. Raine would always bring some sort of animal needing a home on the weekends she spent here. A few of those animals I helped her find during my visits. An injured blue jay, a few baby bunnies, and even a baby fawn who seemed to have lost its mother. Our walks through the woods behind the farmhouse were always adventurous.

Now, the Wileys kept twelve sheep, twenty-one hens, one trouble-making goat, and Daisy on the farm. It's the maximum they can keep up with these days. Even Johanna's garden and greenhouse has dwindled down to a few basic vegetables, fruits, and herbs along with some of her favorite flowers. The thought brings my heart sorrow, remembering how vibrant and full of life this farm once was when I first saw it fourteen years ago. I help when I can, but even that doesn't seem like enough some days.

I finish up the chores, grab my tools from the bed of my truck, and get to work on the front porch. After I fix a few of the loose boards, a loud bang echoes through the front screen door along with Earl's panicked voice quickly behind it. I jump up and rush into the house, through the living room, and find Earl hovering over Johanna's unconscious body on the kitchen floor.

"Jo honey! Jo?!?" he shouts and looks up at me with pleading eyes. "What do I do? She, uh...she just stood up and fell over."

I move quickly and position myself over her. I check for a pulse but find nothing. I begin CPR while instructing Earl to call an ambulance. Time seems to move slowly. I am thankful for the CPR course I took when Annabelle was a toddler and focus on my pushes to her chest and air breathed into her mouth. Minutes flow by, and I don't hear the ambulance, or the sound of stomping footsteps, or feel the hands pulling me away from Johanna.

Earl hops into the back of the ambulance and as Luke rushes down the driveway in his police cruiser, I jump into the passenger seat. We chase the loud sirens all the way to the hospital.

Chapter Four

Now

Raine

I've been awake for two hours, and the sun still hasn't inched above the horizon. I'm sitting on the couch next to the window in my living room with the curtains drawn back and the blinds pushed all the way to the top. I blink up toward what I can see of the sky through the towering buildings. It's filled with the dull, gray light that always comes before dawn, like it's trying to decide how to wake up for the day. I'm attempting to do the same.

I've already showered, put on some light makeup, and slipped into a black pencil skirt with an olive-green blouse. My hair is wrapped into a tight knot at the base of my skull. When I look into the mirror, I don't even recognize myself.

I move into the kitchen to make myself an omelet with avocado toast for breakfast. It feels strange eating breakfast alone. It had become a daily tradition between Samuel and me. We enjoyed spending the morning together before our busy schedules took over.

Behind my eyes is a dull ache from the tears I shed all night and again when I woke up this morning. My eyes feel like sandpaper anytime I blink. When I called Olivia last night, instead of watching a movie together over FaceTime, like we had planned, the movie was left playing in the background, unwatched, as I dished all my feelings out to her. She has always been the best listener, and she also unapologetically gives me her advice whether or not it is something I want to hear—it wasn't, this time.

As much as it pains me to admit, Olivia is right. It devastates me to think that I have spent so many years working toward building this life in Rockdale, something I am very proud of, only to slowly lose interest in it. There are also certain memories that I've worked hard to forget so that I can try to live a more peaceful life. Unfortunately, I never could fully forget. For a while, the past only haunted me when I was alone. But lately, it has clung to my subconscious and surfaces any chance it can.

A thought is a hard thing to control.

I used to want a life that was long-term in the city, and at one point, Samuel felt like the best anchor for that. And then I chose to run away, like I always do when things start to feel too serious, when someone feels too close to my heart.

I can choose to stand here and spend minutes, hours, days, weeks, or even months overanalyzing the relationship I had with Samuel, trying to put the pieces together, justifying what could've or would've happened, or I can choose to leave the pieces on the floor and move on.

A knock on the front door causes me to jump. I walk toward the door, and my breath hitches as I open it and see a familiar pair of crystal-blue eyes staring back at me. Samuel is standing in front of me, holding a cup of GiGi's coffee, wearing dark shadows under his eyes that tell me he hasn't slept much. My eyes sweep across his face, wide with shock from seeing him here.

I take a moment to catalog his face—the lines by his eyes and how deep his frown is. He runs a hand through his short black hair, messing up his styled waves, and lets out a deep breath. Once I feel brave enough to look into his piercing eyes, dread squeezes against my heart.

"Hey," he starts, coughing away his nervousness. "I, uh... wanted to see how you're doing. I brought you a coffee."

A part of me wants to make up an excuse to leave the house in a hurry. Instead, I choose to stay, giving him a nod, and move out of his way. As he passes me, I try my best not to inhale the intoxicating scent of him. He is wearing my favorite cologne, and it makes me feel even more on edge.

Why is he here? He broke up with *me*.

I shut the front door and take five seconds to count as I breathe. It does nothing to help my nerves, but I feel stronger. I turn and catch him watching, his stare burning into me as I walk past him and lean against my kitchen island.

"Why are you here, Sam?" I ask, my heart beating so hard I am sure he can hear it.

"I told you. I just wanted to check on you. It's weird, you know, not having breakfast together." He acts like the breakup has been harder on him than it has been on me. He was the one who chose to end us. I guess, in a way, I did too, when I decided I didn't want to move in with him. "I miss you."

Samuel closes the distance between us and reaches for my face, pushing a piece of loose hair behind my ear, his other hand gripping my hip. I have no time to react when he leans his face into mine and plants his warm lips onto my own. No matter how hard I try to fight it, Ryland's face pops into my mind, as he has been doing lately. Why he has chosen now to resurface in my mind after all these years is beyond me.

Maybe it's because of my frequent beach trips that trigger memories of him. Maybe it's because I finally allowed myself to feed my curiosity and looked him up on social media. Maybe it was when I discovered an old Polaroid photo of him or the rainbow necklace that was in a box of items my Mamaw sent me for Christmas. Either way, the memory of him found its way back to me.

Mamaw's gifts for me this past Christmas were pieces of home: a bottle of local honey, a homemade candle, a small painting made by her, and a photo album she mentioned that she pulled out of my old room and thought I would love to have. It all stirred something inside of my heart, especially with the way she expressed how much she was missing me. She's always been supportive of my move and life in Rockdale—up until the last several months anyway.

I pull away from his kiss and allow my shoulders to sag in defeat. "Sam," I whisper, placing a hand onto his chest and pushing him gently away. I forget all about my uneaten breakfast and start pacing back and forth in between the small space of my living room and kitchen. He leans against the kitchen island, where I once was, as if he needs the extra support after my rejection.

"You miss me?" I ask.

"Yeah," he replies, and the frown finally lifts into a small smile.

"But you broke up with me."

This is so awkward. Why is this so awkward?

He grabs the coffee he bought for me and brings it to me. As our fingers brush against one another, he takes advantage and wraps his whole hand around mine. It's comforting, and I appreciate it. But what I also notice is no spark when our skin touches. The spark has been gone for me for a while now. I hate myself for it.

He leans down and places a small peck on my cheek. I lean into him, begging myself to try to feel more drawn to him than I do at this moment. Samuel has been nothing but good to me. He deserves so much better than what I was able to give him when we *were* dating.

"Let's talk?" He says it like a question and motions to the couch.

I nod and cling to my coffee, inhaling the scent of vanilla, cinnamon, and coffee beans, before taking a brave step toward the couch. I take a seat and he sits down next to me. I take a sip of my coffee, enjoying its warmth, before I dare to look at him.

He's extremely handsome in a well-kept kind of way. He takes pride in his appearance, especially for his job, and that used to be something I never really cared about in a man. It might be part of the reason I was so drawn to him in the first place. Because he is so different from Ryland.

"So," he starts and places a hand on my knee. I tense unintentionally and he removes his hand. Instead, he clasps them together and leans forward, leaning his elbows onto his knees. "I know I broke things off, but maybe I was trying to rush things with us, and that scared you."

I blink, taking another sip of my coffee to keep myself busy, before nodding in response. I'm glad he's starting the conversation, because I'm not sure that I would.

"I figured, after three years, it was time for the next step in our relationship. I thought you were ready and I'm sorry if I made you uncomfortable," he adds cautiously.

I nod a second time, unsure of the words I need to say or what he's wanting to hear. My eyes fall toward the ground, my nervousness buzzing in the air around us.

"It bothered me that you didn't want to take that next step. It made me question our whole relationship, and out of anger, I ended things, thinking that it was what was best for us."

Where is he going with this? What is he wanting to ask? And what am I willing to tell him?

He runs a hand through his hair and squeezes the back of his neck. "I think I rushed into both things—wanting to move in and then breaking up with you. I don't want to be without you, Raine. I'm willing to wait for that next step until you're ready."

"But what if I'm never ready?" I say, my words coming out quickly.

He runs his hands through his hair again and I notice the slightest tremble. This must be bothering him more than I thought. I knew I couldn't run forever, and right now, life is hitting me like a freight train, forcing me to face the music I tried so hard to mute. Every emotion I had tucked away returns at once, and I'm not ready to deal with them all. I'm not prepared for this.

"I, uh...well, I don't know," he stutters, looking down at the carpet.

Tears sting against my eyes and the back of my throat feels like it's about to close in on itself. I do my best to blink the tears away, not wanting him to see how fear is getting the best of me.

"I'm not sure I'll ever be ready for the next step with you, Samuel. I'm sorry," I admit and hate myself for the flash of pain behind his eyes when he looks over at me.

"What are you saying?" he asks.

"I'm saying that breaking up was what was best for us. You were right," I say, the words tasting metallic in my mouth.

The thought of living with him unravels me, and the truth continues to spill out. "I promised myself ten years ago that I would never put my heart in danger of getting broken again. Moving in with you could make things more real, more permanent. When you asked me to move in with you, I realized then that, even after all these years, I'm still not ready for it."

I wipe away the fresh tears that are on my cheek and look at Samuel. His blue eyes bounce across my face, searching for answers I'm not sure that I have to give, before he exhales and cups my face into his hands. "But what if you could be in three more years? You can't predict the future. Unless this is all because you're not in love with me."

If I tell him the truth now, I will be admitting defeat. Admitting that this life I've built for myself in Rockdale has all been for nothing. That even after moving away from home to try to find myself, I have somehow still ended up lost.

I want so badly to be found.

I exhale and do my best to gather my emotions. I remove myself from his touch, and instead, I lean over and place my hands together. I silently pray for guidance, that God will put the words into my mouth that I need to say, that whatever is in His will be done. I pray for peace, but it never comes. My nerves only grow more as silence passes between us.

I open my eyes and look back at Samuel, his dark brows pulling together in concern, and I choose not to run anymore. I choose to speak the truth to him. He deserves to know.

"I gave my heart to someone a long time ago and I never got it back. I never could fully give myself to you, Sam...not all of me. Just the parts I was willing to share. I care so much for you, but I never allowed myself to fall in love with you."

He opens his mouth to say something, but the sound of my phone ringing on the coffee table interrupts me. I look over and see the name *Papaw* on the screen. I could call him back once Samuel leaves, but something deep within my gut tells me to answer now. I hold up a finger to Samuel, signaling that I need to take this call. He frowns, not happy with me for answering.

"Hey, Papaw," I say softly and stand up. I walk into the kitchen and put my back against the counter.

"Raine." I could never forget my mother's voice. Even if I last heard it ten years ago when she told me to leave. Why is my mother calling me from my Papaw's phone?

I clear my throat but am unable to say anything. I've suppressed everything for so long. I don't know how to act around her anymore.

"Raine, it's your mother," she states, like I don't recognize her. "I'm sorry to call you like this, but your grandmother—"

Her breath catches, and I can hear her silent sniffles echo through the speaker and into my heart. *What about my Mamaw?* I want to ask, but my words are trapped inside my throat.

"She, uh... She had a heart attack and..." Another excruciating pause is between us. "And she is in the hospital right now hooked up to some machines. I knew I should be the one to tell you... You probably should think about coming—"

I can't seem to hear anymore. There is a piercing sound vibrating inside my ears and my mother's words are the only thing bouncing inside of my thoughts. "*She had a heart attack.*" She has to be lying. My Mamaw is okay. *She has to be okay.*

God, you told me she was going to be okay.

"Raine?" a voice speaks behind me, pushing through the ringing in my ears. "Is everything okay?"

Samuel. It's Samuel speaking. He's still here in my tiny apartment that is twelve hours away from my Mamaw. I blink and feel fresh tears spill from my eyes. I reach up to wipe them away, noticing the phone is no longer in my hand but is sitting on the floor by my feet. I look down and hear a faint, "Raine?" coming from the speaker.

I reach down to pick it up and say, "I'll be there," before hitting the red end button.

After ten years of living without her as a part of my life, ten years of her never trying to reach out to me, to apologize for what she did, ten years of working hard on repairing my heart from the damage she caused...ten years...and she's asking me to come home.

It hits me in that moment— something bad must have happened, maybe this is more than just a heart attack. What was it she said? Something about machines? *What kind of machines?*

"Machines?" Samuel whispers, his voice laced in confusion. I must have been talking out loud. He is close to me now as I spin around and face him. The uncertainty on his face melts away as he rushes to me and wraps his arms around me.

Samuel takes his large hands and wipes away my tears with his thumbs. His eyes search for answers in mine but I don't want to say it out loud. It will make everything feel real, and I want nothing more than to escape this reality that I seem to have slipped into.

Samuel shakes me lightly and I snap out of the trance my mother's voice put me in. "Babe, what happened? Please tell me what's wrong. You're so pale."

Babe. That one word stabs my heart and unlocks the emotions I'm trying hard to keep trapped inside. Samuel wraps me into his arms and allows me to weep into his chest. I've tried my best to not show my emotions, especially tears, in front of anyone, but most of all *him*. Our conversation from before feels like it happened a long time ago. It's as if days have passed when it's only been a few minutes.

Once I feel my tears stop, I mentally build the walls back up around my heart and try to prepare myself for what lies ahead of me. "Do you feel like talking about it?" he whispers against my ear.

I want to lean against him, nudge my nose into the crease of his neck so I can breathe him in a bit longer, and wrap my arms around his waist to bring him closer. I want to do this all out of comfort; however, it's time to let go of those urges. I can't string him along anymore. I owe that to him.

I remove myself from his embrace and make my way down the hallway. "My Mamaw had a heart attack," I say flatly, feeling myself begin to numb. "I have to go back home."

Samuel's eyes stay locked onto mine and he nods in understanding. I can tell from the look on his face that he wants to ask more but chooses not to. Instead, he asks, "Would you like me to look for flights there? Cove...what's the name again?"

"Covewood, Kentucky," I reply, my back still toward him.

I walk into my bedroom and grab a duffel bag from the bottom of my closet and start piling it full of clothes. I open the drawer to my nightstand and see the rainbow necklace laying inside. The sight of it is enough to send me to my knees. I allow myself one more moment to feel as I place the gold chain around my neck and clasp it together. It brings me a sense of comfort as I place the pendant between my fingertips and give it a squeeze.

My mind goes blank as I manage to turn off all my thoughts and return to packing. It's a defense mechanism I adapted years ago. It's something I used to do growing up. Something that has apparently never gone away.

I zip the bag shut and begin to fill another one with more clothes. A soft knock comes from my bedroom door. I jump at the sound and turn to see Samuel's apologetic expression. "I couldn't find any flights that would be leaving anytime soon."

"Alright," I reply. Driving there seems like my only option at the moment. If I drive, I can pile my car with more of my things, in case I need to stay and— I bite my bottom lip and fight against the new tears that try to form. I take a moment to breathe in deeply and pray for strength. "I'll drive," I add, nodding in agreement with myself.

"Are you sure? I'm not sure if you should," Samuel admits and walks closer to me.

I take a step back and busy myself by grabbing my camera bag and laptop. "I'll be fine."

"Raine." He huffs, and my eyes snap toward him. "It's okay to—"

"I said I'll be fine, Samuel. I have to pack and leave as soon as possible, so I think it's best that you leave now." My voice sounds unfamiliar. Flat. All emotion ripped away and tucked inside a box.

"I don't feel right, leaving you like this," he admits. "Even if you don't love me." Hurt is laced within his words. The last thing that I wanted was to hurt him in this way. Unfortunately, I don't have time to deal with it. I need to go back *home*.

"Sam, I'm sorry, but I need to go."

Samuel's face falls in defeat, and after a few moments of him fighting with himself, he nods in agreement before turning toward the door. He starts to walk down the hallway but stops and spins around to face me once more. "Will you call me when you make it there?"

"Yes," I promise him.

He taps the door frame two times, lost in thought for a moment or struggling to leave me, before he finally turns and walks away. As soon as I hear the front door close, I rush to grab the rest of my things.

Even if I return to Covewood and the past tries to make me a hostage of the painful memories I left behind, I will try my best to be brave. I will fight to be strong. I have lied to myself long enough, and my heart is telling me that it's time to go. It's time to finally return *home* and face the demons that I left behind.

Chapter Five

Now

Ryland

It's been one of those days where the minutes go by too slowly and everything seems to collapse onto one another. Nothing fits quite right and the sunlight shines with no warmth. There is this constant feeling lingering, like I'm forgetting something, but I don't know what.

Twenty-eight hours have dragged by since Johanna arrived at the hospital. For the first few hours, I did everything I could to keep myself busy. I spent my time grabbing anything Johanna's family needed from town and went for multiple coffee and food runs. I returned home for a few hours last night to tuck Annabelle into bed and struggled to sleep myself. I came back to the hospital early this morning after dropping Annabelle off at school, and I have sat next to Earl ever since.

Sooner or later, I'm going to have to think about what happened, and then I'm going to be a mess.

So, I continue to find ways to stay busy. I make small talk with the townsfolk who arrive. I hand out muffins that Olivia brought for everyone. I grab coffee for what feels like the fiftieth time. I make sure that Earl is okay. It's all I can do to keep myself together.

Earl and Johanna have become a big part of my life. I have always made sure to keep a close eye on them. They're family to me. A second set of grandparents I didn't ask for but happily gained. Watching Johanna go through this feels like losing my grandparents all over again.

I fight to contain my emotions, to stay strong for everyone that sits in the hospital waiting room with me, but it's growing harder to do the longer we wait for answers. The last update we were told was that Johanna's body has stopped fighting the machines and has finally settled down. Her heart needs surgery, but the good news is that she is able to have it.

All we need is to get the results of her MRI, which is what they're doing now. The doctors need to see if she's still in there somewhere after ten minutes of her heart stopping.

"I tried my best," I said over and over to Luke on the drive to the hospital and again to Earl, who in return gave my arm a pat as if silently saying, "I know." I never stopped pushing and fighting for her life on that kitchen floor until the ambulance arrived. And yet, I carry this heaviness of *did I do enough*?

Earl told me earlier that Raine is on her way. How do I explain to her that I wasn't enough to help her grandmother? How can I face her after what happened between us all those years ago? I don't think anything could have prepared us for this.

My phone vibrates inside my pocket, stealing my attention. "Hello?"

"Hey, honey. How is she?" Mom's voice vibrates from the speaker. I excuse myself and walk down the hallway, away from everyone.

"I'm not sure. We haven't heard any new updates yet. Some of her family has been able to go back and see her, but...I don't know. I'm not sure I can handle seeing her hooked to machines. It's too much like—"

I hear a sniffle and the clanking of dishes in the background. "I understand. I can't imagine how you must feel being back there and watching them go through this. That's why I don't think I can be there."

I nod, even though she can't see me. "I know. They understand that. Plus, I need your help with Annabelle, and I'm very grateful for it."

I've been a single parent since Annabelle was just an infant. Her mother struggled with postpartum depression, amongst other things, and she left us both. She even signed over her rights, giving me full custody of our daughter. It's not been an easy journey, but it could be a lot harder.

Mom and Zane have been a huge help with Annabelle. Sometimes, Luke comes over to offer a distraction so I can get a few things done around the house. Other times, Earl and Johanna step in and babysit on the days Mom can't. The community Annabelle and I have is such a blessing.

"Of course. That's what grandmas are for." The word grandma stings, and I release a pent-up breath in response. "Are you going to be okay?"

"Yeah, I'll be fine," I assure her, even though my heart tells me otherwise.

"I'll be praying," she says, "and I'll let you know when Annabelle and I are back home after I pick her up from school. If you need anything, please let me know."

"I will," I reply. "Thank you. I love you."

"I love you too, honey. Remember, God is in control."

We end our phone call, and I take a few seconds to collect my thoughts and get a better grip on my emotions. I fight back the hot tears that are stinging my eyes. I have to stay strong. Why does it always seem to take me ten times as long to put myself back together as it does to fall apart?

I inhale a deep breath and turn to take a step back toward the waiting room; however, my whole body halts at the sight of *her*.

Sometimes, it can feel like the past and the future are pressing so hard on either side that there's no room for the present. That is exactly what this moment feels like to me. It's as if I am seeing a ghost, but instead of feeling scared, all I want to do is reach out and touch her. To make sure she's really here.

Raine is running down the hallway in front of me. She's wearing a black pencil skirt that hugs her hips, sending me flashbacks of when my hands used to do the same, and a green dressy shirt. She looks bewildered. Her lips are tucked into a thin line. Her grayish-blue eyes are wide with fear and framed with dark circles.

Once her eyes lock on mine, she slows to a jog, stopping only a few feet from me.

It's been ten years since I've laid eyes on Raine, and that memory has me feeling unsettled. There are certain people who come into our lives and leave footprints on our hearts. Even years later, I can still feel the hurt of knowing that we never really said goodbye. We just kind of ended.

The Raine I see before me is someone different from the woman who used to be my best friend, someone I fell for and loved with my whole heart. I had to let go of that version of Raine the moment she decided to leave Covewood.

Gosh, she is still so beautiful. I'd be lying if I said that I hadn't searched for her on social media from time to time. She doesn't post many images of herself on Instagram, and her Facebook page is private. I never had the guts to try and add her as a friend. It was better that way.

The only time I got to see her over the years was through photos that our mutual friends, Olivia and Luke, had hanging in their homes or shared on their social media, or things that Earl and Johanna would show me from time to time.

The images didn't do her any justice. During the beginning of our friendship, Raine embraced her natural beauty, letting her natural wavy dark-blonde hair hang wildly down her back, and she kept a bare face, never feeling the need for makeup. I witnessed a change in her, as if her natural sunshine became shaded by certain people in her life.

The last few years of high school, she chopped her hair into a short bob and dyed it fun colors. She claimed it was her way of being a rebel, but I always knew that the real reason was because it was something she could control in her life.

Somehow, between then and now, Raine has gone back to embracing her natural hair color and has it twisted into a well-kept bun at the nape of her neck. A loose strand has fallen and goes past her shoulders. It makes me wonder what her hair would look like down. Would she look more like my best friend from the past?

Her body, which used to be a little shorter and thinner, looks toned and cared for. Her eyes seem the same, which brings me a sense of relief, even though the expression on her face is indifferent. It's clear that I'm not able to read her like I once could.

My eyes follow the loose strands of her hair to where the edges touch the nape of her neck, and that's when I notice it—the rainbow necklace that I gifted to her years ago. She kept it? Even after everything that happened between us? *What does that mean?*

"Raine," I say her name, unsure of what else there is to say at this moment. My brain can't seem to catch up with what is happening around me. Having her stand here right in front of me, wearing the necklace, does something to my already broken heart. I'm filled with nerves now, and I catch myself leaning back on the heels of my feet, unsure of what to say or do.

I run a hand through my hair for a second time and stare at her like an idiot. She takes a step forward, blinking a few times, as if she can't believe it's me standing in front of her. "You're here," she says, nearly a whisper.

"Of course I am," I reply, giving her a nod.

"I, uh...thank you for being here for them," she adds and

then looks past me down the hall that leads into the waiting room where her family and some of the townsfolk wait patiently. "Where's Papaw?"

I point over my shoulder down the hall. "He's down here. I can take you to him." I place both my hands inside my pockets, keeping my eyes forward and not on her, as I lead her down the hallway. Once we're in the waiting room entrance, I announce, "I found someone for you, Earl."

It's the first time since arriving at the hospital that I see pure joy on that man's face. Raine is holding back tears as she rushes towards him and practically jumps into his arms. I wish that I could share with her the lightness I feel in my chest or the warmth that floods me with having her here and seeing her smile.

Instead, I take a step back to give them some space. My eyes wander across the waiting room until they land on Raine's mother, Shannon. She's watching Raine closely with an unreadable expression on her face. If only I could read minds. What I would give to know what's going through her thoughts in this moment.

Shannon has changed over the years, especially after she married Preston about four years ago. She seems to have been blessed with a second chance at life. I don't know if she and Raine have spoken over the years, but with the way Raine's eyes are piercing into Shannon's with a look of resentment washing over her, I assume they haven't.

Shannon seems to be fighting an internal battle. Preston whispers something into her ear that calms her and has her relaxing in her seat. This is probably for the best as I see the relief in Raine's eyes. Now isn't the time to try and approach their issues. However, I hope things can be repaired for them in the near future so their heartbreak with one another can be resolved.

Maybe the same could happen for Raine and me.

One issue at a time, Ryland.

I sense movement to my left and catch the sight of Olivia and Luke making their way through the entrance. I walk over to greet my friends. Olivia gives me a small hug and then rushes to Raine's side. Luke places his hand into mine for a tight handshake before following Olivia.

Once Olivia releases her hold on Raine, Luke steps toward her, and his face falls. He wraps her into a tight embrace, and they stand there for a while, rocking back and forth. He plants a kiss on the side of her head and whispers something into her ear before moving away and wiping a tear from her cheek.

The three of them take their seats across from Earl, and I'm unsure of what to do with myself, so I move over to stand next to Felix Grady, one of Pops' and Earl's good friends. He gives my shoulder a quick pat in greeting before returning his attention to the baseball game that's playing on the nearby television.

Normally, when a baseball game is on, I'm hooked. It's even my favorite team playing, the Utah Big Horns, and as Max Hunter hits a home run, instead of cheering, I'm fighting the urge to look over at Raine. I mean, how can I not look at her? I've prayed for years that I would see her in person again. It all feels surreal, and I don't want to take this blessing for granted. But now isn't the time to talk about our history.

She's holding Earl's hand and listening to something that Luke is saying. A slight grin pulls at her lips. I stand in silence, trying not to memorize every softened wrinkle of those lips, the height of her cheekbones, the curvature of her collar bone.

As if sensing me staring, she looks up at me. For the first time since she entered the room, she fixes her gaze intently on mine. Something twists and pulls between us. I feel it as sure as a touch against my arm, a squeezing to my chest.

We're only empty shells of what we could've been, and our eyes are full of unsaid words. She blinks and returns her attention back to Luke, who hasn't stopped talking. I feel the desire buzzing inside of me to walk over there, to sit next to them, and let Raine know that, even after everything, I will always be here for her. But instead, I tell myself that I'm not worthy. I gave that right up ten years ago.

Chapter Six

Fourteen Years Before

Raine

"Should we check on the kid, Little Duck?" my Papaw asks from beside me.

The two of us are swaying together on the porch swing, enjoying the warmth of the morning sun, as he shares stories with me from when he was younger. He learned a lot about raising goats as a teen and explained how he had helped with sixty-seven births before he left the nest. I'm amazed at that number, especially since I gained my first experience this morning at the age of fourteen.

"Yeah, and her name is Anastasia." I smile proudly and hop off the swing.

"I like that name!" Mamaw hollers from behind the screen door, which makes my smile grow. "It suits her."

Before we're off the front porch, a familiar orange boxy truck makes its way down the gravel driveway. Cliff Ferrell, Papaw's best friend, always shows up at the farm on the weekends. He has always felt like a bonus grandpa.

"Cliff." Papaw tilts his head in greeting as Cliff hops out of the driver's side. His bushy dark brows lift with humor as he gives Papaw a wave. "Did you come by to bring me back that trolley jack?"

"Actually, I did." Cliff chuckles and moves toward the bed of his truck, Papaw following behind him. "It only took you twenty times of reminding me until I remembered."

"I only needed it six months ago," Papaw teased.

I take a seat on the front steps, knowing this conversation will last a while. Movement from inside the truck catches my attention, and I see a boy in the passenger seat. I can't quite see his face from the reflection on the windshield, but I'm curious as to who he is. Cliff never brought someone with him before, besides his wife occasionally.

Before I can get a better look, Mamaw opens the screen door, drying her hands with a towel, and says, "Raine, would you care to gather the eggs for me?"

I nod in response before hopping off the porch and making my way to the fence that leads to the chicken coop. Daisy, our six-month-old Great Pyrenees pup, follows close behind me, and I'm thankful because I might need some reinforcements when I encounter Lucy the rooster. I'm not sure what it is about the warmer seasons, but Lucy gets extra protective over his hens. And he terrifies me.

I grab a scoop of chicken feed, open the coop's doors, and toss the feed onto the ground. After I make sure all the chickens are distracted by food, I slip into the coop and gather a basketful of colorful eggs. I love seeing them all together—hues of olive greens, light blues, dark browns, light browns, and whites.

As I'm admiring some of the speckled eggs, I catch movement at the door and look up to see Lucy's red face peek through. His beady eyes see me, and he wastes no time before charging at me. I let out a scream that I'm sure everyone hears back at the house. As I rush outside, I try my best to avoid his sharp beak.

But I don't get too far before I hit something hard, stunning me for a moment. "Ouch!" I grunt and reach up to rub the throbbing pain on my forehead. I look up to see just what I ran into, and suddenly, I forget all about the pain as it is replaced with butterflies in my stomach.

Standing in front of me is a boy I've never met before. He must be the person I noticed sitting in Cliff's truck. What's he doing out here? I look over at the farmhouse and catch Mamaw laughing and giving me two thumbs up.

She planned this. Maybe not the part of me running into him, but as I see her watching us joyfully, she knew what she was doing. *Thanks, Mamaw,* I think as I roll my eyes.

My eyes scan him, taking in the way his seem more green than brown, his hair is a golden-brown color and is parted in the middle and swooping on either side of his head, and he is covered in egg yolk.

"Oh my gosh, I am so sorry!" I squeal, my hand smacking against my mouth and eyes growing wide with embarrassment.

He stares at me for a moment before shaking his head slightly and looking down at his navy-blue hoodie. He goes to wipe away the yolk, but my hand has a mind of its own, because I grab his wrist to stop him. I don't miss the way my fingers buzz at the touch of his skin.

"I, uh…" My voice cracks, and I try to cough away my nerves and drop my hold on his wrist. "There's a towel in the barn. Follow me, and we'll clean you up. I mean, you—you can clean yourself up."

I would smack myself in the forehead if I knew it wouldn't cause the throbbing that's already there to grow. *What is wrong with me? Do I not know how to talk to a boy? A very hot boy, might I add.*

The boy grins slightly, and I forget what I am doing. He waits patiently for me, as if that grin didn't do something to my heart. *What was I doing? Oh yeah, the barn!*

I motion for him to follow me, needing desperately to turn

away from his gorgeous face and what that dimple is doing to me. Once we reach the barn, I push open the door and walk to the tote of towels we had ready for this morning's birth adventure. I turn to hand him a towel and feel my mouth drop as he takes off his hoodie.

My eyes travel down his torso, catching the sliver of skin that is revealed as his shirt lifts up just a bit, and it takes everything in me to avert my attention somewhere else. He straightens the dark-gray shirt he's wearing underneath, tossing his inside-out hoodie over his shoulder, and gives me a wide smile that reveals a set of metal braces over his teeth. This boy even makes braces look attractive.

"Don't worry, it can be washed," he says, his voice surprisingly deeper than I expected it to be, and my knees suddenly feel weak. Stupid teenage hormones. *Get a grip, Raine!*

He tosses a thumb over his shoulder. "Your grandma asked me to help you. Something about an evil rooster?"

"Uh, yeah. Lucifer—Lucy for short—is very protective over his ladies, and for some reason, he hates me."

He chuckles and turns to look out the barn door. "Is he that tiny rooster?"

I nod my head as he looks back at me, the heat rising onto my ears. "Yup," I answer, popping the P and rocking forward onto the balls of my feet.

Lucy is a bantam barnyard mix. Basically, he's a tiny wannabe rooster. It might be why he is so hateful and trying to show his dominance. My grandparents have him and a few bantam hens in our flock to breed and sell them. Surprisingly, they're a popular breed, even though their eggs are the size of a quail egg, which in my opinion is a waste of food. It takes three of their eggs to make one regular egg.

Lucy lets out a miniature crow, and the boy chuckles, returning his attention back to me. "He sounds *so* fearsome. I can see why you're terrified."

I roll my eyes and bite my lip to keep from grinning. "He

tries to prove that he isn't a waste of poultry. I only pretend to be scared to help him win the hens over, and in return, it helps the farm out."

"You're such a good Samaritan," he adds and looks outside for a second time to watch Lucy chase off Daisy, who runs away quickly, whining loudly. *Coward.* He laughs, and it's the most amazing sound I've ever heard.

I look down at my muddy rain boots because looking at him is making my stomach feel like it's flopping around inside of me. I peer down at what I'm wearing and realize how much of a mess I must look right now. I wipe away the dirt that has collected on my jeans, straighten my light-pink tank top, and run my fingers down my long braid.

Once I dare to look back at him, he is staring at me. His grin is gone now, replaced with parted full lips and widened eyes. If I felt self-conscious before, it only grows with remembering how close we're standing to one another.

"I, uh—" I cough away the thick feeling in my throat. "I'm a mess. I've been working all morning." I motion to my body, biting my lip, feeling uncomfortable in a good sort of way with how his eyes follow my movement.

"I— I'm Raine, by the way. Earl's granddaughter," I say fast, wanting to change the subject.

That earns another smile from him. "I'm Ryland Quinn."

Ryland. I like that name. I will probably be doodling *Mrs. Ryland Quinn* on my notebooks later because I'm crushing hard on him. How could I not? My face must be beet red with my growing nerves.

"Would you like to come see a baby goat?" I ask without thinking. It's the first thing that comes to mind. "She was born this morning."

"Yeah, sure," he replies and follows behind me as I lead us through the barn.

"So...how do you know Cliff?" I ask, yearning to know more about him.

Ryland's lips pull into a smirk. "He's my grandpa."

"Are you just visiting?" I add and pray that he is here to stay.

His smirk falls, and his shoulders sag with it, as if that question holds some weight. "No. No, I think I'm here to stay for a while—according to my mom, anyway."

I want to pump my fist into the air and shout, *"Yes!"* but I fight against it, and instead, I say calmly, "You don't sound too happy about that."

"I'm not, honestly. I had a life back in Utah," he adds. "It's hard to start over."

"I wish I could start over most days," I admit honestly.

We stop walking, and I turn to face him in front of the pen. He studies me for a second, taking me in again. I fidget awkwardly by smoothing my braid across my shoulder and tucking a loose piece of hair behind my ear. He fights back a smile and turns his attention to the pen that is in front of us now.

I pull back the gate and lead him inside, pointing to the new baby kid with her mama. I motion for him to follow me as I make my way toward them and bend down to give Anastasia a quick pet.

"What are their names?" he asks as he bends down next to me. I catch a whiff of his scent, *sunshine and mint*, and wish I could bottle it up and sniff it later while I'm alone. Okay, I am acting weird and need to contain myself.

"This is Esmeralda," I answer and point to the mother. "And I named this little girl Anastasia."

He raises a brow, and I study his eyes now that he's closer. They're an enchanting shade of hazel with flecks of gold mixed with green and light brown. A beam of sunlight from a crack in the wood of the barn is hitting his irises, making them even lighter, and my stomach drops.

"Those are interesting names," he ponders. "I like them."

I smile and look down at Anastasia. "I like old-fashioned names."

“Hmm,” he makes an agreeing sound as he pets Esmeralda. “You did a good job, Mama.”

“That she did. I got to watch the whole thing, even assisted in helping to pull Anastasia out. She was giving her mama a bit of trouble, but she got here safely.”

Ryland looks at me and seems to be impressed. He holds a shy smile on his face as he looks back toward the goats. This causes a flicker of bravery to overcome me.

“You know, since you're new in town, if you need a friend... I mean, if you even want a friend, that is... I just, uh... I’m always happy to make new friends is all.” If I could shrink down and hide away from him right now, oh I would. That was not how I wanted to ask him to be my friend, and embarrassment squeezes against my throat.

“Yeah?” he marvels, his face beaming, helping to ease my nerves a bit.

“Yeah....if you want.” My voice rises up a notch on the last word, and I shrug to appear more relaxed than I am at this moment. If he could hear my heart right now, it would give away the panic inside me.

“I’d like that,” he states, like it’s the easiest thing to say, and it fills my heart with so much joy. However, that joy is sucked away the moment the barn doors swing open and reveal Davis, my mother’s boyfriend, snarling toward us.

“There you are!” He spits and stomps his way toward me. He looks over at Ryland, runs his eyes up and down him as if accusing him of something, and then reaches down and grabs my arm.

I notice Ryland flinch next to me before shooting a heated glare at Davis.

Davis jerks me up and starts dragging me toward the barn door. “Your mother has been honking for you. Can you not hear? We don’t have all morning to be waiting on you to be in here flirting with some boy.”

If I thought I was embarrassed before, this moment has set a new record. *Of course* this would happen. It's my life after all, and this sort of thing happens a lot. The farm is my only safe space, and the weekends are the only time I am truly happy.

Ryland stands up and clenches his fists. His eyes land on Davis' hand on my arm before snapping toward mine. I try my best to give him a smile that says *'I'm okay'* but I think it falls flat. Giving him a wave goodbye, Davis pulls me toward the farmhouse

My mother is sitting in the driver's seat of the rusting green Honda Accord, pushing her hand against the horn before holding her head out of the window to yell at me to hurry up. That she doesn't have all day. She never seems to have time for me. I wish so badly that she would allow me to live with my grandparents, but for some reason, she holds onto me, even though she makes me feel like the world's biggest inconvenience most days.

I look behind me and see Ryland closing the barn doors and following us to the house. Once we get closer to Cliff and Papaw, Davis makes sure to release his grip on my arm. Papaw's eyes pierce into mine, holding a soundless question of *You okay?* I shrug my shoulders and open the back door to the car.

"Call me if you need anything, Little Duck," he tells me before wrapping his arms around me tightly.

"I will," I whisper and fight back tears.

It's always hard to leave the farm and to return to my normal life. I can see it written all over Papaw's face that he wants nothing more than for me to stay. But things are complicated, and Mom holds all of the authority since my birth father, their son, passed away before I was born. I often wonder what life would have been like if my father hadn't died. *Would it be better?*

I dare a look at Ryland, who stands next to the orange truck and watches me closely. He holds a knowing look on his face, a silent understanding, as if he grasps how I feel in this moment. This recognition only makes him more appealing to me.

"I'll see you around," he says, and I hear a hint of a promise in his voice.

"Come on, Raine!" Mom hollers from inside of the car, and I force myself to slide into the seat and shut the door.

Chapter Seven

Now

Raine

There is a part of my mind that is always preparing for the worst and another part that believes that if I prepare enough for it, the worst won't happen. That's what I'm hanging onto for dear life as I sit next to my Papaw, clasping his hand tightly, reminding myself that all of this is, in fact, real. I wish I could summon some comforting words to say to him, but this is one of those moments where I choose to be silent, as no words can express what we're all feeling deep inside.

Instead, I choose action and squeeze his hand, letting him know that I'm here with him, and lean my head against his shoulder. A deep exhale escapes him, and he sinks further into me. I know it means a lot to him that I'm here. I can see it in his light-blue eyes and feel it in the way he leans back against me. There is comfort in knowing I made it in time to be by his side during all of this.

What I wouldn't give to have my Mamaw wake up and be back to her normal self. A repeating prayer of healing has been echoing inside my heart since I received the news. She needs a miracle, and I beg God to consider it.

We've been sitting in the waiting room for hours. I've dozed off a few times because the waiting is agonizing. I honestly don't know how Papaw is keeping himself together. He is quieter than usual, lost in thought, but he answers questions when asked and has held a few conversations. He amazes me with his strength.

My phone buzzes in my lap, and I peer down to see Samuel's name on the screen. *Crap*, I forgot to text him. I'm sure he's worried despite us breaking up.

SAM

Did you make it safe?

Yes. I'm sorry for not letting you know sooner.

SAM

It's okay. How is your grandmother?

I'm not sure. We're waiting for an update from her MRI.

SAM

I'm sorry you're going through this.

Me too.

I watch as the three dots shimmy but I click my phone off and turn it upside down in my lap. Felix Grady takes the seat next to Papaw and is whispering something to him. Olivia and Luke walked outside a few minutes ago, and I wish I went with them.

I look around the room, studying who all is left waiting and only find a few others. My mother and her new husband sit in the back of the room along with my Uncle Jack. I turn when I notice my mother's face shifting my way. I'm still not sure why she is here. This isn't her family. I can feel her eyes on me, and it causes a hot prickle of awareness to take over. My composure is starting to crack, I notice the shaking of my hands intensifying.

I understand that my biggest problem, especially with my mother, is that I haven't forgotten what happened in the past—the feeling of abandonment, her issue with alcohol, her poor choice in men. No matter how hard I try to forget, the memories and the pain stick with me. This has been my fatal flaw, and I'm not sure how to keep it from becoming my own destruction.

The agony I'm trying to hide between quiet breaths is starting to eat me alive. Being here in this hospital with the unknown status of my Mamaw, facing my mother for the first time after *that* night, and being around Ryland is all too much.

I shoot up from my seat, and without saying a word or looking at anyone, I beg my feet to move. I push open several doors without thinking of where I am going. I desperately need to put distance between me and *them*. My mind is spiraling, the shaking in my hands getting worse, and I know it won't be much longer until I break. I need a quiet place to let this eruption building inside of me *out*.

I find a small room with a handful of empty chairs. I rush inside and plant myself into one of the chairs. I'm used to wearing a thousand different faces daily, all to hide my own, but right now, I erase them and allow a tear to run down my cheek.

"God, I'm not ready for this," I whisper, allowing the pain to swallow me whole.

I sit here in this tiny room and come undone. I'm not sure how much time passes. I don't care, in all honesty. It feels good to be alone, to allow my true feelings to escape just for a little bit before I have to return the fake mask I plaster onto my face when I'm around others.

The sound of a door opening causes me to jump and jerk my face away from my hands. Standing before me is Ryland with a foam cup in each hand. His dark brows are pushed together in concern as his eyes pierce my own. He places the two cups onto a glass table by the door, and in two swift steps, he sits down next to me.

"Hey," he says softly and reaches his hand out to touch mine. He hesitates for a moment before patting the top of my knee instead and intertwines his fingers together in his lap.

I wrap my arms around my knees and pull them closer to my face. I lean my chin on my arms and wipe my eyes against my forearms. I'm embarrassed that he found me breaking down and train my gaze on his brown boots. He's got a bit of mud clinging to one, right at the toe. I try to distract myself by picturing him in his flannel, covered in sweat, his sleeves rolled to his elbows, like he used to look when he would come over and help Papaw around the farm. The memory loosens something inside of me, and it makes me want to be open with him instead of reserved like I should be.

I let out a sigh. "I'm sorry," I admit and mean it in so many different ways. I sniffle and wipe away a few fresh tears.

"You don't have to apologize. It's okay to feel the way you do right now." He puts his hand on my lower back lightly, and I can sense his nervousness before he removes it just as quickly. "I've seen you in worse shape."

I snort, but there is a heaviness with it. "I doubt that." I return my gaze to the man that used to be *my everything*. The man I've tried hard to forget but have always failed to.

"You'll make it through this, no matter the outcome." He would know better than anyone else after losing both of his grandparents.

I don't know if he can feel it too, but there's this familiar buzz between us. I wonder if he's still hurt by my past actions. Am I still hanging onto his? *That night* has played over and over in my mind, leaving me wondering how things could have been different. Oftentimes, I question if leaving hurt him worse than it did me? Where can we stand today after that?

I feel as if I let go of that heartache a long time ago. We were teenagers, after all. Fresh out of high school with the whole world at our fingertips. We wanted different things, and we both made our choices that night. One of the saddest moments in my life was the love I ran from because of fear. That's the one thing I've hung onto.

It's why I chose to spend many years single, never trusting anyone with my heart. That was, until I met Samuel. He unlocked something in me. He gifted me silent understanding and a fresh start. Yet, I never could open up to him—not fully —or allow myself to truly love him.

I inhale a daring breath and bravely peek at Ryland. His hazel eyes find mine, and his Adam's apple bobs as he swallows. I watch, frustration tightening his expression as he considers me quietly.

I can't get over how different he is now compared to the boy I met when we were teens. Back then, he was loose and comfortable, a little quiet but charming. His smiles were easy and frequent. Here, now, sitting next to me in the small room, the overhead fluorescent lighting painting him in shadows as he sits next to me, he's got a frown on every line of his face from the set of his eyebrows to the downward tilt of his full lips. I wonder how much of that is my fault.

I open my mouth to say something—anything—but instead, I swallow my words, feeling them form a lump in my throat. His eyes never falter from studying me. I feel the familiar swoop, low in my belly, just like I did the first time I saw him. It's like cracking open a memory to take another look. Flannel instead of a school sweatshirt. Messy golden-brown hair instead of a backward baseball cap.

His eyes still look the same, still hold a kindness within their hazel color. I notice the small crow's feet etched into their corners. His hair, messy from running his hands through it, is the same shade of golden brown but is now mixed with a few stray grays near his temples. He has filled out, and the lower half of his face is covered in a brown beard that looks like it could use a trim. Even so, it's rather striking.

His eyes may be familiar, but they don't look at me like they once did. Why does that send a pang through my heart? Something I've told myself to work on while I'm back in Covewood is to finally put the past in the past. To take that step forward, even though forgiveness often feels like a giant leap rather than a step.

"Raine?" Ryland's voice snaps me back into reality as he runs a hand through his hair. "The necklace."

I'm confused at first, but then it dawns on me. I'm wearing the rainbow necklace. In the chaos of events, I completely forgot that I had it on. My hand reaches up, pinching the rainbow in between my index finger and thumb.

"Mamaw sent it with some old photo albums a few months back. I, uh...don't know why, really, but I put it on before I traveled home."

He hums, considering me for a moment, before he looks down at the pendant between my fingers. "I'm glad you kept it."

I give him a small smile, and it seems to loosen something within him. It's enough to snap me out of our little bubble and return back to this horrible nightmare that is our reality. Being here with Ryland is starting to mess with my emotions. It feels as if the past and present are fighting with one another. With an exhale, I stand up and look down at Ryland as his lips part to say something, but the words don't come out. I know the feeling because I don't know what to say either.

"I probably should get back," I say softly and point to the door.

He stands up and bends his head down to get a better look at me. "Yeah. Yeah. Okay," he stutters before adding, "Would you like a hug?"

My eyes travel down his shoulders, across his biceps, to his large hands. Oh, how good it would feel to be wrapped in those arms and receive his comfort right now. To feel safe like he used to make me feel. But I know I won't be able to handle it. Not right now. It's best to keep my distance. I shake my head no. "I, um... I'm trying to keep it together right now. A hug might get me crying again."

Life is hitting me like a freight train, forcing me to face the music I've tried so hard to mute. Every emotion I've worked intensely to tuck away seems intent on returning all at once, and I'm not ready to deal with them. I'm not prepared for this.

"Okay," he replies softly as he moves around me to grab the two styrofoam cups and hands one to me. "It's just hospital coffee, but you looked like you could use some caffeine."

I take it from his grasp and place my hands around its warmth. "Thank you."

He gives me a nod in return and opens the door for me. As we walk down the brightly lit hallway, he stops near a door and asks, "Hey, would you mind if we go in here together to pray over Johanna. I can go grab Earl to join us."

My eyes look past him and see that we are standing in front of the chapel. Ryland and I went to church together often in the past, but the fact that he wants to pray over my Mamaw sends an odd yet satisfying feeling into my heart. I nod in agreement and reach for the door handle.

"I'll be right back," he assures me and makes his way down the hallway. I take a seat near the window and do my best to breathe encouraging breaths. The last thing I want to do is cry in front of Papaw. I have to stay strong for him.

Within minutes, Ryland returns with Papaw close behind him, and I'm relieved when I notice no one else came with them. It's just the three of us. Papaw takes a seat next to me, and Ryland sits next to him. I lace my fingers with Papaw's and give him an encouraging squeeze, reminding him that I'm here for him. He gives me a slight smile, revealing just how strong he truly is.

My heart softens as Ryland takes my Papaw's other hand and bows his head. I can't take my eyes off him as he coughs back his nerves and lets out a breathy exhale. I feel so selfish in this moment when I realize how hard this must be for him as well. I have been so self-absorbed in my own suffering. I forgot how close Ryland is with my grandparents. He's spent more time with them these last ten years than I have. That thought alone twists my gut, and I feel the hot sting of fresh tears fight their way past my eyelids as I shut them and bow my head.

"Dear Heavenly Father, we come to you today to ask that you be with Johanna and her loved ones. Please come near to this family, Lord, and bring them a peace that only you can give. We ask that you place your healing hands upon Johanna and make her whole again. That you usher the medical team into success. Lord, we are not ready for her to leave us," his voice breaks for a moment with a cough following.

My eyes open, and I watch him as he continues his prayer. "I know we can't ask of you something that isn't part of your will, but we're begging you to heal Johanna. Bring her back to us, Lord. Please be near us during this difficult time. In Jesus' name, Amen."

Papaw sniffs beside me and tightens his grip around my hand. "Please Lord, hear us."

This breaks something inside of me. I thought I cried all of the tears that I could on my drive back to Covewood and then again in that tiny waiting room. Despite myself, more tears find their way down my cheeks. We sit in the chairs and hold onto each other's hands tightly as we stay silent in prayer.

As a few moments pass by, a rush of peace falls over my heart. The icy shock of panic is replaced with a flood of warmth. The shaking in my hands and legs stops. The tightness in my chest loosens and helps my tears to stop flowing.

At this moment, something deep inside of my heart is telling me that my Mamaw is going to be okay. I open my eyes and look at Papaw, who turns toward me.

"Did you feel that?" he asks and then turns to Ryland.

Ryland opens his eyes, and I notice a single tear fall down his cheek. I've only seen him cry twice since I've known him. It's hard to see him hurting. I want to move closer to him and show him the comfort that he showed me moments ago. Instead, his eyes seem to light up as he looks at me and nods his head. "Yeah."

"Peace," Papaw whispers next to me and squeezes our hands again. "Thank you for praying, Ryland."

"You're welcome, sir."

Papaw pushes himself up off the chair, his shoulders already looking lighter, and he shuffles toward the door. "I'm going to head back out there."

As the door shuts behind him, I turn to study Ryland more closely. I'm not sure if it's from seeing him for the first time in years or witnessing him like this, but something within him has changed. More than his appearance. It's something much deeper.

"Are you okay?" I ask, feeling the twisting in my gut again with the reminder that he, too, is hurting.

His hazel eyes, looking more brown than usual, pierce into mine as he shrugs his shoulders. "Honestly, I'm barely keeping it together."

In the past, I used to rely on Ryland for his constant honesty. It draws me to him still as I move to the seat where Papaw sat and place a hand into his for the first time since we broke each other's hearts. The skin there is more callused from years of hard work. I try not to enjoy his touch as much as I am, but it feels so comforting.

"I'm sorry," I mumble. "I'm sorry that I didn't think to ask how you were doing."

"It's okay. You have your own pain to deal with."

"That's not a good enough excuse. I know being here doesn't bring you good memories, and Mamaw is just as much yours as she is mine."

Something within him deflates with my words. His eyes gloss over, and I can tell that he is trying to fight back his emotions. It takes everything in me not to cry at the sight of him hurting. "I, uh..." he starts, swallows hard, and takes a deep breath. "I was there...when it happened."

It takes me a moment to realize what he is referring to. I squeeze his hand, encouraging him to continue. It feels like we're in this weird bubble of time where both the past and present are held back behind a closed door, and we've locked it for now, focusing on this moment and nothing else.

"I tried to bring her back. I tried to get her heart to start." He bites his lip and closes his eyes tightly.

My other hand flies up and touches my lips, allowing his words to sink in. He was there when she had the heart attack. He gave her CPR. My heart sinks deeper, the peace I felt moments ago washing away.

"Ry," I whisper, the nickname slipping out of me like a procedural memory.

His eyes open, and another tear travels down his cheek and into his scruffy beard. I remove the hand from my mouth and wipe the tear away, keeping my fingers against the rough texture of his beard.

"I, uh..." He looks down at our hands. "I don't want you to be disappointed in me—that I couldn't save her."

I shake my head. "No, you did everything you could. I'm thankful you were there. And she's here now. We haven't lost her."

I look at our hands together and wonder how we got to this point already. So much hurt and years between us, and yet, somehow, we still have an understanding, this *need* to be there for one another. That part of us never went away, and I find comfort in it.

I open my mouth to say something but I'm interrupted by the door to the chapel opening. We both look and see Bill Hampton, a close neighbor to my grandparents, standing and staring back at us. He waves. "The nurse came back with the MRI results."

Ryland and I shoot up, keeping our hands together, and

chase after him down the hallway. A nurse stands in front of the group of people waiting to hear about Mamaw. When her eyes land on mine, I already know what she is going to say. I stop in my tracks. Ryland looks back at me with a puzzled expression. I don't have the strength to move any closer.

He studies me then looks back at the nurse, then back to me. I can't look anywhere but at the clipboard the nurse holds in her hands. There is a buzzing in my ears as I watch her lips move. I can't make out clearly all of what she is saying, only parts of it.

"Understand that she died for ten minutes."

"Her brain didn't have enough oxygen."

"There's nothing left of her."

"Her body is barely hanging on."

"The family can have a moment to say their goodbyes."

Ryland stands next to me, and I am suffocating. How is this happening? She was fine. Yeah, sure, she died, *but she came back*. She can't leave us. I know she wouldn't want to leave us. God gave us peace. *Why* did he give us peace only to take her away?

My mother's weeping snaps me back into reality. I look toward her, then to my uncle next to her, and then to my Papaw, who is unmoving. A hand is on my shoulder, and I turn to see Olivia and Luke, out of breath from rushing to us.

"Raine?" she asks, and I look at Ryland for a reason I'm unsure of. A mask of despair is hanging on his face, and there's a glossy sheen layered across his eyes like he's holding back a mass of emotions. I allow Olivia to wrap her arms around me and feel two others that I suspect are Ryland and Luke, wrapping themselves around us, and I allow myself to come undone, no longer caring.

Chapter Eight

Thirteen Years Before

Raine

"If I didn't know any better, I would say that Honeysuckle is your favorite friend." Ryland snickers beside me as we walk along the trail that takes us back toward the farmhouse. A light breeze pushes past us, cooling our skin from the intense heat from the sun, and not a cloud is in the sky.

I push my shoulder into his and attempt to hide the smile spreading across my face with my hair. I look down at Honeysuckle, a male mallard duck that has been my pet since I was little, and rub his feathers. He is a tad bit spoiled and lets me carry him everywhere. He's right—Honeysuckle is my favorite.

"If I didn't know any better, I would say that you're jealous," I tease, planting a kiss on top of Honeysuckle's head, who quacks in response.

Ryland bumps back into my shoulder, causing me to trip, and a giggle escaping my lips. "Oh, I'm definitely jealous," he adds, and my heart does one of those flipping motions, stealing my breath for a second. I try not to dissect the meaning behind his comment. He could've meant nothing by it, but I like the idea of Ryland being jealous over me.

Every weekend for the past year, minus a few holidays or illnesses that kept us apart, Ryland and I have been joined at the hip. Our friendship was easy to establish. Like we've known each other for years. We can be silly together one minute and have deeper conversations the next. I love that about us.

I love him.

I'm not sure if I'm *in love* with him or anything, but the feelings I have for Ryland are deeper than the love I feel toward my other best friends, Luke and Olivia. Olivia would be upset if she knew this, but Ryland knows all of my secrets, even things I've never told her—which isn't a lot, but still, she can never know.

It's easy with Ryland. When I open up to him, he does the same in return. Even after months of getting to know one another, I still crave to know more and more about him. I want to know everything.

"Is he the reason why your Papaw calls you Little Duck?"

I giggle again as the memory surfaces of how I earned the nickname and nod my head. "Yeah, actually, he is." I hand Honeysuckle over to Ryland, a quack of protest escapes before he settles into Ryland's arms, and I take the basket full of honeysuckle flowers from his hands.

I grab a handful of flowers into my palm and bring them toward my nose and inhale. Scents of sweet honey, vanilla, and hints of jasmine wrap together in a heady nectarous concoction. It's my favorite scent.

"I was eight years old and went out to pick honeysuckles, like we did today, and I heard a little quack underneath a bush. He was so scared, but he let me pick him up. I tried to find his mama, but I never could, so I took him back to the house and asked Papaw if we could keep him."

"That doesn't sound like something you'd do," he jokes, knowing full well that I have a problem with finding stray animals and bringing them back to the farm. He's helped me a time or two this past year. What can I say, I have a huge soft spot for animals. Why live on a farm if you can't have lots of pets?

"Anyway," I add and bump into him again because I like feeling his warmth on my bare shoulder. "I was trying to get Honeysuckle to trust me, and so I started acting like a duck. Papaw caught me and started calling me Little Duck, and it stuck."

"Please reenact this for Honeysuckle and me. I'm curious to see how you won him over with your duck impersonation." Ryland strokes his feathers and gives me a brilliant smile, revealing his super-straight teeth, thanks to the work of his braces, which were removed last month. I thought his smile before was attractive, but without the metal, I've found myself staring at his mouth more often than I'd like to admit.

What would it feel like to kiss Ryland?

This question keeps popping into my head, and I have to constantly remind myself that he's *my best friend*. Plus, I'm too scared to take that next step to see if we could be something more than friends. He hasn't shown me any clear signs that he feels the same and hasn't made any moves toward me. Instead, I tuck the thoughts away, only bringing them out to mull over when I'm alone.

The scent of charred meat fills the air around us, and so does the sound of my stomach gurgling. "As fun as that sounds, we should get inside. I can smell dinner, and I'm starving."

I give Honeysuckle a pat, Ryland does the same before setting him down on the ground. It makes me grin watching him waddle toward the chickens. Ryland reaches over and takes my hand into his, tugging me behind him until we're up the porch steps.

His hand is callused from all the hard work his grandpa and Papaw have been putting him through lately. I like how it feels and the fact that he's a hard worker. My thumb strokes his rough skin, and he looks over his shoulder, giving me a smirk that makes my knees quake.

Mamaw is at the screen door, eyes snapping to our hands, and Ryland quickly releases his grip. *Thanks, Mamaw!* She grins at me and motions for us to come inside. "Dinner is almost ready. Come in and wash up."

She takes the basket from me and hums in approval. "Thank you for picking these. It looks like we will have enough for me to make some jelly and brew some tea for that old man over there."

We laugh and look over at Papaw, who pushes himself out of his favorite recliner, grunting in protest as he stands. "Now, listen here. Age is just a number. In here"—he pats his chest—"I feel just as youthful as I did when you first laid eyes on me and fell in love with my good looks."

I make my way to the sink and wash my hands, listening in on their conversation because I always love how they playfully bicker back and forth. Ryland is behind me. My skin seems to buzz every time he's near, as if alerting me that he is close. *Attention, Raine. That hot guy you claim is your best friend but you secretly have feelings for is near! Try not to act weird.*

"Did you forget that I despised you at first?" Mamaw deadpans, and Papaw gives one of his intoxicating belly laughs. "You were such a pain in my butt. Still are some days."

"But I was persistent and knew that you would have to eventually give in." Papaw looks over at Ryland and gives him a wink. "Take notes, son. This is good advice."

Ryland shakes his head, grinning at Papaw, and I study his face for a moment, taking in the way Ryland's eyes crinkle as his smile grows, how the gold in his eyes seems to shine in the sunlight, and the honeysuckle that is stuck in his messy golden-brown locks. I reach up and snag the flower, tossing it into his face with a laugh, and run around the kitchen island to avoid his hands as he chases after me.

I let him catch me, his fingers tickling my ribs until he stops and places the flower behind my ear. Mamaw watches us with a sparkle in her eye and motions for me to help her prepare the salad. She hands me a tomato to cut and plants a kiss onto my temple. The scent of her—coffee grounds, dirt, and fresh roses—fills my nose, and it instantly comforts me.

"Ryland, would you care to set the table?" she asks and opens the oven to pull out a peach pie that she made from scratch. My mouth waters thinking about pairing a piece with a scoop of vanilla ice cream. Ryland looks at the pie and licks his lips. He must be sharing the same thought as me. I focus on distracting myself with work, or my mind will start to wonder about his lips again.

I chop up the tomato and place the pieces into the bowl of lettuce. Once Ryland is out of the room, Mamaw walks over to me, leans close to my ear, and whispers, "So..."

"So what?" I ask, keeping my focus on the tomato I'm chopping and not the way my heart picks up its beat.

"You and Ryland seem to have grown closer lately," she adds, nudging me slightly with her elbow.

"Yeah, we've spent most weekends together since he moved here." I know where she's going with this, and I don't want to discuss it when Ryland is closeby. However, my Mamaw is relentless when it comes to girl talk.

"I saw you two holding hands and the way he tickled you in the kitchen."

I roll my eyes and look up at her. She is a few inches taller than me. Just the right height that when I hug her, I fit perfectly within her arms and neck. Her hair is pulled back today, but most days, she lets it lay down past her shoulders. She embraced her whitish-gray color as it began to take over when I was just a baby and gets it permed every so often. I've always loved her hair.

"Friends hold hands and tickle each other," I admit, swallowing back my nerves and look toward the opening that leads into the dining room.

"I often hold your grandmother's hand and give her a tickle too." Papaw chuckles from behind us and grabs a hold of my

Mamaw, tickling her sides, earning a loud squeal from her as she jumps away from his embrace and swats at him.

"Now stop that!" she hisses but doesn't contain her smile.

"You know I can't keep my hands off of you," he adds and gives my Mamaw a pat on the butt.

I laugh at the sight of them. This type of hands-on flirting is normal around my grandparents, and I adore how much they love one another. Even when they bicker back and forth some days, it always ends with a playful comment or a kiss. I'm blessed to have them in my life and want a marriage just like theirs when I'm an adult.

"Stop it!" She swats at him again, and the smile spreads on her face, lighting her up like a Christmas tree. "I was just saying, Raine, that it seems like—"

"Do you want me to carry anything else into the dining room?" Ryland asks, and all three of our heads snap to him. He stops in his tracks and stares back at us, a dark brow rising up his forehead in question. "Did I miss something?"

"Nope," I say quickly and grab the bowl of salad. "Just Mamaw and Papaw being gross."

"Hey now! I'll show you two gross," Papaw argues and takes my Mamaw into his arms and plants a kiss onto her lips. I smile at them and make a gagging sound. Mamaw moves away from Papaw to toss the rag in her hand at me. Ryland laughs, and I can't get past him fast enough as I escape into the dining room.

We sit down and enjoy grilled lamb chops, a salad made with vegetables from the garden, and finish with Mamaw's award-winning peach pie. We are stuffed and stay at the table for an hour afterward, playing cards together. The phone rings and steals Papaw's attention right as I shout, "UNO!" I'm so close to winning my second game in a row.

"How are you so good at this game?" Ryland asks from across the table.

"Because I taught her how to play," Papaw adds before he answers the phone. "Hello. Where ya been today? Yeah. Yeah." He laughs and looks over at Ryland. "He's been a good help today. Alright, I'll tell him. See you soon."

He hangs up the phone and walks over to the table to retrieve our dishes that have been pushed to the side. Mamaw stands up to help him. "Your Pops is on his way to pick you up."

"Okay," Ryland says, a frown taking over his face.

I can feel a frown on my face as well. I know it takes about twenty minutes to get from the cabins to the farmhouse, so we don't have much time to hang out until we see each other tomorrow at school. Ryland is supposed to be a grade ahead of me, but when his family made the move to Covewood, his mother decided to hold him back a grade. He was bummed about it, but I wasn't. I loved sharing a few classes with him and getting to see him in the hallways at school. It makes the time in between the weekends more bearable.

"Wanna come to my room so I can show you that Polaroid camera I thrifted with Olivia and her family last week?" I ask, wanting some alone time with him before he has to leave.

"Leave the door open," Papaw adds. I groan and roll my eyes at his comment. I don't miss the way he smirks at us before we rush up the stairs.

Once we're in my room, I close the door just a bit but leave a crack. Ryland takes a seat in the chair by my vanity, and I hop onto my unmade bed. My room is very girly. I decorated my bed with bright pinks and purples. A few of Mamaw's paintings hang on the light-cream walls as well as photo collages I made from magazine cutouts and photos I've taken with my small digital camera. It's my happy place. At my mom's, I'm not allowed to decorate my room, and it feels more like a prison cell than a bedroom.

I push the dark thoughts away and grab the shoebox from underneath my bed. I set it on my lap, and Ryland moves over to sit in front of me. He removes the lid, and I pull out the light-gray, boxy camera.

"I love that I instantly get a photo when I use it."

"And you've used it a lot," he adds as he starts to sort through the photos in the box.

"It's been fun. Oh, I need a photo of us together," I add and scoot closer to him.

I hold the camera out and bring my face closer to his. Butterflies make their appearance in my stomach as I catch the scent of sunshine, earth, and peaches from Ryland.

We say cheese at the same time, and a bright light blinds us for a moment. The film moves out of the camera, and I shake it until the image starts to bleed through. It's a good photo. We both look happy. He pulls it from my hand and studies it for a moment before placing it into the box.

He goes back to sorting through the photos as I peek out my bedroom window to see if his grandpa is here yet. The weekends fly by too fast. I always dread saying goodbye.

Suddenly, panic zaps through me when I remember that I snapped a photo of him this morning without him knowing, and it's in the box. I have to find it before he sees it, or I'll be so embarrassed.

"Hold on!" I yell, his eyes snapping to mine in confusion. I leap and grab the box from his grasp. I start digging through the images, and I feel him watching me.

Thankfully, I find it. I remove it from the others and stand up to hide it from him, but he's faster than me. "What are you hiding?" He laughs and jumps on top of me. My back hits the mattress, and my nostrils are filled with the scent of him again. His hot breath hits my face, and I would enjoy this if I wasn't so worried about hiding this photo from him.

"Nothing. Ryland!" I squeal and try to hide it behind me without wrinkling it.

His hand squeezes behind me and is able to grab the photograph before he jumps away from me and turns around to look at it. I attempt to jump onto his back, but he dodges me, and I fall onto the floor with a loud *thump.* He starts laughing, so hard that he has a few tears in his eyes, and all I can do is cross my arms and pout.

"Everything okay up there?" we hear Papaw shout from the bottom of the stairs.

In unison, we both reply, "Yeah!" and share a laugh. I use it as a distraction to try to steal the photo from him again, but of course, he's much faster than me.

"What's this?" he asks as he studies the photo, his smile dropping slightly.

My face is burning hot. I try to hide behind my hands and curl into a ball on the floor. Why did I take that stupid photo in the first place? And why did I forget that it was in the box?

"When did you take this?" he asks, and I spread my fingers so I can peek at him but keep my hands over my face. He moves down until he is sitting with me on the floor and tugs my hands free from my face so I can look at him.

"This morning. I just thought it would be a cool photo, like artistic or something."

He raises a brow like he doesn't believe me and goes back to studying the photo. He had his shirt off, dripping with sweat from the heat of the sun and the hard work he was doing with Papaw. I wanted to freeze that moment in time, and once I caught him looking away, I snapped the photo quickly from the kitchen window and ducked down to hide. In my haste, I tossed the photo in the box with my others.

"Cool," he says and hands the photo back to me.

I take the photo from him, glancing at it for a moment before I look up at him. He stills, waiting for me to do or say something. I notice how close we are on the floor. He's only inches away from my face, and I catch his eyes drop to my lips for a split second before returning to my eyes. What is *this*?

It's like we have this magnetic pull between us, and I'm completely absorbed in him.

"Raine," he whispers. The sound of him swallowing fills the air between us, and all I can do is stare.

"Ryland. Your Pops is here!" we hear Mamaw shout up the stairs, breaking our trance, and as much as I love her, I'm so mad at her right now.

Ryland blinks away the cloudiness within his eyes and pulls away from me. He clears his throat and stands up. As he extends a hand to help me up, I panic and push myself up, and rush out of the bedroom without a second glance at him. I take the stairs down, skipping a step to get to the bottom faster, and run outside. I need air. I desperately need some space.

Did we almost kiss?

Was I reading into things that weren't really there?

Could Ryland want something more than friendship with me?

How could he? I'm just...*me*. Simple, plain, Raine. And he's so much more than that and deserves much better too. Am I even willing to test the waters and put our friendship on the line? I'm not sure that I'm ready to chance that.

"Hello, Raine," a deep Southern voice calls from the bottom of the porch. I turn to see Cliff tilting his head in greeting. "Have fun with my grandson today?"

"Yes, sir." *In more ways than you know*, I think to myself.

Cliff's dark bushy eyebrows raise, watching me for a moment before humming a sound and turning his attention toward Ryland, who makes his way down the steps.

"There he is. Ready to go?" Cliff asks and gives Ryland a pat on his shoulder. Ryland flinches, and an apologetic look washes over Cliff's face.

"Hang on, I need to do something real quick." Ryland says.

My Papaw shuts the screen door behind him and gives Cliff a wave. "Smells like you have an exhaust leak."

"No, that's just power steering fluid leaking."

They move into a conversation, like they always do, which means Ryland and I can have a few extra minutes together. He usually calms the storms inside of me, but right now, he is creating one. My stomach is in knots, my heart is about to break a rib, and my palms are starting to sweat.

"Come here," he says, his tone sounding smooth.

Either he's ignoring what just happened, or I was imagining everything. Maybe it's for the best. I don't like how uneasy I feel right now, and I want us to get back to our easygoingness. Ryland points for me to stand in front of the large oak tree that sits in front of the farmhouse. Once I'm standing in the right spot for him, he takes a few steps back, keeping one hand behind his back, and looks me up and down.

"What are you doing?" I ask, rocking back on my heels and lacing my hands together behind my back.

"No, don't stand like that. Here." He walks toward me and places his hand onto my arm and moves it until it's relaxing on my upper thigh. He places his fingers under my chin, tilting my face up just a bit, and gives me a satisfied look. *What is he making me do?*

He takes a few steps back again and pulls the Polaroid camera out from behind him. Before I can argue, he holds a finger up, and I shut my mouth. "Now, I want you to think about that time Lucy chased me up a tree."

The memory is impossible not to laugh at. Ryland thought I was crazy for being so scared of a tiny rooster, but Lucy showed him just how terrifying he can be. He flocked Ryland's legs a few times, making him bleed, and cornered him by the barn. His only way out was to climb up the small tree next to the barn. As I laugh, a flash startles me, and Ryland snatches the photograph from the camera.

"No!" I shout and run to him. He holds the photograph to

his chest, dodging my grabby hands, and cackling at my failed attempt to snatch the photo. "Give it to me."

"Nope. You have a photo of me, and now I have a photo of you. It's only fair."

I drop my hands and feel my jaw go with it. "You want a picture of me?" I ask.

"Yeah, why wouldn't I want a photo of my best friend?" He smiles, but it doesn't quite meet his eyes.

For a second time, we stand there in complete silence, Ryland waiting again for me to say something. But what does he want me to say? I don't get to find out because Cliff is hollering for Ryland to come on, and I have to say goodbye.

I walk him over to the old truck, and he gives me a small wave, promising to see me at school. I stand in the driveway and watch them drive away, not hearing Mamaw's footsteps on the porch.

"Everything okay?" she asks.

I exhale a breath and make my way up the porch. "Yeah. Just tired."

She wraps her arm around me, pushing me against her, and wraps me into her comfort. "Ah...young love is a fickle thing."

Chapter Nine

Now

Ryland

Rain falls softly from above, feeling as if tiny kisses are brushing against my skin. Each droplet touches my skin with just enough coolness to command my mind to the present, to pull myself away from the pain of the past and the uncertainty of what's to come.

The weather matches the grief we're all feeling as we watch Johanna's casket being lowered into her burial site. Grief hangs in the air like a thick wool turtleneck, the kind that clings to your throat in a smothering way. I move my eyes away from the people gathered around Johanna's casket and let them wander over the rows of tombstones.

A few rows back is where my grandparents were laid to rest. When my Nan passed away, the thought of her being buried in a place that is abandoned by society used to give me chills. I knew that it was just her body being placed into the earth and that her soul was in a much better place, but there's something about graveyards that makes a person feel lonely, and I didn't want her to feel that way.

Once Pops was buried next to her, there was a sense of comfort knowing that her body was no longer resting here alone. I'm still working through the grief and pain from their loss. Knowing that Johanna is near them brings me reassurance, just like it did with my grandparents. Unfortunately, saying goodbye to her has stirred up even more grief inside my heart.

I rub the chill away from my arms and lean closer into the embrace my mother holds me in. I'm thankful that Zane stayed home with Annabelle for me. I didn't want her to have to witness another funeral, especially with how hard she took my Pops'. I want her to remember Johanna as the joyful woman she was—always checking in on us, bringing over freshly baked treats, taking Annabelle to the art studio downtown, and filling Annabelle's library full of books.

I study the faces around me and notice that there are no smiles being shared in remembrance of her. I only observe sorrow over the loss of the wonderful person that Johanna was. She has a large turnout. Most of the town is here along with people that, I assume, are her family and friends from out of state. The town really came together to provide everything for the funeral. Zackary and Jerica Huffman, the owners of Enchanted Petals, donated dozens of flower arrangements. Cindy Potter offered her art studio up for the funeral reception. Olivia worked hard to provide the food while Grayson Tompkins offered free coffee. It is comforting, watching the town come together to honor Johanna.

I stand across from Raine. She's standing next to Earl and Olivia with a blank expression on her face. I wish I could read her thoughts, reach a hand inside her heart, and wipe away her sadness.

Raine was always one to keep her emotions locked deep inside. She has the best poker face out of anyone I've ever known, but I used to be able to read the truth within her gray-blue eyes, see the chaos she hides behind her mask. She has a way of appearing strong when around others. However, I *was* the person she would reveal her true emotions to.

What would things be like if I hadn't messed up and became another reason she wanted to run away from Covewood all those years ago.

Becoming an adult, for me, has been learning to live with regret and doing my best to not allow it to consume me. The older I become, the more mistakes I seem to make, opportunities I miss, a longer list of people I've disappointed. Each passing day, I have to remind myself to be kind and forgiving, not just to others, but to myself.

We watch together as the top of Johanna's casket slowly disappears into the ground. I whisper a last goodbye to the woman who was like family, dropping a purple iris flower, her favorite, on top of her casket. I hold a second iris in my hand and plan on giving it to Raine.

My mother takes my hand into hers and leads us toward Earl and Raine. My nerves grow with each step. I look at Raine, but her eyes remain forward, trapped in grief, fully unaware of my presence. I know that feeling all too well.

We wait as a few townspeople give the family hugs with words like "I'm sorry for your loss." Once it's our turn, my mother reaches for Raine first and pulls her into a tight hug. She whispers something in her ear, which causes her to blink away the blank stare she was wearing, and she looks at my mother as if seeing her for the first time.

Earl tugs at my arm and pulls me closer to him. "Can I hitch a ride with you? I want to escape these people," he whispers.

"Yeah. Of course," I tell him and nod toward the truck. "But Raine—"

He waves at me and continues in a whisper, "I can tell that the idea of going to the farm is too much for her right now, so I let her off the hook on taking me home. She's also wanting to skip the reception."

"Is she going back home?" I ask quickly. The thought alone sends my stomach plunging out of my body—a constant reminder that she'll leave again.

"Back to her hotel room for now." Relief floods me with his answer.

Mom reaches up and places her hand on Raine's cheek, giving her a look that only a mother could, before walking away and focusing on Earl. Now is my chance to talk with her. *Why am I so nervous?* We were able to talk decently well at the hospital. Things feel much more fragile now. I'm scared I'll mess things up again.

I take the purple iris in my hand and place it into hers. My hand is trembling slightly, and I hope she doesn't notice. Her eyes follow the flower, up my arm, and land on my face. Her expression is empty, but her eyes reveal the internal pain she's suffering. I want to touch her, wrap my arms around her, comfort her like I used to do. However, I've lost the right to comfort her that way.

I open my mouth to say something—anything would be better than this silence—but I can't find the right words. We stand there for a moment, staring at one another, until someone besides us clears their throat, and then Earl breaks our silence.

"I'm going to have Ryland take me home. Don't you dare leave town without telling me, okay?"

My eyes study Raine's. Would she leave this soon? Leave her grandfather during this time of grief?

"I won't. Thank you for letting me skip the reception. I love you," she mumbles and gives him a quick hug, and he whispers something to her before she turns to walk toward the parking lot. I watch her closely as she makes her way to a white Honda Accord and slides into the driver's seat.

"Let's get going," Earl says and walks to my truck.

As we both hop inside, I look back over toward Raine's vehicle, but she's already backing out and making her way to the main road. "Where is she staying?" I ask Earl and put the key into the ignition.

"Down at the old motel on highway ninety."

"Why didn't she stay with Olivia?" I question.

"I guess she wants to be alone during all of this," he answers, and I can hear the sadness in his voice.

"Oh," I say and pull the truck out onto the main road and turn left. "How long do you think she'll stay?"

I peek over at Earl and see him shrug. I can't help myself with asking the questions, but I sense that he isn't in the mood for much small talk. I keep the rest of my questions to myself as we drive through the curvy roads that lead to their home—now, *his* home. The thought of him sitting alone in the unfinished farmhouse brings back memories of my Pops and the same concern I had for him after Nan had passed.

As if reading my mind, Earl asks, "How did Cliff do it? Find a life after Anna...passed." I can hear him fighting against tears as he speaks.

Why does life have to be this hard? Why does sin have to enter the Earth and allow death to be a part of our world? It's pure torture, seeing loved ones having to learn to walk through life with grief. It becomes a torment, carrying the grief upon your shoulders. Each person that leaves this Earth also leaves a missing piece in our lives.

I try my best to not be angry with death, and instead, I dig deep in my memories for an answer for Earl. It takes me a second, but as I pull into his driveway and put the truck into park, I remember something Pops said to Mom one day. I was eavesdropping, like a typical kid, and was listening in on their conversation about her depression after we first arrived in Covewood.

She suffered for months, could hardly make it through the day without crying, and it held her back from moving on to the life she wanted to have here. My Pops had to snap her out of it, and I remember something that has stuck with me since.

"You just keep living until you're alive again. At least, that was something he said and seemed to do after losing Nan."

Earl chuckles. "Of course he'd say something dumb like that."

"Yeah," I offer and try my best to smile. "It didn't make sense to me either, but it always seems to stick with me during the hard times. Life has to move on. No matter how much we don't want it to."

"That Cliff, he never did give advice that would make sense. To say goodbye is to die a little. How can you keep living when a piece of you is forever missing?"

I wish I had the answers for him. I don't have the words of wisdom or comfort to provide for him, so I decide to stay silent. He's right. When you lose somebody, it's not only when they pass away but each time when you are reminded of them, when memories of them flash across your mind in broad daylight, when you yearn for their presence.

When you lose somebody, you lose them not only once, but over and over again for the rest of your life.

He coughs and takes a moment to collect his thoughts. He reaches over to tug against the door handle but comes to a stop, hovering his hand for a bit before turning back to me.

"You still care for her, yeah?" he asks, and I know instantly who he's referring to.

"Yes, sir," I confess to my friend. There is no sense in denying it.

"Would you look after her for me? I don't know how much help I'll be for her during this grieving process. She was there for you, you know, after Anna. She seemed to help you back then."

I give him a nod. Raine was the only person who could have pulled me out of my sorrow and helped me find the strength to be the strong one for my Pops. "She did. And I'll make sure she's okay."

"Thank you," he says before pushing his door open and hopping down to the ground.

I feel my eyes soften. "You know I'm always here for you. You're welcome to come stay at the cabin if you need to get away. Either way, don't be quiet."

"Alright, Cliff Junior." He manages another soft chuckle, and I know right then that Earl Wiley is the strongest man in the world.

Chapter Ten

Thirteen Years Before

Ryland

It's my favorite time of year. The turning point between summer and fall. The days are long with hints of warmth still clinging to the air. However, anytime a breeze flows by, it sends goosebumps over my skin with the reminder that autumn is near. As I walk along the stone path that leads to the dock, I notice the leaves are starting to show a hint of color as they begin to die. They sway in the wind as if dancing for one last time.

Even so, it does nothing to lift my sour mood.

"Ryland." Pops' raspy voice stops me in my tracks.

Oh, how I would love to have the option to ignore him. Instead, I loudly exhale and turn to face him. We had an argument earlier this morning and again just moments ago when I went inside to grab some snacks. Apparently, he isn't going to let things go. My jaw clenches as I mentally prepare for more lecturing.

"I won't tolerate you walking out when I'm still speaking to you. I'm not trying to be hard on you. I just—"

"Yeah, I know, you want what's best for me. I get it, Pops,

but having you nag at me over every little thing sucks. It feels impossible to live up to your expectations of 'the perfect grandson,' and no matter how hard I try, I don't think I'll ever become who you want me to be." I ball my fists and look at him, silently begging him to back off.

His face falls as the words leave my mouth. He blinks, running his hand over his thick white mustache, and then places the same hand onto the back of his neck. He struggles with finding the words he wants to say, and as badly as I want to turn and storm away for a second time, I fight with myself to remain in place. I might as well allow him to finish what he needs to say so I can get back to my friends who are waiting for me on the dock.

"Is that what you think? That I have expectations of you being perfect?" he grumbles, dropping his hands to his sides, the movement making me flinch.

I hate that it's my first response to the quick movement of someone's hands. It's a side effect of my relationship with my father that I desperately wish I could get over. Pops has never threatened me. Although his tone can be harsh at times, I know he means well. I can't seem to control my defensive reaction.

He notices the flinch, and his brown eyes soften with realization. He takes a step toward me. My instincts tell me to step away, but I ignore them. I allow my grandfather to place a hand onto my shoulder. He bends his face down so he can look into my eyes better, and all the anger he held for me a moment ago disappears. He reaches up and gently places his other hand onto my cheek.

Every nerve in my body is screaming at his touch, but I force myself to stay frozen in place. My father's approach toward Zane and me was always heavy and cruel. He treated Mom the same. Pops has been working hard to show us that he is the opposite of our father. And because of that, I allow him to touch me and remind myself that, even though he's tough on me, he's *nothing* like my father.

"I know what you're going through. I experienced both verbal and physical abuse from my father and my grandfather. When I had a family of my own, I vowed to never be like them and worked hard to break the generational curse or whatever they call it."

He's never told me this before, and neither has my mom. My jaw drops at his confession, and in a strange way, it brings me comfort knowing that if he could end up unlike his own father, maybe I can too. My shoulders relax, and the buzzing within my skin starts to calm down.

His brows pull together, and he shakes his head. "It's hard for me to understand how your mother ended up with a man who was just like them. But she removed you all from the situation, and we should focus on being grateful for that."

He releases his hold on me but not before giving my cheek a soft pat, and then he takes a step back. He exhales before continuing, "Listen, the hard work I give you and the respect I demand is how *I* discipline. Think of this discipline like I'm training you. I want to help you grow into...not a perfect man, but a better man. In this process, I'm going to help you break some of the habits you've learned with your father, and sometimes it's going to be tough, but I can promise you that if you stick it out, you'll be grateful. You just have to work with me, and I promise to be more patient with you. Does that sound like a plan?"

I give him a nod, allowing his words to sink in, and I do my best to release the anger that lives rent free within my heart. The sound of crunching gravel catches our attention. We both look up toward the road and see Earl's green truck pulling into the driveway.

Earl hops out of the truck, and before he goes to close his door, he pauses for a moment, peeks his head back into the truck, and says something to Raine before I hear the thump of the door shutting. I can feel it in the air. Something is off. Earl looks over and sees Pops and me standing in the path and gives us a wave.

Pops returns his attention to me. "We'll talk later, okay?"

"Alright," I reply, paying more attention to Raine, who is still sitting in the truck.

Pops walks up the path, gives Earl a handshake, and they make their way toward his cabin. I stand and wait a few seconds before I see Raine's long hair bounce around as she hops out of the truck. She slams the door, and I see Earl tensing from the sound, but he doesn't turn around.

She catches sight of me and practically drags her feet down the stone path until she is at my side. I watch her for a moment, expecting her to stop and tell me what's wrong, but she doesn't. Instead, she walks past me and makes her way toward the dock.

I take two large steps and twist in front of her, blocking her path. She blinks a few times, as if I broke a trance, and looks up at me. Her eyes look sad today, their bluish-gray color looking like the storm brewing behind them. I place the basket of snacks onto the ground and reach for her hands.

"What's wrong?" I ask.

Raine's nose scrunches up as she blinks quickly and bites her lip. Her hands are shaking within mine. She's been a little distant the past few weeks, and I hate seeing her like this. I raise a brow, a silent plea for her to tell me what's going on.

"What's wrong with you?" she asks instead, averting her attention onto me.

"I'll tell you if you tell me," I add, giving her fingers a squeeze.

She exhales and nods, pulling her hands away from mine, and wraps her arms around herself. "Okay, you go first."

I rub at the tension in the back of my neck. "Pops and I got into an argument. You know how intense it's been between us ever since I started working for him. But we'll be alright. It's just hard to listen to him complain every time I do something."

When I first arrived in Covewood, I carried so much anger

within my heart, and unfortunately, it's something I am still working through. It's not just Pops who knows how to push my buttons. It's also my mom, who loves to stay on top of everything I do, making sure I'm not falling back into my old ways. *And* it's also Zane, who acts like a typical little brother, wanting to be around me every second of the day.

Life can feel heavy sometimes. But not when I'm around Raine. Anytime I'm with her, my worries evaporate. It's been like that since the first time I met her. She has no idea how she has impacted my life.

If I had the guts, I would man up and tell her how I really feel about her. But I want to show respect and follow her lead. I'm not sure if she's interested in turning our friendship into something more. Maybe she just wants to be friends, and I'll take whatever she'll give me.

"I'm sorry he's been hard on you," she replies softly.

"I can handle it. Now, what's wrong with *you*?"

She exhales again, this time allowing tears to gloss over her eyes as she says, "Honeysuckle died."

"What?" I whisper, the shock feeling like it's squeezing my throat.

"I went to clean out his pool this morning, like I always do, and usually like clockwork he would quack—" her voice cracks, and a lip quiver follows. I reach up and use the pads of my thumbs to rub away her fresh tears.

"He wasn't waiting on me this morning, and when I went into his house, he—"

I don't let her finish. She doesn't have to. Instead, I wrap her into my arms and rub circles against her back. Her sobs vibrate against my chest, and if I could absorb her pain, I would. Instead, I know that comforting her is all I can do right now.

She loves the duck so much, and I have grown to love him too. He was a friendly face to see anytime I visited the farm, and it was adorable how he'd always waddle next to Raine no matter what tasks we were doing. The thought of him being gone breaks my heart for Raine.

"I'm so sorry. I know how much you loved him, and he loved you too. You gave him a good life."

"Mamaw said the same thing." She sniffs and pulls away from me to wipe her face with her hands.

She looks down toward the dock, and I answer her question before she asks. "Luke and Olivia are down there. Do you feel like going? We can—"

She holds up a hand. "It's okay. I'll be fine." She wipes her face a second time and takes a deep breath. "Let's head down there."

"I have snacks," I say and pick up the basket, feeling my chest warm at the sight of her smile.

"Emotional eating is just what I need," she admits. I look down and double-check the basket to make sure I grabbed enough snacks. I knew Raine was on her way, so I made sure to have a bag of the fizzle Skittles she loves so much, a Milky Way bar, and her favorite soda, Ale-8-One.

"Thank you," she says softly, peeking up at me quickly before looking down at her light-blue dress, "for always being here for me."

When Raine is at school, she dresses differently. She wears mainly t-shirts and jeans with her hair pulled back into a ponytail. But anytime she's staying with her grandparents, she wears long flowy dresses or skirts. She keeps her hair down and welcomes her natural waves. Most of the time, she is barefoot and keeps her toes painted bright colors. Like this, she's her true self—wild, free, and joyful. I haven't told her before, but I prefer this version of her best.

"You're welcome," I reply and fight the urge to hold her hand. "That's what friends are for."

Once we make our way to the dock, Olivia's face lights up at the sight of Raine. She bounces onto her feet to give her a hug and lets out a squeal. Luke is sitting on the edge of the dock, and as he sees Raine, he is quick to dodge her eyes.

That's weird.

Raine seems to notice but returns her attention back to Olivia. "It's about time you showed up. Luke has been killing my vibe, and I need to tell you about Derick!"

Raine looks over at Luke, who's still avoiding eye contact with her, and a frown pushes against her pink lips. Olivia takes Raine's hand into hers, bringing Raine's attention back to her.

I plop down next to Luke and nudge his shoulder. "Snacks?" I ask, and he hums in approval.

He reaches into the basket and pulls out a bag of Flamin' Hot Cheetos and tosses them to Olivia. She doesn't even break her conversation or look his way. She turns and grabs the bag while keeping her eyes on Raine as she continues to tell her how Derick called her last night and asked her to meet up next weekend. Luke rolls his eyes, which causes me to smirk at him.

I hand Raine the bag of fizzle Skittles, another feeling of warmth spreading in my gut at the smile she gives me. I also hand everyone an Ale-8, and as tradition, we pop off our tabs and clink the glasses together, yelling, "Cheers," before downing its ginger-citrus goodness. Luke lets out a large burp, earning a, "Gross," from the girls and a high five from me.

"I'm so glad she can talk to Raine about Derick. I was about to lose my mind," he whispers to me before shoving a handful of sour-cream-and-chives potato chips into his mouth.

I nod in agreement before popping M&Ms onto my tongue. Before I can ask him what his deal is with Raine, Luke strips his shirt off beside me, tosses it at the girls, and jumps into the water.

I'm jealous of how buff Luke is. When I first met him freshman year, I was told that he had lost close to thirty pounds over the summer. He lost a bit more when we both started working out together at each other's houses. Pops has some standard workout equipment in his garage, and Luke's mom has a basic set of weights that we use.

However, since I started working for Pops, my workouts have slacked a bit, but Luke has kept going. He makes me feel lanky when I'm next to him, and so I decide to keep my shirt on. Luke pulls himself up onto the dock, and I glance over toward the girls, who are both staring at him. Raine is rolling her eyes and popping a Skittle into her mouth while Olivia's jaw drops for a second before she corrects herself, a small blush spreading across her cheeks as she looks away from him.

Luke gives them a brilliant smile before leaping backward and diving into the water, creating a huge splash that hits the three of us. I laugh as the girls shriek and try to shield themselves.

"Luke! You jerk!" Olivia shouts and kicks her legs in the water, splashing him back. He swims over to her, and before she has time to escape, he grabs her legs and tosses her into the water. He goes to grab Raine, but she raises a warning brow that sends him away from her.

They're acting weird. Luke and Raine have been friends since middle school and have always been really close. I always thought they had a brother-sisterly bond with how protective they're over one another. There is a clear distance between them today, and I don't like not knowing why or how my mind wonders if maybe I read them wrong. That maybe they were something more, and that's what has created the tension.

I try to push the assumptions out of my head.

Olivia, however, is oblivious to their tension and hops onto Luke's back, attempting to dunk him into the water but fails. He grabs her again and slings her over his shoulders. The water is shallow enough that his feet can touch the bottom, and the water comes up to his chest. "I bet Derick can't do this." He laughs.

"No, because he isn't a jerk." Olivia squeals before splashing into the water.

"We need more mature friends," I say and scoot over to Raine.

She hums in approval while laughing at Luke and Olivia. I reach into her bag of Skittles and pop one into my mouth with a smile. The powder coating on the candy begins to fizzle in my mouth, and I try not to make a face. She giggles and pops one into her mouth.

My eyes are naturally drawn to the powder it leaves behind on her lips and how her tongue is quick to clean them off. I swallow loud enough to hear and have to avert my eyes. A heat spreads up to my ears.

"I don't understand why you like these things so much," I say and reach in her bag for a second one just to be closer to her.

"Because they're one of the greatest candies ever invented!" she snaps and holds the bag up for effect and points to them.

"It's like a rainbow explosion in your mouth!" Olivia exclaims as she climbs onto Luke's shoulders. "Who wants to play chicken?"

"I was about to take Raine out on the pedal boat," I say quickly, wanting to have her alone to myself again.

"Yeah. That'd be nice," she replies and waves at Olivia, who jumps off Luke and floats on her back.

"Whatever, you're just avoiding being beaten again," Olivia adds before splashing us with water.

Luke laughs, but I can tell it is forced. His dark brows are pushed together in concern as he looks over at Raine, but she pays no attention to him. He's quick to recover, placing a smile onto his face as he looks up at me and gives me a salute before diving into the water.

I hold Raine's hand to steady her as she places a foot into the small boat. I follow close behind her, and within minutes, we are in sync with our feet as we push against the pedals. She's silent, keeping her focus over the water.

The wind picks up as we move farther out onto the lake. Her hair begins to blow across her face and into her mouth. I laugh as she spits it out, and more pieces fly into her mouth. "Here," I say, tapping her shoulder and nudging her to turn around. Once she has her back to me, I take her hair into my grasp and start braiding.

"Since when do you know how to braid hair?" she asks, moving her head, and I place my hands on either side of her head to keep it still.

"Maybe some things are still a mystery between us." I reply, teasing her because we tell each other everything, and wrap the hair tie she keeps on her wrist onto the end of her hair.

She turns back around, placing her feet back onto the pedals, and we move through the water again. She's quiet for a moment before she adds, "Yeah, maybe so."

"What's up with you and Luke?" I blurt, feeling heat raise into my cheeks as the words leave my mouth.

She twists her face toward me and tries to act innocent, but I see right through her mask. "What?"

"You and Luke have been avoiding each other. Are you two —?" I can't finish my sentence. Instead, I pray silently that it has nothing to do with them secretly dating each other or having deeper feelings for one another.

"We don't have those kinds of feelings for each other, if that's what you're thinking," she admits and rolls her eyes. "He's like a brother to me, Ry—even more so now."

I wait for her to elaborate, watching her closely as she bites her lip and stares out onto the lake. After a moment, her shoulders drop, and she returns her attention to me.

"Things have been a little weird between us since his dad moved in with my mom. Now, Luke is living with me every other week," she confesses.

I know that Raine's mom is dating Luke's dad, Davis, but I had no idea they were planning on moving in with each other. Although, they've been dating for almost two years. From the dread on Raine's face, I can tell it bothers her, and in return, it does me too. Davis is a hateful and controlling person.

Davis reminds me a lot of my father. I've witnessed how he treats Raine a few times. It doesn't take much for him to snap at her. He demands to know what she's doing at all times when she's with her mom. Raine has told me that her mom's drinking problem has become worse since they started dating.

Luke informed me of his dad's life of crime and how he has control in every part of the town. The police turn their heads anytime Davis does something illegal, and he walks around as if he runs the place. In a way, he kind of does. I can't stand the guy and pray daily that he gets served justice.

A frown takes over my face. Raine knows how I feel about Davis, and the idea of him living with her unsettles me. "Why didn't you tell me Davis moved in?"

She shrugs her shoulders, keeping her eyes on her lap where she picks at the skin by her thumb nail. "I don't know. I didn't want you to worry."

"Of course I'm going to worry. He causes problems in your life already—Luke's too. I don't like to think about how living with Davis must be for you." I huff and run a hand through my hair. "I'm glad Luke can be there for you, but it sucks that it's only every other week, since he goes to his mom's."

She rolls her eyes. "Yeah, he's lucky that he has an escape. I guess I resent him for it, and he's picked up on it."

"But you have your grandparents. Have you thought about living with them?" I add, seeing the worry that flashes in her eyes as she lifts her head toward me.

"I have. Many times. Before Davis, I wanted to keep an eye on Mom and make sure she was okay. But now...I just want to run away."

"We'll find a solution. It's going to be okay," I promise her, praying that my words will become true.

"How do you know it'll be okay?" she asks as she runs her fingers along her braid.

The thing is, I don't know. But there is one thing that I am a hundred percent sure of. "Because you have me, and I'll always make sure that you're okay."

She drops her braid, eyes finding mine, and gifts me with a beautiful smile. The kind that lights up her whole face. Being the reason for that smile sends a surge of confidence running through me.

A boat nearby is playing music loudly, distracting us for a moment, and an idea hits me. I place my hands onto the side of the boat and do my best to balance myself as I stand up. Raine watches me, raising a brow in question.

"What are you doing?"

I ignore her question and sway a bit as I turn to face her. I extend my hand to her, and she looks at it with concern. "Grab my hand."

"What?"

"Just grab my hand, Raine!" I snap playfully and give her a winning smirk as she grabs my hand and slowly pulls herself to stand. "Now, dance with me."

"What?" she repeats, and it takes everything in me not to laugh at the look on her face. "They're playing a rap song. I can't get low on a pedal boat—or anywhere. I can't dance."

Although I would love to see her attempt that, I place one hand onto her hip and the other in her hand. "Just dance with me." I look at her with a grin.

"You're crazy." She chuckles, the tension releasing as she removes her hand from mine and places her arms around my neck. "Who dances in a pedal boat?"

"Us. We do."

"We're officially crazy, then," she adds as she places her head onto my chest, and I pull her closer by placing a hand onto the back of her head.

I'm crazy about you, I want to say, but instead, I tighten my lips together and place my cheek onto the top of her head. We stay like this for the rest of the song until the boat is far enough that we can't hear their music anymore. The tightness in her back relaxes as she snuggles into me more and begins humming a song for us.

I rub circles on her back, silently telling her that everything is going to be okay. I can't take away her grief from losing a pet or remove the worry in her heart of knowing Davis is always going to be at home waiting for her. But I can distract her for the moment and take her mind away from it all.

We are both so wrapped up in one another that we fail to hear a boat speeding by us. It's close enough that the waves push against the boat, yanking us apart and sending us both into the lake. Panic hits me as the sound of water bubbling around me fills my senses. I reach out to search for Raine in the water before I push my way up to the surface.

I find her clinging onto the boat with her back to me. My arms push through the water until I'm at her side, and once she turns to face me and I see the smile on her face, relief washes over me. We both start laughing as we work together to get back into the boat.

We're both soaking wet, our clothes clinging to us, and my laugh evaporates and is replaced with nerves as I try to avert my eyes from looking at her. I can hear the splash of water hitting the bottom of the boat as she wrings out the fabric of her dress.

"Thanks for making me feel better—even though you almost killed us," she says softly as we put our feet back onto the pedals and begin making our way back to the dock where our friends are waiting for us.

"That's what friends are for," I say, but the word *friends* comes out a little hoarse this time. Because in my heart, Raine is much more to me than just my friend. And I wish I knew how to tell her that.

Chapter Eleven

Now

Raine

My world is falling apart and I don't know how to stop it.

It's been three days since Mamaw's funeral, and I haven't had the energy to do anything but lie in an uncomfortable hotel bed, drinking metallic-tasting water from the bathroom sink and snacking on vending machine food. I desperately need a shower because I can smell the musty scent of myself.

I'm thankful that my job has given me bereavement time off along with a few personal days that I used when I traveled here. I know that I can't stay like this forever. I need to collect whatever pieces I have left of myself in order to be there for my Papaw.

I've called him each day to check in on him, keeping things short and simple, understanding that we both need some time to accept reality. I've ignored every other call and text message I've received since the funeral. I'm not ready to talk to anyone about it. I might not ever be.

I roll over to my left side, reach down toward the rough carpet that looks like it was designed in the early '70s, and grab the cord to my phone charger. My phone died a few hours ago, so I plug it back in and watch as the Apple logo pops into view. I place it face down so I don't have to watch all the notifications pop up at once.

Exhaling, I flop back onto the bed. Even doing that simple task seems to drain my energy. Grief sucks the life out of anyone within its grasp. I'm pretty sure I passed through three of the stages of grief within the past few days. The first day after we said our goodbyes, I was in denial that it even happened.

It felt like a dream and that I would eventually wake up, and there Mamaw would be, sitting at the kitchen table, folding dough to bake a fresh batch of sourdough bread. However, each day I wake up to the reality that she isn't here. How could God allow my Mamaw to die like she did? He gave me peace! Why would he give me peace and then just take her away?

The second day, I entered the bargaining stage and pleaded with God through my tears. I felt so alone, and that peace he once gifted me never returned. And so, I slid right into depression, which is where I feel stuck currently. I've ignored the alerts on my phone. I've ignored the knocks at my hotel door. I've ignored reality. But I know I *can't* stay like this.

Bang. Bang. Bang.

A knock on the hotel door sends me jumping and sprawling onto the floor.

The sound is loud and impatient. Someone is going to beat down the door. Is it an intruder? The second they catch sight of my mess, I guarantee they will turn around and walk right back out—I hope, anyway.

"Raine! Open this door right now!" Olivia's voice shouts through the wood.

I'm too scared to get up. When she gets mad—which is very rare—she's terrifying. The angriest that I've ever seen her was in eighth grade after she witnessed a boy bullying Luke. She went up to him and said, *"I don't know how to say this nicely, so I won't,"* and then punched the kid in the throat.

"Don't make me break the door down! You know I will give it my best efforts!"

I take a deep breath and sniff my armpits for good measure. She's probably seen me in worse shape, however I'm still embarrassed. Before I can reach the door, I hear the sound of a key being inserted into the door, the doorknob twists, and I'm blinded by the sun. I want to hiss like they do in vampire movies and pull the covers over my head, but the sight of Luke's large form coming toward me has me halting in place.

Really? She had to bring him? Fully dressed in his police uniform, might I add.

Olivia must read my expression, because she says, "What? I didn't want to go to jail for breaking and entering, so I called in backup."

Her face softens once she takes me in, and then her green eyes scan the hotel room. I peer up at Luke, who is doing the same, and I cannot contain my embarrassment. I place my hands over my face, not wanting to see their pity.

"Come here," she says softly, and I peek through my fingers to see Olivia extending her arms open for a hug. I oblige and walk into her embrace, glad that she has stopped yelling at me. However, when she pulls back, she scrunches her nose and adds, "I love you. But you smell."

I know I do, but I still give her an unamused expression.

I look at Luke, who has a hand running through his dark hair, leaving it a mess. He reaches over and takes one of those bags that hotels leave for ice and begins picking up my pile of wrappers off the floor. My friends are always there, ready to pick me back up when I'm a complete mess—*literally*.

"I know. I'm gross." My voice sounds foreign, like grief transformed me into someone else. Maybe it has. I certainly don't feel the same.

"Did we know she was this messy?" Luke asks, looking over at Olivia.

"Unfortunately, yes," she replies with a smirk.

"You both know I'm standing right here, right?"

"You know, if she would have just answered our calls—" she adds, but I interrupt her with a loud groan, earning a chuckle from them both.

"I know I suck right now. But I won't apologize. I can clean up my own trash," I proclaim and reach for the—*now full*—bag in Luke's hands. He moves the bag away from my grasp and ties a knot before tossing it toward the door. Behind me, Olivia is grabbing my suitcase and packing everything she can find. "What are you doing?"

"You're leaving this disgusting hotel room. Then, when we get back to my place—which you will be staying at, by the way, and how dare you not even think to ask me if you could—you'll be taking a nice hot shower because, girl, you smell like you've been laying in onion juice and look like one of those goblins from *Harry Potter*."

I shake my head in protest, but the look I receive from her quickly shuts me up. She makes a face at Luke, and before I have time to react, he picks me up and slings me over his shoulder. I'd hit him in protest, but he could throw me in jail for assaulting a police officer—not that he would do that, but he could if he wanted to.

"She wasn't kidding about that shower."

"Shut up. I don't stink that bad! Wait. Are you serious?" I shout as Luke places me into the backseat of his police cruiser.

There are a few people walking down the sidewalk, who turn their attention our way, and my embarrassment grows. A frown spreads across my face when the door is locked and won't open. There are also bars that prevent me from climbing into the front seat and escaping. Luke's lips pull at the corner in a smirk that I'd love to smack off his face.

"She's rubbed off on you! You know that, right?!" I shout, but he ignores me and returns to the hotel room.

A few minutes pass, and I watch as my friends take the trash to the dumpster, check me out of the hotel, and drag my belongings behind them and place them into the trunk. Olivia giggles as she slides into the front passenger seat. She looks back at me and snaps a photo with her phone. I make a mental note to steal her phone later and delete it.

"I never thought I'd see the day that you'd be sitting in the back of a police car. I take that back. We pulled a close one that time we stole Ms. Johnson's lawn gnomes."

"*You*. You stole them. And you were planning to blackmail me if I didn't help you," I add, biting my lip to hide my smile. I'm supposed to be angry with her right now.

"Wait a minute. That was you two?" Luke snaps as he shuffles into his seat.

"They were creepy. We did the citizens of Covewood justice." Olivia shrugs her shoulders while snapping her seatbelt into place.

"But you placed them all throughout the school. One in particular in my locker, which scared the crap out of me!"

Olivia's shoulder's bounce as she laughs hysterically. Luke looks back at me as if I betrayed him and points a finger at me, adding, "You earned your place back there for causing me nightmares after that." His words only feed into Olivia's laughter.

"Olivia was the one who suggested we pull a senior prank and that we mess with you in the process. You should have never shared your locker combination with her."

"I didn't," he adds, giving Olivia the stink-eye.

"But Raine was the one that picked Mr. Gnome Chomsky for the job! He was the scariest of all forty-seven gnomes."

Luke shudders at the memory and points a finger at Olivia. "I'm about to stick you back there with her if you don't stop laughing. It was traumatizing. I expect some comfort food to help me cope with this traumatic news."

"You already get comfort food for free all the time!"

"That's the only reason why I'm not shoving you back there with Stinkalicious."

"You both are unbelievable! You didn't have to drag me out

of there like I'm a crazy person!" I hiss and twist my arms together in a pout.

"Have you looked in a mirror lately?" Olivia makes a judgy face and points toward what I suspect is the bird's nest of hair I have on top of my head. "Don't make that face at me!"

"I am not responsible for what my face does when you're yelling at me."

"You're the one yelling!"

"Alright, calm down, ladies, or I'll handcuff you together." Luke growls as he puts his car into drive and pulls out onto the highway.

"Wait! My car! Can't I just drive to your house?"

"No. That takes away from our fun," Luke announces as he turns on the red and blue lights and begins speeding in the direction of Olivia's house.

"Now, this has to be breaking some sort of law," I snap and wish I could reach through the bars and smack him in the back of the head. Olivia giggles and lets out a joyful squeal as she blasts the "Bad Boys" song from *Cops* through the car speakers. I hate them right now. But I also love them so much for making me laugh as we speed down the road.

It doesn't last long, unfortunately. Luke turns off the lights and returns to normal speed once we're on the main road. A quiet spreads throughout the car, and I'm reminded that they're hurting too, and guilt fills my heart as I realize I abandoned them the last three days.

I look out the window and watch as we drive through downtown. Lining the street are colorful dogwood and redbud trees starting to bloom. The brick buildings look the same and yet different all the same time. I notice new businesses lining the streets as we pass by.

Before I know it, we're at Olivia's house. Luke jumps out first, making his way to open my door. I step outside and admire the cute yellow bungalow that I'm ashamed to admit I haven't seen in person yet, even though Olivia moved in several years ago.

I place my hands onto the porch railing, taking the steps, and admire the twin white rocking chairs I've seen her sit in during our FaceTime conversations. Underneath each window sits matching flower boxes that hold several different herbal plants. On each of the four corners of the porch is a large plant that I don't know the name of.

I place my feet onto the welcome mat, bold and colorful to match my best friend, and the tears hit me again as life's heaviness seems to sit on my shoulders. I turn around and see Olivia standing a few steps behind me, blinking in confusion, and studying me. "What is it?"

"I, uh..." I take a breath, hoping that it'll help steady me. "I feel awful for never seeing your house in person before. It's so cute."

As the words leave my mouth, a sob follows, and Olivia is quick to swoop in and wrap me into a tight embrace. There's no snarky comment this time, only the sound of her shushing in my ear.

"It's okay. Don't start beating yourself up over it. You're here now. Let's focus on that, okay?"

We pull away from one another, and I wipe my eyes as I nod my head. I want to agree with her, but the guilt seems to keep building the longer I'm in Covewood. Maybe things would be better if I go back to Rockdale soon. But not before I make sure that my Papaw is going to be okay.

Olivia opens the bright-blue door, the smell of sweet baked goods fills my nose, and my stomach growls, reminding me that I haven't eaten real food in days. Behind us, Luke carries my bags. He places them next to the couch and sticks his hands into his pockets.

"Is there anything else you need from me?" he asks and shifts on his feet. "I, uh... I need to get back to the station."

"Nope," Olivia says, making the P pop as she says it. "We are all good here."

She gives him a salute, and he rolls his eyes in return. He walks over to me and wraps me into a big bear hug, one that I didn't know I missed so much until I feel the warmth of his arms around me. I have always felt safe with Luke around, even before he became a cop. He smells like fresh air, pine trees, and aftershave. I breathe him in and squeeze him back and then let go.

Olivia has been my best friend since elementary school. Once Luke moved to town when we were in seventh grade, Olivia and I kind of claimed him as our own after the whole Olivia-throat-punching-a-bully-for-him thing. It was always the three of us, until Ryland joined our crew freshman year of high school. Luke was once a chubby kid with a messy black mop of hair on his head and round black glasses.

I watched him grow up a lot during high school. Literally, the guy bulked up like the Hulk after the summer of eighth grade. He didn't have any issues with bullies after that, but we always made sure to stay close. The man that stands before me is still the same Luke and yet so different. It pains my heart, knowing I missed a big portion of him growing up into the Luke I see now.

"Are you going to be okay?" He tips his head down toward me to get a better look at my eyes.

I do my best to give him a reassuring smile. He pats my shoulder and seems to accept it as my answer. "Sorry if we had a little too much fun today. We were just trying to take your mind off...you know. And if you're worried about running into Davis, he's not coming back to Covewood. I made sure of that. I promise that you're safe here," he says before kissing the top of my head, which I'm sure is a giant mess. It doesn't seem to bother him. His words are comforting and I finally allow myself to relax.

Olivia tosses a muffin toward him, and he catches it effortlessly. "Let me know if you need anything—both of you," he says. "I will come back after my shift, okay?"

His eyes are on me, and I reply with a nod.

Once the door closes behind him, I look towards Olivia, who is still looking at the door with a grin on her face, and say, "In that uniform he looks so..."

She returns her attention to me, the grin falling from her face, and she sighs. "They grow up so fast," Before clapping her hands together and stepping towards me. "Ok, grab some comfy pajamas and go take the longest, hottest shower of your life. When you're done, I'll have some lunch made and we can finally watch *Bridesmaids* since we didn't the other day."

"Have I told you how much I love you?" I say, grinning at my best friend.

"Not lately, and I will gladly take all the praise from you, but right now, you must shower before I lose my appetite, okay?"

"Okay, okay! I'm going! Do I stink that bad?" I ask and grab one of my bags.

"Yes! Now go!" She chuckles before making her way toward the kitchen.

Chapter Twelve

Thirteen Years Before

Raine

The sun is hot against my back, covering me like a comforting blanket. I pick at the petals of a dandelion flower, allowing the wind to sweep them away from my fingertips, as I sit on the porch steps outside of my mom's house and wait for Ryland to pick me up. Waves are crashing inside my stomach as each second passes. He's never seen my home before, and I'm embarrassed for him to see where I live.

It's a small brick house near downtown in a small neighborhood. My grandparents helped my dad buy the house right before he married my mom. They were supposed to start a family here, but instead, the world had other plans.

The landscaping could use some work, weeds have taken over the flowerbeds, the lawn is four weeks past due for mowing, and the bushes have grown over most of the front windows. Not to mention all the junk that is laying around that Davis brought over with him once he officially moved in to live with us. Thankfully, Davis isn't home at the moment.

It's rare that I get to see Ryland outside of school during the week. However, he got his license a few days ago, and Pops told him he could celebrate by picking me up. But Pops is tagging along since it's his truck that Ryland is driving.

I hear the familiar purr of the engine before I see the boxy orange truck pull onto my street and into my driveway. I practically run toward it, not able to contain the huge smile that spreads across my face as it does anytime I'm around Ryland.

Pops opens the door for me to hop inside, and I'm sandwiched between him and Ryland. It feels odd seeing Ryland behind the wheel. And yet, somehow, it makes him appear more grown-up and confident. I like this look on him, probably more than I should, but I keep the feelings locked deep inside.

We're just friends, my subconscious likes to remind me.

Ryland's full lips pull into a grin, and the way he looks down at me makes my heart feel like it's falling down onto the floorboard of the truck. I take my eyes away from him because I don't like how it makes me feel. Okay, I do like it, but his Pops is right next to me, and I also don't want to complicate things

"I made us a CD for today," he says, holding up the shiny circle so I can see his handwriting over the silver surface. The title says, *Raine and Ryland's Epic Mix*, and on the sides he wrote each song title. It has a mixture of nineties country and early two-thousands pop—a little bit of him, a little bit of me. The thought of him putting the music together for *us* sends warmth into my gut.

"Do people still burn CDs? It's 2011," I say, turning to face the windshield so Ryland can't see the pink spreading across my cheeks.

"Only the cool people still do." He hitches a shoulder, grinning at me when I tuck my hair behind my ear and peek up at him through my lashes. "Plus, an MP3 player won't work in Pops' old truck."

We share a laugh when Pops rolls his eyes and grunts at our choice in music, but he allows us to play whatever we want. We decide to go to some of our favorite spots at the edge of town. Our first stop is Matty's Meats. I know the name is strange, however Matt loves to cook all types of meats. He offers burgers, steaks, pork tenderloins, and more. One weekend a month, he even offers exotic meats. It's interesting, and the townsfolk love it here, including Pops. It's his favorite restaurant.

Once we take our seats, Ryland dares me to try to eat the "Mighty Matt Burger", which is made up of four thick hamburger patties with melted cheese between each layer and triple the toppings. It's huge. I agree but only if he will try it too. Somehow, we talk Pops into joining the challenge, and before we know it, a crowd begins to form around us as the three of us chow down.

I have to admit, it's the best burger I've ever eaten in my life. However, I'm the first to tap out without even finishing a quarter of the burger. Ryland has a little over half of his burger eaten before he has to quit. Pops surprises us all as he keeps going and going until the very last greasy bite is gone.

The whole restaurant cheers as he swallows the last bite. They place a fake gold metal around Pops' neck and take a picture of him, hanging it up on their wall of *Mighty Meat Lovers*, which holds three other photos. The proud look that spreads across Ryland's face fills my heart with so much joy. He insists that we go and get ice cream to celebrate.

Pops looks sickened by the thought of eating anything else but doesn't protest. We drive across town to Frozen Scoops, singing as loud as we can to the music and sharing giggles as we catch Pops bopping his head to a few of the songs.

I never want this day to end.

Ryland wrinkles his nose at my choice of ice cream. "How can you enjoy mint in ice cream form?"

I roll my eyes, pretending to ignore his comment, as I take a lick of the tingly flavor. My cheeks burn as I catch him watching me. "It makes it taste extra cold and refreshing. It's the perfect flavor for hot days," I reply and shrug my shoulders, trying my best to ignore the lava running through my veins. The ice cream does nothing to help me *chill*.

"Cookie dough is by far a better flavor." He raises a challenging brow before pulling his ice cream to his lips, licking his towering two scoops from top to bottom, and now I'm the one watching his movements closely. He smirks knowingly, and it's enough to snap me back to reality, and I avert my eyes. Why does my best friend have to be so hot?

"Have you ever tried mint ice cream before?"

"Why would I even think to try it? I bet it tastes like brushing your teeth right after eating chocolate." He shudders at the thought, and I let out a giggle.

"Try it," I tell him and hold out my cone. I laugh as Ryland wrinkles his nose. "Please."

He rolls his eyes, leans over, and takes a lick of my ice cream. My eyes widen at the sight, and I wait patiently for his response. He smacks his lips together, using his tongue to wipe the ice cream at the corner of his mouth, and gives me a thoughtful look. "Nope. Not for me."

Before I can argue with him, Pops walks up with a cup in his hand and points a spoon full of dark-pink ice cream toward us. "That's because the best flavor of ice cream is sherbert."

Ryland looks over at me, and we both burst with laughter. "Pops, you're showing your age with your choice in ice cream flavor," Ryland deadpans before taking another bite of his cone.

Pops rolls his eyes and takes the empty seat next to me. "You kids have it all wrong with your chocolate-flavored everything. Sherbert is where it's at."

Ryland and I steal licks from each other's cones, refusing to admit that we like the other's flavor, before finishing up and hopping back into the truck. Pops requests a quick trip to the nearest Walmart so he can pick up a few things. Ryland and I choose to load up on snacks. How we are still hungry is beyond me.

Driving around with Ryland and Pops has been one of the best days I've had in a long time. Unfortunately, it's a school night, and we both need to head home before it gets too late.

Ryland pulls the truck into the driveway of my house, and I freeze as soon as I notice Davis' black truck sitting in the driveway.

Ryland senses my hesitation, his eyes searching my face when I turn and look at him. "I'm going to walk her to the door," he says to Pops, his hazel eyes never leaving mine.

Pops hums an approval, his eyes closed and a hand on his stomach, clearly uncomfortable from our choices today. "See you around, Raine."

"See ya," I say softly before following Ryland out of the truck through his door.

He reaches down and takes my hand into his as we walk toward the door. My heart is pounding so loudly in my chest, especially when I see the curtains to the living room window move as someone watches us. I close my eyes, inhale a breath, and wait for Davis to stomp outside and cause a scene. But he never does.

I tug Ryland toward one of the overgrown bushes, where I know we'll be hidden from watchful eyes. I've wanted a moment alone with him all day. Even if it's only a minute. He wraps his arms around me and pulls me into a tight hug. "Thank you for today," I whisper and give him a gentle squeeze.

"You're welcome. Oh, hey, I snuck and got you something at Walmart when you were in the restroom." His lips curl over his teeth as he reaches into his pocket and pulls out a small gold chain that has a rainbow pendant dangling from it. I raise a brow, taking it into my hands to study, before he explains. "Remember in church, last Sunday, when they were talking about Noah and how the rainbow brings us hope and beauty after a storm."

I stare at him, my lips parting in surprise. "Yeah."

If I could bottle up one look of Ryland's to have forever, it would be the way he is looking at me right now. His eyes, greener in the setting sunlight, hold a sparkle to them as they dance with my own. The side of his lip is turned up into a shy grin, one that speaks so much more than words could ever say.

"You're like that. You bring a rainbow wherever you go. So, I just, um...wanted to give you this."

This is the sweetest, kindest thing anyone has ever done for me. To know that he saw this and wanted to gift it to me makes me feel like I'm floating in the clouds. He probably meant this as a nice gift between two friends, but to me, it feels like so much more.

"Will you help me put it on?" I ask, handing the necklace to him and turning around.

He hesitates for a moment until his fingers graze the back of my neck, sending goosebumps across the exposed skin. "Yeah," he says, his voice raspier than before.

My hands hang loosely by my sides, and I feel his fingers run down my arm until they snag the hair tie I keep around my wrist. He slides it off and runs his fingers through my hair before pulling the strands into a braid. I love it when he does this. Once the braid is finished, he allows it to fall over my shoulder. He places the necklace around my neck, and the rainbow pendant falls against the dip of my collarbone once it's fastened.

"Thank you. I love it," I announce and touch it with my fingers. I'll never take this necklace off.

"I'm glad, Rainbow."

"Is that my nickname now?" I question, and he gives me a grin in return.

"Yeah. I want it to be a special nickname just for me."

I practically jump into his arms, almost causing us both to fall down, and the plastic bag in my hand swings as it bumps against his back. He chuckles and wraps his arms around me in another hug before I pull away and move my braid over my shoulder. He looks down at me, his brows pinched together in a discomforting look, and he parts his lips to say something.

"I—"

The words seem to be lodged in his throat. He coughs, his shoulders tensing up, and the glossiness in his eyes washes away with a blink. “I’ll see you at school tomorrow.”

I wave goodbye as he leaves and watch the truck back out of the driveway, the sense of dread hitting me as soon as he is gone. As I shut the front door behind me, Davis' voice fills the space.

“Where the hell have you been?” he shouts, and I cringe at the sound.

Beside him on the couch sits my mom, who is clinging to a bottle of beer. She pulls it toward her lips and looks over at me with empty eyes and says nothing. She has never stuck up for me before. I’m not sure why I still hope that she will, but instead, she allows Davis to do and say whatever he wants to me. Even though she's physically here, it's as if she’s abandoned me.

“Ryland has his license now and took me to get something to eat.” *Since we don’t have anything to eat in this house*, I want to say but bite my tongue. “His grandpa went with us,” I add.

“You don’t just leave without telling your mother where you’re going. She was worried sick.”

I’m not sure what comes over me at this moment, but something inside of me snaps, and my anger toward my mother and Davis lashes out. “Yeah, she seems really worried. She was passed out drunk when I went to ask for her approval. I thought since it’s okay for her to be unconscious around her child, it wouldn’t matter if I left for a little while.”

My mother’s eyes widen once the words leave my mouth. She cowers deeper into the couch as Davis twists around and looks at her with disgust. Her eyes snap back to me, a little bit of emotion sparking back to life inside her.

“Raine, go clean up the kitchen and then go to your room,” she growls, trying to sound demanding, but all I hear is fear laced within her words.

I roll my eyes, ignoring his words about how I’m worthless and disrespectful, and head into the kitchen where I find Luke at the sink, washing the dishes.

"Hey," I say, feeling relieved the instant I see him. I'm so happy he is here, even though I know how much being here makes him unhappy. It does for me too, but at least we have each other—some of the time, anyway. His dark eyes look dimmer today, the usual light in them gone. Davis does that to those around him.

"Want to share?" I add, holding up the plastic bag in my hand, hoping I can make Luke's day better.

He blinks, as if recovering from a trance, before looking at the bag. "He's been in a bad mood since finding out you weren't here. He kept demanding that I tell him where you were, and he had his goons out looking for you."

The color drains from my face. I didn't think about the consequences of leaving. I just left at the first opportunity that I could. "I'm sorry," I whisper. "You could've gone with us if I knew you were coming over," I add as he dries his hands off with a towel.

"It's okay. Mom dropped me off about an hour ago. I'm not allowed to go into my room until I do the chores." He huffs, and I instantly feel regret.

"I took off the second I could. I was going to do the dishes when I got back home."

"It's okay. It's not your fault my dad is a jerk who's apparently obsessed with you."

I swallow hard at his statement. Davis is controlling over the both of us, but I have noticed he's harsher on me, always demanding to know where I am at all times. The fact that he had his friends out looking for me makes a chill run deep into my bones.

Davis stomps his way into the kitchen, his bloodshot eyes snapping between the two of us before they land on the bag in my hand. He walks over, and I flinch with the movement, not missing the way Luke places his hands onto my shoulders and moves me to stand behind him.

"The next time you decide to leave without telling me, there will be consequences. Do you understand?" he hisses before he eyes the bag again. "What are you hiding?"

He shoves Luke out of the way so he can snatch the bag from my hand. He pulls out two containers of ramen noodles, a Snickers bar, and two bags of chips before tossing the bag back toward me.

I look inside, and all that's left are three Milky Ways. I'm surprised he even left those. As I always do, instead of yelling back at Davis, I keep my true feelings buried deep inside and turn to rush off into my room, dragging Luke behind me. I shut the door behind us and feel my tears trying to betray me.

"He's such an—" Luke mumbles but stops once his eyes land on me. "Hey..."

"Why is it okay that he treats us like this?" I say, my voice trembling, and I take a seat on my bed.

"I don't know. But it won't be forever," he says and sits on the bed next to me.

"Here." I reach into my jeans pockets, thankful they're a little baggy, and pull out a few bags of candy, beef jerky, and ramen packages from my back pocket that I hid before coming inside. We both laugh softly.

"You're awesome," he whispers before unwrapping a Milky Way and taking a big bite.

"I'm glad you're here," I add, his eyes piercing into mine with a knowing look behind them before we return to our dinner.

I cling to the rainbow necklace around my neck and think about the hope Ryland was speaking about. I pray for God to place hope into Luke's and my hearts that, one day soon, we can both get away from Davis. And that no matter what, we will always have each other.

Chapter Thirteen

Now

Ryland

Normally, on Sundays after church, Mom, Zane, Annabelle, and I go to Matty's Meats and order their "Mighty Matt Burger" in memory of Pops. We all split the humongous burger and reminisce on our favorite memories and stories of my grandparents. We started the tradition shortly after we lost Pops. We're still learning how to cope without my grandparents in our lives.

I love a good tradition. However, today, I don't feel like participating. After the church service this morning, I felt drained. Everyone around me seems to be carrying a heaviness with them, knowing it was our first service without Johanna.

When I mentioned to my family that I wanted to head home, Annabelle didn't want to leave my side. I try to limit how much screen time she has, but today, I turn on *Bluey* and snuggle up on the couch with her. She fell asleep a few minutes ago, and yet, here I am, continuing to watch the show.

I secretly think this is a cartoon for parents too.

I shake myself out of a *Bluey* trance, especially since it's the episode where Bluey and Bingo's aunt visits, and it always tugs at my heart. I need some fresh air, so I gently move away from my sleeping daughter, successfully not waking her as I do, and make my way onto the porch.

I take a seat on one of my rocking chairs, and the creaking fills my ears as I rock back and forth. I peek through the glass of the back door and see that Annabelle is still sleeping peacefully on the couch. Her mouth hangs open just a little bit, reminding me of how her mother would look while she slept. I ache for Annabelle anytime I think about Maggie. I've had seven years to try to understand her reasoning for leaving us, but even so, it still breaks my heart for my daughter.

After Raine left Covewood, I started drinking heavily and partying every chance I could. It was the most broken I've been in my life. Two years after Raine left, I met Annabelle's mom. Maggie's family rented the cabin next door one summer. Maggie and I ran into each other at one of the bonfire parties people held at the lake, and we hit it off. Our shared brokenness drew us to one another, and we became the perfect distraction for each other.

One thing led to another, and she ended up getting pregnant. I didn't know for months. After summer ended, Maggie and her parents returned home to Colorado, and even though we'd exchanged phone numbers, we had a silent agreement that things would end after that summer. Three months later, she called me and told me she was pregnant.

Her parents weren't supportive, and after a pep talk with Mom and Pops, we all drove to Colorado and picked Maggie up to come live with us. I should have known that she wasn't doing well mentally, with how she seemed unattached during her pregnancy. I tried everything that I could think of to excite her and assured her that I would always be there for her and our child.

After Annabelle was born, Maggie's postpartum depression took over, and a few months later, she told me she was leaving. When I begged her to at least keep in touch with Annabelle, she suggested signing over her rights so that she wouldn't have anything keeping her tied to us. At the time, I thought that burying my Nan or losing Raine was the worst pain that I would endure. But I was wrong.

Knowing that my daughter's mother wanted nothing to do with her completely destroyed me. I reached out to Maggie's parents and asked for help, but they only turned away from us. They, too, wanted nothing to do with Annabelle. I was so angry and originally refused to allow Maggie to sign over her rights. But finally, my gut told me to let it be done.

Once everything was finalized, she returned to Colorado. I gave it a few years before I felt brave enough to reach out to Maggie again. Her phone number had changed of course, but I was able to get a hold of her parents, who informed me that they hadn't spoken to Maggie in over a year and, sadly, still showed no interest in Annabelle. They told me to not call again and hung up.

I let it go after that and decided that, in order to heal from it all, we needed to move on. Now, if Maggie were to show up tomorrow and want a relationship with Annabelle, I wouldn't say no. What kind of a father would I be to take that away from Annabelle? But until that day comes, it'll just be her and me. And I'm content with that.

Annabelle changed me for the better. She helped me grow into a much better man and find my faith again. She's my little angel, and I feel so lucky that God chose me to be her father. I know that when the time is right, he will bring us someone who will be willing to step up and be the mother figure Annabelle needs.

We just haven't found her yet.

"There you are," I hear Zane say from my right.

I jump slightly, ripped away from my deep thoughts, and throw an empty cup toward my little brother. He dodges it and paints a smirk across his face.

"Did I almost give you a heart attack, old man?" He chuckles when I scowl at him.

He takes the empty rocking chair next to me and lets out a sigh. "We missed you today. I think it was the first Sunday you've missed since..."

He doesn't finish his sentence. He doesn't have to. I shrug and exhale some of the weight that's been sitting on my chest.

"Yeah, I know."

He reaches over and gives my shoulder a comforting pat. Zane might give me a hard time some days, but he has a heart of gold. I'm thankful to have him as my brother.

When we were younger, especially back in Utah, we would fight so much. We had to share a room back then, and because we spent so much time together, it caused a few issues between us. Once we moved to Covewood, we not only gained our own spaces, but we also kept the fighting to a minimum, thanks to Nan and Pops. They wouldn't tolerate it.

Once we grew up, so did our friendship, especially after Annabelle was born and Zane became "The World's Coolest Uncle" as he likes to claim. He even bought himself a coffee mug that says so. He helped me a lot during those first few—very hard—years of raising a child all on my own. I learned just how important family is during those times.

I still do.

"I'm sure it's a lot. Losing Johanna. Running into Raine. I'm here for you. You know that, right?"

"I appreciate it," I reply.

He claps his hands together and leans back into the wooden chair. The sound of it creaking fills the silence as we both peer out toward the lake. After a moment, he seems to remember Annabelle and looks through the back door.

"She's taking a nap," I tell him, and he relaxes next to me.

"I brought her some leftovers." He holds up a plastic bag I hadn't noticed before. He plasters on a goofy grin as he sets the bag onto the small table next to me.

"Are you trying to sneak her some sugar?" I question accusingly.

He widens his eyes innocently, but I know better. "I would never." He proclaims.

My family thinks it's funny to sneak Annabelle sugar behind my back. Now, don't get me wrong, I let my kid enjoy treats from time to time. However, when Maggie was pregnant with Annabelle, she had gestational diabetes, and I started doing a ton of research. I became a bit of a health nut after that, maybe a tad bit protective.

Raising a tiny human on your own will do that to you.

That doesn't mean we don't enjoy junk food from time to time. There's a time and place for it. I take pride in knowing what my child is ingesting. After all, food is medicine.

Zane loves to poke fun at me for it, but I'm the parent, not him. He just gets to be the fun uncle who sneaks my kid what looks to be a chocolate chip cookie in the bag. I reach inside and pull out the very large cookie and hold it up to my face for size reference. Zane shrugs his shoulders as he chuckles.

"Does a seven-year-old really need a cookie that is the size of a human skull?"

"Absolutely not," he says, folding his arms behind his head and leaning back in the chair. "I intended for her to share it with you, unless you're scared of gaining some weight and not being able to impress Raine. Newsflash, brother: your massive Santa beard will already do the trick. Might as well gain the jolly belly to go with it."

"Don't you know to never disrespect a man's beard?" I roll my eyes and shove a piece of cookie into my mouth, not missing the way Zane's eyes twinkle with glee when a piece falls into said Santa beard.

I run my hands through my long facial hair. Maybe I should shave? At least trim it a bit.

"I'm jealous that you can actually grow a thick one, is all."

He smiles, but it doesn't touch his eyes. After a beat, he says, "So..."

I glance at him, raising a brow in question, but he doesn't finish his sentence. "So...?"

He watches me for a moment, the smirk slowly dripping away from his face and is replaced with a hint of concern. I don't like it. The pressure from his gaze has my skin buzzing.

"Are you doing alright? Really?"

It's a loaded question, one I'm not sure how to answer. I exhale, hoping the knot in my chest will go away with the breath. I lean back in my chair and run my fingers over my beard again.

"I'll be fine," I manage to say, but with the way he tsks at me, I can tell it isn't what he wants to hear.

"But—"

Just in the nick of time, Zane is interrupted by the sound of a police cruiser beeping in the driveway. I turn and see Luke's large form moving out of the driver's seat and give him a wave.

"Hey." Luke huffs as he stomps up the porch steps, swinging a paper bag in his left hand, and reaches out to shake my hand.

"Hey, bud," I reply and gesture to the empty chair to my left.

He nods at Zane before sitting down. "Where were you this morning?" Zane cuts to the chase.

Luke lets out a breath and runs a hand through his jet-black hair. His dark eyes snap to mine, the look making my stomach do one of those back-flip things.

"I was at Olivia's this morning, making sure Raine was getting settled. I ended up staying."

Raine.

One word. One name. That's all it takes to grasp every ounce of my attention and cause my chest to constrict.

"She's still here?" I'm puzzled, shocked even, that she stayed.

"Yeah. Olivia and I had to remove her from the hotel she was at and talked her into staying with Olivia for the time being."

Zane's brows raise as he asks, "Remove?"

"Uh, yeah. It had been days since anyone had seen her, and we were worried. I literally had to pick her up and carry her out of the room and stick her into the back of my police cruiser." Luke smirks and points behind him toward his car.

A frown takes over my face at the thought of Raine being forced to ride in the back of a police cruiser, and Luke catches my disappointment. "It was all a joke. She was totally cool with it." He holds his hands up like he's the guilty one—ironic, with him being a policeman.

"Some people never grow up," Zane utters, and both Luke and I whip our faces his way and glare at him. "What?"

Luke exhales loudly next to me. He shakes his head, and I can see the worry written on his face, deepening the lines by his mouth. He looks exhausted.

"What's wrong?" I ask, the question pulling him from his thoughts.

"I just hate seeing her like that. She clearly hadn't been taking care of herself, and I wish there was something that I could do to help."

"Like forcing her into the back of your police car?"

"It lightened the mood. She laughed about it." Luke waves a hand at me.

"So, she's staying at Olivia's? For how long?" The question comes out fast, my need to know overtaking me.

Luke shrugs his shoulders, his eyes moving toward the back door. I hear the sound of it sliding open before a small squeal leaves Annabelle's mouth. I turn and open my arms for her, but she completely ignores me and rushes toward Zane.

"Uncle Z!!!"

I glance over at Luke, whose outstretched arms drop beside him, and a look of defeat washing over his face. I chuckle, but it's cut short with his fist on my shoulder. I rub against the skin, frowning at my best friend.

"There's my girl!" Zane howls with joy, wrapping Annabelle into a tight hug. "Guess who brought you a cookie."

Annabelle's face lights up as she begins to jump up and down. Zane gives me a smug look that I wish I could wipe off his face. She searches for said cookie in Zane's hand and turns at the crackling sound from the plastic bag I hold.

"Yes, he did, but you have to wait until after dinner."

Zane and Annabelle groan in defeat. Luke, however, beams and holds up the bag in his hand. "Aunt Liv made you an organic, naturally sweetened muffin that I'm sure Daddy will approve of." He looks at Zane, lifting a brow that says *I win*.

Annabelle's squeals return as she runs toward Luke, leaping into his arms, and his smile spreads like the Cheshire Cat from *Alice in Wonderland*. Zane huffs in defeat as Annabelle peeks into the bag.

"If I let you have half of it, do you promise me you'll eat all of your dinner?" I say, giving in to the pouted lip she has mastered.

"Yes, yes, yes!"

"Uncle Luke, break off half for her please."

Luke does as I ask, but he gives Annabelle the piece that is bigger before placing the rest back into the bag and handing it to me. I roll my eyes at the pleased look on his face before going into the house to hide the treats. I check inside the crock pot and see that the roast I put in this morning is just about ready.

I jump at the sight of both Zane and Luke peeking their heads inside the back door, both of them sniffing the air. Annabelle skips her way inside, grabbing Zane's hand and pulling him into the living room.

"Is that roast I smell?" Zane asks, his mouth practically watering with the question.

"Yup."

"Is there enough for me?" Luke asks, slipping past me and

raising the lid to get a better sniff. I swat him away and shove him out of the kitchen.

I did, in fact, make plenty in hopes of having some for leftovers this week. If I'm going to share my food, they will have to earn it. A thought crosses my mind, and now I'm the one with a Cheshire Cat smile. Luke's brows draw together in question.

"Hey, Annabelle. This is the perfect time for you to use your new nail polish set I got for you. I'm sure your uncles won't mind helping you practice."

"You traitor," Luke whispers as Zane releases the hold Annabelle had on him, as if her hands are on fire. She giggles and claps her hands together before running down the hallway toward her bedroom.

"Come on now, it's an uncle's job to keep the princess happy. Don't you want to win at this little game you two are playing for the title of favorite uncle?" What I don't say is how my toes are currently painted bright yellow and it's time for someone else to be Annabelle's canvas.

"Oh, it's clearly me, seeing that I'm blood-related and all," Zane proclaims and takes a seat at the dining room table.

Luke takes a seat next to him, shoving him a bit with his elbow, and adds, "Yeah, but blood doesn't always make you family."

I keep myself busy in the kitchen to avoid having my nails painted again. This is going to be entertaining. I welcome the distraction, knowing that once they leave and Annabelle is in bed, my mind will be wandering back to its usual dark spiral.

Chapter Fourteen

Now

Raine

An early two-thousands pop song is blasting from the yellow cylinder speaker that sits on top of Olivia's kitchen counter. Beside me, Olivia is singing along to the music —*off pitch, but I will never tell her that*—and dancing while stirring a bowl of dough. I watch her for a moment, amazed that this is how she chooses to work, and can't contain my smile as she looks over at me and begs me to join her.

"How do you work in these conditions?" I yell as I try to pull my hand away from her, but her grip is strong. She spins me around and forces me to jump up and down with her. Her bright-red hair smacks me in the face, making me laugh. I give in and sing along with the lyrics.

After a few minutes, the music changes into a soft R&B song. She reaches over and turns the music down a few notches, which I'm thankful for because my head is beginning to pound but so is my heart in the best of ways. There is something about being around your soulmate, or soul sister as Olivia calls us, that's the best cure for depression.

I've been staying with Olivia for the last two days, and she has been putting me to work. She and I were able to prepare double of her orders and deliver her *goodies,* as she calls them, to the local businesses who wholesale with her, as well as personal orders. I asked her if she would ever want to open up her own bakery, but she told me she loved working from home and having the opportunity to help other businesses out by wholesaling to them.

She receives custom orders from clients, but if anyone wants to grab one of her amazing muffins, scones, and other tasty baked goods, they have to visit the local coffee shop or a few other businesses in Covewood. I admire her hard work and how she always finds a way to help out the community. My best friend really has grown into an amazing woman, and seeing it all in person has made me emotional.

Since I'm still on bereavement leave from my job in Rockdale, working with Olivia these past few days has been the breath of fresh air that I needed. Yesterday, we had a photoshoot to update her headshots for her website and social media accounts as well as photographing her while she was baking in her kitchen and taking staged photos of the baked goods she offers.

This is the type of work I've been aching to do.

"Don't judge the process, my friend. Judge me by how amazing these macarons turned out," she says, taking a bite of a blueberry-lavender macaron before shoving the rest into my face. I take a bite and hum in approval after the flavors hit my tongue. Who knew lavender mixed with blueberries in a macaron form would be so heavenly? The woman is a genius.

"This is so good," I say through a mouthful.

"It's doubly good because it's delicious and nutritious all in one. You can thank Ryland for that."

His name sends a zing throughout my veins. I perk up, raising a brow in question. She smirks at me, still dancing around to the music.

"Thank him for what?"

"Since becoming a dad, he's cared more about ingredients. He's started ditching as many processed foods as he can and makes a lot of things from scratch. One time, he made a honeysuckle lemon pound cake with all organic ingredients, and it was one of the best pound cakes I had ever eaten. It inspired me to do my own research, and now I want to make sure I provide healthier but still delicious options for my clients."

"Honeysuckle?" I whisper, a faint memory of Ryland and me picking honeysuckles together plays in my mind. I wonder if he thought of the same memory as he made the cake.

She gives me a shy smile. "Yeah. I found that cooking and decorating with botanicals also helped my business to grow. People loved what I was making and appreciated having healthier options."

So many thoughts are running through my head right now. There is a new version of Ryland that I know nothing about, and I feel this tug within my heart, urging me to get to know him again.

My heart begins to shift at this moment. For the first time in ten years, the thought of being back in Covewood doesn't repulse me. Especially with knowing that Davis isn't returning and Luke can make sure of it.

It finally feels safe and I'd like to stay longer. I'm just not sure how.

Olivia's dance halts as she glances over at me, her expression going from playful to worry in an instant. I feel guilty for dampening her mood. *Do I do this to everyone?*

"What is it?" she asks, searching for answers that I'm quickly trying to hide behind a mask.

"It's nothing." I smile and point behind me, where Olivia's next-door neighbor lives in a little light-blue townhouse. "I was just wondering about Edna. She doesn't mind your loud racket?"

She doesn't look convinced at my change of subject but answers anyway. "She doesn't mind it. Edna can hardly hear without her hearing aids. If I get too loud, she just takes them out. Sometimes, she even comes over and joins me for dance parties. She says I help keep her young."

I begin to clean up the mess we've made, attempting to distract myself from the sudden jealousy I feel for a seventy-something-year-old woman.

"Thank you for your help these past few days. I can't wait to work on revamping my website and posting new photos on social media." Olivia practically skips toward me, and the scent of her wraps around me like a warm hug—cinnamon, lavender, and her expensive all-natural shampoo. "You know, you're really good at what you do." She sneaks beside me and bumps her hip into mine. "I think you could make a career out of this."

"This?" I ask, raising a brow and handing her a plate to put away.

"Working with small businesses. It's something that you complained about not being able to do in Rockdale. You should quit your job and start your own photography business." She smiles.

The thought has crossed my mind a time or two, making me feel both excited and terrified. It would be a huge risk—one I'm not sure I'm willing to take.

"I've worked too hard, dedicating years of my life to moving my way up to the position I have now at *The Rockdale Journal*. I don't think I can just drop something that I've chased after for so long," I say, but the words taste stale in my mouth.

Years ago, I started at the bottom. I made coffee runs and prepared proposal after proposal with my photographs, until finally, one day, I was able to get a promotion. And then another. It's been my sole focus, distracting me from the past and giving me something to look forward to in my future—until, one day, I stopped looking forward.

I don't want to admit that I lack the same joy or drive that Olivia seems to have with her business. When I look at the photographs I've produced for *The Rockdale Journal*, I'm not proud of what I see. Have I been so blinded by my drive to keep myself moving that I forgot to stop and find the happiness in the now? Maybe that's why I've been feeling like I've been standing on unsteady ground for quite some time.

"I understand that, but sometimes you just need to take a leap of faith and see where it takes you. It could bring you more success and happiness. You'll never know until you give it a try," she adds, the words hitting me harder than I want them to.

I place a dish into the drainer and reach for a towel to dry my hands off. Olivia opens the oven and places a tray of raspberry-rose macarons inside and sets the timer before motioning for me to follow her. We walk out onto her front porch and take our seats on her matching white rocking chairs.

Olivia lives within walking distance of the downtown area. She likes being close to some of the businesses she works with, making it easier for deliveries. I look out toward the rows of small and colorful buildings that sit in front of her house, the tips of the Appalachian mountains peeking over the horizon, the occasional car driving by with a honk. A few townsfolk even shout, "Good evening," to us.

It's completely different than my view back in Rockdale. Even though I can look down from my third-story window and see the constant movement of life, it will never be as comforting as this.

"I heard you on the phone with Samuel this morning," Olivia announces, no remorse written on her face for being nosey.

"Nothing has ever been private with you." I shake my head, a grin spreading on my face. "What about it?"

She eyes me for a moment before scrunching her nose as she ponders her words. "It's okay to admit that love fades sometimes."

I think back on Samuel's and my conversation from this morning. He asked me when I would be back in Rockdale, I told him I was unsure, and then he expressed how unsettled he felt after our argument. I didn't want to discuss the future since it currently feels like the past is trying to suffocate me. My world feels completely unraveled after losing Mamaw.

"I don't think I ever allowed myself to love him. Not like he deserved."

Olivia lets my words sink in before she continues. "Maybe while you're here, you can work on healing the parts of your heart that *need* repairing so that you can finally love the way *you* deserve," Olivia adds.

My eyes snap toward hers, her words making my heart feel like it skips a beat and takes my breath. I knew what she's referring to—or better yet, *who*. I have some unresolved issues with a certain ex-boyfriend who has been on my mind a lot since returning to Covewood. But how can Ryland and I fix the damage that was done over a decade ago? Is it something worth trying to fix? And even if we do, what will that mean for us?

"I'm not sure I want to deal with that while I'm also trying to move through this grief," I admit, welcoming the hug that she pulls me into.

She rubs small circles on my back as I lean closer to her. I remind myself to soak this in, the warmth of my best friend, the comfort she provides, and I hold onto her a little tighter. Olivia has helped me try to work through my heartbreak these past few days, and the thought of leaving her and returning to Rockdale sends my stomach plummeting to the ground with dread. How can I miss Olivia while I'm within her embrace?

She gives me an encouraging smile as I pull away. I know my bereavement time off from work will be up soon, and eventually, I will need to return back to the real world. However, the last thing I want right now is to be away from my loved ones during this difficult season. My mind starts pondering on how I can extend my time here when my thoughts are interrupted by the sound of my phone vibrating from inside her house.

"I'll be back," I say as I stand up and make my way back into the living room to pick up my cell phone. A photo of

Papaw and a nine-year-old me holding my favorite pet duck pops up onto my screen.

"Hey, Papaw."

I've purposely avoided visiting the farm since Mamaw passed. I've been scared of how much the house will remind me of her and that her memory will be the only thing I have left of her. I'm not ready to face that just yet, but my Papaw needs me, and I can't avoid certain things any longer.

I remember the drive to the farm like it's something I could do with my eyes closed, allowing my instincts to lead the way. In the past, when I thought of the farm and my grandparents, it was a safe haven. My place of escape. And then, one day, I decided that it wasn't enough for me.

I think that's what I'm most ashamed of. The fact that I thought leaving this place would be better for me. Better for everyone. The first few years felt freeing to be somewhere new, to have the fresh start I always dreamed of having. I was safe to be who I wanted to be with the distance between me and *them*.

But then, something changed, and life started to weave together a blanket that didn't comfort me anymore. Instead, it scratched against me, revealing just how uncomfortable I've truly become in my own skin.

My soul has been longing for the rolling green hills that lead down the pathway toward my grandparents' home. Toward *my* home. I yearn to feel my bare feet against the earth, inhale the scent of fresh-cut grass and morning dew, and watch the changing colors in the sky at sunrise while sitting on the front porch swing.

I want to be home, but how can I return when I'm not the same girl anymore, when I tried so hard to bury her deep beneath the ground, never ready to face the pain that I'll find waiting for me if I dig her back up.

I can feel her slowly clawing her way to the surface as I inch closer and closer toward the dirt-covered road that leads through the canopy of trees. I inhale and hold in a breath for a few seconds as I pass the green gate that has *Wiley* written across it. As my car moves along the road, the trees start to thin, revealing undulating slopes that seem more orange than green as the sun begins to set into the golden hour. I can see the roof of the farmhouse through my windshield.

I release my breath and feel the squeeze in my chest as my anxiety builds. The trembling in my hands grows, and I tighten my grip against the steering wheel. Acting on instinct, I hit the brakes, and dirt from the road puffs around my car in a poor attempt to hide my arrival. I need a moment to collect myself before I face Papaw.

I place my forehead against the steering wheel and close my eyes. Even though I've slacked on praying lately, I know I need his help to get through this.

"Please help me, Lord. I feel so weak, and I need the type of strength that only you can give. I need to be strong for Papaw. Please, help me do this for him."

I allow the words to repeat in my mind over and over again, until I feel the buzzing of anxiety start to evaporate. The tremble in my hands stops, the squeezing in my chest loosens, and I can take in a deep, calming breath.

When I feel ready, I put my car into drive and push my big toe down on the gas pedal. The farm slowly comes into view and looks like a piece of art, painted with oils and pressed into a canvas with rough fingertips. Bold strokes of burnished gold and bright whites and deep forest greens. I can see why my Mamaw was often inspired to paint landscapes of the farm.

I traveled to Covewood a few times over the last ten years, always to visit here and nowhere else. Each time that I returned, I noticed how there were less and less animals, how the garden started to dwindle down to something more attainable for my Mamaw, and how the house seemed to age right along with my sweet grandparents. The more I visited and saw the differences, the harder it became to accept just how much I was missing out on.

But today, the farmhouse has a fresh coat of white paint, the front porch has been completely redone, and the roof is layered in black metal. It looks brand new.

I shut the car door and take a step toward my favorite place in the whole world. "Hey, Little Duck," Papaw says in greeting. I walk toward him, my eyes still studying the changes of the house before I wrap my arms tightly around his soft form.

Home.

This is what home feels like. Warm, comforting, and familiar. Home smells like peppermint, earth, and coffee. Papaw places his hands on the side of my face and pulls me away from him to get a better look at me. His glassy blue eyes take me in as a smile deepens his wrinkles. This is what home looks like.

Papaw moves his hands to my shoulders before stepping away and waves for me to follow him onto the porch. We take a seat at a small farmhouse-style table, and I try not to notice the vase of spring flowers—daffodils, jonquils, and wild blue phlox—that sits in the center.

Flowers that are withering away.

Mamaw liked to keep fresh flowers everywhere she could and always made sure to replace them when they were starting to wilt. Seeing the dying bouquet is another reminder that she's no longer here, and I fight against the sting that it sends to my heart.

As if Papaw can sense my thoughts, he picks up the vase and discards the old flowers over the porch railing. He takes a seat across from me, scooping up the fallen petals, and tosses them over the railing to meet their friends. I smile at him appreciatively.

He sucks in a breath, his round belly rising as he does, and begins tapping his fingers on top of the table's surface. As he exhales, he looks at me, and I can see how much this grief has been weighing on him. The bags under his eyes are heavier, circled by dark shadows from lack of sleep. His face seems thinner, as I'm sure he hasn't had much of an appetite. My face softens, and I reach out to hold his hand.

The gesture causes tears to form in his eyes, and it's a punch to my gut. Where have I been these past few days? Hiding away in a hotel room. Distracting myself at Olivia's. All the while, my Papaw has been here, trying to learn how to live life without his soulmate. What kind of granddaughter does that? I should have called and checked in with him more, met him for a few meals in town, but I all but abandoned him here.

God give me strength, I pray again as I try to blink away the hot tears I feel behind my eyes.

"I'm sorry," I whisper and clear my throat. "I'm sorry I haven't been here since..."

He waves his free hand at me and shakes his head. "You don't have to apologize. I understand."

I squeeze his hand, wishing I could find the words to bring him comfort as he lets out a shaky exhale. "I know how hard it must be for you to be here without your grandmother. It's been the hardest days of my life. I can't go anywhere without a constant reminder of her. Although it's somewhat comforting, it also keeps breaking my heart over and over again. Not just over your grandmother but also stirring up feelings after losing your father."

His voice breaks, and tears begin to stream down his face. I often forget that my grandparents still walk through the grief of losing a child. No matter how many years go by, or how hard they try to hide the internal struggle, they will always carry that with them. And now Papaw has to carry it alone.

I feel ashamed that I hadn't thought of that before. About how Mamaw's grief could also make the loss of my dad worse for him. The strongest man that I know is breaking before me, and there's nothing I can do to repair him.

"I, uh..." He clears his throat, keeping his gaze on the table. "I was vacuuming this morning and found her hair in the—"

Tears begin to blind my vision, and I try my hardest to hold back my own sobs. I know that if I cry it'll make things harder on him. I inhale and blink as fast as I can before his eyes find mine. He places his other hand on top of mine and gives it a comforting pat.

"I've decided that I can't be here anymore," he admits, and my breath catches, "in this house. I've talked with your Uncle Jack, and he's agreed to let me come stay with him for a bit until I figure out what I want to do. He has that shed in the backyard. You know the one you used to play in with your cousins? He turned it into a guest house and said that I'm welcome to it."

I shake my head and look toward the front door. "But what about the house? The renovations? The animals?"

"Everything in the kitchen and living room was removed this past week so that the renovations there can be started on. I need to be out of the way, anyway. I'll have to travel back and forth to take care of things, but I can't stay here right now. It's too much." His voice breaks again, and guilt slices through me like a sharp knife. "I'll figure it out. I just wanted to be able to tell you in person before you return to Rockdale."

I left ten years ago because I was terrified. I only return to visit when it's convenient for me. I barely speak to my mother, all because I think I'm protecting my heart. I've missed out on so many things and haven't been here when my grandparents needed me the most. What if I could have helped, and my Mamaw could still be here? What if—

Before I realize what I'm doing, I blurt out, "I'll do it."

My heart stops. Or at least it feels like it stops. I look down at my feet where I'm sure I will find it laying, beating, waving goodbye. *What am I doing?*

His eyes widen, completely shocked at my words. Heck, I

am too. The guilt mixed with grief is eating me alive, and knowing that Papaw has been having such a hard time, I have to do something. I need to think about someone other than myself.

"Do what?" he asks, his brows raising.

"I'll stay here. I'll help oversee the renovations and make sure things are getting done. I can take care of the animals and everything else. I want to help."

An idea strikes me. I can work remotely for a while. A lot of what I do for the company can be done from my laptop. I wouldn't be able to photograph for them, which isn't a big issue with Thomas trying to use his images over mine anyway. I might return to a demotion, but I couldn't care less if it means that I can help my Papaw.

"How? You have—"

"Papaw, I can make this work. I will talk with my boss about working remotely. I can stay here if that's something you'd like me to do for you."

He shakes his head slightly, his brows coming together in concentration as he considers my offer. "Raine, I couldn't ask this of you. You have a life in Rockdale. You shouldn't have to stay here and deal with my mess."

"*Our* mess," I correct him. "I might have had a job and a tiny apartment in another state, but my life will always be wherever you are. I hate that I haven't been here for everything that has happened and the things I've missed out on in the past. But I want to be here now for you."

A flashback pops into my mind. The moment in the hospital where I had to squeeze my Mamaw's hand while she lay there hooked up to tubes, unresponsive. I bent down and gave her a hug and whispered into her ear that I promise to take care of Papaw. I expected the memory to cause me to come undone; however, peace wraps around me, letting me know that I'm making the right decision.

"I told Mamaw I would take care of you, and that's what I'm going to do," I say with determination.

He looks out toward the front yard, his eyes scanning the farm before huffing and shaking his head. "It's a lot for me to ask from you."

"I'll just tell you that it's happening, then." It feels like a small victory when we both face each other and share a smile that seems to help release a bit of the tension building inside me. "You trained me for this growing up. I'm telling you I got this."

"I know you do, Little Duck."

Chapter Fifteen

Twelve Years Before

Raine

"Quit acting like you give a crap about what I'm doing!" I can hear the tremble in Luke's voice.

I had every intention of staying here with my bedroom door cracked open, but knowing that Luke is on the verge of tears has my feet moving toward the living room. Luke has his back to me. He's clenching and unclenching his fists.

This is bad.

I look over at Mom, who's sitting on the couch, tension written on her face. She notices me then and flicks her head, silently telling me to leave, but I don't listen. I'm not leaving Luke, especially with how fiercely Davis peers down at him.

"You will not speak to me that way in my house!" Davis hisses, the words weaved together in a threat. "Go to your room before you regret your actions."

"No!" The sound of Luke's shout makes me flinch. My mother does the same and stands up quickly, moving toward me.

"Raine, go to your room," she whispers in my ear.

It's not a room in this house. It's a prison cell. Davis wants us to be trapped with nowhere to go—a punishment I'll never understand. But I refuse to leave Luke, so I shake my head and stay planted.

"I'm done with you," Luke says before shoving his way past his father and grabbing the knob of the front door.

Davis reaches for Luke's wrist, but Luke is quick to escape, making his way out the door before Davis can grab him a second time.

"If you walk out that door, don't you dare come back!" Spit flies out of Davis' mouth, like snake venom, the words sounding just as deadly.

"I don't plan on it." Luke's words are just as lethal, and even though I know he didn't mean to, they hit me like a blow to the chest.

He's leaving me?

How can Luke leave me here? *Alone*? I can't be here without him. If he's leaving, so am I!

I rush toward the front door, not missing the way my mother's fingers brush my arm in an attempt to stop me. Before I can open my mouth and shout for Luke to wait for me, Davis' broad chest meets my face. I crash into him, and before I can move backward, he grips my forearm tightly and yanks it up. I hear a *pop* in my shoulder and grit my teeth as pain shoots down my arm and into my back.

"Where do you think you're going?" he practically hisses like the serpent that he is.

"You can't keep me here!" Now my voice decides to tremble, but I blame the pain, not the panic currently rushing through my veins. "I want to go with Luke."

"See, the thing is, I can keep you here. And if you try to leave, there will be consequences. We don't want that, do we?"

I look over at my mother, who has made her way back to the couch, and beg her silently to put a stop to all of this. To, for once in her life, *fight for me*. Instead, she cowers, keeping her eyes on the ground, running a shaking hand through her messy blonde hair. Davis laughs beside me, knowing that my mother isn't going to help me, before releasing his grip.

"Now be a smart girl and go back to your room."

I want to run. I want to chase after Luke and beg him to take me with him. Beg him not to leave me here with this monster. But I have a better idea. I turn without looking at either of them and run to my room. I shut the door softly behind me, grab my cell phone, and pull on a thick jacket and a pair of tennis shoes. It takes me a while to push open my window without creating too much noise and remove the window screen before hopping out and landing in the bushes.

I run toward the street, ignoring the sting in my lungs from the cold air and the pain shooting down my arm, and I search wildly for Luke in the dark until I finally see movement across the street.

"Luke!" I whisper-yell, air puffing from my lips. He stops in his tracks and looks over his shoulder at me. I make my way over to him, and without second-guessing, I slap his arm.

"Ow! What was that for?" he asks, rubbing against the spot dramatically, even though I know it didn't hurt him through his thick jacket.

"You left me back there." I hadn't noticed the tears until I hear them in my voice. "Why would you leave me with him?"

His face falls, defeat pulling down his shoulders, and he runs a hand through his messy black hair. "I can't do this anymore, Raine. I can't deal with him. I'm done. I'm sixteen and can make my own decisions for my life, and I'm finally choosing what's best for me."

"But what about me?" I say, hating how weak I sound. "Luke, I can't live there without you."

"Then don't," he replies, his eyes lighting up with an idea. "Go live with your grandparents."

As if I hadn't thought of that before. I would love nothing

more than to live with them. To wake up feeling safe every day, to be able to help them throughout the week rather than just the weekends. Especially since Davis moved in. But I didn't want to abandon Luke or my mother.

Before my mom met Davis, things weren't as bad as they are now. She still had a drinking problem, but our relationship wasn't as strained. So, I stayed for her. And once Davis moved in, I stayed for Luke. If Luke is gone and my mother couldn't care less about how Davis is treating us, why should I stay?

"What if your dad follows me and makes a big deal out of it? I don't want to cause my grandparents any problems," my worst fear slips out. Luke eyes me for a moment before replying.

"What can he do? He doesn't care about us. We'll be doing them a favor by leaving." Luke waves a hand in the air, like this isn't a big deal, and I want to believe him.

"What about my mom?"

His brows furrow in confusion. "She made her choices, Raine. It doesn't mean you have to suffer right along with her."

My gut is telling me otherwise. Part of me doesn't want to leave her alone with Davis. What if I leave and my choices end up hurting her even more than she is hurting herself? But in a way, Luke's right. She has chosen this for her life, and I'm done suffering. I refuse to live here without Luke. I'm choosing to listen to him and ignore the sickening feeling that's swashing inside my stomach.

Headlights shine toward us, and out of reflex, I move to stand behind Luke. An unfamiliar red car pulls up beside us. Luke opens the passenger door and hops inside.

"Where are you going?" I protest, placing a hand onto the door to keep it open.

I look inside the car and see that it's Jake Himswell from school—one of the punks Luke has been hanging out with lately. I roll my eyes at the sight of him and the fact that I can smell weed flowing from his vehicle. I glare at Luke.

"Really?" I question, not understanding why Luke chooses to hang out with a guy who used to bully him in middle school.

"I gotta go. Call your grandparents," is all he says to me before he wiggles the door free from my grasp and shuts it in my face. He doesn't give me the chance to beg him to take me with him. I watch the car drive away, and my heart breaks from Luke's betrayal.

I was upset at first when Davis moved in. However, knowing that every other week Luke would be there with me brought me a sense of relief. All of that vanishes along with the red headlights of Jake's car.

I stand on the sidewalk, frozen in place, not knowing what the right thing to do is. I know I don't want to go back inside the house so my only option is to leave. I could crash at Olivia's house, but I really don't want to cause her family any issues. At least my grandparents are family and will understand my situation better.

I make my decision and pick up my phone to dial Ryland's number. As the phone rings, I walk down the street, pulling my jacket closer to me and putting distance between me and *them*. I can see the tiniest hint of snowflakes trying to fall from the sky as my breath puffs out from my lips with each fast-paced step I take.

"Hey, Rainbow. What's up?"

The sound of his voice is like soothing ointment over a wound. Luke left me bleeding, and I know I can count on Ryland to help bandage me up. He's the one person I can always rely on. And besides Luke, he's also one of the only people who understands what I'm going through.

"I, uh..." I clear the dryness from my throat. "Could you come pick me up?"

I hear shuffling in the background—a click of a lamp, feet hitting the floor, fabric moving around. "What's going on?" he asks.

I exhale, hating to relive the last twenty or so minutes, or the fact that I know how upset he's going to be at Luke. But right now, I'm upset too, and it would be nice to have someone on my side for once.

"Davis and Luke got into an argument. Luke left, but Davis wouldn't let me leave too, so I snuck out of my window and chased Luke down, only for him to leave me on the street and take off with Jake Himswell."

I can hear his teeth gritting together. "He did what?"

"It's fine," I lie. "I don't want to go back there. Could you—"

"Where are you?" his voice rings with urgency, and I can hear the jingling of his car keys.

I look around in the dark and can barely make out which street I'm on. I know at the end of this road there is a Dollar General store. I tell Ryland to meet me there before we hang up. Fifteen minutes later, I see Ryland's dark-green Honda Civic pull into the parking lot. I rush toward it, wincing as the pain in my shoulder grows, and hop inside.

Ryland spent his summer working for his Pops and was able to save up enough money to purchase this slightly beat-up used car. It needed to be fixed in several areas, and last month, they were able to get her running. Today, I am incredibly thankful for it.

His familiar scent floats in the warm air and finally I feel safe. I relax against the seat, welcoming the sense of security before I turn to face him. I open my mouth to thank him, but before I can get the words out, he reaches for my face and pulls me toward him.

For a split second, I think he's going to kiss me, and all sense of calm is replaced with the pounding of my heart. It's not a rush of panic, more like a surge of adrenaline. *Of want.*

But instead of kissing me, he runs his thumbs over my cheeks, wiping away the evidence that I cried earlier. His hazel eyes look almost black in the shadows of his car. They dance around my face, studying me for a moment before he finally speaks.

"I'm going to punch Luke in the face for leaving you."

"Not before I can," I add, a grin pulling against my lips. I don't miss the way his eyes flicker to them, just for a moment, before returning to my face.

"It's freezing out, and he just left you? What has gotten into him?" He releases his hold on me and pulls out his phone.

I reach my hand out to stop him but hiss as pain shoots through my shoulder. Ryland's eyes snap to mine, a sudden urgency within them. He drops his phone and reaches over to tug my jacket off.

"I'm fine," I say, but he ignores me, determination written on his face as he removes my arm from the fabric.

I try not to wince, but my face fails me when my arm moves toward him. His eyes search my face, silently apologizing before he's back to examining me. I peer down at the skin on my forearm as Ryland traces his fingers around a very purple bruise I didn't know was there.

"I'm going to hurt him," he says through his teeth, releasing my arm before gripping the steering wheel.

"I'm fine, Ry."

"No, you're not, Raine!" he shouts. It's the first time Ryland has ever raised his voice at me, and I blink back the shock.

"I'm sorry," he's quick to say, releasing the steering wheel and taking my hands into his. "I know what it's like. To have someone who abuses you like he does. It's not okay. You don't deserve this. And I can't believe Luke..."

My heart sinks, knowing Ryland's history with his father and how he's still healing from it. I squeeze his hand, bringing his attention back to me, and I do my best to give him an encouraging smile.

"We'll deal with Luke later, but for right now, I'd like to go to my grandparents'."

"You'll leave your mom?" he asks, knowing that I never wanted to leave her behind. But I have no choice. She should want me to be safe, and this is the only way how—at least until I'm eighteen and can finally move away from this town, far away from *him*.

"I have to." I shrug, wincing for a third time.

"Okay, then." He nods and shifts back into his seat before putting the car into drive.

We pull into the driveway of the farmhouse, and nervousness settles into my stomach. I haven't told my grandparents the truth of what has been going on at home—how bad Mom's drinking has become or how Davis treats me. But I know they can sense it. I've shrugged off their questions, wanting to somewhat protect them from the truth, but also not wanting to cause any issues with my mom. Tonight, the truth will set me free.

Or so I hope.

I catch the glimpse of light coming from behind us, and when I turn around, I see a vehicle at the bottom of the hill. The color drains from my face, and when I look over at Ryland, his expression matches my own.

"Davis," I croak.

Ryland acts fast, shifting his car into reverse and turning us around within seconds. He drives fast down the driveway, causing gravel to dust around us, and I pray my grandparents don't wake up from the noise.

Midway down the driveaway, Ryland jerks his steering wheel to the left, driving through the grass in order to miss the vehicle that passes us by. Just when we think we can make a break for it, at the edge of the road, a black truck pulls out in front of us and blocks our way.

Ryland swears under his breath and punches the steering wheel. My breathing picks up as fear grabs hold of me. What was I thinking? I shouldn't have listened to Luke, and now I have put the people that I love in danger.

"Ry, I'm sorry," I cry.

He looks over at me, confused, before we both jolt in our seats from the tapping on his window. A man in a black jacket is standing outside of Ryland's door, and I turn to see Davis standing outside of mine. He's practically snarling at me as he tries to open my door.

"Open the door!" he shouts through the glass, and I can't believe this is happening.

"Don't," Ryland pleads, but I have to make the right decision in order to keep him safe. "Raine!"

I unlock the door and swing it open, but as I move to step outside, Davis yanks me from my seat. My shoulder feels like it's on fire from the pull, and Davis drags me toward his truck. I catch a glimpse of Ryland chasing after us.

"Ryland, don't!" I scream, but he doesn't listen.

"Let her go!" he shouts, causing Davis to stop in his tracks and turn around to face him.

God, please don't let him hurt Ryland. Please keep him safe.

"Go home, kid." The man in the black jacket grabs Ryland's shoulder and shoves him back.

"I can't. Your stupid truck is blocking the way. And I'm not leaving here without Raine."

Davis' cold eyes scan Ryland up and down before an evil laugh escapes his disgusting lips. I catch the sour scent of alcohol on his breath, and it makes my stomach want to hurl. "Please. What are you going to do?"

"I'll call the cops!" Ryland shouts and balls his fists together, nostrils flaring in rage.

Now, both Davis and the other man bark out in laughter,

and Ryland's face falls. Davis tightens his grip on my injured shoulder, and it takes everything in me not to cry out in pain. I bite my lip, close my eyes, and pray again.

"Go ahead, kid. I'm sure the cops would love to know that you helped a child run away from home. In the meantime, I have a little girl to return to her mother."

Ryland looks at me, and I can see the panic in his eyes. I know he won't leave me, and I love him so much for it. But I need him to leave and get far away from Davis. I inhale a breath and try to muster up as much courage as I can.

"It's okay. I shouldn't have left my mom. It's better that I go back home."

'But—" I hate how Ryland's face falls, his arms dropping in defeat at my words, but it's better this way. This way, he stays away from Davis' wrath.

"You heard her. Now leave," Davis growls as he takes a step back, pulling me with him.

I feel the heat of tears stinging my eyes, and I try my best to blink them away. I hate how heartbroken Ryland looks right now, knowing that he isn't able to protect me. But I know if I cooperate with Davis, allow him to believe that I want to go back home, he'll let Ryland go.

The man in the black jacket hops back into his truck and drives back onto the main road, vanishing into the night. Ryland, however, doesn't move a muscle, his eyes stay firmly on mine. His breath comes out in quick puffs of clouds, dissipating as fast as the hope in my chest.

"I'll be okay. I'll call you as soon as I get home, okay?"

Sensing that there's no other way around this, Ryland nods and returns a heated glare at Davis before turning and hopping back into his car. I release a breath as I watch him drive down the driveway.

"Get in!" Davis shouts and shoves me toward the passenger side door.

He watches me closely until I'm inside and is quick to lock

the doors once he's in the driver's seat. I half expect Luke to be in the backseat or that we would go after him next. However, Davis lets Luke go, and I'm not sure how I feel about that. Why did he have to come after me, but Luke is allowed to do whatever he wants?

Once we pull into the driveway, Davis turns off the car and twists toward me. "Here is how this is going to go down. You're going to climb back into your window and act as if you've never left this house. Do you understand me?"

What?

"You will not speak of this again. And you sure as hell won't be trying to run away again. Do you understand?"

I bite the inside of my cheek, keeping the words that I wish I could say to him inside, and instead, I frown at him. He can't keep me locked in this house forever. Can he?

"If you try, I'll start with that little boyfriend of yours. I know where he lives, where his grandfather works, and can make him wish that he never met you. And if that doesn't work, then I will start slowly destroying your grandparents' farm and—"

"I get it!" I cut him off, not wanting to hear any more of his sickening threats. "I won't run away again."

Please just let me go to my room.

"And if you even think about getting the police involved in this, think again, sunshine, because I got men on the inside, and there isn't anything the police can do to me. So, you're better off keeping your mouth shut and keeping your mother happy. Understand?"

I nod because it's all that I can do. He gives me a *humph* before I hear the door unlock. I'm quick to remove myself and rush toward my window. He watches me, making sure that I get back inside before he shuts his door and walks into the house. As I close my window, I make sure to push my dresser in front of my bedroom door.

I don't care that he can keep me here. It doesn't mean that I can't have a barrier between him and me. Once I feel like I'm safe, I pull out my phone and dial Ryland's number again. He picks up on the first ring.

"I'm outside."

"What?" I whisper, covering myself with pillows in hopes that it'll keep them from hearing me.

"We can run away. I'll get you far from here, I promise."

I close my eyes and can picture how perfect that would be. But it can't happen. Davis will never allow that to happen. And that realization finally crushes me.

"Ry—" I say before a sob escapes my lips.

"Raine, please." I can hear the fear in his voice. "I can't stand the thought of not being able to protect you."

"He threatened your family. He threatened my grandparents and their farm. He threatened you. I can't..." I exhale, trying to find the right words. "I have to stay. It's the only way to keep everyone safe."

"He can't do anything if he's behind bars. We can go to the police, show them the bruise on your arm, and they'll arrest him for abuse. You'll be safe."

"But he said the police can't touch him."

"What?" he says in defeat.

"The police won't help. I have two years until I'm eighteen. I can put up with him until then."

I hear the jingle of his keys in the background and the loud exhale he releases out of frustration. "You shouldn't have to do that."

"I know, but it's the only choice we have right now. Okay? Just promise me you'll get home safe and let me know when you get there."

"I really don't want to leave you."

Luke, who I consider more than a best friend...he's family... left me behind tonight. But here is Ryland, someone who has made such a large impact on my life in a matter of a few years, refuses to leave me. I'm falling for him.

I'm in love with Ryland.

I want to tell him, but I keep the words lodged in my throat. Instead, I say, "I know. Thank you. You came to my rescue, and I'm forever grateful for you."

"Yeah, some rescue it was."

"I mean it. I'll take you up on that getaway when I'm a legal adult," I promise, meaning every word. I have two years to form an escape plan, and I'm going to make sure I get as far away from here as possible. It's not just for myself anymore.

Chapter Sixteen

Now

Ryland

The strong aroma of ground coffee beans drifts in the air, soaking into my clothes as I close the front door behind me and make my way toward the front counter. The smell of coffee always brings me a sense of calm, and that is exactly what I need this morning.

The usual gentle murmur of voices can be heard above the stomach-churning sound of the coffee machine as it struggles to produce the hot steaming liquid beloved by the customers, and the soft sounds of Fleetwood Mac flowing from the speakers immediately remind me of Johanna and her love for the band.

If I close my eyes, I can envision her swaying to the beat of the music, a mug of fresh coffee in her left hand, a paintbrush in the right, as she squints at a blank canvas in her art studio. She always said Stevie Nicks helped her to see the art before she was able to paint it.

I look around the coffee shop, taking in the late-'60s style with the collection of warm earthy colors and antique-style furniture that create an inviting feel. Anyone who steps inside The Groovy Bean feels as if they have stepped into a time machine that serves amazing coffee. It's become one of my favorite places in Covewood.

In front of me, I recognize August Banks' long dark-brown hair worn in her usual low ponytail. She catches sight of me and waves. "Hey, Ryland. How are you?"

"As good as I can be," I reply with a shrug.

She gives me a look that's a mixture between understanding and pity. She opens her mouth to say something but is cut off by the sound of a bell and Grayson Topkins, the coffee shop owner, letting her know that her order is ready.

"How's Jessie been? I haven't seen him around lately." I take a step toward the counter and wait for Grayson to return to take my order.

"He's good. He went to stay with my sister, Samaira, last week during spring break. He's back at the farm today, helping Dad with the goats." She grabs a drink carrier, and I reach out a helping hand with the four drinks she ordered. She mutters, "Thanks," as she balances the carrier in her arms.

"Farm work is always a good way of teaching kids responsibility," I say, and she hums in approval. "We'll have to get the kids together sometime. Annabelle has been wanting to play with Jessie, and your husband owes me some barbecue."

She chuckles. "Yeah, about that. I'm pretty sure he mentioned something about you hosting a cookout soon. He must think that it's your turn. And I've been wanting some of your famous smoked brisket."

I grin and shake my head, knowing that Thomas is trying to get out of having to cook but not minding an excuse to host a gathering. It's getting warm enough outside that cookout season can begin. "I do have a brisket in the freezer. I'll check my schedule and see what I can throw together sometime soon."

"Alright, that sounds like a plan, then. Maybe you could invite Raine Wiley to join us?" She gives me a knowing smile.

Of course the small-town gossip has made its way around.

Earl called me late last night to inform me of Raine's decision to take over the farmhouse renovations for him. I tried to ignore the jolt of excitement I felt at his words. I could hardly sleep last night and felt the tightness of nerves this morning with the anticipation of seeing her at the farm this morning.

"News travels fast around this town."

"It does." August nods in agreement. "How has she been?"

I shrug my shoulders for a second time, not sure how to answer her question since I haven't seen Raine since the funeral. "I'll find out in a few minutes."

"Oh," she replies with a sympathetic smile. "You should grab her a coffee, then. Coffee makes the day a little brighter."

I hadn't thought of that, but that would be nice. A peace offering. A let's-have-a-fresh-start coffee—if that's even a thing. An idea strikes me, and I'm thankful to have a female friend to confide in right now.

"Yeah, okay. Do you think I should get her a muffin too? Maybe a gift card to use while she's in town?" I'm rambling like an idiot. August's smile spreads across her tanned skin, and she reaches out with her free hand to point at me.

"I have an idea!"

* * *

When I pull up to the farm an hour later, I see Raine's white car in the driveway. There is a buzz of anticipation building inside my gut as I shut the truck door and do my best to cradle the gift basket in my hands.

August and I ventured to different small shops that line the downtown streets. She had the bright idea to put together a basket of things to show Raine what Covewood has to offer these days and to focus on items that could bring her some comfort during this time of grief. The town has grown a lot over the last ten years, and this basket will be a way to welcome her back, even though it's only temporary.

I hope this will be a way that I can brighten her day, as I can only imagine how hard it has to be for her to be back at the farm without her grandparents living here. It still breaks my heart, remembering what Earl explained to me the night before about why he didn't want to stay at the house any longer.

I make my way up the porch steps, and Raine turns to look at me, taking me in with her wide grayish-blue eyes. I do my best to contain my own expression as I refuse to admit the hurricane of emotions that is currently giving me whiplash as I take her in as well.

It's weird seeing her here again. It was easier to be around her at the hospital, but being here on the farm, where so many of our past memories were created, has my head spinning with a weird sensation of deja vu.

She seems to be feeling the same way with how her light brows pinch together and her eyes dance around my face, searching for an answer to an unspoken question that is hidden within her stare. We stay silent for a long moment, both looking like we want to say something, but neither of us knowing where to go from here.

"Hi," I finally say to break the deafening silence, taking in just how familiar her eyes are, yet reminding my brain that everything else about her is unfamiliar.

Proceed with caution, my heart warns me.

"Hi," she repeats back to me suspiciously and looks at the basket in my hands.

I take the few steps between us and set the basket on top of the table she's sitting at. I hold up a finger before she can say something and jog back to my truck to retrieve the coffees that I picked up before I drove here. I'm thankful I decided to wait so that the coffee would still be hot by the time I arrived.

I make my way back to her, giving her a nervous smile as I place the coffee into her hands and attempt to ignore the way my skin buzzes at the feel of her fingertips grazing my own. I take a step back to give us some space and bring my cup of coffee toward my lips, giving my shaking hands something to do.

"What's all this?" she asks and sorts through the basket. She pulls out a bar of soap that August helped me pick out from her family's store, Soap and Hope. Raine brings it to her nose, inhales the scent, humming in approval, and a grin tugs at my lips.

"That's handmade lavender goat's milk soap from a little shop downtown." My free hand finds the back of my neck, giving it a quick squeeze to help release some of the tension I feel.

She smiles brightly while she sorts through more of the items in the basket. I know I should give her some space, but I can't ignore the pull I'm feeling, so I take the seat across from her.

"This basket is from a store called Preloved Finds. It's a small thrift shop downtown. The jar of honey is from a locally owned apiary. This tea blend is supposed to help support your sleep. And—"

"All of these things came from small businesses from town?" she questions, something unknown flickering behind her eyes that I really want to ask questions about. Instead, I nod, my smile falling as I see hers do the same.

"Is it too much?" My voice betrays me, giving away my self-consciousness.

"No, it's not that. I love this so much. It's just..." She eyes the items again, picking up a handmade mug from Potter's Art Studio. "How did you know?"

My brow arches in confusion. "Know what?"

She exhales before looking up at me with a skeptical expression, like she doesn't believe that I didn't know whatever it is that she is coming to a conclusion about. After examining me for another second, she shakes her thoughts away.

"Back in Rockdale, I recently suggested to my bosses that we should focus on promoting the small businesses that are in the city. It's a little passion of mine—discovering the family-owned businesses and supporting them when I can. I saw an opportunity to help the community with my work; however, my bosses turned down my idea, wanting to highlight the bigger popular businesses that bring more tourists there instead. It seems like they are more worried about the dollar signs that it would bring to the company."

I take another sip of my coffee, allowing her words to sink in, and put the pieces together. "So you enjoy supporting small businesses?"

Her expression lights up. "Absolutely! I made it my mission to try to only shop from locally owned businesses in Rockdale. I love being able to know where my money is going and the opportunity to help support a person's dream instead of a corporate-owned business with hundreds of employees and locations all over the United States."

I look down at the cup in my hands, reading the logo for The Groovy Bean, understanding where she is coming from. "There are a million Starbucks. However, there is only one The Groovy Bean. I get it. I'd much rather support a friend."

She looks at me and a bright, dazzling smile crests over her face like a sunrise, and causes my chest to constrict. I never thought I would feel this way again, and yet, somehow, it's like my heart has been preserved to react this way only for her.

I nudge her cup toward her. "Try it. It beats Starbucks any day. I hope it's still warm for you."

The buzz inside my veins grows as her eyes light up after she takes a sip. I feel a satisfied smile take over my face, knowing how amazing Grayson's coffee is.

"Oh, wow," she says and looks at the cup in her hands and studies the logo. "Olivia was telling me about this place, and she wasn't lying about it being the best coffee she's ever had."

"It's groovy, right?"

She chuckles softly. "If Jesus had turned water into coffee, I think this is what it would've tasted like." I share a laugh. "Thank you. You didn't have to do any of this, but I appreciate it. It's exactly what I needed," she says softly before taking another sip from her cup.

"You're welcome." I feel the swell of pride fill my chest.

She tips her cup back for a third time, and my eyes betray me as they study the way her black dress pants hug her hips and long legs, the loose strands of her hair framing her face, the small coffee stain on her white silk blouse. I notice that her neck is bare, the rainbow necklace no longer there.

There's a pause, a moment where our eyes lock on each other, the gray flecks bright and welcoming, but there's a speck of something I don't recognize. Maybe it's because as familiar as Raine might feel, she's a stranger now.

"Wait, I don't know how I didn't put this together." She sets her cup down and places a hand onto her forehead. "You're the boy." She waves her hands in the air as the realization hits.

I'm confused. I point to my chest. "Boy? I thought twenty-nine meant I was a man?"

She faces me, and her eyes travel down my face, to my chest, up my arms, until they land back on my face again. I can see from her expression that she's agreeing with me and is quick to turn her attention back to the basket in front of her. She exhales in defeat and starts bouncing her knee in nervousness.

"Papaw didn't tell me it is you that's helping him. He would refer to 'the boy' whenever we talked about it. I feel silly for not even thinking of you as an option. My head has been so..." She stumbles over her words, running a hand through her hair, messing up her perfectly pinned-back style. "I need to make a phone call."

She stands up, cell phone in hand, and walks swiftly toward the stairs past me. I can see the city version of Raine written in the way she walks confidently. It makes me wonder if the Raine from my past is still in there somewhere.

I turn, watching her hips sway for a moment before asking, "Is it a problem that I'm here?"

She twists around to face me. "No," she stutters, pink tinting her cheeks, and she shifts on her heels. "I just can't believe he didn't tell me."

"And is it an issue?"

Her lips part, and momentarily, I'm frozen in place, studying their pink shade and every crevice that lines them. I think I'm asking the question more for myself, because it has only been a few minutes and my brain is flustered from being around Raine again. However, I hate the idea of *not* being around her more.

So much unknown is etched on her face as her mind ponders my question until she finally answers, "No."

There it is, the slightest twitch around her eye that always gave away her lie. It's a good thing her grandparents never figured it out when we were teens, because we would have been busted on plenty of occasions when doing something we weren't supposed to do. But I picked up on it when I was fifteen.

I decide not to call her out on it. Instead, I enjoy the fact that I just witnessed a piece of the old Raine underneath her professional exterior. Maybe pieces of her are still there after all.

She looks down at her phone and then back up at me before exhaling in defeat. Her heels click as she makes her way back up the steps and sits back down at the table across from me. Her eyes return to mine, a silent question behind them.

I need to stop staring at her, so instead, I scan the table, noticing a few notebooks, pens, an appointment book, and a laptop sitting to the side of her. "Working remotely?" I ask.

"Yeah, at least until the renovations are complete. I've felt guilty for not being much help to Papaw and Mamaw over the years, and when Papaw explained how he couldn't be here anymore, I knew I had to help somehow, and before I knew what I was doing, I volunteered to take over the renovations."

"Like Katniss," I proclaim, remembering how much she loved reading *The Hunger Games* books in high school.

She chuckles, her nose crinkling just like I remember. "Yeah, I volunteered as tribute." She smiles, a sense of nostalgia hitting me before she takes another sip of her coffee. "Thankfully, my boss is okay with letting me work remotely starting Monday."

She's staying.

Relief fills my lungs, helping me to inhale a little deeper. My stupid smile betrays me, and I try to hide it by looking away. I turn my attention toward the barn and see that the chickens are already out and scratching the ground, the sheep are loose in the field, and Daisy is barking and guiding them.

"Are you staying here?" I ask.

"I've been at Olivia's, but I probably need to. It would make doing the chores a lot easier. I just... I haven't gone inside yet," she admits, and for a second time her leg bounces nervously.

I wonder if she needs a little encouragement to go inside. The place doesn't look like the same home, and maybe the changes will bring her some comfort—I hope, anyway. I point behind me toward the house.

"Would you like me to come with you? I can show you some of the changes we've made."

You'd think I asked her to hit a beehive like a pinata with the expression she gives me. She fights through her discomfort and pushes to stand, giving me a nod of approval. I do the same and make my way to the front door. I catch the smell of vanilla drifting off her as she walks inside before me, and I take a deep breath, hoping she doesn't notice, before following her.

What was once a small hallway leading into the living room is now completely open. Raine inhales quickly, and a shocked expression washes over her face. She places a hand on the walls, which haven't been painted yet, and walks into the living room.

"It's been months since I've come to visit. Before the renovations started." Her words are laced with embarrassment, and I can see a hint of pink forming on her neck. Her eyes are traveling over every change that's been made. "It doesn't even look the same."

The living room and kitchen furniture were covered in protective plastic and carried off to the barn for temporary storage a few weeks ago. The carpet was ripped up recently, revealing hardwood floors underneath that I haven't had the time to refinish just yet. There was once a wall separating the living room from the kitchen, but that has been removed, revealing one giant living space that allows for more natural light to filter in.

"Ryland," she whispers, and I can hear the emotion that she's trying to hide. She coughs, regaining her composure before continuing. "I can't believe this is the same house. It looks like something Chip and Johanna would design."

I beam proudly as she walks over to the built-in bookshelves and the shiplap that lines that wall as well as the fireplace. Everything is primed for paint. "It's beautiful. You're amazing. Who would've thought that you would take over the family business?"

My smile doesn't reach my eyes, and I know there's a trace of sadness in them that she catches onto when she returns her gaze to mine. "Pops did."

"Yeah, I guess he did, didn't he? He would be very proud of you."

The sting of grief is familiar. The fact that it'll never end is exhausting to comprehend. It may become softer over time, more gentle, but some days feel sharp. Grief lasts as long as love does. *Forever.*

"Yeah, he was," I reply.

She walks into the kitchen and places her hands onto the newly installed granite countertops, shaking her head softly as she studies the white farmhouse sink Earl and I installed a few weeks before.

"I wish she could enjoy this."

I come up behind her and lift my hand to place on her arm

but pull away. How does it feel so natural to want to reach out and touch her even after all this time?

Keeping my hands to myself, I stand next to her and follow her gaze toward the small window that sits above the sink. Outside, we can see the white fence that lines the forest area, the sheep are grazing softly, the sun beginning to touch the top of the trees. It's breathtaking.

"I wish she could too," I add, feeling the ache in my chest, longing for the ones we've lost. "But she'd be thrilled to know that you're here and able to enjoy it."

Raine looks at me, her eyes growing larger, taking my words in. "Maybe so," she whispers before turning and making her way toward the sunroom.

I try to stop her, at least give her a warning, but I'm too late. Raine sucks in a breath as she looks around the untouched room. Originally, Earl and Johanna requested that the only room that we wouldn't renovate was Raine's old bedroom. However, since Johanna passed, I can't bring myself to even think about touching the sunroom.

Raine takes a step inside, the sunrays coming in through the windows casting golden light against her fair skin as she walks over to the easel holding an unfinished painting. It's a piece that Johanna was working on slowly, before she got sick. Raine's fingers reach out and trace the swirls of paint that form what I think is the start of an iris flower.

Raine's fingers are trembling as she brings them to her lips. She bows her head, and a sob escapes. I rush to her, ignoring the warning bells in my brain telling me to give her space and, instead, follow my heart that's desperate to comfort her. She turns away from the painting and buries her face into my chest. We stand there in the memorial room, clutching each other for support until her crying slows.

"I'm sorry," she whispers, coughing away the emotion lodged in her throat, and pulls away from me.

My body reacts naturally to her as my hand reaches over and

wipes the tears away from her cheek. Since I'm already touching her, I place my fingers onto her chin and urge her to look up at me. "You don't have to be sorry for your grief, Rainbow."

Her eyes widen at the sound of my old nickname for her. I clear my throat, reminding myself that I *need* to move away from her. But it's hard. Even with all of the years separating us, I still find myself feeling as if I'm right back where she and I once were, especially standing here in this home together.

"Come on, want to see your old room?" I add, hoping she'll take the bait for a distraction, and motion for her to follow me.

We walk up the stairs, through the hallway, past the guest room and bathroom, until she stops in the doorway. "They refused to change my room."

"Yup, that was their one rule," I add as I lean against the doorframe and cross my arms, watching her closely.

She sits down on her old pink comforter, patting its softness, and studies the posters and collages of photos that line the walls. "I'm glad they didn't."

I reach over and point to an old photograph of her and me sitting on the boat dock by my house.

"That was a good day," I say. Her eyes drift to where I'm pointing, and a small smile pulls against her lips. I move my finger to another photo of Olivia with a chicken sitting on top of her head, a look of terror sculpted onto her face. "And this was when Olivia knew she wasn't cut out for the farm lifestyle."

She chuckles and adds, "Especially after the hen pooped in her hair. I never heard her scream so loud in my life." She points to a photo that's close to her bed. I study it, seeing that it's a photo of me standing next to my grandparents' cabin. I feel like that photo was taken a lifetime ago. Maybe it was. "It's hard to believe this kid has a kid of his own."

"Yeah, I can't grasp it some days either." I grin and scan her room.

Twice in one day, I feel like I've stepped into a time machine. Johanna and Earl kept everything the same in Raine's old bedroom, from the white dresser to the matching vanity that's covered with her old notebooks and makeup bags. Her fingers reach over and trace a line of dust that sits on top of its surface before her eyes find mine again.

"Olivia told me everything."

"Everything?" I ask and take a seat next to her on the bed. It's a bad idea. I forgot how small this bed is, and I'm sitting so close that I can see the hint of freckles lining the bridge of her nose, and our knees press together. I don't feel uncomfortable, but it's hard to not want to reach out and hold her hand like this.

"I guess not everything, but she told me when you became a father. It sounds like Mamaw was pretty smitten with your daughter too, and I know Papaw is too. It's sweet, knowing there's a miniature you in the world."

I smile at her words. "Maybe you can meet her while you're here."

She shifts on the bed and reaches down to pull out an old shoebox that I know is full of Polaroid photos. "Yeah, maybe," she adds, returning her eyes to mine for a brief moment before sorting through the stack of photographs.

I see the ghosts appear in her eyes as she sifts through the memories. I'm reminded of a hazy gray morning, a storm rolling in on the other side of the lake, sinking to my knees as I realized she is gone. I shake my head, willing the memory to fade.

"We could talk about that night...if you want to."

She nods her head, but I can tell she doesn't want to—not yet, anyway. There are two reasons why people don't talk about things: either it doesn't mean anything to them, or it means everything. And by the way she has been looking at me, I know the past is still everything to her.

"Whenever you're ready," I quickly add, and relief washes over her with my words.

We sit in silence for a moment, and I feel the uncomfortable shift in the air between us. I rub the pads of my fingers through my beard and say, "Well, I'll leave you to it. I need to get started on those floors."

"Yeah, okay," she replies, keeping her eyes down on the box of memories in her hands. It's the lock of hair that keeps slipping from behind her ear, the hue of pink on her cheeks, the weight of her knee that's been pressed against mine that has my heart warning me that I still care for Raine. I always have. I always will.

Chapter Seventeen

Twelve Years Before

Raine

Olivia is leaning against the bright-red lockers, hugging her algebra book to her chest as she continues her story about… I don't even remember. Her smile widens as she continues, her eyes scanning through the moving crowd of teenagers, searching for someone, but I don't have the energy to care who it is. I give her an occasional nod or, "Uh-huh," to let her think that I'm listening, which I know makes me sound like a horrible friend, but teenage gossip is the least of my worries.

"And then my grandma's hair caught on fire."

"Yeah—" My eyes snap toward Olivia, her words sinking in. "What?!"

She rolls her eyes, giving away that the last part is a lie, and playfully shoves me. I try to hide my wince but the pain in my shoulder has been a constant reminder today that last night did in fact happen, and it wasn't just a nightmare. It's real life.

"You weren't even listening. Were you?"

I shrug in response as I place my English book into my locker, my eyes landing on a photograph of the four of us together at the lake, and seeing that version of Luke in contrast with the one from last night makes my stomach churn. I slam the locker shut and mimic her stance.

"What's going on?" she demands, her overly plucked brows pulling together, silently letting me know she isn't going to let this go until I tell her where my mind is.

"Luke?" Olivia hisses, her attention locked on him as he does his best to avoid eye contact with us. "What happened to –" she continues but he picks up his pace.

Olivia is petite, but she never allows it to stand in her way. She can also be surprisingly strong when she needs to be. She grabs the back of Luke's leather jacket and pulls back as hard as she can, causing him to crash through a group of girls, and then his back slams into the lockers. Eyes are watching us, and I feel the heat of their stares. Olivia, however, is oblivious with her gaze searching Luke's face.

She squeezes his chin, bringing his face close to hers, and he does everything he can to not look at her. She swings his face side to side, inspecting the swollen skin, tsking in disapproval before she releases him. If I wasn't so hurt by Luke's actions last night, I might find this spectacle to be somewhat comical.

"Who did this to you?" she practically growls, her hands closing into tight fists at her sides, like she's ready to attack whoever hurt her best friend.

And I have no doubt that she would. Her loyalty is something I admire about her. But when she learns about how Luke abandoned me last night, will she still feel the same way? Where will her loyalty lie then? I don't want to come between my two best friends, even if one of them broke my heart.

"I did," a raspy voice announces from behind us.

I turn and face Ryland, unable to hide my shock. "What?"

He places his arm around my shoulders, like it's the most natural thing he's ever done. We've hugged before, even had an occasional playful wrestle. But standing in the hallway with his arm slung over my shoulder like we're—dare I say it —more than friends. Yeah no, this isn't like us. My internal alarms are screaming as the warmth of him seeps into my skin.

Warning! Warning! Ryland is touching us. Central nervous system shut down! I repeat, shut down!

I'm wrapped in the scent of him: spearmint gum, evergreen trees, and wood smoke from his fireplace at home. My instincts take over, and I lean into him, welcoming his embrace. My hand raises up until it's planted on his chest, locking me into the first sense of comfort I've had since I was in his car the night before. Just the mere presence of him erases all my anxieties. My alarms hit the snooze button. *How does he always do that?*

I look up at Ryland, who's glaring at Luke, and I'm reminded of what he just admitted to. I don't have it in me to move away from his comfort, even with the puzzling look Olivia is giving us. Her face is jumping from Ryland, to me, to Luke as her brain puts the pieces together.

"You three follow me right *now*!" she commands in full drill-sergeant mode.

The three of us stand firm in our place, the boys in some sort of a glaring standoff, me looking back and forth between them, not knowing what to do. Olivia's bright-red hair swings into our line of sight again as she turns and points to us.

"Now!" She grabs Luke's arm and begins dragging him behind her.

"Should we make a break for it?" Ryland whispers into my ear, sending goosebumps down my spine.

"She'll hunt us down and make us regret it," I add, earning a small chuckle from him before we follow her and Luke down the hall until we're in the stairwell alone.

Ryland removes his arm from my shoulder and places his hands inside his pockets. I try not to miss the weight of his arm around me, but it's hard to do. Olivia shoves Luke until he's leaning against the wall. She then places me by the stairs so no one can escape her wrath. And she makes sure to stand in front of the door. Poor Ryland is left in the middle of us. I can practically see steam rolling from Olivia's nostrils as they flare in anger like a bull ready to charge.

"Talk." She points to Luke, and we all watch him closely. Inside, I'm dancing with joy that she picked him first.

He shrugs his shoulders and shoves his hands into his jacket pockets, making sure to keep his eyes downcast. "I deserved it," is all he says.

My eyes widen with his honesty, and I wish he would look at me. His broad shoulders slump in defeat. I want to release this anger that I have toward him. I'm tired of carrying it around. But it will stay inside of my heart, rotting away, until he apologizes to me. It feels like he doesn't care that he hurt me.

Olivia's green eyes study the three of us for a moment before returning to Luke, and she asks, "What did you do?'

No one says anything for a moment, and I'm not sure that I want to be the one to tell her what happened last night. Ryland exhales loudly and removes a hand from his pocket to point at Luke. "Well, to start, this idiot left Raine alone on the street last night in the freezing cold."

Olivia's brows pinch in confusion, and she looks at me for clarity. "Luke and Davis got into an argument last night. Luke stormed out and left, but Davis wouldn't let me leave. So, I snuck out of my window and chased Luke down, but he ended up leaving with Jake Himswell. I called Ryland to come pick me up, and—"

I can't finish. I don't want to admit out loud what Davis did. Luke finally looks at me, pain shining in his eyes, and it takes everything in me not to crumble under the weight of it.

Olivia smacks Luke on the shoulders. "Seriously, Luke? Jake? Why are you still hanging out with that jerk?"

"That's not all," Ryland adds, and his eyes bore into Luke's.

Luke studies Ryland for a moment, and it's then that I realize Luke has no idea what happened last night after he left. So, when did Ryland punch him? I wanted to take Olivia's place and start demanding answers, but when Ryland reaches over and tugs the sleeve of my hoodie up to reveal the evidence of Davis' anger, I freeze.

Olivia inhales sharply, one hand covering her lips, the other reaching out to touch my wrist as she examines the bruise on my arm. "Are you okay?" she whispers so softly I can barely hear her.

I give her a nod. "I don't think Davis meant to hold my arm so tightly, and I bruise easily."

"Don't make excuses for him," Olivia adds, her fingers tracing over the purple tint in my skin.

"A bruise for a bruise," Ryland adds, looking at Luke.

Luke's expression drops along with the color in his face. He pushes himself from the wall and goes to move toward the door, but Ryland is quick and stands in his way. Luke is much larger than Ryland and easily could shove him out of his way, but he has respect for Ryland, and it shows in how he backs away.

"You forget, Luke, that your choices don't only affect *you*. You made the decision to leave Raine, and look what happened because of that," Ryland snaps, pointing toward my arm that Olivia is still examining with tears in her eyes. "I took her to her grandparents' house, but Davis followed us. He even went out of his way to block our way out and threatened not only her Mamaw and Papaw but my family as well. He won't let her leave so now she's stuck there without your protection."

"Who's to say that's my responsibility?" Luke adds, color returning to his face as his anger rises.

Olivia blinks back her tears and looks up at Luke. "We did when we chose to become friends, Luke. Since middle school, the three of us have always made sure to have each other's backs. When bullies, like Jake, try to get to us, we put a stop to it and are there for each other. You're supposed to protect Raine, not cower away for your own benefit."

"Who's going to protect me, then?" he adds.

"Me," I say. "I walked into the living room to have your

back, Luke, but you turned your back on me when you left me there with *him*."

He turns to face me, shoulders falling for a second time. "He's only been in your life for a little while. I've had to deal with him my whole life, Raine. I don't want to do it anymore."

"I get it, Luke. I don't want you to have to suffer anymore. I just—" It hits me then, hard like a baseball bat to the back of my skull, that I'm the one being unreasonable.

Davis has tormented Luke his whole life, and I should want him to escape that pain. I want Luke to be safe, no longer suffering at the hands of his father, and yet I've kept things one-sided this whole time. I'm being selfish, and that's not fair to Luke.

If I want to protect Luke, I need to let him go. If I play my cards right and walk on eggshells at home during the week, then in two years, I will graduate high school and be able to leave for college. I can apply to colleges that are far away from Covewood and finally be free. It won't be like this forever. I just have to bide my time.

"I made a mistake in underestimating Davis last night. It won't happen again. I'll be careful from now on. I'll follow the rules and make it through the next two years. You shouldn't have to suffer with me, especially if he's leaving you alone."

"What?" Ryland says, but I ignore him and reach out to touch Luke's arm, bringing his attention to me.

"I'm sorry I didn't think about your feelings, Luke. And I forgive you."

A single tear falls from Luke's good eye, and guilt tries to suffocate me. How did I not see just how much he's hurting because of his father? The pain I felt last night doesn't compare to what he's endured for years. He reaches out and pulls me into a hug, placing a faint kiss on top of my head before nuzzling his face into the crook of my neck.

"I'm sorry I left you. I was scared," he whispers.

"It's okay."

He pulls himself away from our embrace, sniffing away evidence of getting emotional, before he gives me a nod and releases his hold on me. I peek behind Luke to see Ryland and Olivia both watching us with uncertainty. And then Olivia asks the question that's been nagging at me.

"So, when did you punch him?"

Luke winces at the memory. Ryland's face doesn't hold as much anger as it did before. His shoulders bounce once as he says, "This morning. In the parking lot."

"He pulled me out of Jake's car, shoved me against the hood, punched me, and walked off without explaining all of this."

"I figured you'd put two and two together."

"I mean, somewhat, but you could've explained the parts I didn't know." Luke shakes his head and makes for the door, clearly still upset with Ryland. By the looks of his swollen eye, I would be upset too.

We all move out of the way and allow Luke to slip past us. Olivia swings around to face me, her eyes silently asking a question, and I jerk my chin toward the door behind her. "Go. Make sure he's okay," I assure her.

Before she leaves, she gives Ryland a scolding look, scrunches her nose, and pokes his chest. "Me and you are not done. Okay?"

He holds up his hands in defeat, a hint of fear etched in his expression—and for good reason. Everyone knows you don't mess with Olivia, and he's in for an earful from her. Once Olivia's gone, the stairwell falls completely silent. It's so quiet I can hear each breath escaping Ryland's lungs.

"You were quick to forgive him," he proclaims, leaning against the wall.

"Well, I learned from the best," I say. "It's not right for me to want him to suffer too. I didn't understand that before." I exhale, wishing I felt better after forgiving Luke, but the same dread stays firm in its place inside me.

"I get that. I made some sacrifices in order to take the pressure off Zane and Mom when Dad had his episodes. It doesn't mean that what Davis is doing is okay. He shouldn't be allowed to get away with it," he shouts, swearing under his breath.

My mouth drops as the swear leaves his lips, and he apologizes. I know he's angry at the injustice of it all. He hates that I'm learning firsthand how his father was once to him. However, Ryland's dad sounds much worse. I wish I could erase the scars I know his father left behind.

"Are you okay?" Ryland asks after a moment of silence. I meet his gaze and notice a hint of heat behind their hazel color.

"I will be," I say breathlessly and give him a small smile.

There is something buzzing between us, making me feel unsteady. I shift on my feet nervously, twirling the strings from my hoodie around my fingertips, and ask, "So you punched Luke?"

It's not really a question because we both know the answer, but I need to say something to help root me here, by the stairwell, instead of closing the distance between us. Ryland's hands are in his pockets, and he's leaning against the wall across from me, and yet with the way his eyes are looking at me, it feels as if they're touching my skin.

"Yup," he states, allowing the P to pop.

My eyes shamelessly watch as his lips move, and the urge to taste them takes over. Something has shifted between us, and I'm not sure when or what caused it, but Ryland has never looked at me like this before. I'm enjoying it way more than I should.

"Are you mad at me for it?" he asks, the heat in his eyes dampening just a bit.

I tug the ends of my hoodie string, trying to look anywhere but at him, and attempt to ignore the flow of lava that is currently splashing around in my gut.

"Kind of. You shouldn't have hurt Luke. But I also understand why you did it."

"Do you?" he quickly asks, taking a step away from the wall.

"Yeah?" It comes out more like a question with the way he's studying me, begging me to answer correctly, but words have yet again failed me. I swallow hard, but it doesn't help the dryness in my throat.

"I don't think you do, Rainbow." Another step toward me. "Or you just don't want to admit it."

"Admit what?" I ask, and there is a brief look of desperation on his face. An invisible string between us, pulling tighter as the seconds tick by, and my feet involuntarily take a step toward him.

"That I care about you." His words start a fresh ache in my chest. My lungs hang on to the air within them, and I stop in my tracks. He closes the distances between us but doesn't touch me. My skin hums with desire, but I'm too scared to move. I don't want to mess up this moment.

"I know you care. You're my best friend," I finally say. Friends care about each other. That fact alone was just displayed right here in this stairwell moments before. It does nothing to keep my heart from hammering so hard in my chest that I'm sure he can hear it.

He reaches out and places his hand onto the side of my face. I can feel him shaking, and my expression softens, knowing that he's just as nervous as I am. Is this how we've decided to let each other in? Slowly healing each other's wounds. Being each other's source of light when the world gives us nothing but shadows. I've chosen to give Ryland my trust, and now he's deathly close to my heart.

"It's more than that. Always has been."

More.

That simple word bounces inside my head a few times before I allow it to sink into my heart. It's making my head spin. My eyes flutter at the tingle his fingers are leaving against my skin, and I lean into the palm of his hand.

"After last night, I—" His words quiver, and he takes a

second to swallow back the emotions he's trying to contain, but I decide right here that I'm done holding back. I don't want to be scared anymore. I want to give Ryland my heart. "I can't stand the thought of not being able to protect you. I want to always be here for you, more than as a friend, because I—"

I run my hand up his back, over his shoulder, until I thread my fingers through his hair. The movement has his breath hitching. It's a silent plea, one I've been waiting to make for years, as I tug him closer to my face. I'm desperate to hear what he has to say but not as badly as I want to feel his lips on my own. I watch as his lips part and his eyes widening as my mouth inches closer.

"Raine, I—"

"What are you two doing in here?" a deep voice shouts from behind us. We both jump and release our hold on each other. "Get to class before I send you both to the principal's office!"

I never liked Mr. Philips, with his bad attitude and the way he always spits when he talks in class, but I especially don't like him now. He ruined something I've been praying for since I was fourteen years old. Ryland and I both frown as we sulk our way through the door and walk into the hallway. I give Ryland one last small smile before I have to head in the opposite direction to class.

Chapter Eighteen

Now

Raine

Yesterday was my last day at Olivia's, and even with the farm being just down the road, it felt like another goodbye. Luke spent the day with us, and I soaked up every last moment of that dedicated time with them. I know my time will be spread thin between the renovations, working remotely, and taking care of the chores. I helped with those same chores for years when I lived here, and I took care of them just fine yesterday, but when Papaw and I met at the farm earlier he still insisted on showing me exactly how he does everything.

Once he left, I kept busy with cleaning where I could around the construction and ended up sorting through my Mamaw's clothes. They still smelled like her. It was strange, how just the familiar scent of her helped me to envision her better.

When I closed my eyes to finally go to sleep, I could hear the sound of her laughter, picture her giant smile, and see every small element of her face. If we could forget our loved ones who have passed, it wouldn't hurt anymore. But I don't want to forget her. I'd rather endure the pain in order to keep her alive within my memories.

My phone rings beside me on my nightstand and I roll over and see Samuel's name light up the screen. I haven't talked to him in days.

"Hey," I answer and push myself to sit up.

"Good morning. Did I wake you?" he asks. I can hear the sound of his coffee maker in the background. My feet hit the ground, and I shuffle my way into the kitchen to do the same for myself.

"No, I've been lying in bed, being lazy, but I need to get up and take care of the animals."

He snickers. "That sounds so weird to hear you say."

Maybe it is to him, but it isn't to me. Falling back into the old habit of taking care of the animals and garden is like riding a bicycle, especially since my grandparents run the farm pretty much the same way they did in my youth. I could complete each task blindfolded if I want to. However, Samuel doesn't know this version of me, so of course it would feel strange to him. It's another reminder that he doesn't know me, not really.

"Yeah, I bet it does," I admit, pulling my comforter around me to stay warm, I make my way down the hall.

"Olivia doesn't have a farm, does she?"

It's my turn to snicker. The image of Olivia handling the chores, especially the task of scooping out the droppings from animal stalls, sends me into another fit of laughter.

"Gosh no. Although, I'd pay good money to see her try it out for a day."

"Oh. So, you're staying at your grandparents, then?"

Grandparents.

The single word stings in a way that's unfair. It's no longer my grandparents' home. I'm not sure if it will even be Papaw's by the end of the renovations. I need to think of a way to convince him to keep the farm. I can't fathom the idea of losing this place. It's my safe haven.

"Yeah. It's easier to keep up with everything if I stay here."

"How long do you plan on staying?"

"Probably for a few weeks. I'm going to take it day by day. I start working remotely on Monday, and I don't know how long I can push my luck with my bosses. I don't want to take a chance of returning to no job at all."

The thought of losing all the hard work I've done for the last decade sends a rush of anxiety through me. Coffee probably won't help my nerves, but I ignore that fact and push the button to start the brewing process.

"They won't fire you. They need you and your amazing photography skills."

Yeah, tell that to do-no-wrong Thomas. He'll take this opportunity to brown-nose his way to a promotion for sure. Oddly, the thought of that doesn't bother me as badly as it probably should. I shrug those thoughts away and study the calendar hanging on the fridge.

"Anyway, I just wanted to call and check in with you."

"I'm doing better. Thank you." I know to some people it's probably frowned upon to still talk to their ex after they've freshly broken up, but Samuel and I always had a trusting friendship between us, even if I kept pieces of myself hidden from him. I hope that we can still keep our friendship after everything.

"I'm glad to hear that," he says, and I know he means it. "I'm sorry for how things ended between us, but I want you to know that I'm still here for you."

"I appreciate that, Sam. And I'll be here for you also."

"I better get to work. Stay in touch, okay?"

"Alright. Have a good day."

As we end our conversation, I catch the time on my screen and see that Ryland is running late today. I check the calendar a second time to make sure it's Thursday. Ryland made sure to mark the dates that he'll be working at the house before he left the other day. I appreciated the heads up, knowing I need to mentally prepare my heart to be around him again. My original plan was to try and avoid him at all costs while I'm in Covewood, not wanting to stir up old feelings, but it seems like God has other plans.

I make my way to the counter and smile at the basket Ryland put together for me. He has no idea how much the kind gesture would mean to me. Olivia told me a little bit about how the town has grown over the years—sometimes as a way to try to persuade me to venture past the farm whenever I came to visit Mamaw and Papaw. Spoiler alert: it never worked. My reasons for avoiding the town are starting to feel really stupid the longer I stay in Covewood.

The sound of tires on the gravel catches my attention and I peek out the window to see Ryland's truck pull into the driveway followed by a red truck. I look down at my pajamas and pat the rat's nest on top of my head. Terror washes through me like a cold shower, and I rush to my bedroom.

I'm tossing clothes into the air but have no luck finding anything quick to change into. I touch something soft, and the floral pattern catches my attention. It's one of my Mamaw's dresses I brought into my room last night. I just wanted a piece of her with me as I fell asleep, and now I'm tugging the dress over my head without second-guessing. I run my fingers through my hair as I rush towards the living room and slip into my boots by the front door just as I hear the sound of footsteps on the front porch.

I swing open the door, and Ryland halts in place. He trimmed his beard, which was looking a bit wild before, but is now closer to his face, enhancing his incredible jawline. I can see a hint of his dimples that used to drive me crazy and feel the familiar itch to reach out and brush my thumb against the indention in his skin.

He also had his hair cut. It's shorter on the sides but still long enough on top that he can run his fingers through it to move the strands from his eyes. As if Ryland Quinn could get any more attractive, he shows up on my doorstep looking like a lumberjack hero from a romance novel.

Be still, my heart. I'm not prepared for this.

His mouth falls open, just the tiniest bit, but I notice. His eyes skim down my bare face until they land on my Mamaw's dress. Suddenly, I feel self-conscious and look down to make sure I put the dress on the right way.

"Hey," he says, the words catching in his throat.

I stare at his lips, the same way I used to as a teenager, and it's like the past and present are mixing together, creating a recipe of their own. It's such a surreal feeling, and it takes me a moment to come back to reality.

"You shaved," I say, my voice sounding throaty. Why is that what I chose to say? Not, '*Hey, Ryland. Good morning.*' Gah, I could slap my forehead in embarrassment.

"I told him the *Duck Dynasty* look wasn't working for him," a familiar voice says from behind him.

I peer over Ryland's broad shoulders to see Zane and a wide smile fills my face. I haven't seen Zane since he was fifteen. He sent me a friend request on Facebook a few years ago, which I accepted, so we've exchanged messages back and forth a few times.

Regardless, seeing him in person tugs at my heart, and I can't stop myself before I'm rushing into his arms for a welcoming hug. "Zane," I say softly and squeeze him in return before moving back to get a better look at him.

I pat his shoulders, noticing that he's bulked up since I last saw him as a skinny boy. He's wearing a Mossy Oak ball cap over his golden-brown locks, and a hint of waves peeking out from beneath that he inherited from his mother. Like his big brother, he's grown a beard and keeps it neatly trimmed and cared for.

It's surreal seeing him like this, all grown up instead of the little boy who used to follow Ryland and me around everywhere. I take in the paint-stained shirt he's wearing and the tool belt around his waist and remember that he, too, stayed in the family business. Pride swells in my heart for the two of them.

His eyes, the same hazel color as Ryland's, shine brightly toward me, and his smile widens as he says, "It's so good to see you."

"Likewise."

"Big bro couldn't handle the job alone today, so I came to save the day." Zane rolls his shoulders back proudly.

"Hey, Daddy, look! That goat is stuck in the hammock." A tiny voice giggles, and now I'm looking over Zane's shoulders to see a blonde-haired little girl standing in the front yard.

Behind her sits two large oak trees, and between them is Buck, the billy goat, tugging his head with no luck at getting his horns free from the hammock netting. I look back at her, and she's giving me a wide, toothy grin, revealing a hole where one is missing. Her blonde hair is pulled back into two braids, and she's wearing overalls over a light-pink shirt.

There is no doubt that this is Ryland's daughter, Annabelle. I've seen a few photos of her before. However, seeing her in person has its own effect. She looks so much like Ryland. Same hazel eyes, same cute freckles on her nose, and they even share the same cackling laugh.

"There's a teacher's day at her school, and Mom wasn't able to watch her, so I had to bring her along. I'll make sure she minds and doesn't disrupt your day," Ryland says, gripping the back of his neck nervously.

"Nonsense. She won't be a bother. I'm happy to finally meet her and have her here."

Ryland's shoulders sag with relief, and his mouth tugs into a small grin.

"You dumb goat. How'd you get in this mess?" Zane chuckles behind us.

I watch as Zane pulls out his phone to snap a few pictures,

one including himself pointing toward the goat. He then tugs on Buck's horns and gets one loose; however, Buck doesn't seem to like it and jumps, almost knocking Zane over. Ryland rushes over to help, but Buck is not a happy camper. He jumps up again and tries to headbutt Ryland. He's able to move out of the way but not before falling back against Zane.

"I *goat* you, brother." Zane cackles at his own wit, earning a head shake from Ryland and a laugh from Annabelle and me.

"You have *goat* to be *kidding* me. We're trying to help you, Buck," Zane hisses while he's struggling to get the other horn to release. Once he does, Buck takes off as fast as he can, kicking and spitting as he runs away. "What an ungrateful grump."

I move over to where Annabelle is standing and give her a wide smile when she notices me.

"Papaw Earl's goat is silly," she says.

Papaw Earl.

Why does hearing her call him that melt my heart?

Ryland smirks at me, as if reading my thoughts, and bends down to pick Annabelle up. She squeals with joy when Zane comes up behind them and gives her a tickle. As if my heart couldn't melt any more.

"This is my baby girl, Annabelle," Ryland says, cradling her into his arms like she's a baby.

"I'm not a baby!" She giggles.

"You'll always be his baby, and don't you forget it," Zane adds, pointing at his adorable niece.

"He's right," Ryland says before planting a kiss on her cheek and placing her down. "This is Daddy's friend, Raine."

I bend down to extend my hand toward her. "It's nice to meet you." She gives me a sweet smile and tugs my hand. "I love your braids. Did your Daddy fix your hair?"

She runs her tiny hands down her braids and looks up at Ryland. "Yup. I wanted to look like Anna from *Frozen*."

I look up at him, knowing he's sharing the same memory as

I am, before I add, "Your dad used to braid my hair when I was younger. It seems like he's put those skills to good use."

A pink tint seeps into Ryland's cheeks, and my smile grows even more. Something warm and liquid bubbles inside my chest as I watch him bend down and give Annabelle a hug and kiss her cheek before walking over to where Zane is standing.

"Would you like to help me with some chores this morning?" I ask her.

Annabelle jumps up and claps her hands excitedly, and I wish I could say I have the same energy about doing farm chores. She'll definitely make them more fun this morning. I look up to ask Ryland if it's okay, but he's already giving me a nod of approval.

"Let's get to work, Zane."

"Whatever floats your *goat*, bro," Zane says as he bends down to pick up the toolbox he had set on the ground.

"That's enough with the goat puns," Ryland grumbles before planting another kiss on top of Annabelle's head and walking toward the house.

Scratch the whole lumberjack comment. Seeing Ryland Quinn as a father is the most attractive thing I've seen. If I could get away with it, I'd fan myself. My heart is in trouble.

Annabelle turned out to be the best little helper. She collected the eggs by herself, watered the garden, and helped me with the sheep. We collected strawberries and harvested some redbud blooms too. Now, we're standing in the kitchen, waiting for water to boil in a pot so we can make redbud jelly.

It's a sweet feeling, sharing a family tradition with Annabelle. She has been telling me stories of Mamaw and how they used to make art together with Ryland's mother. Mamaw told me her own stories of Annabelle, but I had no idea how often she was around her. Hearing Annabelle share her memories brings me so much joy.

"You know. Mamaw and I used to make redbud jelly every spring. I always looked forward to the end of March to do this with her. We'd blast some music and sing and dance as we waited for the blooms to steep."

Annabelle's face lights up. "I want to have a dance party!"

"Well, show me your moves, then!"

We spend the next forty-five minutes dancing and singing and taking breaks to snack on strawberries dipped in homemade whipped cream. I tell Annabelle tales of growing up on the farm and how I loved the weekends when I could visit Ryland and his family. She stays quiet, listening, and laughing with me when I share something funny her father or uncle used to do.

I didn't realize how healing it would be to share things with Annabelle about Mamaw as well as Ryland's grandparents. It's a way to keep them alive. It's also a sweet way to bond with her.

As we pour our mixture into jars, I tell her, "One time, I tried to make a double batch of jelly, but it turned out to be a big sticky mess. It was more like honey than jelly."

"That still sounds yummy."

"It was but not exactly what I was trying to make. I was so disappointed, but Mamaw Jo made me feel better by using the honey on some toast, and it still tasted delicious." I smile at the memory. "She always had a way of finding the good in any situation."

"Knock, knock!"

I'm not used to this new open floor plan in the farmhouse, even as I turn around and am able to see the front door from the stove. It's still bright outside, so I have to blink to adjust my eyes to the light that is bouncing in from the windows. As I squint, I can see Ryland and Zane's mother making her way toward us.

"Maribelle!" I say

At the same time Annabelle yells, "Nannie!"

Maribelle makes her way into the kitchen and opens her arms to allow her granddaughter to jump up and give her a hug then she looks at me, giving me a small smile before looking back to Annabelle.

"I came to pick you up. Have you been good today?"

"Yes! Raine showed me how to make redbud jelly!" Annabelle squeals and points toward the jars sitting on the counter.

"Did she?" Maribelle smiles and takes a step toward me and brings me into a hug.

I smile and close my eyes, soaking in this moment. As she wraps her thin arms around me, I feel a sense of warmth. She squeezes me tight and plants a small kiss on my cheek before pulling away from our embrace. Her warm palm finds my cheek, and her eyes study me for a moment.

"Look at you! All grown up. Johanna and Earl loved any moment to brag about you. They are so proud, you know? You always knew that you wanted to travel and see the world outside of this small town, and you did it. You made something of yourself, and you should be proud." She places her hand onto my shoulder, giving it a small squeeze. "I have to admit though. I'm happy you found your way back home."

Found my way back home. I did, didn't I? Even if it wasn't in my plans, it was for sure in God's. Movement catches my attention at the front door. When a pair of hazel eyes meets mine. I'm hit with the realization of what God wants from me while I'm here.

"Hello, ladies," Ryland says softly, the crinkles by his eyes showing. He'd taken off his brown jacket at some point while working, now revealing a gray long-sleeve shirt with the sleeves rolled up to his elbows and a tool belt attached to his blue jeans. I stare a little too long at the three buttons going down his chest and how the first one is unbuttoned, revealing a peek of his flesh. For the second time today, I'm feeling flushed.

"There he is." Maribelle beams at the sight of her first-born and brings him in for a hug and kiss on his cheek. "The house is looking absolutely stunning."

"It's coming along nicely." His eyes find mine for a second before he looks down at Annabelle and picks her up into his arms. "This one seems to have been a big help for Raine today."

"She was the best helper." I add, loving how Annabelle beams at my compliment.

"Hey, Mama," Zane says sweetly as the front door shuts behind him. He moves into the space and joins in on all the hug giving going on.

I stand in the kitchen, watching them all closely. Having Ryland and his family here in front of me begins to feel like a blast from the past. My heart sends a small pang right into my gut with the reminder that I chose to leave them ten years ago. How could I have done that?

I mean, I know how and why I chose to leave. At the time, it seemed like the best choice for us all. And I've put so much effort into building myself a life away from Covewood. Yet those lines I drew years ago between me and the past are starting to slowly fade with each passing day.

I observe the four of them as they talk to each other in the living room and instantly feel like an outsider. What would life be like if I had stayed in Covewood? The guilt of choosing to not include these people in my own life hits me all at once and starts to smother me.

I need to get out of this house.

I grab a few jars of the jelly Annabelle and I made, placing the leftover strawberries in a bag, and walk over to the group. "Here, take this home with you," I tell Annabelle, doing the best I can to keep my face from giving away the panic I feel inside.

"Look at what Raine taught me how to make, Daddy," she exclaims and holds up the jar.

Ryland studies it for a moment, a memory touching his eyes, and he turns to face me. The smile on his face drops when he looks at me, and I push my hair out from behind my ears, using it as a curtain to hide behind. How can this man *still* read me so easily?

"It was so good to see all of you today. Truly, it, uh... I hadn't realized how much I missed everyone." I'm panting now, my words coming out faster than I can think. I'm raw and on edge. "I apologize, but I have to run a quick errand that I forgot about. Annabelle, I enjoyed our time together. Thank you for all your help."

"You're welcome," she says sweetly.

I grab my purse, giving everyone a wave goodbye, and avoid everyone's eyes as I pull the door open. I'm practically jogging toward my car, praying to not lose the hold I have on my emotions. What is wrong with me? I'm such a mess, it feels like whiplash after how calm and strong I felt earlier today. But witnessing the Quinn family all together dug up the guilt I've been trying hard to keep buried.

"Raine, wait," I hear Ryland shout from behind me right as I place a shaky hand onto the door handle to my car. Of course he followed me.

I exhale and turn to face him. There's concern written all over his face, and he reaches out to place a gentle hand onto my shoulder. Why can't he just let me have my space to fall apart in solitude? I can't hold it together much longer.

"What's wrong?" he asks, his hazel eyes dancing with my own, so close that I can see the hints of golden flakes within their color.

"I forgot— I need to go do a thing— I just need to go." I'm not making any sense and I can feel my eye begin to twitch.

"Hey, talk to me. Please," he adds softly, daring a step closer to me.

I catch the scent of him. It's familiar and yet unknown. Hints of pine and woodsmoke covered with cologne. It's another reminder that the past is mixing in with the present.

"I'm a mess, Ryland," I admit softly, feeling my shoulders slump in defeat, and I lean against the door of my car for support. "It's been a lot to take in."

"I'm sure it has been. No one expects you to have it all together," he says, lacing his fingers with mine, using the pad of his thumb to rub against the inside of my hand. It's oddly comforting, and I'll gladly welcome the touch to keep me grounded instead of spiraling like my mind seems to do these days.

I close my eyes and focus on inhaling three deep breaths. When I peek up through my lashes to look at him, I'm met with understanding instead of judgment. It's refreshing to always be seen by him.

"I've been carrying around a heavy weight of guilt ever since losing Mamaw and being back here," I add, releasing his hand to gesture toward the farmhouse. "Being around *you*."

Admitting this out loud opens the door for the old Raine to see everything I've allowed to slip away from my life. She's shaking her head at me, disappointed in the choices I've made, especially with my biggest regret standing right in front of me.

"You're not the only one carrying around guilt." His eyes dance with my own, a pool of truth, as if he's speaking from experience. "It's been living in my heart since the day I lost you. So, I get it, Raine. You're not alone in this. Maybe you're here not to bring up guilt from the past but because God knew you needed your family and friends to help you get through this difficult season."

He reaches out, wrapping his big arms around me, and pulls me into a hug. "Pray about it. Ask God to work on changing your heart, and then give your burdens to Him. The rest will come together after that."

"You make it sound so simple, but it's not that easy," I

proclaim and bury my face in his sturdy chest, welcoming the scent of him this time.

"I don't think it's supposed to be easy—not all the time, anyway. It's the hard times that truly help to shape us. We all have to walk through seasons of pain in order to grow. You might not be able to see it right now, but there's a rainbow waiting for you on the other side of this storm. And the best part is, you don't have to endure it alone."

As his words sink in, all the fight drains out of me. The flame of hope that was burning bright in my chest earlier flickers. Embers, really—cooling in the pile of ash that has taken up residence in the open space between my lungs. Every breath seems to burn.

If I can still breathe, I'm fine.

Being here in the embrace of Ryland's arms, the timelines of us combining...it leaves me feeling confused. The feelings I had for Ryland in the past have chosen to linger whether I want to admit it or not. Somewhere deep inside my heart, I still crave him. I left so much of myself, who I truly was, with him. And being around him again is slowly bringing those pieces back together.

The real question is, have I completely stood in the way of what we once had since I chose to run away?

Ryland pats my back before removing himself from our embrace. He gives me a small smile, one that I wish I could reach out and grab and tuck into my pocket for later. I don't really need to leave, so now what do I do? Putting some space between us sounds like the smart thing to do so I can breathe and think without his intoxicating presence hindering my thoughts. Another part of me never wants to leave him.

"Thank you," I say and tug the driver's side car door open, making the decision for myself.

"You're welcome. Hey, uh... We're having a cookout on Saturday out at the cabin. Around noonish. You're welcome to come...if you'd like."

Silence hangs in the air as I ponder his invitation. It would be nice to be by the lake and to see the cabins again. "I'll think about it," I say.

"Please do, because I'd like you to be there. Well, not just me, everyone will enjoy having you there too." Now it's his turn to ramble, and I have to bite my bottom lip to keep from smiling.

"Yeah, okay. I'll see you there," I promise.

Chapter Nineteen

Twelve Years Before

Ryland

It's Saturday, and Raine is hanging out with me in Pops and Nan's living room. Pops and Earl left early this morning to go hunting. Why they chose to go hunt in the freezing cold is beyond me. They invited me to tag along, but I gladly turned them down, especially knowing that I would get to spend time with Raine.

However, I wasn't anticipating Nan sitting between us for most of the visit. But she hasn't been feeling her best, and I'm not about to leave her alone. Plus Raine is happy to share her snacks and watch *The Golden Girls* with us.

I peek over at her as she laughs at something Sophia says.

"You grow old, you sag, and you get over it. I've never heard a wiser statement."

"Ain't that the truth. Sophia is my favorite," Nan admits, grabbing a handful of popcorn and shoving it into her mouth. Earlier, I couldn't get her to eat anything, but once Raine sat down next to her, she started sneaking some of Raine's snacks. "I think Sophia would approve of your new hairstyle."

Raine's smile brightens as she reaches up to run her fingers through the short strands. She recently cut her hair into a short bob style, and it's taken everything in me not to run my fingers through it.

We haven't had a free moment to talk about what happened at school a few days ago—or more like what *almost* happened. The unknown has been floating around in the air between us, and it's been driving me crazy not knowing what could've happened if the teacher hadn't interrupted us.

I was going to kiss her. And I was going to tell her how I truly feel.

"Honey, would you care to grab me some more water? This popcorn is making me so thirsty."

"Of course. Ry, do you need anything?"

Just you, alone, so I can finally see what your lips feel like against mine.

"No thanks," I say instead, watching each step that she takes toward the kitchen, admiring the way her hips sway as she moves. She's wearing a pair of tight blue jeans and a cream-colored sweater. She looks happier today, and I hope that it's because of me. I guess I can give Nan a little credit.

I look over at Nan, who is staring at me with a wicked grin on her face. "What?"

"I think you know."

"Know what?" I play dumb and study the popcorn in my bowl before placing a piece into my mouth. I try to focus on the buttery flavor instead of the ever-growing grin on my grandmother's face.

"What's going on between you and Raine?" She nudges me with her bony elbow, right in the ribs. I frown, and my brows pull together. "Oh, don't give me that look. I've seen how you've been staring at her."

"I have not been staring—"

"Yes, you have. Listen, I know a thing or two about love. I've been married to your Pops for almost fifty years. I know the signs." She waves her hands in front of my face with a soft chuckle. She's enjoying this a little too much. "And I know she feels the same way about you."

I perk up at her words, and suddenly, I'm done with playing dumb. "Really?"

"See, I knew it." She smirks, and a grin spreads across my face. And dare I say that I feel heat grow in my cheeks. Am I blushing? With my grandmother? "Just tell her how you feel already."

"I'm scared," I admit, feeling my shoulders slump with the weight of the truth.

"Of what? That girl is just as crazy about you as you are with her. There's nothing to fear."

How can she be so sure? I want to ask her, but Raine waltzes back into the room, and immediately, it's a little stuffy in here.

"Thank you, dear. I might try to rest for a bit. Why don't you and Ryland go play in the snow and give me some quiet time."

"Yeah, sure," Raine says, bending down to give Nan a quick hug before grabbing her thick coat. "We won't be far, in case you need anything."

"Oh, don't worry about me." She swats the air and gives me a wink when Raine isn't looking.

"You're trouble," I whisper to Nan before giving her a peck on the cheek. "I'll be back to check on you."

"Go get your girl."

Once we're bundled up and walking down the stone path that leads to the lake, all courage leaves me. We fall silent, our shoulders brushing as we walk, and I press my lips together to keep my thoughts from tumbling out. There's a strange feeling in the pit of my stomach, like after a dip on a roller-coaster.

A light breeze is blowing, making the air feel much colder, and it brings the scent of snow with it. The sound of large snowflakes hitting the ground and the crunching from our feet echo around us. After a few moments, Raine's voice fills the air between us.

"Wanna hear the weird dream I had last night?" she asks. It's become something normal between us, deciphering each other's dreams. I hum in approval, thankful for the distraction.

She giggles, and the sound is contagious. "Okay, don't judge me for this one. So, it starts out with you and me eating ice cream. We seem to be having a fun time. But then I smack my lips together and notice I have a clump of hair in my mouth. I look down at my ice cream cone and notice it's not ice cream—it's a kitten. I was licking a kitten, Ryland."

I grin and turn to look at her. I take in the way her eyes sparkle, how she wrinkles her nose and is animated with her hands as she continues.

"And the weirdest part is that I continue to lick this poor little kitten. I look over, and you're doing the same. So, there we are, licking our kitten cones—" She snorts as a laugh escapes her lips.

I laugh with her because how can I not? Her eyes widen as she peers over at me, and I find myself tracing the lines of her lips with my eyes as she continues to laugh. How easy would it be to reach over and brush mine against hers?

"And then someone walks in and grabs a puppy-cone, but when the puppy sees the kittens, it starts chasing our kitten-cones all around the ice cream shop. And we just sit there, smiling at one another, like everything that is happening is completely normal. Please, Ry, try to decipher that crazy dream."

Her bottom lip is tucked between her teeth as she restrains herself from giggling, and all I want to do is reach over and run my thumb across her mouth. I want to hear her laugh for the rest of my life. I don't know how she does it, but she always brings a light with her everywhere she goes. And it's refreshing to see after the past few heavy weeks we've had.

It's crazy to think that Raine and I have been best friends

for three years now. The first moment that I met her at the Wiley farm, something in me became lost in her. I think it took some time, but after we spent a few months getting to know one another, my heart started to feel more for her. I found myself falling in love with her.

It's more than just three words that I ache to say to her. It's the way I always seem to laugh harder when I'm with her. It's how I feel *more* when she's around. It's trusting her with me—the real me. It's how she's the first person I think about in the morning and who my thoughts drift off to during the night.

I want to be her friend—the friend she falls hopelessly in love with. As I watch her face light up with a smile, the reflection of the sun in her eyes, the wind blowing pieces of her hair, I want to tell her that—that my heart is full from the love I have for her.

"I mean, where do I even begin?" I laugh.

She shoves against my shoulder, shaking her head but giving me a soft smile.

We make it to the dock and stand next to one another, looking out over the still lake. Not a boat is in sight with it being in the middle of winter. I always like this time of year, when the lake is silent and layered with white fluffy snow.

"Okay. Maybe it means..." I begin, keeping my eyes on the water as I try to explain what I'm feeling inside. "No matter what we're doing in life, even when life gets a little crazy, we'll always have each other. We'll always be happy when we're together."

I reach over, feeling brave, and run my hands down her arm until I can lace our fingers together. I look at her, watching her smile slowly fade as she watches our hands become one. I wonder if she feels the prickle of energy up her arm in the same way that I do?

"Only you could find something meaningful in an unexplainable dream like that," she whispers.

"Only you can make me feel happy when life is full of chaos."

Her eyes dance with mine before rolling down my face and landing on my lips. She stands there in silence, snowflakes gathering in the strands of her hair, and I realize I've never been more sure about something as I am at this moment.

I lean toward her, keeping our hands tightly wrapped together, and I press my lips against hers. Our eyes flutter closed at the same time, and I use my free hand to reach up and slide a strand of her hair behind her ear, gripping the side of her face to bring her lips harder against my own. She takes in a deep breath before pulling away.

"Ry," she says breathlessly.

"I'm in love with you, Rainbow."

Her gray-blue eyes widen with shock at my sudden confession, but I can tell by the way her lips turn up into a grin, revealing the dimple that always drives me crazy, that she already knew. I think we've both known for a while now but were just too scared to admit it to one another. Too fearful of messing up the friendship we've built.

"Who knew all it would take was for me to dream about licking kittens for you to admit that you love me."

Raine is looking at me differently now, all droopy-eyed and parting lips, heavy breaths and a blush coloring her cheeks. It feels like honey dripping inside of me, warm and liquid, pooling in all the places that I'm absolutely desperate for her.

"There have been so many times that I wanted to kiss you," I admit out loud, my eyes landing on her lips again.

"Like in the stairwell the other day?" she says, the words a mere whisper in the wind around us.

"Yeah," That one word is all the encouragement she needs. Raine wraps her arms around me and pulls me closer.

"I love you too."

Raine smashes her lips against my own with no sweet introduction. No gentle learning. Instead, she reaches up, scratches her nails into my hair, and tugs me closer. There's a certain demand in the way her mouth works against my own. She kisses me like she's hungry, like she's been dreaming of me the same way I've been dreaming about her.

Kissing Raine has never felt more right than in this moment, on the dock where we've shared many memories, with her wrapped tightly in my arms. Our touches are careless; every point of contact between us feels important.

We hear the sound of a car door shutting which snaps us both back into reality. We separate but refuse to hide the happiness written on our faces. I wish I would've done this sooner. A seed of gratification takes root in my chest and blooms, spreading throughout my body.

"We should check on Nan," she says, keeping her hand entwined with my own.

We hold each other's hands and jog toward the cabins. Raine's giggle rings out, and it sounds like music—the kind you can only get in nature, the kind that feels like peace. From the look on Raine's face as she looks over at me and smiles, I know she feels it too.

We see Pops' truck outside of the cabin and make our way inside. We were only gone for maybe thirty minutes, but I feel guilty for being caught away from Nan when I told him I would look after her.

"We were letting her rest," is the first thing I say when both Earl and Pops turn to see us shedding our jackets at the front door.

"I told them to go outside and let an old lady get some shut-eye, but I couldn't sleep." I peer behind Pops to see Nan wide awake with a cardboard box opened beside her. "Come here, Raine. I want to give you something."

Nan's glassy brown eyes dance over Raine's face, and her expression must give Nan the answer she is looking for because she looks over at me and gives me a thumbs up. Raine studies her for a moment, confusion etched in the way she looks back at me then she reaches out and takes something that Nan hands to her.

"A camera?" Raine says. Her voice is soft, and the look that washes over her makes me wonder if she's about to cry.

"Yes. This is something I've had for years, but it's been sitting inside this box, unused. It needs someone to take care of it and use it again. You're the perfect person for it with how much you've been loving that Polaroid camera of yours."

"Oh, Nan, I don't know what to say."

"You don't have to say anything. The way you love my grandson is enough for me." Raine's eyes widen, and she swings her head to face me, giving me a bright smile.

"That's kind of you, Anna. Thank you for giving this to Raine," Earl says, studying the camera, as if her comment about Raine loving me was nothing new to him.

After he gives Nan a hug, Earl turns and gives me a wink before following Pops into the kitchen, leaving the three of us standing in the living room until Nan finally laughs and shrugs her shoulders. "We all called it."

"Called what?" Raine asks.

Nan chuckles and says, "You two finally getting out of that pesky friend zone. Took ya long enough."

Chapter Twenty

Now

Ryland

I should've known that word would travel around town. This cookout was supposed to be just my crew—Mom, Zane, and Annabelle—as well as August, her husband, Thomas, and son, Jessie. Obviously, Luke, Olivia, and Raine were invited. Zane invited his best friend and our co-worker, Ashton. But those are the only people who were expected to be here.

I'm cooking a big enough brisket to feed the eleven of us as well as have some extra in case anyone wants to have seconds. However, there are seven other people who have shown up within the last thirty minutes. Every person did at least bring a side dish or dessert with them, which has me a little less aggravated.

I open the smoker and check on the brisket, my mouth watering as the smoky scent puffs around my face. A speaker is sitting on one of the picnic tables nearby, blasting a mix of 80's rock and 90's country music, courtesy of my Spotify playlist. I walk over to the white foldout table that Mom set up for the side dishes and check out the options.

I see that Zane made his "famous" potato salad, which is

just regular potato salad that he swears he makes special. Mom baked two loaves of fresh bread. Felix Grady brought one of those boxes full of an assortment of chips and also a few boxes of Capri Suns, as much as we expect of him.

I see that Bill and Hope Hampton, August's parents, brought some of their homemade goat cheese and crackers to go with it and their award-winning goat milk fudge. But the holy grail of sides is the basket of fried morels, also known as dry land fish, that Ashton brought. I've already snuck a few because they're bound to disappear quickly

I look out over what we've claimed as *the picnic area*, which is just a cleared spot of land between the cabins and lake. Three wooden picnic tables sit in the middle. Several blankets and camping chairs fill the spaces in between them.

Luke has set up his volleyball net, and a few people have gathered in teams to play. Annabelle and Jessie are playing on the trampoline. Even though I planned for this to be a small family gathering, a smile tugs against my lips at the sight of everyone mingling together.

My grandparents would have loved this. They always enjoyed hosting events, having people over, and valued the closeness this town brought to everyone's lives.

"Well, so much for a small gathering," Mom says as she places her arm around my hips and pulls me in for a side hug. "But you know how your grandparents loved cookouts like this."

"I was just thinking that," I admit, looking down at her with a grin.

She reaches up, pats my cheek, leaning her head on my shoulder. I welcome her comfort. The warmth of her body pressed into mine, her signature scent of lemons, and the tickle of her long golden-brown and silver waves against my neck.

In the past, my mother and I had some pretty bad fights. But once we moved to Covewood, those arguments slowed down and then came to a stop altogether once Annabelle was born. Becoming a father really showed me how much my mother sacrificed for Zane and me. She still makes sacrifices in order to be there for the three of us. I'm forever grateful for her. I wrap my arms around her and give the top of her head a quick kiss. "I love you, Mom."

"I love you too," she says back.

She releases me as she catches Annabelle trying to sneak a cookie. I can see Jessie's black-and-white tennis shoes from under the tablecloth. His and Annabelle's giggles stop the moment Zane tiptoes behind them and shouts, "Got ya!"

The kids squeal in unison, clinging to the cookies in their hands, and they take off running toward the trampoline.

"That's stealing! Did you kids forget that we have a policeman here?" Zane says after the kids zip shut the trampoline's safety net.

"Yeah, but he's my uncle, and that means I get a 'get out of jail' card," Annabelle proclaims and sticks her tongue out at Zane, earning a booming laugh from me.

"I'm pretty sure that isn't how it works." Zane crosses his arms over his chest and raises a brow in question.

"Yeah-huh! I have the card in my backpack. I can go get it and prove it to you."

"It's true," Luke says from behind me, clasping my shoulder, and then he opens the smoker for a peek, but I swat at his hand.

Annabelle inhales sharply, clearly disappointed in me, and points toward us. "Daddy! That's assaulting an officer!"

"It's okay. Luke gave me a 'get out of jail' card too," I throw back at her and cross my arms. I have several of the cards in a Monopoly game that she doesn't need to know about. I fully plan to use them in the future. "And also, I agree with Uncle Zane. You don't need to be stealing cookies, especially before we eat lunch."

Zane walks over to me, gives me a fist bump, and whispers, "Justice is served."

Behind us, we hear a frustrated huff escape from Annabelle as she hops down from the trampoline. Luke, however, must have every intention of turning my daughter against us, because he takes off running, snatching Annabelle into his arms. He hands her a cookie and, somehow, is able to flash us his badge as he makes a beeline toward the cabins.

"He might as well have been flipping us the bird," Zane grumbles beside me.

"That has to be an illegal way of showing a badge," Ashton's deep voice catches our attention.

Zane smiles at his friend and gives him a firm handshake. "Hey, man, I'm glad you showed up."

"Me too," I add, shaking his hand.

"Ah, you just wanted some of my morels. I hit the jackpot this year." He chuckles.

Ashton moved to Covewood about eleven years ago to reconnect with his dad, and about five years ago, we hired him to work for us. He's made a great addition to the company with his impressive work ethics. He and Zane hit it off instantly, and I'm glad my brother found a good friend.

"Hey, there she is!" Zane beams at someone behind me.

I turn and see Olivia and Raine making their way towards us. My body instantly reacts to Raine, a zip of electricity whipping through me as soon as she's near. I turn towards her and my eyes trail her body. She's wearing a long pink dress that flows against her ankles. Her hair's hanging down in natural waves past her shoulders, and sitting against her chest is the rainbow necklace.

She gives me a shy smile and waves in greeting. She looks at Ashton and reaches out a hand. "Hi, I'm Raine."

"Oh, *the* Raine. I've heard a lot about you." Ashton announces.

"All good things I hope." She adds, glancing at me shyly.

Ashton gives her his signature charming smile before eyeing me. "Yes Ma'am. It's nice to finally meet you in person. Now if you'll excuse me, I have some food I want to sample before everyone else comes over and steals all the good stuff."

"Alright! Who brought the Morsels?" Olivia shouts and follows him.

"I brought some sourdough cookies," Raine says, eyes flowing up and down my body, and I catch the hint of pink growing on her cheeks.

"Please tell me they're like the ones Johanna would make," I ask excitedly.

"They are. She had some discard left in the fridge," she says, her voice cracking, my heart cracking with it. People have always told me that time heals all wounds. But not this one. Not yet.

"I like this look on you," I announce, trying to change the subject, and give her another once-over.

"What? *Little House on the Prairie*?" she jokes and pushes her hair behind her ear.

"It's more *you*. Like, the old you, anyway."

"How'd I look before?" she asks curiously, her brows raising.

"When you first came to town, you were all 'city business woman.' Now you're..." I wave my hands in front of her, unsure of what to say.

"Maybe I should dye my hair bright pink again?" she tosses back, and I laugh.

"It kept me on my toes, not knowing what color your hair would be each time I saw you back then."

I reach out and catch a strand of loose hair between my fingers. She tenses slightly but keeps her eyes locked on mine. Despite the heat outside, goosebumps prickle against my skin, especially when her mouth parts and her eyes land on my lips.

"I guess I've felt more like myself the past few days," she admits, her blush deepening on her cheeks. There's simple honesty there, a thin thread of hope from her heart to mine. I release her hair and my hand finds hers without thinking, trailing up the length of her forearm before sliding back down to link our fingers.

"I'm glad," I say softly and begin to tug her closer toward me, but I stop when I hear someone approaching us. Annabelle and Zane are looking at us with mischievous grins on their faces. I open my mouth to ask what they are up to but feel the words trap inside my mouth once I feel a gush of cold water splashing against me. Raine squeals, and her hand leaves mine.

I wipe the water from my face, and Zane is laughing so hard he's gripping his stomach. Annabelle holds a large water balloon in her hands, and I attempt to snatch it from her, but she's quick and takes off running. I face Zane, my nostrils flaring in frustration, and he holds up his hands in surrender.

"I'm just trying to win Annabelle over."

Thankfully, I took most of the blow, only a few drops of water having found Raine's dress and hair. I, however, am soaking wet. I look Raine over one more time and say, "I'll get you a paper towel."

I walk over towards the tote Mom brought out that holds some extra supplies like plates and utensils. Thankfully, there's also paper towels. I grab a roll as Luke walks towards me, pointing in the direction of where Zane and Annabelle took off.

"Some people never grow up." He shakes his head, a playful smile spreading across his face.

"You're one to talk." Olivia shouts from our left and before we can react, she throws a large water balloon at us. Her laughter echoes along with the people around us. Luke races after her, catching up to her quickly. He picks her up, runs towards the dock, and tosses her into the Lake like he used to do when we were teens.

I do my best to dry my shirt and head back to the smoker but don't find Raine where I had left her. My eyes search through the sea of people until they land on her, helping Edna, Olivia's elderly neighbor. My heart softens at the sight and recognition that Raine still has a serving heart.

After I check on the brisket, which just needs a few more minutes, my eyes follow Raine closely as she moves through the crowd, talking with several townspeople. I feel like a stalker, so I turn my attention to the lake, at the rolling hills and faded mountains in the background, vibrant green and drenched in the bright-yellow sunshine of the early afternoon. The blinding light that's shimmering off the lake catches my attention. I look toward the dock and am reminded of the first time Raine and I kissed.

"Is that brisket done yet?" I hear Luke's gruff voice ask from behind me.

I lift up on the lid's handle, revealing that the brisket is finished. Its sizzling sound brings me back to reality, and I start preparing everything. Luke wraps his arm around his girlfriend, Beckah, before making the announcement that the food is ready, and a line forms around the tables.

After I reach over and wrap Annabelle into my arms, I try to catch a glimpse of Raine but am cut short by August and her husband making small talk with me as we wait in line. I try to stay engaged in the conversation as I make a plate for Annabelle, but my mind is still trapped in the past, on the dock that sits a few feet away. My hands tingle with the memory of Raine's skin, itching to feel her once again.

"I see that our basket idea was a success," August leans in and says softly beside me before nudging me with her elbow. "I'm glad Raine was able to make it."

"Yeah, me too," I reply.

"You, sir, worked hard on this meal and should be the first one to eat," she adds.

"We both know this little princess gets to eat first." I bend down and press my lips to her ear. "Even though you haven't been listening very well today. I'd like you to eat every bite of the food I give you, okay?"

"Yes, Daddy." She bats her eyelashes and gives me her most innocent smile.

However, August and I share a look that says, *We know she won't.*

I place Annabelle down, her small hand in mine, and she follows closely behind me. After I make Annabelle's plate, I find her a seat near my mother before returning and making my own. It takes about fifteen minutes before everyone is through the line and stuffing their faces. Raine is sitting a few tables away, and my eyes keep drifting to her. I really need to get a grip on myself. But who can blame me? I've spent the last decade wishing I could see her again, and now here she is, only a few feet from me, and every cell in my body is completely drawn to her.

To my surprise, Annabelle finishes her plate. I guess her uncles did a good job of helping her work up an appetite. "Can we go say hi to Raine?" She doesn't have to ask me twice.

"Yeah, sure," I reply.

We walk over to where Raine is dumping her empty plate, and her eyes look over my shirt that is still wet, which I notice is revealing the curves of my pecs. Before I can say something to her, Annabelle jumps up and gives her a hug.

"Hey, Raine! Come jump with me," she insists, tugging Raine toward the trampoline. Raine's eyes find mine, seeking permission.

"Have fun, ladies." I wave at them and take a seat in a nearby camping chair.

Raine climbs onto the trampoline and takes Annabelle's hands into her own before they begin jumping together. Annabelle squeals with glee, and I enjoy watching them play together. It's the first time I catch myself wondering what it would be like to have a motherly figure in Annabelle's life and if it could be Raine. The thought feels dangerous for my heart and I remind myself that she's only visiting Covewood. Her time is limited here.

I try to distract myself by looking around the crowd of mingling people. It's the kind of day that leaves you feeling nostalgic, like I'll miss the memory even though it's still happening.

A few minutes pass, and the sound of a nearby argument catches my attention. I turn my head to the right and see Luke shoving his hands into his pockets, his head hung down, and Beckah shouting angrily at him.

Luke isn't much for drama or confrontation in his personal life, so he stands still, allowing her to say what she needs to say to him before she stomps away toward the rows of vehicles. Luke stands still for a moment and then seems to sense me watching him. His eyes find mine, and he begins walking my way. I grab a chair that's near me and tug it closer, motioning for him to take a seat.

"What was that about?" I ask and clamp my hand down onto his shoulder. "You okay?"

"Yeah, I'll be fine," he replies flatly and runs a hand through his messy dark waves. "She felt left out today. Said Olivia always demands my attention whenever she's around."

"Ah, so she got jealous." I put it together and release my hand.

"Yeah," he agrees, exhaling deeply. His shoulders slump as he leans forward onto his elbows, his eyes scanning the crowd around us until they land on Olivia. "If she can't handle that Olivia is my best friend, then I don't think I can date her."

"Isn't that the same issue your last two girlfriends had too?" I proclaim, raising my eyebrows in questioning.

He swings his head to face me before leaning back in his chair. "Yeah."

"Why do you think it's a recurring issue?"

"People don't understand Olivia's and my friendship, is all." His knee starts bouncing up and down, and I can tell this is really bothering him. And I know the truth behind it all.

"Why don't you just tell her how you feel?" I state, and his eyes shoot daggers my way as I declare the truth out in the open.

"We're just friends," he says through his teeth, growing frustrated with me. Luke and I are close. Close enough that I'm not scared to tell him the truth or push his buttons.

"Yeah, and that's because you're too chicken to tell her the truth."

Luke pushes himself from his chair and flexes his fist. "I'm done with this conversation," he growls and stomps his way toward the lake. At the same moment, I see Raine walking toward me, and from her expression, I know she witnessed Luke's temper tantrum.

"Is he okay?" she asks, her eyes following Luke. I push myself up from my seat to stand next to her.

"Yeah, he'll be fine," I assure her and search the area for Annabelle. "Where did my daughter run off to?"

"She saw your mom walk by with a plate of apple pie and took off after her." She grins and points to the two of them shoveling bites into their mouths.

"She's got such a sweet tooth." I shake my head and return my attention to Raine.

"I remember her dad having one too," she tosses at me, causing my lips to tip up in a small smile.

"Yeah, she definitely gets that from me. I became sort of a health nut after she made me a dad, though. I try my best to limit processed junk when I can."

She smiles knowingly. "Olivia was telling me about that. She said you inspired her to use organic ingredients with her business."

"Huh, she didn't tell me that. Everyone thinks I'm a little excessive because of it, but I'm in charge of taking care of and raising this tiny human on my own. I want to do the best that I can, you know?"

"I don't think you're being excessive. You're doing a wonderful job. You're an amazing father, Ry."

Hearing her say that does something to my heart. When Raine smiles, it's bracketed by the faintest of dimples, little indentations that you can feel better than you can see. "Thanks for saying that."

A few moments of silence go between us before she starts another conversation, her eyes studying the lake.

"The dock looks the same."

"Yeah, it holds a lot of good memories too," I say, my eyes returning to hers. "I was thinking about one earlier."

"Oh yeah? Which one?"

"The day we first kissed," I deadpan, and her smile falls.

"That's a nice memory," she finally adds, her eyes flowing back toward the dock.

"I remember it being more than nice."

She takes in a deep breath of air and pinches her brows together as if swallowed by a deep thought. She still picks at the skin around her thumb when she's nervous, I notice. I reach over and take her hand into my own, giving in to temptation more and more when she's around.

"Can we talk about it?"

Her head swings to face me, her eyes wide in panic, and when she opens her mouth to say something, Olivia rushes by and asks, "Have you seen Luke?"

"Last I saw him, he walked off that way." I point toward where I saw Luke, hoping Olivia will walk off so Raine can say what she was about to tell me.

Olivia's gaze follows where I'm pointing, and her frown deepens when we don't see him anywhere. "Will you let him know to call me later? I have to head out." She motions for Raine to follow her since they arrived together.

Raine raises her brows, and Olivia gives her a look that says, *I'll explain later.*

I run a hand across the roughness on my jaw and say, "Some other time, then."

Raine nods and waves goodbye. "I'll see you Tuesday?"

I give her a wave and watch as she leaves. Just before they

reach Olivia's vehicle, Raine turns back and smiles at me. I feel my heart swell with hope.

Chapter Twenty-One

Twelve Years Before

Raine

The lake is like a mirror during the night. I can see reflections of the bright light from the moon, the twinkling stars, as well as Ryland's form as he sits at the edge of the dock. Kentucky's weather is always strange. It's in between the spring and summer season where some days are comfortable and warm, while other days there's a promise of cooling rain. Thankfully, today we were blessed with some warmth.

I walk across the dock, the wood creaking with each step. Looking down at my reflection I watch as it sways with the water. My skirt flows in the slight breeze, and the bright-pink color of my hair stands out on top of the dark water. I smooth down my skirt before taking a seat next to my boyfriend.

My boyfriend. It never gets old saying that.

I sigh and slip off my sandals, sinking my feet into the lake. I hiss, feeling how cold the water is but keep them in anyway. I need something to focus on besides the fact that there is nothing I can do to help take Ryland's pain away.

It's been a few weeks since his Nan passed away. What we thought was a simple cold ended up getting much worse. He told me on the phone this morning that he's still having a hard time processing the loss. For him, it feels like she's still everywhere—everywhere but here with us, and the realization hurts. Ryland's family has quickly become like my own, and losing Nan is the first time I've experienced a loss.

It feels extra heavy knowing that Ryland is feeling even more pain than I am. What can I even do to help him? He leans over and places his head onto my shoulder. I do the same, leaning my head onto his, and slide my hand underneath his.

"It's nice that you have your own car now and can drive over here," he says softly, giving my hand a squeeze.

"Yeah, at least on the weekends."

Over the winter, on the days that we're nice, Papaw let me drive down the back roads in his truck. I also got a job during the week, working at MJ's Diner downtown. The owner is good friends with my grandparents and agreed to let me have off on the weekends. It's been a nice change.

The job gives me something to do during the weekdays after school. Mom and Davis don't question my job's schedule. For him, the more I work, the more money I can give him since he demands half of my paycheck for what he calls 'a lesson in responsibility'. It's a price I'm willing to pay for the little taste of freedom it brings me. I only go home to shower and sleep during the week.

A few days after Nan's passing, Pops showed up to the farm and handed the keys to her Honda Accord to Papaw. He said that Nan wanted me to have it. It was on her list of demands that she made during her last days with us. It felt strange accepting the vehicle, but I know it was her way of taking care of me.

There's no way that I could afford a car on my own with the dent in my income that Davis has caused. With the car being gifted to me and my grandparents insisting they put it on their insurance policy, I only have to worry about gas and food.

Everything else I have saved and kept safely in my room at my grandparents' house.

"Yeah, Nan wanted to make sure I could be here for you more," I reply.

"Yeah," he says with an exhale.

We sit for a few moments of silence, wrapping our arms around each other, and I say, "I hate that I can't take the pain away."

"I wish the same for Pops. I hate seeing him like this. He said this morning that it feels like an amputation."

"I say it does."

I can only imagine the loss Pops must be feeling right now. I can't fathom the thought of losing one of my grandparents and having to watch them grieve in the same way. If I've learned anything about grief these past few weeks, it's that it creates an unbearable pain that will never fade away. It's something we have to learn to carry with us, until we return to heaven and can be reunited with our loved ones.

"I hate this so much. I feel so angry with God," Ryland admits.

"You shouldn't be mad at God for this. I know your Nan wasn't."

He removes his arms from around me and twists until he can see me. "How do you know?" He raises his brows.

"Because she told me," I proclaim and give him a small smile. "The last time I came to visit, we were watching *The Golden Girls,* and you got up to help your mom with something. Nan turned to me and told me she was thankful that the doctors gave her a heads up about her possibly leaving us. It gave her a chance to say goodbye and help prepare everyone. She seemed at peace with it all."

I remember how weak she looked during that last visit. She mainly slept the last days away, but she was having an unusually good day during my last moments with her. I'm forever thankful for it and for her sharing that with me.

We swish our feet through the water below us, the temperature not feeling as cold anymore. “I had a dream about her last night,” he says, bumping his foot into mine.

“What about?”

He exhales, turning to face the water, his mind in another place. “I was sitting right here, on the dock, and she took a seat next to me and told me everything was going to be okay. I somehow knew it was a dream, but it felt so real, especially when she reached over and gave me a hug. I could even smell her perfume. It was surreal.”

When his eyes find mine, he studies me closely before adding, “Want to decipher that one?”

I stay quiet for a moment and ponder on his question. “I know you miss her. It could be why you dreamt that. But maybe she was also visiting you in a way. She wants you to be okay.”

“It’s not easy.” he admits, his eyes dancing with my own.

A light breeze is blowing, cooling the warmth in the air and bringing a scent of the water and fresh grass with it. After a few moments of silence, I add, “I don’t think losing someone is supposed to be easy. Remember what they said at her funeral? That even Jesus wept with those who were mourning.” I reach a hand out and move his hair away from his forehead. “But do you know why he was mourning? It wasn’t because someone died.”

I let my fingers travel down his cheek, tracing the edge of his jawline before landing on his shoulder. He watches me closely, waiting for me to continue.

“He wept because he had to bring someone back to Earth. They were in heaven, walking the streets of gold where there’s no such thing as pain or grief. And Jesus took them away from heaven and brought them back *here*. If we could see what heaven is like, I don’t think anyone would want to come back to Earth. And when you think of it that way, it helps put things into perspective.”

My Mamaw shared that with me on our way home from Nan's funeral. It has stuck with me ever since, and in a way, it helps me with my own grief. I pray now that it can bring a sense of comfort to Ryland like it has to me.

The moonlight casts shadows onto Ryland's face but helps highlight just how breathtaking he is. His mouth opens slightly, his dark brows raising up his forehead, and his eyes widen as my words sink into his heart. His lips touch, tilting upward into a grin, before he shifts and lays back against the dock.

I mimic him and lie down too, making sure my hand is intertwined with his. We stare up at the stars, watching them twinkle, a huge galaxy full of questions staring down at us. We're just two teenagers trying to learn how to navigate this thing called life. And I'm thankful we're able to do it together.

"I think that's what she was trying to tell me in my dream," he finally says, breaking the silence.

"I think so too," I agree. "We have limited time here. She has forever. To her, it must feel like a quick and simple blink before it's our time to join her in heaven. She won't have any time to miss us."

Ryland moves until he's hovering over me. He keeps his body sitting on the dock, but his arms are on either side of my head. "Thank you. You always know what to say to make me feel better." He lowers himself down until his nose brushes mine and all thoughts vanish and are replaced with the thumping of my heart. His eyes travel over my face before they land on my lips.

"Since we have limited time on Earth, I refuse to waste another second not kissing you."

He moves his lips closer, barely touching the sensitive skin, while his eyes lock onto mine with a silent question. I nod, letting him know it's okay, before his lips touch my own. My eyes flutter shut as I rake my fingers through his thick strands and pull him closer to me. It's a sweet kiss. One that says so many things.

Ryland moves back just a touch, keeping his nose a few centimeters from my face. He runs his hand through my hair, cupping my jaw, and smiling down at me. "I love you."

His voice is strained, and I wonder how often it's been like that in the past, how many times I didn't notice. Now that I know he loves me, I can see the evidence in everything he does. I'm not sure how I missed it for so long.

His confession makes warmth spread throughout my stomach. I smile as his words sink deeply into my heart. I want to carry them with me always and remind myself of the truth in them.

"I love you too."

"I promise you that I'll do everything in my power to give you the life that you deserve."

As if my chest couldn't swell any more, it proves me wrong with the growing tightness. My smile, however, falters with his sweet confession. It's such a huge thing to say, coming from a seventeen-year-old, but I know he means it.

"And I'll do the same for you."

He smiles, bending down to place soft kisses all over my face and neck. I giggle, pushing his chest until he hovers over me again. "Then we have an agreement. We'll make the most of our limited time here. And we'll do it together."

"Together," I agree, the words leaving my lips, a promise I intend to keep.

Chapter Twenty-Two

Now

Raine

Getting up each morning and accomplishing the farm chores is like riding a bike for me. The memories from my childhood are still fresh of what all I need to do. However, today has been a different story.

I'm covered in chicken poop. I have dirt all over my dress. A fresh bump is throbbing on my forehead, and mud is caked on my knees from where I tripped over Buck, the goat, who yet again escaped the fence.

I also smell, thanks to Buck peeing on my boots when I wasn't looking. When I did notice, he spat at me and lifted his upper lip, clearly happy with himself. I'm very close to turning him into dinner.

I'm kidding of course...*kind of.*

I shoo Buck away, shaking my head as he spits and kicks his legs as he runs off. I wipe the sweat from my brows before bending over to pick up a bag of chicken feed. I heave it over my shoulder, and as I take a step backward, my leg hits something furry, causing me to lose my grip on the bag and sending my body plummeting toward the ground.

The chicken feed rains down all around me as I try to regain my focus. Before I have a moment to scold Daisy for knocking me over, the sound of scattering feet fills the air. I turn and see the chickens running at me with their wings flapping and beaks ready to peck their breakfast.

"Ah! No! Shoo!" I swat away the tiny dinosaurs and wince at the throbbing ache in my backside. I thrust myself up from the hard ground and rub against the bruise I know is already forming. How did my grandparents do this every day?

And without complaining?

I hear a husky laugh and see Ryland walking through the gate with the biggest smirk across his face. I feel heat rise up my neck and settle into my cheeks. I exhale loudly, annoyed that he caught my morning of epic failure.

"You're here early," I state and bend over to try to save the rest of the feed.

"Yeah. I decided I'd like a head start on that master bedroom today. Totally glad I did." His smirk deepens as he makes his way over to me. "Are you alright?"

He wipes away the dirt and feed dust from me, his thumb doing a circle around the bump on my forehead, making me hiss in pain. "Those chickens really came at you," he says, fighting against a grin.

"Yeah, like the raptors in *Jurassic Park*. I won't be able to watch the movie without traumatic flashbacks now."

He chuckles and I shove against his shoulder, fighting against a grin myself.

"Do you remember the first time we met?" he says, dusting my shoulders. As soon as the chickens hear the sound of the seeds hitting the ground, they're quick to peck around our feet.

"Nope. I have completely blocked that embarrassing moment from my memories," I lie and shoo the chickens away.

"You were terrified of that tiny rooster."

Ryland doubles over, laughing at the memory. His laughter is contagious, and I can't help but join in. I remember that day very clearly—the look on Ryland's face when I slammed into him, what he was wearing, the way his eyes did something to me that I had never felt before. How do they still have that effect on me fourteen years later?

I busy myself to avoid looking at him. I bend down, removing one of the hens who managed to get herself inside of the feed bag and I roll the top down so it doesn't happen again. "I remember that you, too, were scared of Lucy."

"And I owe so much to that tiny rooster. I had never been so happy to be covered in eggs," he adds. I can hear the sound of his hands running through his beard. "Would you like some help?"

Before I can argue, he takes the bag from my hands and carries it over to the feeder. I dare a look at him, trying *not* to notice the shape of his biceps or how they grow as he pours the chicken feed into each feeder. I stand and watch as he rubs his hands against his pants and removes his hat to wipe his arm across his forehead.

I catch the gleam of light that reflects off his sweat-damp hair, sticking up every which way. He places his hat back on *backward*, a faded-black snapback, and I watch as it slides into place over the red mark it left behind across his forehead. I stare at it as he looks at me with lowered lashes, a sheepish look taking over his face.

"I can see that your chore skills are the same," he points out, the barest hint of a smirk curling at the corner of his mouth. I swallow hard, a lick of heat dripping down my spine.

"I'm just a little rusty this morning," I proclaim before walking into the coop, mainly to get away from his stare but also to grab my empty baskets. I can't ignore what his stare does to my insides. I really like the way Ryland looks at me, especially when he thinks I'm not paying attention. There's a softness he tries to hide. A special look that I've realized is only for me.

As I walk out of the coop with a basket of eggs, I almost run into him. *Again.* Just like the first day we met. It's like a weird sense of nostalgia. Ryland reaches up and steadies me with his hand on my upper arm, keeping me from hitting him. A knowing look washes over his face.

It's short-lived once we stand there for a moment, our eyes searching each other for the truths we're too scared to reveal out loud—or even to ourselves. He clears his throat, taking a step away from me, before adding, "You have chicken poop in your hair."

Way to ruin the moment, Ryland.

I reach up and touch my hair, gasping as I feel the stickiness. I blow out a frustrated breath, ready to give up for the day. The farm is out to get me. And so is my heart.

"I better get cleaned up," I say and limp my way over to the barn and open the door for the sheep to come out and graze the field for their breakfast. Daisy takes off, switching from pup to working dog in an instant. I should have done that first this morning so Daisy would have been out of my way. "Buck escaped the fence again."

"That goat lives to torment," Ryland says from behind me.

"No *kidding*," I say and peek over my shoulder to see if he got my cringy goat pun.

"Zane has rubbed off on you." He chuckles.

I make my way back to the coop and return all the baskets to their normal spots before I head back to the farmhouse with Ryland by my side. "I desperately need a shower," I say, more to myself.

Ryland's nose scrunches as he nods in agreement. I swat at him playfully, and he makes sure to bump his shoulder into mine. I've missed this. Our playful banter while working on the farm together. Being back here with him, it feels almost like I left all the best parts of myself with Ryland. I didn't realize how much of myself I left behind when I moved away. Or how much would be left with him.

He didn't give you much of a choice back then, my subconscious reminds me.

Since being back in Covewood, I've realized I would have been better off moving forward with my life. Rather than staring at my old wounds, doing nothing to help them heal. However, it was easier to ignore the wounds and keep my distance.

Mamaw is probably in heaven right now, watching everything unfold, standing next to Ryland's grandparents, everyone rubbing their hands together with glee. The image makes me smile.

We make our way up the porch steps, and I stop dead in my tracks as I notice a blue hummingbird feeder hanging from the porch post closest to the table. My mouth drops slightly, and I walk toward it just as a hummingbird lands for a drink. I watch the small, majestic bird fly toward us and swarm around our heads for a second before it's gone again.

"You put this here?" I ask, pointing to the feeder and looking at Ryland.

He smiles shyly. "I remembered hummingbirds were Johanna's favorite, and I thought you might like to see them while you're out here working."

It's the little things that tug my heartstrings. Gestures or words that are so simple. A hug right when you need it, picking a bouquet of wildflowers, hanging a hummingbird feeder.

Witnessing the man that Ryland has become these past few weeks...the way he cares for the people around him, the father he has grown into, the fact that even though we broke each other's hearts he's still here for me...it has reawakened my heart for him.

I've been trying to ignore it ever since I ran into him at the hospital, but as each day goes by, I'm falling back into my old feelings for him. Maybe they never left to begin with.

"Ry, thank you," I whisper, unsure of where to begin with how much his gesture means to me. My eyes travel back to the feeder and then to the vase of freshly picked wildflowers that's sitting on the table next to my laptop, until they find their way back to Ryland's golden irises.

"I don't think I told you this, but when I was eleven, Mamaw was diagnosed with breast cancer. I remember her sitting out here on the swing and watching the hummingbirds that would come visit her feeders. I asked her that day if she was scared, and she had this radiant smile on her face. She told me that she was at first, but then God sent her a sign of peace, and she knew He was going to take care of her."

"What was the sign of peace?" he asked.

"A hummingbird had flown and stopped right in front of her face, and it looked into her eyes for a few seconds before flying off. She said, at that moment, she just knew she was going to be okay and that she would be healed. And a few days later, she found out that she was cancer free. The doctors were amazed and had no explanation for how it could have just vanished. She had no doubt that Jesus touched her and took away the cancer."

I exhale as a flood of emotions washes over me all at once. In typical Ryland fashion, he senses my heartache and takes a step toward me and laces his callused fingers with my own.

"I felt that peace too," I add, the slightest quiver moving my lips. "The day before she had the heart attack, I was sitting at the beach, and I prayed over her. Right when I was done praying, I saw a dolphin in the ocean. In that moment, I just knew she was going to be okay."

Ryland wipes away a tear with the pad of his thumb.

"I felt peace again when you prayed in the hospital chapel. But—" My words lodge in my throat. Ryland's hand trails down my neck, squeezes against my shoulder, and pulls me in for a hug.

"I don't understand. Why would God give me peace only to take her away?" I cry, releasing the words I've been hanging on to for weeks, and bury my face into his chest.

He runs his fingers through my hair, and they get tangled in the mess. I remember how disgusting I am and push myself away softly and wipe away the wetness on my cheeks. "I'm sorry. I'm a mess all the way around today."

"Your messes never bother me, Rainbow," He says, the nickname squeezing against my heart in the same way his fingers squeeze against my own. "Maybe God gave you peace because she was okay. That she was already with him and she was safe, no longer in any pain. She returned home but not in the way we were asking for."

I nod in reply. If I try to speak, I'm scared my words will tumble out and not make any sense. Words that have been locked behind a cracking dam for too long.

He continues, "A wise teenager once told me"—he smirks, lifting the heaviness just a little bit—"that our time on Earth is limited. Your Mamaw won the lottery, and we should celebrate, not be sad. That same lottery is promised to us, and because of that, we'll see them again. Carry that truth with you, and I promise you, you'll get through this."

I tug him closer and wrap my arms around him. As I bury my face in his shoulder, all I can think about is how much I need him. I need his arms around me, need him to hold me and whisper that it'll be okay.

I pull back to look up at his handsome face. I can feel the tension build between us. Our bodies are pressed together so that I can feel our heart beats pumping quickly, signaling a growing need for each other. Ryland's eyes bounce between my own before they land on my mouth, and my mind begins to scream at me to lean toward him.

And oh, do I want to feel the softness of his lips on mine and feel the warmth of his skin against my own. Our souls seem to create a force of gravity when they're close, clinging to one another without any effort. How has it always felt like this?

How did Ryland let this go? And more importantly, how did *I* run and leave this behind?

I can feel the broken pieces of us laying on the ground, shatters of what we used to have together. I can't force myself to forget what it feels like when sweet, tender love turns rancid. However, I know in order to put the pieces back together, I have to face my demons. I don't think I'll ever be able to move on without confronting Ryland.

My hands trail up Ryland's spine, a strong column bound with lean muscle. His body is conditioned by work, hardened and cut by days spent under the sun and lifting heavy equipment. I pull him closer, not caring that I might stink and am covered in filth.

There is something about being held by the right person that is enough to cure anything. However, before I can give in to my temptations, there is something that Ryland and I need to discuss. His expression softens, as if he can read my thoughts, and he steps back, giving us both some space.

"I, uh...should get to that shower," I say, an uneasy feeling splashing around inside my stomach.

"Alright," he replies, taking another step back and slipping his hands into the front of his jeans. "I'll get to work on the fence before starting on the bedroom."

I give him a small smile before making my way inside and taking a long shower.

The sun is starting to set later in the day as we reach mid-spring and I'm grateful for it. Ryland, however, takes it as an opportunity to *work* longer hours. The fence is fixed, trapping an angry goat behind it who has been looking at me like he's plotting his revenge. Ryland also knocked out the wall to a small utility closet in the hallway in order to expand the master bedroom closet, making it into a walk-in—something my

Mamaw requested that is now another reminder that she isn't here to enjoy the improvements on the old home.

Today, he has the closet formed with new drywall. I enter the room with a fresh glass of fruit-infused water and I stop in my tracks as I peek around the corner and witness Ryland's bare back. He still has his hat on backward, and I selfishly enjoy the view.

Sensing me, he turns around, and his lips tip up in a smirk that says *I caught you gawking*. And then he does something that practically makes my knees weaken...*he winks.*

Ryland steps over his tools and makes his way to me. He slides his hand over the glass that I'm holding, his fingers lingering for a moment, before he pulls the glass to his lips. I stare at his throat, watching his Adam's apple bob as he swallows, and then he grimaces.

"What's this?"

"Strawberry-and-lemon-infused water." I shrug, looking anywhere *but* at his shirtless torso.

"Fruit doesn't belong in water," he says and pulls the glass back to his mouth and guzzles the rest. He wipes his lips, my eyes following the movement, before he adds, "But thanks."

It just became ten degrees hotter in this room. What's the matter with me? Olivia must be rubbing off on me because the song "*Hot in Herre*" by Nelly pops into my mind, which only intensifies this moment.

"You got a lot done today," I say, making sure I keep my eyes on the space and not on Ryland.

"Yeah, it wasn't hard to do. I need you to pick out some shades of paint for the bedroom, the master bathroom, and also the living room and kitchen. Maybe Thursday morning, we can go to Lowes and get them together?"

"Yeah, okay," I say and toss a thumb over my shoulder. "I'm going back to work on the porch. I'll let you finish up here."

Before he can reply, I'm out the door and practically taking two stairs at a time to put some space between us. My hormones have taken on a mind of their own, and being around Ryland shirtless is not helping. *He's not mine to ogle*, I have to remind myself.

But he could be, my subconscious tosses back at me.

It's as if my heart and brain are at war with one another. One wants me to admit that I still have feelings for Ryland and that we could have it all, while the other keeps me aware that we have issues to discuss and the fact that I have a whole other life we haven't mentioned in weeks.

I reach the porch, drinking a sip of my water to help cool me off, and almost spit it out as I see my mother making her way up the stairs to the porch. She clutches the railing and sucks in a sharp breath of air, as if I caught her off guard. She sure did me.

"Mom," I state, the name feeling stale in my mouth.

I've done a great job at avoiding her for the last few weeks, not to mention the years I've lived in Rockdale. Somewhere in the back of my mind, I knew that my time to confront her was coming. Even so, I don't feel ready to face her. I may never be. Because no matter how much time has passed, the pain still throbs inside my chest as a constant reminder of her neglect.

Whoever first said that time heals all wounds was full of crap. My wounds are still very much a part of me. I've come to realize that all I did was cover the trauma with scar tissue to help lessen the pain, but it was never gone.

Knowing that Ryland is upstairs brings me a little sense of comfort.

"I'm sorry to just show up here without an invite. I, uh... I don't have your number to call, and I—" She takes a shaky breath, and as much as I don't want to do this, my heart is overwhelmed with compassion.

She studies me before she continues. Her once dark and lifeless eyes now appear lighter and vivacious. They take me in from my head to my toes, and the expression softens on her face. She takes the last few steps until she's facing me. I notice her hand twitching, as if wanting to reach out to me, but I flinch involuntarily, and her smile falters a bit.

"I know I'm probably the last person you want to see," she admits, looking down at her feet, and I want to tell her that she's wrong. She's second to last. Davis is the last person I would want to see, but thankfully he's not an issue since he no longer lives in Covewood or is welcomed here.

"Want to have a seat?" I ask, my voice sounding unfamiliar, and I point toward the table.

She nods, her eyes lifting to mine for just a second before returning to the ground. She takes a seat, and I follow her, sitting down across from her. I move my laptop and items for work to the side, trying to keep my hands busy, and my eyes focus on something other than her.

Bile is rising into the back of my throat, and panic is itching its way up my spine. I smooth my skirt over my lap and place my hands under my legs to keep them from shaking. My leg starts to bounce uncontrollably, and I remove my hands from under my legs and begin picking at the skin on my thumb.

Calm down, Raine.

I say a silent prayer for strength to get through this.

"I won't stay long. I know you're busy," she tells me, and I bravely look at her.

She's wearing a flowy pink shirt with a white cardigan over her shoulders and arms. She has on a pair of white jeans and black flats. Her light-blonde hair hangs down, touching her shoulders, smoothed down by heat. Around her neck is a pearl necklace that she's twisting around with her fingers—a nervous tic, I assume.

I take a deep breath, attempting to calm the raging storm inside of me, and as I release the air, a hummingbird begins to swarm above us. It hovers over the feeder for a moment before buzzing in a circle and stopping beside us. It lasts for maybe a second, but it feels like time slows down.

I feel it right then, a sensation of warmth washing over me

from my head and landing into my toes. The pressure in my lungs releases, and I suck in a full breath of air. My leg stops bouncing, and I steady my hands as the feeling of calm travels through every nerve in my body.

It's *peace,* just like my Mamaw experienced, and I know in my heart that it's a sign from her. Her way of communicating from heaven that she wants my mother and me to mend our relationship. That I need to forgive her in order to let go. Not just for me, but for my mother as well.

The hummingbird flies away. My attention returns to Mom, who is watching me with tears in her eyes. She brings a shaky hand to her mouth before wiping away the wetness on her cheeks. She points to where the hummingbird was and opens her mouth to speak, but she takes a second to regain herself.

"She told you the story?" I give her a small smile, tears blurring my vision.

She nods her head before wiping her face again. "Yeah, a few months before she passed, actually. We've been working on repairing our relationship. Raine, I don't even know where to start with how sorry I am for everything."

There they are. Words that I desperately need to hear. It's like rubbing an ointment over an open wound. It's not healed yet, but it helps with the healing process. There's still a part of me that wants to be angry with her. A little voice that whispers that she doesn't deserve my forgiveness. But I ignore those negative thoughts because I know they're from the enemy.

"I have no excuse for my choices in the past. That version of me feels like a complete stranger. Finding God completely changes you into someone new." She shrugs her shoulders, rubbing her hands together. It brings me a sense of comfort knowing she has found a relationship with God.

She continues, "But even though I've asked him for forgiveness, it has been hard to forgive myself, especially since I haven't been brave enough to confront you. I want so badly for us to have a relationship—one that I should've given you when you were growing up. I can't change the past, but oh, if I could... The things I would wipe clean and do over. But it's out of my control, and I have to learn to walk with this guilt for the rest of my life."

I never sat down and tried to understand her side of the situation or took the time to learn the reasons why she chose alcohol over most things in her life, including me. I hang on to this truth as I let her continue, hoping that it calms my heart for what lies ahead for us and our relationship.

In order to move forward, we have to talk. I have to face my fears, push past my insecurities and discomforts, and try my best to look past the pain. With both my mother and with Ryland.

I place my hand onto the wooden table, and I silently pray. I pray for strength, I pray for guidance, and I pray for God to mend the brokenness between us. Because I know I can't heal on my own, but I can with His help.

"I just...there's a lot to discuss, and we don't have to get into it today, especially since I kind of barged in on you. I can see you have work to do." She waves a hand toward my laptop. "I did want to ask if you would like to come over for dinner this weekend? I'd love to have the chance to explain some things and answer any questions you may have. I don't want to avoid you any longer. I've let my shame and guilt stand in the way of trying to connect with my one and only daughter. I know your Mamaw and your father would want me to try."

Her voice quivers, revealing the emotion she's trying to keep at bay, and I move my hand to hers, and as soon as our skin touches, sympathy fills my heart. "I'd like that. Very much," I admit, more to myself than to her.

She flips her hand over so she can squeeze mine. Relief washes over her face as she looks at our joined hands and releases a shaky breath. It's a good feeling, knowing that she cares enough to try to fix our relationship. It's all I've ever wanted.

A cough breaks into the silence, pulling our attention

toward the doorway. Ryland stands completely still, mid-stride, eyes wide as he looks between my mother and me. Thankfully he has his shirt back on. His lips part as his eyes pierce into mine, a question reflecting within their hazel color.

"Ryland. It's good to see you," Mom says, releasing her hold on me and giving him a slight wave. "I better be off."

She gathers herself and stands. Ryland and I don't move a muscle. She nods, her head bouncing between the two of us, before she nods a second time and walks to the stairs.

I blink away the haze before standing up. "Wait," I shout and rush to her. She turns, eyes large with surprise, and stops on the bottom step. "Let me put my number into your phone."

She smiles and pulls her phone from her pocket and hands it to me. I type my number into her contacts before giving it back to her. Her smile widens, and I see the twitch of her arm, as if she wants to reach out and give me a hug, but she pulls back. I'm relieved, not yet ready for that step, but I'm willing to work on getting there.

Ryland and I stand on the porch while my mother gets into her vehicle and leaves. It's not until the dust from the driveway begins to settle that I finally turn and look at him. He raises a brow, shock still written on his handsome face.

"What just happened?" he asks.

"She apologized and asked if I wanted to come to dinner this weekend to talk things over."

His body remains tense, eyes glued to the driveway, his jaw twitching in discomfort. I tug at his hand and bring his attention back to me. When he looks down and studies me for a moment, his body relaxes.

"Are you okay with doing that?"

I nod, smirking as he deepens his frown. "Yeah. I think I should work on things while I'm here."

"Yeah?" He weaves his fingers around my own, tugging me an inch closer to him.

"Yeah. But can we wait on our talk, though?" One issue is

enough for the day. I'm already feeling drained and ready to take a nap. Sometimes you need to rest in order to help the healing process. Plus, I'm not ready to pop this comfort bubble Ryland and I seem to be in. Not yet anyway.

"Yeah, okay. Whenever you're ready."

Chapter Twenty-Three

Eleven Years Before

Raine

MJ's Diner is *the* popular hangout spot in Covewood, Kentucky. It sits on the very edge of downtown, across from the building where the farmer's market is held during the spring season until the end of fall. The diner was opened in the late fifties by the Loveitt family.

The fact that the original owner named the diner after his wife gives the place a romantic feel. That and their last name literally has the word *love* in it. It's a no brainer.

It's decorated in warm colors that create a cozy atmosphere, and the walls are covered with photographs of the original owners and their family over the years. Each day, I see couple after couple snuggling close in the booths, sneaking kisses when they think no one is looking, sharing food, and causing my coworker, Stefanie, to gag.

"I don't know why I choose to work here and torture myself," she snarls from behind the register, straightening the bills in the drawer, and rolls her baby blues.

"Because you're part of the Loveitt family, so naturally it's tradition that you work here."

Stefanie Loveitt is a few years older than me and went through a bad breakup a few months ago. The idea of being in love is repulsive to her. So anytime Ryland enters the diner to visit me, I tell him to keep the affection to a minimum—only when she's around, of course. Every night when I end my shift, Ryland and I have been sneaking an hour or two together before I have to go back home.

I stretch the truth, you could say, and tell Mom and Davis that I'm working longer shifts. Davis hovers over everything that I do, making sure Ryland and I don't get to see each other throughout the week. What they don't know won't hurt them. Ryland and I spend our evenings hanging out at the diner, walking the streets of downtown, catching a movie at the theater across the street, or we sit in the car and talk.

"Quit being such a Debbie Downer, Stef. You know working with me is the highlight of your day." I bump my hip into hers.

"That and the tips. I can't complain about the tips."

"Agreed." I've been saving every tip that I can since Davis knows nothing about them.

As she continues organizing the cash register, I scan the diner to make sure everyone looks accounted for. That's when I notice an extra person sitting in my section. Panic squeezes my throat as soon as I recognize who it is. Matt, one of Davis' gophers, is watching me with his dark eyes, his lips turning into an evil smirk as soon as he notices me looking his way.

I turn and rush into the kitchen, allowing the swinging door to hit my backside and push me forward a few steps. Carl, the cook, looks over at me and raises his bushy eyebrows.

"Everything okay?"

"Uh...yeah. I just—" *Just what, Raine*? No need to panic here. Matt lives in Covewood, and there aren't many restaurant options to choose from. He's probably just here to eat. Not to spy on you. Surely Davis wouldn't send Matt here to spy on me? To make sure that I'm at the diner? Well, I'm here, so maybe it's a good thing Matt has seen me working.

Unless...

Unless Davis has caught on to my lies.

"Hey, there is a—" Stefanie says from behind me. I whip around, eyes wide with fear, and face her. "You're looking pale. Are you feeling alright?"

"Stefanie, would you do me a huge favor and take over the table in the back corner? Please, I'm begging you. I'll do anything you want." I beg her, the words escaping me so fast.

Stefanie watches me for a moment, hesitating at first, and nods her head and slips out of the kitchen. I take a moment to breathe in deep breaths, attempting to calm my heart, which is currently trying to escape my chest cavity.

A few minutes later, Stefanie is walking through swinging doors with an order to give to Carl. "Okay, since I'm waiting on the creep, could you grab the family that just came in?"

"Yes, absolutely. Thank you."

"You'll explain this to me later?" she asks, pointing a finger at me with a determined look in her eyes.

"Yeah, sure."

And I do. I haven't told Stefanie anything about my home life but as soon as Matt leaves the diner, I fill her in on everything. She stays quiet as she listens, her eyes growing wide occasionally, pity overtaking her face.

"I'll never complain to you again," she finally says, wiping down the last table as we prepare for the nightshift to take over. "I'm sorry you have to deal with that."

I shrug my shoulders. "It is what it is. Only a year left, and I can get the heck out of here."

Once our shift is over, Stefanie and I part ways, and I rush toward my car when I see Ryland waiting for me. He's leaning against the passenger side door, legs crossed, and arms open. I crash into him, wrapping him into a hug, inhaling his comforting scent.

"Wow, now that's a hug. I missed you too." His hands slide up my back, over my shoulders, until they land on the sides of my face.

A shiver runs through me, as it always does when I feel his touch. He pulls my face away from his chest until I can meet his gaze. I can't hide how happy he makes me feel. Why would I ever want to?

My smile falters at the memory of Matt watching me at the diner. Ryland, always attuned, senses the change in me. His eyes search my face for a moment before he asks, "What is it?"

I take a step back and look around us for any sign of being watched. He does the same, even though he has no idea why. Once I feel secure, I step back into him.

"I saw one of Davis' *friends* at the diner tonight. The same one that was with Davis that night." I don't have to explain which night I'm referring to, because I can see the memory written on Ryland's snarl. "I had Stefanie cover the table for me, so I didn't talk to him. I could have been overreacting, and he was just there to eat."

"Or Davis sent him there to check up on you."

Ryland looks around us again, his body tense with alertness. I don't understand how Davis can be okay, knowing how he has emotionally damaged the people around him. It makes me sick. I'll never understand what drew my mother to him in the first place.

"I don't think he's here anymore," I say, trying my best to brush off the sudden chill I feel, even though it's the beginning of summer and I can feel the sticky heat clinging to the night.

Ryland returns his eyes to me, flickering down to the rainbow necklace dangling from my neck that I never take off, and a hint of a grin shows on his lips. He places his fingers on the pendant and tugs lightly on it until I follow his lead. I lean up onto my tippy toes and touch the edge of our noses together.

I kiss the curve of his smile, and the simple touch makes me feel like I'm floating. Like I'm in the middle of the lake, drifting in the water and staring up at the sunbeams dancing through the trees. Ryland has always had that effect on me, even before we started dating.

I let my lips leave his to start trailing along the sharp line of his jaw until they land on his chin. Exhaling all the tension in my body, I nuzzle into his chest and wrap both my arms around him. "I love you." The words slip from my lips, like it's the easiest thing I've ever said.

"I love you too." His words sink into my skin in a rough whisper. He leaves a small kiss on my collarbone before releasing a sigh that loosens his chest. He takes two steps back and begins leading us into a walk.

We follow the sidewalk that takes us toward the center of downtown where a large fountain sits, spraying water into the night sky. The sun has officially crested over the distant mountains, the purple and blue hues of sunset bleeding into vibrant orange. We stay silent, the only sound coming from our footsteps, echoing off the buildings around us. Ryland keeps an arm tightly around my shoulder and his head leaning against mine as we take in the scenery.

My mind is consumed by Ryland, even with him right next to me. All I can think about is how much I love being with him. How much I love our talks. How he looks like pure sunshine when he smiles. How hearing his laugh feels like a cozy blanket. I often daydream about us, pieces of our conversations replaying in my mind, giggling at something funny he said or did. I can close my eyes and see every feature of his face perfectly because I've memorized the details of him, especially the way he looks at me before he kisses me.

I catch myself smiling and wondering when the next time will be that I'll see him again. Even though we never know what the future will hold, I do know one thing for sure: that Ryland is the best thing that has ever happened to me, and I never want to let go of what we have together. It's as if God created the two of us perfectly for one another.

Downtown Covewood is small, and I wish there was more to do. A handful of lawyers' offices sit amongst the different buildings along with a few banks, one barbershop, the movie theater, and a tacky gift shop. The scene isn't romantic at all. If anything, it feels stale, and I'm ready to turn around and suggest we do something else.

"I'm so ready to get out of this boring town," I admit.

Ryland removes his arm to slip his hand into mine. He gives me a little squeeze and looks down at me. "One more year and we graduate high school."

"Does it bother you to think that you could've graduated already?" I ask, remembering when he first moved to Covewood, and that his mom thought it would be best to hold him back a year because of how poorly he did the previous year at his old school.

"Nope. Because I get to graduate with you. Plus, I would be here waiting for you anyway," he answers, bending down until he plants a kiss onto my temple.

"Are you sure about that?" I tease, elbowing him gently in the ribs, loving the sound of his laugh.

Ryland's eyes twinkle with mischief. His playfulness has always been infectious. I bite the inside of my cheek to try to keep from laughing as he tugs my hand, leading me down a small alleyway, until we're hidden between the shadows. He walks toward me until my back touches the scratchy brick wall, arches an eyebrow, and asks, "This okay?"

At my nod, his fingers curl around the swell of my hip, gently pulling me closer, and his other hand finds mine. I feel like I can't breathe, in the best possible way. I'm frozen and waiting for his next move.

"There's no way I could ever leave you, and you're the only reason I'll ever need to stay. I'm not going anywhere unless it's by your side." His words calm the storm inside me.

Ryland has never given me a reason to doubt us, but his reassurance means more to me than he'll ever know. I reach up and run my fingers through his hair and tug him until our lips are against each other. It's my silent way of promising him that I will never leave him.

His lips part, and I stifle a groan when his tongue trails across the seam of my mouth, parting it. The first taste of him is always sweet, like the whipped cream on top of a hot fudge sundae. I want to tilt his face for a better angle, but I let him lead.

He's the first one to pull back, panting, and places his forehead on mine. I can feel the magnetic pull between us. This heated need for one another, to keep kissing, to want more from each other. However, we've done a good job at knowing when to pull back and not rush into things.

Ryland clears his throat, inhaling a deep breath, and takes a few steps away from me. I hate the distance between us, but I know it's necessary. I give him a shy smile and motion for us to continue walking back to our vehicles.

"So, now that it's officially summer break, are you staying with your grandparents?" he asks, the question catching me off guard.

Every summer vacation I spend with my grandparents. However, this will be the first summer Davis has lived with Mom. I predict that he'll want to control the situation, especially since he's been making me pay him rent. If I'm not at the house, I won't have to pay him rent, and I know that will be an issue with him.

"Who knows what Davis will allow," I say, and the worry quickly overwhelms me, as if it's about to swallow me whole.

"He can't keep you from staying with them during the summer. You've always spent the summers at the farm." Ryland's face pinches, a look of displeasure crossing his features before disappearing.

"I know, but he's been relying on my rent money. I'm surprised he even listened to my Mom's request of letting me keep half my paycheck. What teenager has to pay rent to live in their own home?"

"He'd probably make Luke do the same if he was still coming around," he adds, and I hum in agreement. Luke was lucky to get away when he did. He's blessed with a mother who knows when not to take Davis' crap. My mother, on the other hand, bends in fear.

"Like you said, one more year and we can get out of here." That statement alone is all the hope that I need.

"Where am I taking you?" he asks.

We've had a few discussions of what colleges we want to apply to and agreed to pick one together. He's been saving every dime he can and has been working extra lately to help his Pops keep his business afloat, which has been slowly falling apart since Nan passed away. I've tried to not allow that to worry me.

I've been saving everything I get from my paychecks too. Surely, between the two of us, we will have enough to help us move away from here. As we walk back toward our cars, we discuss our plans more, and the excitement of the future builds inside my chest. That excitement is ripped away at the sight of a dark form standing in front of my car. He takes a step forward into the light casting down from the pole in front of the parking lot. Matt smirks at us, clearly pleased to have caught us together.

"What are you doing here?" Ryland growls, moving me behind him, as if he has to shield me from Matt.

"Just taking a nightly stroll," he says, his voice slithering with each word.

"It's not a crime for me to take a walk downtown after my shift. Davis doesn't have to send you here to spy on me." I roll my eyes, anger lighting up every nerve in my body, and I move around my car until I'm standing by my driver's side door. Ryland never leaves my side or takes his hand off me. His eyes watch Matt's every movement like a lion ready to pounce.

"No, but he's not happy that every night after your shift you've been spending time with *him*."

Ryland tenses beside me. "Raine is allowed to do whatever she wants."

"See, that's where you're confused, because Davis specifically told Raine to stay away from you. Now that he knows she's been lying about her work hours to sneak off with you, he's going to be making some changes." Matt's words sink into the pit of my stomach. "You better get on home, Raine."

We stand in silence for a moment as Matt walks over to the black truck sitting a few parking spaces down. His truck turns on, and not until I see its red taillights disappear down the street do I release the breath I'm holding. Ryland pulls me to him, cradling me in his arms, as if I am something breakable, something fragile. Maybe I am.

He stays quiet, rubbing smooth circles onto my back, never moving to leave me. He doesn't try to solve my problems or remove my pain with empty words. He knows how bad this situation is, and it's out of our control until we can move away. Instead, he lets me fall apart without trying to put me back together.

Chapter Twenty-Four

Now

Ryland

It's been a very productive week. Wednesday, I oversaw the construction happening over at the local apple farm. Thursday, I finished up the master bedroom at the Wiley farm, then Raine and I picked out the paint colors for each room and primed all the walls together. Friday, I took Earl out to dinner after work to fill him in on the renovations. After I finished up on Friday, I called and invited Raine to come with Annabelle and me to the Spring Festival that's happening downtown today.

I place Annabelle on my shoulders once we reach the heart of downtown to help search for Raine. Taupe-colored two- and three-story buildings sit on both sides of the street, and in between them is a line of colorful food trucks, small businesses set up under canopies, and a stage that is standing at the end of the street.

I walk to where Enchanted Petals is located and see that they have a 'build your own bouquet' booth. I let Annabelle pick out her own bouquet, which is made of every pink flower she can find. Then we work together to create a bouquet for Raine, choosing an array of wildflowers.

"Oh, she's going to love it, Daddy!" Annabelle squeals as we pay the worker.

Annabelle begs to be lifted back onto my shoulders and I can already feel the soreness spreading into my muscles, but I want to enjoy this while I can before she is too grown. A mix of eighties country and rock is blasting from the speakers nearby, and I dance to the music, sending my daughter into a fit of laughter as I bounce her on my shoulders.

Downtown is already packed. The whole town shuts their businesses down after three p.m. to make sure that everyone is able to attend the festival. Although the small businesses are technically working at the festival, it's the best way to kick off the tourist season, which is usually from spring until the end of summer. The local lake brings in a variety of people. I've noticed the traffic picking up over the weekend as everyone is returning to their lake homes or renting the local Airbnbs.

I catch Luke in his work attire, looking grumpier than usual. He despises this time of year. Our small town doesn't normally have a lot of ruckus going on, especially since Luke has joined the police force, but the tourists bring in some crime for him and his team to deal with. I slap a hand to his shoulder in greeting. He tenses up at first, but he lightens up once he sees that it's Annabelle and me.

"Uncle Luke!" Annabelle shouts as she wiggles against my shoulders, and I gladly place her into his arms and roll my shoulders back to relieve the strain. "Look at the flowers Daddy got me."

"Well, they're almost as pretty as you are, Princess." He gives her a bright smile, and she melts into him as she wraps her tiny arms around his neck.

"You're such a softy." I chuckle and shake my head.

He shrugs. "Only for this one." He places his fingers into her armpits and gives her a tickle.

"How's work?" I ask, already knowing what he's going to say.

He huffs before placing Annabelle back into my arms. "I hate summer."

"Uncle Luke, you said a bad word!" Annabelle shrieks, and my smirk grows, especially when Luke slaps a hand to his mouth, his eyes growing wide, as he plays into her accusation. Annabelle is oblivious to actual bad words because she rarely hears them, but to her, *hate* is on her bad list.

"I mean, I *dislike* summer. Very much. Like the most ever."

A flash of red weaves through the crowd until Olivia bumps into Luke's shoulders. "Faye Grady and Mrs. Calaway are having a heated argument over by the mac and cheese truck. It's pretty epic! You might want to go take care of the situation before the mess gets worse."

"Gets worse? Are you kidding me?" Luke grumbles and jogs away from us.

Just then, the song "Pour Some Sugar on Me" by Def Leppard starts playing over the speakers, and I'm pretty sure the song is inappropriate for this crowd. However, Olivia lights up next to me and starts clapping with excitement. She sings, "Pour some mac and cheese on me!" and I burst out laughing. She stands on her tippy toes, peeking over to where I assume Luke is heading, and says, "This song is perfect for the fight. I hope someone is recording it."

"I might need to take Annabelle somewhere else," I admit through my laughter.

"But I love mac and cheese," she admits in my arms.

Olivia reaches over and takes Annabelle into her arms. She gives me a wink and points over toward *Honey and Tasty,* where I see Raine standing, observing jars of honey. "Mind if Auntie Liv takes this little squirt over to the bouncy houses for a bit?"

"Daddy, can she please?!"

As if I could say no to those puppy-dog eyes Annabelle has learned to master, thanks to her Uncle Zane. "Alright, but when

Aunt Liv says it's time to go, you can't argue with her, okay?" Annabelle nods her head quickly, practically tossing her bouquet toward me to hold onto, before waving her arms in excitement.

"Let's go!" Annabelle squawks and jumps down from Olivia's arms to grab her hand and tug her toward the courthouse where the bouncy houses are set up. I smile, thankful for this found family Annabelle and I are blessed with, before I turn my attention back to Raine.

Instead of walking toward her, I grab my phone from my pocket and send her a quick text.

Did you make it to the festival yet?

I watch her pull her phone from her back pocket and take in the brightness of her smile as she reads my message. Her thumbs go to work in texting me back.

RAINE

Yes, did you?

Yup. I've been here for a while now. I've been searching for this girl I used to date in high school.

Raine's smile grows, but she tries to hide it by biting her bottom lip. I remind myself that slow and steady wins this race, and I'm all about winning when it comes to Raine. I plan to ask her this evening what she wants to do after the renovations are done to see where we go from here.

RAINE

Oh yeah?

Yeah, but there's this woman wearing a pair of tight blue jeans and a pink floral top that has me distracted.

She snaps her head up and begins searching through the crowd until her eyes land on me. And boy, do I love how she beams as soon as they do. It's as if time slows down, just for a moment, etching in a private moment for just the two of us. I've been trying to ignore the gravitational pull between us, as if it was never severed from the past. But as I watch her jog toward me, her dirty-blonde curls bouncing around her, I know there is no way I can ignore my feelings for this woman.

Who am I kidding? I never could ignore them in the past either.

Once she reaches me, I wrap her into a hug. Having her in my arms feels just as natural as it did back when we were dating. There is something magical about being at the Spring Festival. I can't help but give in to the temptation of touching her, treating her as if she's mine again. I know we still have some big discussions to cover before we can define what we might be to each other now but it can wait until later.

So much time has already passed between us, and right now, I want to focus on being in the moment with her.

I pull back to hand her the bouquet of flowers. "From Annabelle and me," I say, and her smile widens before hiding behind the flowers as she gives them a sniff.

"They're beautiful. Thank you," she replies, searching the crowd behind me. "Where is she?"

"Olivia took her to the bouncy houses."

"I was looking forward to seeing her. Speaking of Olivia, me and her had dinner at Matty's Meats yesterday," she says and leads us into a walk.

"Yeah? Is it still as good as you remembered?"

She smirks, raising a brow at me. "Even better. Especially since I saw what looks to be a pretty recent photograph of a certain someone who made the Matty's Meat Lover's wall of fame."

I chuckle, remembering how sick I felt after finishing that massive burger. I was surprised my face wasn't green like a cartoon character in the photograph. I haven't been able to eat a burger since because, once I got home, I threw up every bit of that meal. But I'm not about to admit that to Raine.

"I finally finished the whole thing."

She smirks and adds, "You puked afterward, didn't you?"

"Yup." I chuckle, shrugging my shoulders like I'm not embarrassed to admit it. "The family and I eat there often in honor of Pops. I don't know how he finished the burger back then *and* didn't get sick. Do you remember that?"

She laughs, shaking her head, before she replies, "How could I forget the moment he became a superhero to us? The fact that he ate ice cream afterward still blows my mind."

Oh, how Pops would love to see this sight right now. Raine and I, hand in hand, looking at each other like we did when we were lovesick teens. He knew how much I loved her back then and always said he had hope that one day we'd find our way back to each other.

"The man was one of a kind," I add, feeling the familiar pang in my chest as I'm reminded that he's no longer here with us.

Raine bumps her shoulder into mine as she adds, "So was your Nan. I still watch *The Golden Girls* from time to time, especially when I think of her. In a way, the show makes me feel close to her."

I'm not sure why that little piece of information causes my heart to do a backflip, but it does. I know how important my grandparents were to her. Knowing Raine still thinks of them means a lot to me.

"I kept that red Honda of hers for years until I finally had to upgrade to the car I have now. Oh, and the old film camera she gave me...do you remember it? I still use it from time to time."

I stop in my tracks unintentionally. Hearing her admit to keeping a piece of my Nan with her throughout the years makes me wonder if she kept pieces of me too. Or did she toss them all away when I chose to let her go? I inhale, attempting to steady my heart, realizing that our conversation about that night might need to happen sooner than I'd like it to.

But not today, I remind myself. *You can enjoy this day with her.*

However, it's hard to do when the past stays lurking around us, waiting for a moment to pounce and tarnish what we're slowly working toward. We stay quiet for a moment, our hands still clinging to one another, as we look everywhere but at each other.

"This place has changed so much," Raine says, finally breaking the silence.

I smile down at her. "Let me show you around."

We spend the next hour moving from store to store that line both sides of the street. We taste-test goat milk fudge and caramels from Soap and Hope. Raine picks out a few gardening books from Covewood Literacy, and even though I'm not a big reader, I end up getting a few coffee table books about classic cars. Raine practically squeals when we walk inside Covewood Botanicals, and she sees their elderberry syrup and walls that are lined with glass bottles of homemade spices and herbs.

We both pick up a few articles of clothing from Lakeside Connections Boutique, some locally inspired candles from Covewood Candles, and end up at The Groovy Bean for vanilla-cinnamon lattes—her choice, not mine. However, it's surprisingly delicious.

She bumps her shoulder into mine, wiggling her eyebrows as I look down at her. "I told you it would be yummy."

"If you say so." I smirk at her before searching the crowd for the next place I want to take her. I point across the road to the brick building on the corner. She follows my finger, and once her eyes land on MJ's Diner, another squeal leaves her.

"Oh, I was hoping to go there today! Olivia says it's one of the only places in Covewood that has stayed the same. Although, the outside looks freshly painted, and the sign has been updated." She grabs my hand, and we make our way through the crowd.

I place my hand onto the gold handle and open the black door for Raine to step inside. A small bell chimes from above, and a waitress behind the counter welcomes us. Raine steps forward, her head turning in all directions to take in the diner. I step around her until I'm standing in front of her.

My eyes flow down her face until they land on her pink lips, watching as they part and whisper, "Whoa." I swallow back a lump that found its way into my throat, the past once again pressing against reality. Being here at the diner with Raine is causing a wave of memories to hit me. "It's updated but yet the same."

She walks past a booth, her index finger tracing the dark wood of the table until her hand spreads against the brown leather seat. The walls, which used to be a dark red, are painted a burnt orange. However, the walls toward the front of the diner and side remain exposed brick. They're decorated with old newspaper clippings, pictures of the building from when it was a lawyers' building, as well as the Loveitt family through the generations.

Several booths line against the windows and walls, and the middle of the diner is filled with round wooden tables and black metal chairs. In the center of each table is a small vase of fresh flowers that they change with the season and LED candles that create a warm atmosphere.

"It still feels like a scene from a romance movie," she whispers, more to herself, but I hum in agreement. "I used to stand behind the counter and wish I could photograph people. Couples would come in and get cozy in the booths, as if this place helped to melt away the rest of the world, leaving just the two of them together. Or the families that would fill the space with laughter, sharing funny stories while they enjoyed their meal. I loved how happy everyone seemed to be when they came into the diner."

"They still are," a cherry voice chirps from behind us.

We both twist around, and Raine drops her shopping bags to the floor and gasps in surprise. "Stef!"

I try to remember the spunky version of Stefanie from when Raine worked here a decade ago. She still looks familiar, but parts of her have changed. She looks healthier now, no longer has bleached hair, and stopped wearing eyeliner that looked like it was applied with a wide-tip Sharpie. No one looks the same as they did ten-plus years ago.

"Raine Wiley!" she says, a smile lighting up her heart-shaped face, holding her arms out in a welcoming way. Raine moves quickly, wrapping her arms around Stefanie, and she practically bounces with joy.

"Oh my goodness! You're still here? How've you been?" The words fly out of Raine's mouth.

"How long do you have?" Stefanie laughs and points to a nearby table. Raine looks back at me, silently asking if this is okay, and I toss an encouraging smile her way.

Stefanie was never one to tell a quick story. I remember the nights I would be sitting in a booth, waiting for Raine to clock out after her shift, and share some interesting debates with Stefanie. She would start explaining something and then somehow end up sharing another story before turning it back around to the original topic. However, today, she only keeps Raine for twenty minutes before people from the festival start making their way into the diner for a meal.

Raine swaps numbers with her, promising they can catch up while she is in town, before she makes her way back to me. "Sorry about that." She shrugs her shoulders shyly.

"No need to apologize."

"Downtown Covewood looks so different now, and yet, walking back into this place feels like being back in the past." Her lips turn up into a sad smile.

It does something to my heart. Before I can think of what I'm about to do, I place our bags onto the floor to free up my hands. I take a small step forward, the toes of our shoes tapping with the movement, and slide my hands up her jawline until they find her hair. Raine's eyes flutter, and I want to kiss her so badly.

Instead, I tug her close until her head lands against my chest and wrap my arms around her. The fact that the bad memories overpower the good ones for Raine causes this protective force to wash over me. Ten years later and all I want to do is keep Raine happy and secure.

"I know what you mean," I whisper into her hair before pulling back, retrieving our bags in one hand and taking hers in the other.

Chapter Twenty-Five

Now

Raine

"There you guys are!" Olivia's voice chimes over the crowd.

Zane is following behind her with Annabelle on his shoulders, and it's adorable. Witnessing Zane and Luke take on the role of fun uncles has me in a puddle of mush. I give Annabelle a wave before Zane places her on the ground, and she runs toward me.

"Raine! Did you like the flowers Daddy and I picked out for you?" She points to the bouquet I'm clutching.

"Absolutely! Thank you so much for them." I bend down to her level, my knees cracking as I do, and I bring her into a hug.

"Wanna go have some girl time?" Olivia whispers into my ear.

I nod, waving goodbye to everyone, and wrap my arm around hers. A little space would do me some good, because being around Ryland has me feeling confused. I keep having to remind myself that I can't rekindle a bad breakup over a few weeks. Things are strained between us, and I don't know how to properly manage my emotions around him. Everything feels so foreign and yet familiar all in one.

I also have to return to Rockdale at some point. I have a job and an apartment that I can't just run away from to chase down the idea that maybe he and I can finally have our happily ever after. Putting all my eggs in that basket is foolish and I need to make smart choices for my life. I'm just not sure what that is at the moment.

Olivia tugs me forward through the crowd of people, and I catch a peek at Ryland over my shoulder. He is watching us, and I give him a smile before turning away and following Olivia.

We venture into a few shops and end up back at The Groovy Bean because can you really have too much coffee? We're in the bathroom, and I catch a glimpse of my reflection in the mirror. I feel breathless from laughing so much with Olivia. My cheeks are flushed, and my face holds a grin that almost has me unrecognizable. It's been so long since I've felt like this.

Even in the midst of grief, joy can be found.

"I'm so glad you're here," Olivia says next to me and gives my reflection a wink.

With iced coffees in our hands, she leads me down the street toward the opposite end of downtown where I haven't ventured yet. As we make our way down the busy streets, she bumps her shoulder into mine and asks, "So...how are things going with Ryland?"

"What do you mean?" I reply, acting dumb.

She lifts a brow, silently telling me she knows better.

"Okay, okay. I'm honestly not sure where we stand. The past few weeks, we've sort of gravitated slowly back to each other, sharing hugs and holding hands. That's it, though. I'm scared to take it anywhere else seeing as I don't live in Covewood anymore, you know. Even if we rekindled something, what could come of it when I'm back in Rockdale?" My fears are all laid out, and an unreadable expression passes over

Olivia's face for a split second, there and gone, before I can decipher it.

"Spit it out," I say. It's my turn to lift a brow at her.

"Well, what if you moved back here?"

I'd be lying if I said I haven't thought about staying a dozen times a day. It's scary, thinking about giving up one life to gain another. However, the more time that passes with me being back in Covewood, the less I want to return to Rockdale. I haven't allowed myself time to really sit down and think about it, though.

Before we dig into the issue at hand, Olivia waves her hand in a showy way toward a small storefront with large windows and a gorgeous mural painted on white brick, with a large sign that reads *Potter's Art Studio*.

"Here we are!" Olivia announces.

The name triggers a memory. I know this place and that it's owned by Cindy Potter, who was one of my Mamaw's favorite students. Mamaw taught an art class at the local community college and had mentioned how proud of Cindy she was and that she loved this place. Before I know what I'm doing, a bell chimes above my head as I enter the studio with Olivia trailing close behind me.

The studio is bright with white walls filled to the brim with art and photographs. Wooden shelves line the walls, holding pieces of pottery. I notice a familiar photograph of blades of grass and yellow flowers surrounding the camera, looking up toward the sky. The photograph is one of mine. One I printed and gifted to Mamaw when I was in high school.

"Your grandmother insisted that I hang this photograph in the studio. I always loved the perspective you had in your photographs. How you see the world around you," Cindy's friendly voice echoes across the room as she makes her way toward us.

I feel the stinging of tears at the mention of Mamaw and fight against them. Once Cindy is in front of us, she gives me a sympathetic smile and brings me in for a tight hug—one that I really need and appreciate. As we pull away, she blinks away her own tears.

"Johanna was incredible," she states and looks around the space. "She was the one who pushed me to open this studio—a dream I told her about back in college. She even donated some money and artwork to get this place up and running. I—" her voice cracks, and it's enough to break me and force the tears to stream down my face.

Being in this space makes me feel so close to her. The colors, the possibilities, how she helped Cindy's dream come true... It makes me so proud to be Johanna Wiley's granddaughter.

"I miss her," Cindy admits and wipes her cheeks. She takes a deep breath and gives us a sad smile. "I'm still torn up about her passing. I know you are too. Gosh, I'm a mess. I'm sorry."

"I am too. It's okay." I give her an encouraging smile, the best that I can. "She left behind a huge hole in this world after she passed. It's not the same without her."

Cindy nods her head, agreeing with me, and I feel Olivia's hand slide into mine. She gives me a knowing smile and squeezes my fingers. My eyes wander around the room once more, and I'm drawn to the two large paintings on the far-left wall. One is an oil painting of daisies. The second is a watercolor of wildflowers.

"She always loved painting flowers," I say, more as a whisper, but Cindy smiles in agreement.

"I refuse to sell these. I know that sounds bad for business, but I love having a piece of her here, you know?"

"I do." I think of the sunroom at the farmhouse that has turned into a memorial room for Mamaw, the piece of art that will always stay unfinished sitting on the wooden easel. I plan to leave it right there as a reminder of her for as long as I need.

"She was always so proud of you. There was never a day in class that she didn't mention you. She would share stories or show a photograph you captured. She always kept some in frames along her bookshelf in her office."

Fresh tears blur my vision. Mamaw always made sure that I knew how proud of me she was. But hearing someone else say it, after losing her, really touches my heart.

"Thank you," I say softly, and we give each other another hug. "I needed this. Needed to see you and this amazing place. I'd love to come back soon," I admit, my heart already beaming with the thought of spending more time in this happy little space. "I've always wanted to learn pottery," I add, pointing toward the potter's wheels in the corner.

"You're welcome anytime. Hey, actually, I have been wanting to host a class about photography for the community. I want to start hosting a free class once a month. If that's something that would interest you while you're here, maybe we could work on something together?" Cindy pulls out a card from her back pocket and hands it to me. Once it's in my hand, I feel my spirit move.

It's as if Mamaw is standing right next to me, her hand in mine instead of Olivia's, giving me a little nudge that says *stay*. That I'm needed here. That I can find my place in Covewood again, answering all the questions I have been pondering for days now.

"I'll be in touch," I tell her before Olivia and I make our way back outside into the sunshine. I turn to look at the building once more, noticing the *For Rent* sign in the building next to the studio, before following Olivia down the street.

We walk in silence as we make our way toward the stage. The scents from the coffee shop and freshly bloomed flowers that sit in pots along the street fill my nose. The wind blows softly against us, carrying with it fallen blooms from the nearby dogwood and redbud trees that line the sidewalk.

My name is tossed out in greeting with a wave, and I realize something. I knew Rockdale was missing something before, but

I wasn't sure what. Now, I recognize it's missing foundation—belonging, stories, and community.

I didn't have Felix waving at me from across the road with a half-eaten burger held between his fingers. Or Luke patrolling the crowded streets, sneaking a hug as he walks by. A chorus of friendly whistles when I wave to the guys who work at the garage down the street and are friends with Papaw. People here value family and love.

Olivia must see the worry written on my face as she places her hand on my shoulder, giving me a comforting squeeze. Friendship isn't a big thing. It's a million little things. Like how Olivia knows just how to make me laugh or when to comfort me. Or how she always seems to know how to read my mind and how to say the right thing at the perfect moment.

"Let's go find the others," she says, leading the way.

Moments later, we are close to the stage. Streets have been blocked to provide a safe area for people to mingle together. We spot Zane, Ryland, Luke, and Annabelle all huddled together, sharing the biggest onion petal I have ever seen. Ryland, as if sensing us near, looks up first and tries to smile over his mouthful of food.

"There ya are," Zane says in greeting, and I reach over and give him a side hug.

"Luke, how bad did the mac and cheese fight get?" Olivia asks and hops over toward him.

He groans at the memory, which causes a fit of laughter among the group again. "I don't want to talk about it."

Zane steps closer to Ryland and makes a silly face at Annabelle, which gets her to giggle, before pulling out his phone to show us a video. "I live-streamed the whole thing. It was epic."

"I knew I could count on someone to get it!" Olivia laughs and pushes against Zane's chest.

"I texted the guy who was working the music to play a more

appropriate song for the fight, and he chose wisely," he adds, winning Olivia's smile again.

"You're the best!" she chimes, and Luke stiffens as Olivia gives Zane a hug and then shows him something on her phone. They laugh together, going into their own little world. Zane and Olivia are a lot alike. I wonder why they've never dated before. Or have they and I wasn't told? I make a mental note to find out later.

We all enjoy a few songs together before Luke has to get back to patrolling. I peer over at Annabelle who's snuggled in her dad's arms, looking like she's about to fall asleep. Zane nudges Ryland before saying, "She's looking tired. Want me to take her home?"

"I can take her," Ryland replies, but Zane is already shaking his head, his eyes flickering toward me, and gives a wink. "Are you sure? You don't—"

"Annabelle, Uncle Zane is going to take you home," he says and reaches over to grab her from Ryland.

Annabelle doesn't protest as she leans her face on his shoulder and wraps her arms around his neck, her eyes already shutting. Ryland thanks his brother, gives Annabelle a kiss, and promises to tuck her in soon. She doesn't respond, already crashing from all the sugar and excitement of the day.

Olivia announces that she's going to go find Luke. Ryland and I are left by ourselves, and he takes the lead, quickly wrapping his arms around me, pressing my back close to his chest. He draws me closer, as if even a centimeter of space is too much for him. My back is on fire from where his chest is touching me through my cotton shirt.

We listen to a few more songs. I make sure to act as obnoxious as I can with my dance moves just to get him to laugh and dance along with me. We chuckle at the eye rolls we receive along with others who join in the dancing. He makes sure to keep me close as we dance to the slower songs, and he sings the lyrics into my ear for only me to hear.

The tension between us builds. Maybe it's the music, the twinkling lights strung above us, or the fact that I've decided to push aside my worries and doubts, but having his hands on me, in a place that is so familiar, makes me feel like we are the old Raine and Ryland.

Maybe pieces of them are still alive after all.

Ryland pulls me closer to him until my nose reaches his chin. He has one hand gripping my hip while the other is tracing the side of my cheek. The shining light from the stage is reflecting in his multicolored irises, and I catch the hint of gold and green woven together as his eyes dance with mine....right before they land on my lips.

My heart is hammering so hard in my chest I'm sure he can feel it. Ryland leans down, inching his lips closer to mine, and in a panic, I lean my forehead onto his and grab a hold of what little control I might have left. I place a hand onto his chest, pushing away just an inch.

"I'm sorry," I whisper, not quite understanding why I'm holding back when I've wanted this for so long.

"It's okay," he says, backing away to give us both space.

The last part of the show is an encore of fireworks blasting into the sky above us. Ryland looks up, the light reflecting off his eyes, and I keep staring at him. This moment carving out a nook in my chest where I know it'll sit, like a time-worn fragment of magic I'll remember it even when everything else starts to fade.

Chapter Twenty-Six

Eleven Years Before

Ryland

I've decided that if Raine and I can make it through our senior year, we can make it through anything. Davis put an end to our dates after Raine's shifts at MJ's Diner during the week. I try my best to make the most of our limited time together at school, squeezing in kisses in the hallways, behind the bleachers, or in the stairwell.

We text and call each other every second we could until the weekend would come, and we'd either spend time together at the farm or at the lake. Little by little, I see Raine's light begin to dim. The weight of Davis' control is starting to get to her. Him constantly putting her down, making her feel like everything she does is wrong, and I've caught her often mentioning how worthless she is.

It's emotional abuse. I make it my mission to remind Raine of her worth as often as it takes to help her heal from the damage he's caused. Only a few more months, and we will taste freedom together.

The ding from my cell phone catches my attention. I rush

into the kitchen, pick up my phone from the table, and read the text from Olivia.

OLIVIA

We're fixing to head that way.

A wave of nausea hits me, and I begin pacing the room. The unknown of how Raine is going to react to what I have planned has been eating at me, and keeping this secret from her for the last few weeks has been the hardest thing to do.

"Ryland, what did I say about biting your nails?" Mom's voice booms, causing me to jump slightly and rip my fingers away from my mouth. She gives me a sympathetic smile before closing the distance between us and places her hands on my shoulders. "I've never seen you so worked up before."

"I've never gone behind my girlfriend's back before."

"She'll be thrilled. Trust me. Now, I'm going to go upstairs and get things ready for the girls. Holler at me when she's here, okay?" she says before giving me a little squeeze and patting my cheek softly. "You look handsome."

I release a pent-up breath after she leaves the room and return back to my pacing. What if she's mad at me? Surely she wouldn't think about breaking up with me because I changed our plans. Why is it so hot in this house?

I take off my suit jacket and loosen my tie a bit before making my way onto the front porch of the farmhouse. I'm met with a cool breeze, and I take a seat on the porch swing. I reach into my pocket for the paper towels I placed there earlier and dab against the sweat dripping down my brow.

"Getting cold feet?" Johanna asks as she steps up onto the porch, a basket of flowers from her garden in her hands.

"More like a hot flash," I say, earning one of her snort laughs that I've grown to love.

"Mind if I take a seat?" she asks, and I shake my head, gesturing next to me. She studies me for a moment as she sits down, giving me a small smile, and turns her attention onto the flowers in her basket and gets to work on making them into a corsage.

She pieces different kinds together, holding them up to my chest, and hums a sound of approval. "You have nothing to worry about. She's going to love that you're doing this for her."

"You don't think she'll be mad that I did this behind her back?"

Johanna exhales, shaking her head, and a sad smile pulling on her slightly wrinkled lips. "No. I know deep down that she wants to go to prom with you. My sweet girl deserves some normalcy in her life. That Davis...he's ruined so much. You know, in the past we've tried to reason with her mother. Just when we thought she was going to let Raine live with us full time, she met Davis and he made sure to not allow that to happen. Earl and I have felt hopeless with the situation but are thankful that her mother has allowed us to have our weekends with her. I hate witnessing how she's wilted these past few years."

My jaw twitches, and my hands ball into fists. I inhale a deep breath to try to calm the storm brewing inside of me at the mention of Davis' name.

"God knew that she would need you."

Those words draw my attention back to Johanna. The breeze picks up, swaying her white curls over her shoulder, and the scent of flowers hits my nose. Her hands keep moving as she wraps string around stems and looks up at me, a smirk deepening her smile lines.

"You bring the sunshine into her life. When she's with you, she blossoms." Now it's my turn to smile. I like knowing that I make Raine happy. That she can let loose and be herself around me. "Ryland, can you promise me something?"

I nod, confident in knowing that I would do anything for Johanna.

"That you'll make sure she gets out of this town." She's still smiling, but I see the worry that fills her brown eyes and draws her brows together.

"You'd want her to leave?" I ask, knowing the answer before she replies, but it feels necessary to ask.

She places the flowers down in her lap and turns slightly so she's facing me. I feel the warmth of her hands slide over top of mine, a slight tremble in her fingers telling me all that I need to know. My spine stiffens as I prepare myself to listen wholeheartedly.

"Selfishly, I want her to stay so I can keep her close and see her every day. But I understand that when you love someone, sometimes you have to choose to let them go. If she stays here, it'll smother her. She needs to be replanted somewhere new so that she can truly grow."

I let her words sink in, knowing that she's right, and I make the promise to her because it's the promise I've already made to myself and to Raine. I will do whatever it takes to get her out of Covewood and away from Davis. Johanna pulls me in for a quick hug.

"You're such a blessing." She grins before standing up and disappearing into the house. I stand up to do the same, but the sight of headlights making their way down the driveway has me freezing in place. I blink away the nerves and go into action.

I toss my jacket back on, tucking everything into place before fastening each button and tightening the tie around my neck. I swing open the front door, and I pop my head inside to yell that Raine has arrived. My hands are trembling with the nerves growing inside of me. I feel like I look weird. Should I lean against the post by the steps? Go inside and stand by the stairs? Hold my hand out like Leo did in *Titanic*?

Before I can turn and run inside, I catch sight of Raine at the bottom of the steps. Her eyes widening in shock as she takes in the sight of the black suit I'm wearing. Her pink lips open, and naturally, I'm drawn to them. I want to rush down the steps, tell her I'm sorry, and wrap her into my arms.

She's wearing a hoodie and a pair of blue jeans. Her honey-blonde hair with purple tips is worn in waves that touch her shoulders. My fingers twitch with the need to run them through her strands. Her eyes are wide, taking the sight of me in, as if she, too, is frozen in place. Olivia bounces beside her and squeezes Raine's arm.

"Surprise!" she squeals, shaking her arms out in excitement before pointing to me. "We're going to prom!"

"We're what?" Raine asks, her voice picking up at the end, her light brows furrowing.

"You know what, I'll let Ryland explain, but you have to hurry! We don't have a lot of time to get ready. So, make it snappy, and then meet me upstairs."

Olivia rushes past me in a blur, and once the door shuts, Raine starts making her way up the front porch stairs. I can't get a read on her, and I pray silently that she's not upset. What should I say? What do I do with my hands?

She stops in front of me, her grayish-blue eyes staring up at me, and I want to reach out and touch her so badly, but what if she doesn't want me to? For the first time since we started dating, I don't know what to do around her.

"We're going to prom?" she finally asks, breaking the silence.

I swallow hard and pull out another paper towel to dab at my upper lip. She smiles

then, big enough to reveal all her white teeth, and it's enough to lift the weight off my chest. She takes the paper towel from my hands and starts to pat against my whole face.

"Yeah," I reply, my eyes staying on hers, watching every expression that passes on her face.

"We are going to prom even though Davis basically took all my paychecks lately and refused to let me buy a prom dress? Even though we both agreed that prom is dumb and we'll just hang out here instead?"

"Yeah," I repeat because apparently all other words have left my brain.

"And you're sweating because you think I'm going to be upset with you?"

"Yeah." This time, I'm able to give her a smirk. "Because I knew deep down that you didn't think prom was dumb and that you actually wanted to go."

"You know me too well." She places the soaked paper towel into my hand before wrapping her arms around me and pulling me closer to her. "How are we going to prom? I don't have a dress or—"

"I took care of everything," I admit. Her smile drops, and she goes to take a step back, but I won't let her. I bring her closer to me and run my hands up her jaw until I can finally run my fingers through her hair. It feels like a small victory as I see her skin pebbling beneath my touch.

"How?" she asks, but before I explain, I pull her head toward me until our lips are together. She doesn't need to know that I spent some of my savings on renting this suit or how I asked her grandparents for help to pull this off. Or that Johanna and I went and picked out her dress together, finding the perfect one, and had Olivia help find the right accessories and whatever else girls need for prom.

All she needs to know is how much I love her and that I would do absolutely anything to bring a smile to her face. Like the one she's blessing me with right now as I pull away from our kiss.

"I'd do anything for you, Rainbow," I say, tracing her cheek with the backs of my fingers. "Now, you need to go get ready. They're waiting for you upstairs in your grandparents' room."

It took the girls an hour to get ready. An hour. I didn't think we were going to make it in time for dinner before the dance started. It took me all of fifteen minutes to pull on my suit, have Pops fix my tie, and Earl made sure my shoes were shiny and ready to go. I added a bit of gel in my hair to keep it in place and squirted a bit of cologne on. Things are simpler for men, I guess.

All my complaints go out the window the moment Raine makes her way down the stairs. Much like those slow-motion scenes from the chick flicks Raine's had me watch with her a few times, watching her walk toward me in the flowy rainbow-colored dress I picked out has the same effect on me. She has her hair pulled back into a braid with some of the flowers Johanna picked placed throughout her hair.

Pops reaches over and pushes my mouth shut, chuckling with Earl and earning a scolding look from me before I return my attention back to my girlfriend.

I hold her gaze as she makes her way toward me. I take this rare moment and memorize every detail, because if this is all I ever get with Raine, I want it seared in my mind like a cattle brand to become a permanent part of me.

"What do you think?" she whispers, her trembling hands finding mine.

I bend down to say in her ear, "Things I shouldn't say in front of the old men."

She giggles before Earl walks over and steals a hug from her. His eyes are a bit misty, and Pops and I share a grin. "Quit hogging her, you old sap," Pop grumbles and pulls Raine into a hug, whispering something in her ear before pulling back and patting his best friend on the shoulder.

"Now, don't you dare leave without us getting some photos!" I hear my mom announce as she jogs down the stairs with a camera in her hand. Olivia follows behind her, wearing a shimmery green dress, her red hair in waves that flow down one shoulder. She gives me a wave before making her way to stand next to Raine.

"Hang on, you all need these corsages before we get photos!" Johanna shouts from the top of the stairs.

My patience is running a bit thin as it takes ten minutes to get the corsages right, another fifteen minutes to snap photographs, and another five for hugs to be given. Raine laughs as she looks up at me, sensing my frustration, and gives my hand a light squeeze, grounding me with her touch.

Finally, we make our way toward the door, tossing a last goodbye over our shoulders, only to come to a halt at the sight of Raine's mother walking into the living room.

"Mom?" Raine freezes next to me, her fingers clamping down on mine, a look of panic washing over her.

My first instinct is to look for Davis but I don't see any signs of him. My next move is to place Raine behind me, to protect her from whatever her mother is about to do or say. But to my surprise, her mother gives everyone a nervous wave and smiles at Raine. I peer over at Johanna and Earl and see the small smiles that spread across their faces and feel the tension leave the room, at least for me anyway. However, Raine stays completely still.

"I'm sorry to show up at the last minute. I had to—" she starts, her voice shaky. "Anyway, I wanted to see you before you left."

"You did?" Raine questions, her words soft.

"Yeah. I can't stay long," she adds, and we know what she means. Davis will know that she's gone or that she's here. The last thing we need is him involved. "You look beautiful. I hope you all have fun."

The breath Raine is holding whooshes out slowly, making her body deflate like a balloon. She runs a hand down her braid nervously, giving her mother a shy smile, before thanking her for coming. Her mom waves goodbye to us all before disappearing as fast as she came, leaving us all shocked and frozen in place until we see the red lights of her vehicle leaving the farm.

"We called and asked if she could sneak and come see you. It's what your father would have wanted. They went to prom together, you know. Plus, you deserve to have your mother see you off to your own prom," Johanna announces, giving Raine's arm a small squeeze before leaning over and planting a kiss onto her cheek.

"I'm ready to dance the night away!" Olivia shouts as Raine and I follow her through the door.

We give everyone one last wave goodbye before shutting the door behind us and once we are down the front door steps I take a moment to sneak in a quick kiss. "You look beautiful." I whisper into her ear, soaking in the smile she gives me, and lead her towards the car.

Chapter Twenty-Seven

Now

Raine

My spirit feels stirred today after such a powerful message at church. I was nervous at first, but as soon as the music started playing, the buzzing within my veins settled, and I finally was able to breathe. I closed my eyes, exhaled, and imagined myself releasing all the bad that was pent up within my heart. Oddly enough, the preacher's message today was about forgiveness.

God likes to talk to us within the quiet moments, and other times, like today, I hear him loud and clear. He knows exactly what I'm going to be facing today and sent the words that I'll need to carry with me to get through. I'm so thankful.

I'm picking at the skin on my thumb as Papaw drives us to my old childhood home. I'm thankful he agreed to come with me. I need the comfort his presence brings. I haven't seen this house since the day I left, and I'm not sure what to expect.

As we pull into the driveway, my jaw drops. What was once an old brick home, littered with junk on the porch and under the carport, is now bright and updated, complete with an added garage.

My Papaw looks over at me with a large smile on his face, the kind that always seems to soften my heart. "Doesn't look the same, does it, Little Duck?" he states and points at the house.

I'm speechless. The brick has been cleaned up and painted a dark gray. The cracks on the edge of the home, right where my bedroom used to be, have been repaired. The shutters have been restored and painted white. The broken-down wooden porch with missing steps is newer. I close the truck door and take the three white steps that lead up to a closed porch with matching rocking chairs to the left of the door.

There's nothing here that reminds me of my childhood, and I'm thankful for it. However, I still feel the whirl of nerves in the pit of my stomach. Just because the outside of the home is different doesn't mean the inside will be too. The same goes for the people.

I bite my tongue the moment Preston, my mother's husband, opens the door and reveals a completely redone living room behind him. My eyes return to the man standing greeting us with a smile so big I'm pretty sure I can see all his teeth. "Hey, guys! Come on in!"

Preston's baby-blue eyes stay on me as I enter the house. Papaw and I take our shoes off at the door, and I reach over to wrap my arm through his, keeping him close for support. He gives my hand an encouraging pat before we make our way through the living room.

"Shannon is in the kitchen, getting dinner ready. Everything should be done in just a few minutes."

Papaw and Preston move into an easy conversation, but their words are tuned out as I scan the living room. The walls aren't an old yellow color any longer. The light-gray paint gives the room a modern feel along with the black leather couch, wall of bookshelves, and refinished wood furniture. What happened to the old coffee table that I spun around and accidentally broke when I was eight? The small bookshelf we turned over to make a TV stand?

There's nothing left from my childhood. Yet, memories start to flash behind my eyes nonetheless. Memories of Mom lying on the couch, passed out with an empty bottle nearby. Davis tossing an empty beer can at my head. Mom staring at me with blank eyes. I shake my head, willing the memories away.

The past cannot be healed if I choose to stay there. I can only heal if I stay living fully in the present. I need to accept that my mom has changed and that Davis is no longer a threat to me. I cling to my Papaw a little tighter when I see Mom enter the room. She takes me in from my head to my toes, and her expression softens on her face.

"I'm so glad you came," she whispers, placing her hand onto Preston's arm.

"Thanks for having us," Papaw replies. "Dinner smells good."

"We made homemade chicken and dumplings," she announces, her eyes finding mine, a smile crinkling the edges.

Chicken and dumplings was a childhood favorite of mine. Before Davis' and Mom's drinking became uncontrollable, she used to cook chicken and dumplings every Saturday for me. The memory stings my heart, especially seeing her like this. Healthy and happy. I don't think I've ever seen her so lively. Not even back when things were at their best.

I try to give her a smile, but it's a weak one. My nerves having found me once again. Papaw and I follow them through the hallway and into the dining room and take our seats at a beautiful wooden table. This room used to house Davis' boxes of junk. It was never used for hosting dinners. My eyes roam the room and take a peek into the kitchen.

"We completely redid the whole house several years ago," Mom says as she sets a basket of rolls in the middle of the table. "Right before Preston and I got married, we knew we wanted to keep this home, but it needed a lot of updates."

"I lived in a tiny apartment two towns away, and Shannon wanted to stay in Covewood," Preston adds with a grin. "She always hoped you'd come back, Raine. We're happy to have you here."

She always hoped I would come back?

"You all did a fantastic job. Johanna and I loved seeing life being brought back into this old home," Papaw says, and I catch the sadness within his voice at the mention of Mamaw.

I turn to him and take his hand into mine. I don't know why I feel so clingy to him, but knowing he's here is helping to keep me grounded instead of spiraling. He gives me a small smile and another encouraging squeeze. I bow my head, close my eyes, and say a silent prayer for God to bring me strength to get through this dinner.

As I exhale and look up, I see Preston studying me. He's quick to smile, but I catch the worry in his eyes. Am I making him as uncomfortable as I feel being here?

I can already tell that Preston is nothing like Davis. He's the complete opposite, actually. His body is slim, and his thinning hair is a sandy blond mixed with gray. He's wearing a sweater vest and black round glasses on the bridge of his nose. He doesn't look anything like my mother's typical "men."

I've only spoken to him a few times since I returned to town —once at the hospital, once at the viewing, and once at the funeral. But I've kept my distance since then. I haven't really given Preston a chance. However, I can tell he's safe to be around and that he truly loves my mother with the way his eyes seem to twinkle when he looks at her.

She looks happy and joyful during dinner, sharing stories about how Preston and her met and how they made things work long distance for a while until he finally proposed. It seems like Preston was her saving grace, and it brings me a sense of reassurance seeing her like this.

After we finish eating, Preston goes to help Mom clean up

the dishes, and Papaw takes that opportunity to whisper in my ear, "Talk with her, will you?"

"I will." Even as the words leave my mouth, I can feel the weight of what's to come pressing onto my shoulders.

"It'll all be okay. I promise. I'll go and distract Preston to give you some time to hash things out. This will be good for you, Little Duck. Remember what was said in church today. Use those words to guide you. I want to see you healed from this, and we both know it won't happen until you confront it. I'll be right outside if you need me."

I give him a nod as Preston and my mother enter the room. I need a moment to breathe and prepare myself for this conversation. Excusing myself, I make my way to the bathroom down the hall.

Inside, once the door is shut and locked, I brace against the sink and take in a few deep breaths. I spent a lot of my time growing up locked in this bathroom, mainly because the lock to my bedroom had been damaged and no longer worked. However, the bathroom was the only place I felt safe in this house, and somehow, it still brings a sense of comfort to me.

I wash my face in the sink and dry it with a hand towel. As I pat my skin, my eyes find my reflection in the mirror, and I remind myself that I'm not that same scared little girl who used to live here. I moved on with my life. I made something of myself. I proved to them that I'm not worthless. I am strong. I am capable. I am worthy of happiness. And this will all be okay.

As if sensing that I need him, my phone dings with an incoming text from Ryland.

RYLAND

How is everything going?

It's going. We finished dinner and now I'm about to talk with my mom.

RYLAND

I'm praying over you. It will be okay, I promise. I'm proud of you for pushing past your fears and working towards a better relationship with your mom. Maybe we can celebrate later with some ice cream?

Only if you'll have mint chocolate chip?

RYLAND

Only if you'll have the best flavor that was ever invented!

Which is cookie dough by the way unless you forgot?

Oh I didn't forget. We can settle this debate once and for all.

RYLAND

It's a date.

I grin at my phone, thankful for the little distraction, and don't miss how a cluster of butterflies begin to take flight in my stomach at the mention of Ryland and I going on a date. I fix my hair and pat down my light-blue maxi dress. With a quick inhale, I feel much better as I open the door. But as my eyes drift toward the door to my old bedroom, my body seems to take over, and I find myself pushing the door open.

My eyes widen at the sight of the white walls littered with my grandmother's paintings, some that were from my own collection that I left behind in this room. Everything else is different, yet the memories still seize me.

I stop in my tracks just outside the door. My eyes studying the wall next to a queen-sized bed, right where my dresser once was, and see that the hole is no longer there. However, the memory fights its way to the surface, and I'm reliving that night all over again.

It still haunts me, no matter how many times I try to push it out of my mind—the thoughts, the touch, the smell. Everything still feels alive. Being here in this room brings it all back. My throat feels the ghost of Davis' tight grip, and I reach a hand up to my neck to make sure he's not really there. I back away from the room and bump into something warm.

"Raine?" I hear my mother say behind me. I turn around and see her–her from before–staring at me blankly and walking away from me as I cried out for her to help. Crying for her to finally choose *me*. I blink away the hot tears that pool in my eyes, and the old version of my mother is gone, replaced with a stranger. "Are you okay?"

"I'm sorry. I, uh..." I croak and cough to clear my throat. "It's hard. Being back here."

Guilt takes over the worry in her eyes. She takes a step back, as if my words have physically pushed her away. I wonder if she even remembers the night I left. I feel every cell in my body screaming at me to run, to get far away from this place and to avoid this whole situation, but I fight it.

Instead, I inhale and blink away the tears. I might have chosen to run away ten years ago and leave her behind, but I've always wanted her to be a part of my life. I'll always love her.

I desperately want my life back. I want myself back. I can't achieve this without healing.

"I'll be okay," I assure her, swallowing away my discomfort, and I motion to the living room.

She turns, and I follow her down the hallway that's now covered with picture frames. A lot of them hold photographs of Preston with groups of people I assume are his friends and family members. There are a few that contain photos from my childhood, all before Davis came into our lives. At the very end, sits an image of my mother and father.

They look to be in their early twenties in this photo. Their faces pressed close together, cheek to cheek, a suit and tie on my father and a white wedding dress on my mother. They had wide joyful smiles, their eyes squinting slightly because of it, but within them, I can see pure love and happiness.

The sight of it has me halting in my place. I didn't even know my mom had a picture of him. I look like him. I have his eyes, dirty-blonde hair, and wide toothy smile. My grandparents always told me that I acted like him too. I carried a matching big heart and wanted to rescue any and all animals like he did as a child. I even have his laugh, they've said.

I saw home videos during my weekend visits at the farm, which helped me to feel connected to him even though he was no longer with us. Stories from his childhood are all that I truly knew of my father. How he met my mom and the years after were stories my grandparents always said should come from her.

However, she never wanted to talk about him, and I learned quickly that when I did bring him up, she would reach for a bottle to drown away the pain. I knew she loved him. She loved him so much that the grief of losing him consumed her.

She must sense what's on my mind, because once I turn to face her, I see the frown deepen on her face. "I know I never spoke much about your father."

"Can you talk about him now?"

She gestures to the black leather couch, and as I take a seat, she walks over to a nearby table and grabs a tray of snickerdoodle cookies and two cups of milk. As she places the tray onto the coffee table, I notice the slight tremor in her hands. That's something I inherited from her.

"I remember these used to be your favorite," she rambles and takes a seat on the couch, making sure to leave some space between us. She seems as uncomfortable and nervous as I am, and in a way, it helps to ease my own discomfort—just a bit.

"I'll never say no to a cookie." I grab a snickerdoodle and inhale the scent, instantly thrown back into a memory from my childhood—thankfully a good one this time. After I take a bite, I add, "It's delicious. Thank you."

She shifts in her seat, rubbing her hands together before releasing a breath and turning to face me. *Here we go, Raine. Hold it together. You can get through this.*

"Losing your father was something I wasn't prepared for. The bottom of a bottle was my only escape from the grief he left behind," she begins, wetness beginning to build within her eyes. "Our love story was like a dream. We met in high school, separated during college for a few years, only to find our way back to each other, and then marrying shortly after. We bought this home, and then we became pregnant with you."

Her eyes glaze over as she shifts through her memories, almost like she drifts off to another place. Her complexion pales, and the shaking in her hands picks up slightly as her fingers fidget with the throw pillow beside her. She keeps her eyes on the coffee table, exhaling as she moves on with the story.

"We had big hopes and dreams for our little family. I treasure those memories with him. He was excited to be a father, and I was more than ready to witness him with you. The day we found out that you were a girl, we were driving home through a rainstorm, and I remember him looking over at me with so much love in his eyes—the same eyes I see on you." Her eyes shoot to mine, but just as quickly, she is looking back down at the floor.

"And he told me that he wanted to name you Rain but spell it with an E on the end. And before I could even respond, the tires hit a pothole in the road, and the car lost control. An oncoming car crashed into our vehicle, killing him on impact." My fingers lift toward my mouth. I knew my father died in a car crash, but I never knew the depth of the story. I never knew that not only was my mother in the vehicle but so was I. I want to ask questions, but all I can do is nod. I'm worried that if I try to speak, the words will tumble out and not make any sense.

She reaches for her glass and chugs the rest of her milk

before she continues, "That car literally wrecked my whole world. I blinked, and suddenly, I was a widowed single mother. Back then, I couldn't see the miracle that it was that you and I walked away from that crash alive. It was a miracle, Raine. However, I saw it as a death sentence. The postpartum depression that I experienced after your birth only made my grief worse."

I have the urge to reach out and hold her hand, to let her know how sorry I am that she had to go through that. But I stay quiet because I know what happens next in the story. I lost my mother the same day I lost my father.

"You became this constant reminder of him. Even saying your name would instantly send me back to that day. I barely made it those first few years after his death. I think the continuous task of caring for a newborn distracted me, but on the third anniversary of his death, something in me snapped. I needed a break, and while you stayed with your grandparents one night, I went to a bar a few towns away and found a way to numb the pain.

"I didn't know that alcohol would consume me or that I would develop an addiction to fading away from the world. I drank in order to make it day to day without him here. I'm telling you this because I want you to understand where I was mentally. But it wasn't okay, Raine, the way I chose to mother you. I regret it every single day," her voice breaks, and I feel mine burning from my own tears.

"And I know that when I met Davis, he only caused more tension to build between us. He created even more problems that I couldn't fix. He had me fooled into thinking he could help take care of us, help take care of you since I was incapable of being the parent that you deserved. I was blinded by that hope, but he showed his true colors the moment I let him move in with us.

"When you were able to leave, I was so relieved. I knew you would be better off living far away from him—and from *me.*

Once I found the opportunity to leave him, I hid away in the nearest rehab facility for as long as I could. Davis was gone once I was released. I was able to work on rebuilding my life again, and I didn't want to contact you until I felt worthy of having a relationship with you. But the thing is, I never felt worthy. I still don't."

Hearing this story from her perspective and learning more about my dad...it's breaking my heart all over again. I can't imagine what she had to go through. My hands start to shake from the emotions I'm keeping at bay.

She wipes her eyes and inhales a breath as she fights to regain her composure. The woman who sits before me is a broken one. Broken from so many different versions of grief, and I feel just as broken.

She reaches across the coffee table and grabs a tissue before speaking again. "My heart has ached with the thought of never seeing you again, Raine. But it also pains me to see you, knowing I can't change the past or will never be able to forgive myself for the choices I made. Knowing I'll never be worthy of your forgiveness. How can I even begin to fix our relationship?"

She looks fragile, a silent plea in her eyes, and compassion replaces all the hurt I have in my heart for her. Having a relationship with Jesus will do that to a person. He brings you strength right when you need it the most and helps you let go of the hurt. I'm ready for us to move past this with His help.

"Since I've been back home, I've felt God working on my heart. He's slowly healing my old wounds. It helps that you were brave and opened up to me. Thank you for sharing your story and the reasoning behind your actions. I'm proud of you for what you've overcome and for working on your own heart. Together, I think we can move forward."

She crumbles in front of me and places her face into the palms of her hands. Her shoulders shake as she sobs, and I move over to sit next to her. I place an arm around her and put my forehead against the side of her face. My hand rubs circles against her back, trying my best to comfort her and whisper that things are going to be okay. After a few moments, she starts to calm down.

I hand her a few tissues and wait for her to dry her eyes before I lean over and give her a hug. We stay there, wrapped in each other's arms for a long moment, and for the first time, I feel the heaviness lift away from my shoulders. I hope she feels it too.

When we pull back, she reaches out and touches my cheek, her thumb rubbing against my skin, and she gives me a look that only a mother can. That look alone is everything I've prayed for and more. "Can you tell me what I've missed over the last decade?"

A soft laugh escapes me, relief that we can move past the hurt and actually have a normal conversation. "Where do I even begin?"

Chapter Twenty-Eight

Now

Ryland

In my rearview mirror, the cabins are swallowed up by the trees, rolling hills, and distant mountains. I follow the winding back roads toward the Wiley farm, rolling down the windows to let in the smell of wildflowers and freshly cut grass. Over the whir of the engine, I can make out the sound of the babbling creek that leads toward the driveway.

Earl's truck is sitting next to Raine's vehicle by the garage. A bright-red lawn mower is making its way across the front yard. I greet Earl with a wave before grabbing my tool belt and box from the bed of my truck and walking over to him.

"Rough morning?" he asks as he turns the mower off, his pale-blue eyes giving me a once-over, the edge of his mouth twitching as he fights a smile.

"Do I look that bad?"

Earl rubs my head, a smile spreading across his face, before a bark of laughter escapes him. I always found Earl's laugh to be one of the best sounds in the world. He has the type of laugh that causes his whole stomach to bounce, the sound more of a roar than a chuckle. It's contagious.

"It took a lot of effort to get Annabelle to school on time this morning. Sometimes, she acts like a teenager instead of a seven-year-old."

What I didn't mention was the fact that I hardly got any sleep last night after my ice cream date with Raine. We talked for hours, discussing how things went with her and her mom, and catching up on things we missed through the years. Something felt different with Raine, a light shift in the air, like she could be thinking about staying. I wanted to ask her last night if that could be a possibility for her but I chickened out and because of that, I tossed and turned all night.

Earl grins, shaking his head, and gives me a knowing look that tells me he understands. "Rusty was the same way." His smile fades just a bit, as it always does at the mention of his deceased son, but he's quick to tuck it away.

He points behind him, and my eyes follow. I see Raine holding a basket in one hand and a camera hanging down her neck as she shuts the door to the chicken coop behind her. She's wearing a long cream floral dress that fits her body a little loosely. I try not to gawk, especially while standing in front of her grandfather, but my lips part on their own, and I can't seem to take my eyes away from her.

Her gaze lands on me, her eyes always holding an appreciation for many things. Somehow, I got lucky enough to be one of them.

I peel mine away from her and return my attention back to Earl, whose grin has grown into a smirk. Heat rises up my neck as Raine approaches us and watches me curiously.

"Rough morning?" Her Southern accent is making an appearance this morning. She shakes her head, biting her lip to keep from laughing.

"Like grandfather, like granddaughter," I reply with a chuckle. I run a hand through my hair, and sure enough, its' sticking up everywhere. I hear the sound of a click and look up to see Raine's camera pointing at me. As she moves it down, peeking out from behind the lens, the grin she gives me warms every cell in my body.

"I didn't sign up to be your model today." I point at her, and the edge of my mouth spasming as I hold back a smile, remembering how she used to have her lens pointed at me a lot as teens.

"Clearly," she tosses at me with a mischievous grin. "Actually, I was photographing the animals and garden in the morning light. I woke up feeling inspired."

"The farm will do that to ya," Earl adds with a sad smile. "Your Mamaw loved how the flowers looked with morning dew still on their petals. After our morning coffee, I would sit on the porch and watch her walk around, gathering inspiration for her next painting. She would have that look of awe in her eyes, and when that morning light would hit her, it always took my breath away."

Raine shifts on the balls of her feet and slips her bottom lip in between her teeth. I want to reach out and hold her hand, but Earl beats me to it. He motions for her to do a little spin, and a shy smile spreading across her face as she twirls, the dress flowing around her legs. "You look so much like your grandmother, especially wearing her dress."

I agree with him. It's easy to compare how my heart feels for Raine with how Earl and Johanna loved one another. The same type of love that my Nan and Pop had. A kind of love that so many people pray for. The truth hits me hard right then, that I'm still in love with Raine.

"I hope it's okay that I'm wearing it. I was looking through her things, and wearing her dresses makes me feel closer to her."

He nods his head in understanding. "It's okay. It suits you. She'd want you to wear it and be here to take care of things."

We stand there under the shade of the old oak tree and discuss the rest of the renovation plans. The home will be finished by the weekend. A familiar sense of panic finds its place in the pit of my stomach, knowing that once the house is finished, Raine will be returning to her life in Rockdale.

I've let time slip away, and I don't want to make the same mistake I did in the past. Would it be wrong of me to ask Raine to stay? Would she want to stay in Covewood and give us a second chance?

She's hinted lately that she's not looking forward to returning to Rockdale. How her job doesn't feel as satisfying as it once had. She lives by herself in a small apartment. She doesn't have close friendships besides a few office buddies. And since returning to Covewood, I've noticed how much happier she seems. *She has blossomed*, Johanna's words vibrate in my mind. But this time she was able to blossom at home.

Lord, give me strength. I want to ask her if she's thought of staying. I don't want to let her go again.

"It all sounds good. The three of us can meet after church on Sunday to discuss the next steps. I'll leave you both to it," Earl says, reaching a hand out, and I give him a firm shake. "You all have a good day. I love you, Little Duck."

"I love you more," Raine replies, and we watch him walk to his truck and drive down the driveway before we turn toward each other, an awkwardness buzzing between us.

The things that go unsaid are often the things that eat at you, whether because you didn't get to say them, or because the other person never got to hear what you truly wanted. My mouth opens to say something, but it's like a scratch is in the back of my throat, itching its way to the tip of my tongue, yet never quite reaching. There's no amount of tea or honey to soothe these thoughts that I can't quite choke up.

"I can't believe it's almost done," she says, breaking our awkward silence and looking up toward the house. I study her face for a moment, taking in the freckles that are starting to appear on her nose and cheeks, flowing across her exposed shoulders. A slight redness of a sunburn has appeared on the skin of her shoulders and chest.

She seems different today. She is smiling more freely, her shoulders holding a lightness to them. She releases a breath as a brilliant smile taking over her lips, and I'm captivated by them.

"Mamaw would be proud. It's perfect." She hums in delight before turning to me and wrapping her arms around my back, as if she'd been waiting to hug me all morning. I have a list of things to get finished today, but I will greedily take any moment to feel her against me.

"When I first started on the project, I wanted it to be everything Earl and Johanna needed, but I also want it to be perfect for you," I whisper into her neck.

There is a deep sense of ache that always seems to find my heart when I think about the potential of hers intertwined with mine. I must be mad to have these relishing thoughts and dreams, allowing the *what ifs* to torment me. It only took a few moments of Raine being back in my company to set my heart ablaze, restoring some hidden hope I buried ten years ago.

I bring Raine closer to my chest, and she presses her body in, soft and warm. My mind feels at peace for the first time in a long time.

I inwardly thank God and hug her even tighter. The type of love she and I had before was something to be cherished. And finally, she's here. She's home.

Raine takes a step back to look up at me, the effect of my words clear in her expression. She reaches up and places her hands onto the sides of my face, like a prayer in which no words exist. With each embrace that we've had since she's been home, it's as if our hearts are rediscovering something familiar.

She releases a breath, her stress evaporating before she pulls away but not completely. Her arms slide down until they land on either side of my hips, and she's blinking at me with those mesmerizing blue eyes, and the words slip right through my lips.

"Stay."

Her eyes widen with shock, and nerves twist the inside my stomach. I don't want to cause her to run, but I need to get these words out before they suffocate me. And the words keep tumbling from my mouth, completely ignoring the warning bells going off in my brain.

"I mean, you could stay if you wanted. Not that your job isn't important in Rockdale. It's just... Never mind. I'm butchering this, aren't I?"

Raine lifts a hand and places it on my elbow. With a gentle squeeze, she gives me a reassuring smile. I expect her to back away and retreat. Instead, she watches me for a moment before saying, "Take a breath, Ry, and try again."

I inhale and feel myself relax just a bit. "I have this whole speech I've been working on," I admit and run a hand through my already messy hair.

"You were never good at speeches." She grins and points to the porch, signaling for us to take a seat. Space would probably help me regain my composure. I could never think straight with her body touching mine.

"Remember that time in history class—I think it was our junior year—and you had to do a speech in front of the whole class," she adds after running inside to pour us both a cup of coffee. She hands me a mug, and the warmth and scent of hazelnut help my nerves to calm down.

We take a seat at the porch table, and I reply, "I'm pretty sure I blacked out because all I remember was walking out the door."

"That's what you did. You stood there, stuttered for a moment, and then just bolted out the door." She laughs at the memory, and the noise loosens some of the tension in my shoulders.

"Yeah, that sounds about right," I add and look down at the table's surface. "The house is almost done, and I know you have a life back in Rockdale to return to, but I don't want to miss this opportunity to tell you..."

So many feelings are running through me as I stare at her, mouth open to say the words, and yet they're trapped in my throat. *Again.* I don't want to scare her. I want to do things right this time. My chest burns, my stomach contracts, the blood seems to rush to my temples, and I try my best to breathe.

Do I have the courage to let her go again? Could I stitch the shattered pieces of my heart back together for a second time? Simply seeing her again has brought back years of memories, and listening to her talk—the trusting and knowing sound of her voice—is like time jumped backward or like we haven't been away from each other that long.

Raine squeezes my hands, guiding my attention back from the table to her open and eager face. "Tell me what?"

"That I love you. I always have, and I've never stopped."

There it is, all laid out on the table between us. As my words hit her, I watch her eyes grow glossy, and her bottom lip slightly quivers. I want to lean over and place my lips against hers, and without thinking, my body takes over. I stand up and walk to her side of the table. I reach for her hands and gently guide her up toward me.

I place my hand against her cheek before guiding her face closer to mine. Our noses brush together, and I find my lips curving into a grin as I see the skin on her neck grow goosebumps. It gives me the courage to ask her, "Do you still love me?"

My bottom lip barely touches hers, and she shivers, closing her eyes. Her hands find my stomach, inching their way up my chest, and one remains there as the other slides into my hair. It's such a natural thing, her hands on me, her lips this close, our breaths becoming one.

"I never stopped," she repeats, eyes opening and locking onto mine, and that's all I need to finally come undone.

I run my fingers through her hair and smash our mouths together. The rest of the world fades away. Her lips part, welcoming me inside, and I deepen our kiss with all the power I can muster to make up for all of the seconds, minutes, days, weeks, years that our lips have spent not touching. This feels right. Like my soul is saying I'm home.

I run my hands down her arms, down her stomach, until they find her hips. At the same time that I lift her up, Raine hops and wraps her legs around my hips. Her lips find my neck, and she plants tiny kisses upon my skin, starting a fire within me that no one else could ever ignite.

I place her on top of the table and lean my body over hers. Our bodies unable to get close enough. I taste her, and I realize I've been starving for the last ten years. I've felt love with others, but it was never like this. I only have this with her. I've kissed others before, but it didn't set every nerve ablaze like it always has with Raine. This kiss contains years of all the things we've wanted to say to each other and all of the feelings we've kept buried for only each other.

I'm the first to pull away, as much as it pains me, but I know if I don't stop now, I never will. Raine places a hand on my chest, pushing slightly, silently agreeing with me that we both could use a moment to collect ourselves. Her eyes flutter open, and she clears her throat. Her eyes look at my lips, disappointment washing over her face before she seems to come back to reality and moves away from me.

"So..." she says, smoothing out her dress and walking over to the porch swing to put some distance between us.

My eyes follow her every movement. The way her hair is slightly messy from where my fingers were just tangled, the red blotchy skin on her chest and neck caused by the heat between us, the way her lips are swollen from our kiss. I need to get a grip on myself, but all I want to do is march over there, pin her against that swing, and kiss her all over again.

I exhale, clamping a palm to the back of my neck, squeezing away the tension. "I kind of lost control there for a second. I'm sorry."

"Don't be." She smirks, her fingers touching her lips, a

dazed look washing over her face. "Waiting a decade will do that."

"So, what now?" I ask.

She winces as reality hits her. "Well, we still need to talk about...everything. I've avoided it long enough."

I've been avoiding the conversation just as much as she has, if not more, because there is something I haven't told her about that night, and I'm terrified that it might ruin what just happened between us. Wanting to hang on to this feeling for just a little bit longer, I suggest, "Would you like to come over later? I could cook us dinner, and we could talk after?"

She purses her lips together, considering my proposal, and gives me a soft smile as she replies, "Yeah, that would be nice."

Chapter Twenty-Nine

Now

Raine

I pull my car into the driveway that leads to Ryland's cabin. I caught a glimpse of it when Olivia and I attended Ryland's cookout. However, being this close gives me a sense of familiarity as I take in its worn wooden exterior. It looks like a typical two-story cabin in the woods, but the updates Ryland has made over the years have brought it back to life.

The roof has been redone, now the same color as the updated dark-green front door. A wooden balcony on the top floor has been added to match the refurbished front porch that wraps around to the back. I've always loved the large windows that allow the people inside to enjoy the gorgeous landscape of evergreens and the blue water of the lake.

Covewood brings a variety to its people and travelers. Where there are rolling green hills full of farmlands, there are also flourishing wooded areas next to the large lake. People come from all over to escape while visiting Covewood. My life before was spent despising this place and wanting to run away from it, only to find my soul secretly yearning to return to my roots.

"Hey," Ryland says softly, the crinkles by his eyes showing

as he makes his way down the porch steps. He's wearing a gray long-sleeve shirt with the sleeves rolled up to his elbows and a pair of blue jeans. My gaze trails up his veiny forearms to the swell of his muscular shoulders and up to his multicolored irises.

He waltzes toward me, placing his hands onto my waist, and leans in to press his lips against my own. I grin, closing my eyes, and wait. However, a tiny squeal interrupts us.

"Raine!" Annabelle rushes past her dad and wraps me into a hug before pulling me toward the cabin. "I helped Daddy cook dinner! Come see what we made."

I giggle and allow her to lead the way, catching a glimpse of Ryland as he shakes his head. Annabelle leads me through the living room and into the kitchen. Once we're at the stove, she prompts me to pick her up.

"We made chicken poop." She beams and points toward the skillet.

"You made what?" I ask, my eyes growing wide.

Ryland barks out a laugh as he shuts the front door behind him. "That's what Pops named the meal years ago."

My eyebrows raise when I look down to study what exactly is for dinner. Whatever it is, it smells amazing and thankfully looks nothing like chicken poop. I can make out small pieces of cooked chicken and sliced browned potatoes with shredded cheese melted on top.

"I cooked this for Pops, and he loved it. One day, I asked him what he'd like for dinner, and he told me to whip up some of that chicken *poop* he loved." He chuckles at the memory. "However, Pops said a bad word instead. So, we started calling it chicken *poop*. Annabelle has a fun time telling people we eat chicken poop for dinner, if you couldn't tell."

Ryland slides in behind us, his hand finding the spot on my lower back, and smiles down at me. "Just trust us, you'll love it."

Annabelle giggles, pressing her fingers by her lips before

adding, "Yeah, trust us." *I can trust them with my heart*, a little voice sings in the back of my mind.

"Okay," I reply, and Annabelle's smile completely melts me.

I realize that I never asked Ryland about Annabelle's mother or why she isn't a part of their life. It makes me sad for Annabelle, knowing how it felt to have an absent parent. But that sorrow is replaced with joy as I watch her hop from my arms and run into her father's. She's nothing but a ball of happiness and love, a reflection of her father's parenting. The sight of them together makes me swoon.

I take out my phone and snap a quick photo of them, wanting to freeze this moment in time. While the two of them finish preparing dinner, I walk around the living room. One of my favorite things to do in someone's home is look at the photographs they hang on their walls. To me, it tells a lot about someone's heart with what they display in their home. I wish that photographs were like tunnels, that you could crawl inside them and go back to that moment.

Photographs of Ryland's younger years hang near the hallway that leads to the bedrooms. Zane and him hiking together. Ryland sitting next to his Nan on the porch. Ryland's mother wrapping her two boys in a tight hug and smiling so brightly. Pops looking proud as the boys hold up a large fish. So many sweet photographs I've seen before.

Then I move through the living room and see moments I've missed. A grown Ryland with his Pops next to their company office. Many photographs of family members with Annabelle, always surrounded by love. The ones that tug my heart the most are, of course, the photographs of Annabelle throughout the years, watching her grow through each image.

Behind his couch sits a large canvas of Ryland holding a newborn Annabelle in his arms. I don't know why it's bothering me at this moment, knowing how much I have missed since leaving, but it does. Here we are, days away from the farmhouse being finished, and I'm expected to return to my life in Rockdale. However, I don't want to leave.

I want to stay.

I sense Ryland behind me. The scent of him wraps around me, filling my nose. I turn and look at him as he reaches into his back pocket and pulls out his wallet. As he unfolds the leather and pulls out a small piece of paper, I notice it's not paper but a photograph. It's the Polaroid image of me at fifteen, standing in front of the oak tree at the farm that Ryland captured what feels like a lifetime ago.

A bashful grin tugs against his lips as his hazel eyes move from the photo to my face. "I've carried this with me ever since the day that I took it." he admits.

My heartbeat picks up, a growing reaction my body seems to have when I'm around Ryland. He brings his arms around me and places my head perfectly onto his chest. I breathe in his scent again and close my eyes, allowing myself to enjoy every bit of this embrace.

"I love you," I whisper, loving how comforting it feels to say it.

I feel his breath catch, like my words affect him just as much as his do to me. He gives the top of my head a kiss, the gesture zipping down my body and tingling my toes. "I love you, Rainbow."

We hear Annabelle shout that dinner is ready, and we make our way to the table hand in hand. She catches our hands together and gives me a grin as she points to a chair. "Raine sits here."

I take my seat, folding my long skirt under my legs, and notice the plate she sits before me has Disney characters decorating it. "You broke out the fancy china tonight, I see."

"Fancy china?" she asks, scrunching up her nose.

She points to the chair that sits in front of me and has Ryland take his seat. "Sweet, I scored the Aladdin plate," Ryland states and beams at his daughter.

"It's your favorite," she says matter-of-factly before sliding into the seat next to me. "Daddy knows all of the songs and likes to act like the Genie."

My eyes widen. "Oh, I would love to see that!"

"I bet you would," Ryland adds before taking a drink from his cup, which also matches his plate.

We reach out and intertwine our hands together before bowing our heads and thanking God for our meal. Then, we dig in. And the food is absolutely mouth-watering. Ryland filled a toasted tortilla with the chicken, potato, and cheese concoction along with sour cream and picante sauce.

"Oh my gosh," I mumble through a mouthful. I don't miss how Ryland's eyes brighten with satisfaction. How they trail down my face until they land on my neck as I swallow. "This is delicious."

"Told ya!" Annabelle shouts, tossing her hands in the air with a beaming smile, earning a chuckle from her father that slithers down into my heart.

After we finish up dinner, I help Annabelle wash the dirty dishes. We end up soaked in water with beards made out of bubbles. Ryland laughs and snaps a few photos of us before snatching Annabelle away to get her a change of clothes. When he comes back into the kitchen, I have the dishes dried and put away.

He hands me a Kentucky blue sweatshirt to change into. I go into the bathroom to change and inhale his scent, knowing there is no way I'm giving this back to him. I take off my soft-pink tank top and pull the sweater over my head. Thankfully, my skirt is just a little damp. As I step back into the living room, Ryland's eyes are heavy-lidded at the sight of me in his clothes.

"I'm keeping this," I tell him before Annabelle jumps between us, clothed in *Bluey* pajamas, and pulls us to the living room couch.

"Can we please watch *Aladdin* before bed, Daddy?"

Ryland looks at his watch and then to me before asking, "Want to watch *Al—*"

"Yes!" I say a little too loudly, earning a laugh from him.

"Alright, then I'll go get us some cookies to eat while we watch." He winks at me, and I swear I have one of those moments you only see in Hallmark movies where my knees become weak, and I flop myself onto his couch with a sigh.

Annabelle places her tiny hand into mine, scooting in close beside me. She turns, looks at me, and from her expression I expect her to ask a serious question. However, I can't hide the laugh that escapes me as she asks, "Okay, if you had to choose between marrying Aladdin or Kristoff, who would it be?"

"Most definitely Aladdin," Ryland says to her, winking at me as he sets down a plate of cookies.

"Good, because I wanted Kristoff." Annabelle crosses her arms and gives me a proud smile before shoving a cookie into her mouth, much like her father does at the same time.

Ryland leans back against the couch, making sure his arm is across the back so he can place a hand on my shoulder. Annabelle is squeezed in between us. He hits play on the movie, and Annabelle wasn't lying about Ryland knowing every song. I haven't laughed this hard in a long time, but watching him mimic the Genie, word for word, including the gestures, is the best thing I've ever witnessed. I make sure to record a video to watch later.

Once Aladdin sinks to the bottom of the water, we hear soft snores coming from Annabelle. Her head is leaning against Ryland and her hand is still wrapped in mine. Ryland notices and gives me a gentle smile as he whispers, "I'll get her into bed. Want to hang out on the porch?"

"I mean, I'd like to see you finish your performance, but I guess we can save that for another time."

"Another time," he repeats before pulling Annabelle into his arms. "There's some Ale-8's in the fridge. Why don't you grab us some, and I'll meet you on the porch?"

I grab two bottles from his fridge and make my way to his back porch. I take a seat in one of Ryland's wooden rocking chairs, and as I take my first satisfying sip and inhale the scent of the forest, nostalgia hugs me. I've always loved it here, being surrounded by these woods and the lake, a teenage boy deciphering my dreams and promising to make them come true.

Ryland slides the back door closed behind him and scoots his chair closer to me before picking up his drink. We hold our bottles out, clink them together, and say, "Cheers!" like we used to do. He pops open the lid and takes a big glub. I shamelessly stare as he closes his eyes, throat bobbing with each gulp, a joyful, "Ahh," sound escaping his full lips afterward. He looks at me, his smile moving slowly across his face like a moonrise.

"So," he says, rubbing his hands together and leaning his elbows onto his long legs.

"You've done a great job with Annabelle," I tell him before taking a swig of my drink, savoring the familiar flavor.

"Thank you. I can't take all the credit, of course. Mom helps a lot. She's had great influences in her life. Pops, Zane, your grandparents..." His eyes glance over the lake, looking as if his mind is far away in the past.

I finally ask the question I've been dying to have an answer to. "What's the story with Annabelle's mom?"

He lets out a whistle and pushes himself to lean back against his chair, his hazel eyes lightened by the reflection of the moonlight. He hesitates for a moment before looking at me.

"If you feel comfortable sharing it with me," I add, pulling my legs up to hug them close to my chest.

He drags a palm down his jaw, exhaling deeply, and his shoulders drop from the weight this topic must bring him.

"When you left, my whole world fell apart. I was depressed. Any free moment I had, I'd drown my pain with alcohol. Whiskey was easier for me to swallow than accepting that I messed up and you weren't coming back."

My breath hitches at his words, not expecting him to start the story with us.

"Raine, you were everywhere. Everywhere but physically with me. And it *hurt*. I couldn't go to certain places without memories of you coming to the surface. I couldn't listen to certain songs. Even certain scents brought you back to me. And it broke me over and over again."

There are some memories that are unforgettable that remain vivid. I can tell this is one for Ryland. His choices after I left took a toll on him. It's hard accepting how badly we broke each other.

"I met Maggie, Annabelle's mom, two summers after you left. She was staying at the rental cabin with her folks, but we met at one of those bonfire parties people like to throw at the lake. I had no intention of finding someone else, but once we started talking and I realized she was just as broken as me, we bonded over our shared love of whiskey. I didn't know it at the time, but we were very toxic to one another. Thankfully, she was only visiting for a short time—or so I thought.

"After Maggie left that summer, we had no plans of keeping in contact, but after a few months had went by, she found me on Facebook and messaged me to call her. It seemed urgent, so I did, and that was when she told me she was pregnant."

Ryland's face falls, and he runs a hand through his hair. His eyes find mine again, and my chest tightens. Ryland places his elbows on his legs, his hands folded together, as he continues.

"I was so scared. I kept thinking, who am I to try to raise a kid? What if I ended up just like my father?"

"You'll never be like him," I say, my voice sounding small.

"I was very close to being like him back then. But after I told Pops and Mom, they reminded me that it wasn't about me anymore and that I needed to get right in every aspect of my life. They basically gave me an intervention, and after a lot of prayer and guidance from the man upstairs, I drove all the way to

Colorado and begged Maggie to come live in Covewood with me.

"Her family was not supportive of her decision, but my family was. So, Mom and Zane moved in with Pops and they gave this cabin to me and Maggie to live and raise Annabelle in."

"Did you love Maggie?" the question leaves my lips. I'm not sure why I need to know, but I feel it in my core. I have to know if he loved her. I want to know everything I've missed in his life since I left.

"I cared. I had respect for her, but I don't think I ever allowed myself to fall in love with her. *I couldn't.*" His eyes pierce my own.

I feel the weight of what he is saying. Ryland is looking at me with such tender affection that it feels like a kiss. A knuckle under my chin, pulling me toward his face.

He looks out toward the lake and continues, "I did, however, fall head over heels for a tiny little girl. Annabelle stole my heart the moment I first held her in my arms. I never understood how she didn't steal Maggie's heart, but after a few months, Maggie started leaving for long hours and would come home either high or drunk. I believe she was suffering from postpartum depression, but she refused any help that I offered her.

"One day, she told me that she didn't feel like she could be a mom and said she wanted to sign her rights over. I tried to argue with her, but she had made up her mind. Annabelle was nine months old when her mother chose to leave her. It has been the two of us since, and I made sure to turn my life around after Annabelle was born. She saved me. She gave me my life back."

We stay silent for a while, a storm slowly brewing within my gut from his words, as I realize how self-centered I have been this whole time.

"I'm so selfish," I whisper, allowing the words to hang between us for a moment before I continue. "I chose to leave because of my own fears and selfish reasons. I didn't think about how it might affect others. I honestly thought everyone would be fine without me."

His expression softens as he replies, "It wasn't your fault, Raine. I was the one who tore us apart."

Ryland deserves to know that I no longer hold the mistakes of his youth against him. "You were scared, Ry. I get it now. I didn't have to leave, but I was so hurt and living in constant fear. I just—"

The sound of his exhale catches my attention. I watch as he runs a hand over the hair along his jaw before meeting my eyes. "There's more to the story."

Chapter Thirty

Ten Years Before

Ryland

The moonlight bounces off the lake's surface, reflecting in Raine's eyes as she looks up at the stars above us. I bite my lip and fight against the urge to kiss her. Kissing her always enchants me, and I don't want to lose my focus. I brought her to the lake for a reason. I want her to be surrounded by the calmness as I break the news to her.

Our feet are pedaling in sync together as we move through the lake water in the pedal boat. I wrap my arm around her and bring her close, enjoying the scent of her floral shampoo as her hair hits my nose. I give her head a kiss and try to muster up the courage that I need to get this off my chest. I've held onto this news for weeks now, lost countless hours of sleep, and know that this isn't going to be an easy conversation.

But it needs to happen tonight.

"It feels surreal that we finally graduated," she whispers and snuggles closer to me.

There's so much joy laced in her words. The moment we tossed our graduation caps into the air, I saw the weight lift from her. The world around us seemed to move in slow motion as I watched her smile grow and a cheer leave her lips. I've never seen Raine as happy as she was today.

I hate myself for what I'm about to tell her.

"The future is ours!" she shouts, throwing her hands into the air and smiling brilliantly at me. Her smile falters the moment she takes in my expression. "What is it?"

"I have something that I need to talk to you about," I admit.

Raine brings her arms down, and her body grows stiff with anticipation. I think she knows what I'm about to say, but I'm not a hundred percent sure. Either way, this all sucks and is unfair.

She shifts her weight, turning so that she's facing me, and watches me closely as she waits for my explanation. The rainbow necklace is between her fingers, and she's twisting it nervously. I run a hand through her hair, playing with the brightly colored strands between my fingers, hoping to calm her. She's absolutely beautiful.

And she deserves so much more than what I can give her.

Her eyes dance with mine, searching for the answer, and as her eyebrows draw together, I know she has found a piece of the truth lying within them. I inhale deeply, allowing the murky water scent to fill my lungs, and I take a second to prepare what I have to say to her.

I reach for her hand, thankful that she allowed me to pull her closer, and lock my eyes onto hers. "Pops isn't doing so well."

I try to hide the quiver within my voice, but as Raine's brows pinch together, I know she heard it. The pain written upon my face reflects on hers. She grabs my hand tighter, bracing the two of us for what's to come. She already knows what I need to say without even speaking the words. With us, silence has always been a conversation.

"I— Zane and I— We talked for a long time last night about how we could help Pops. With Nan gone, it's like his broken heart has been too much for him to handle. It's made things worse for him knowing my plan to leave after graduation. The past few months, Pops' business has been falling apart, and he can't seem to keep any reliable or trustworthy help."

She squeezes my hand. "You want to stay and help him."

I nod my head. I know what this means for our plans. We are supposed to use our savings, find an affordable place to live, and go to college together in a town that would give us distance from here. One that would be close enough that we can travel back home to visit family and friends. Raine would finally have her freedom, and with that, we can be together without Davis coming between us.

However, I can't ignore what my heart is telling me. I have to do what's best for the ones that I love. I have to let Raine go.

"I can't leave him, Raine. Not right now. Not like this. He's —" The words are lodged in my throat as emotions swell inside me.

Raine reaches up and places a hand against my cheek. "I know how important Pops is to you. I think you should stay. We'll figure something out together."

Growing up with a selfish father who was abusive helped me to appreciate just how good of a man my Pops is. He stepped into my life and did everything he could to heal my heart. Pops is my hero. If anyone shined the light of Jesus, it was him. He doesn't deserve to walk through this grief alone.

Watching him have to say goodbye to the love of his life has been *the* hardest thing I've ever been through in my nineteen years of life. I wouldn't be able to live with myself knowing that I abandoned him when he needed me the most. I owe him more than that.

But to hinder Raine's plans of freedom...that hurts just as bad, if not more. Because I know if Davis continues to control her—and he's made it clear that he will—she won't be happy. And what if she resents me afterward?

"I don't want to change our plans," I admit, leaning my cheek into her palm.

"I know that. But right now, you need to be here for Pops," she whispers as a large tear rolls down her cheek. I can't watch her cry, so I look down at our hands. "So, we'll stay, and we can reevaluate after six months and go from there. I want to be able to help Pops too, if I can."

My head snaps up to look at her. "What?" My nose crinkles in confusion.

"I'm not leaving you, Ryland." Raine's eyes soften to warm, bright puddles of blue.

"You have to. There's no way that I'm going to let you stay and suffer any longer. You have to go. We can try long distance for a while until I get Pops back on his feet and feel comfortable leaving," I plead and wipe away the wetness from her cheeks.

"Long distance will suck," she says softly and moves her focus onto a boat that's drifting in the distance. The waves find their way toward us, crashing against the pedal boat, rocking us back and forth, much like how life is treating us at this moment. "I don't want to be miles away from you."

"I know. I don't want that either," I add, taking both of her hands into mine. "But I refuse to let you—"

"No. That isn't going to work with me because wherever you are, I'm going to be. Wherever you decide to go, I will follow. I love you, Ryland, with every fiber of my being, and I can't imagine a life where you aren't a part of it. And not just on the weekends but daily! I'm done with limiting my time with you. I want every second of every day to be consumed by you. That's what I want. That's what I need in my life. I know you want me to be free, but it would be a life of prison without you. Don't you get that?"

Raine fists my shirt in her hands and pulls me forward until our lips touch, hands against skin and bodies fusing together. Kissing her feels like lighting a match and watching it go up in flames. Raine's hand slides into the collar of my shirt, and my eyes roll to the back of my head.

She sighs against my mouth, and I take advantage, kissing

her harder, until we're both gasping. I let my mouth slide along her collarbone. Not kissing, but just feeling, memorizing. Because for some reason this feels like it could be our last kiss, and I don't want to waste it. Raine's breath comes in loud, panting gasps, and when I look up at her, I don't think I have the strength to let her go.

Here she is, willing to sacrifice her dreams and freedom because of how much she loves me. And here I am, trying to convince myself that maybe if she stays, everything will work out. I don't know how I ended up being so selfish.

"We're going to miss the party," I say breathlessly, desperately wanting to cling to anything other than the uncertainty of our future together. "Let's enjoy the rest of the night, and we can talk about this tomorrow," I add, giving her hand an encouraging squeeze.

A cool breeze blows around us, pushing her hair across her face, hiding her expression from me. I wish I could crawl inside her mind at this moment, to know how she feels, to see what she sees. To understand better.

"Alright," she replies.

A half hour later, I drive us to the location of our graduation party. The unanswered questions vibrate between us, eating me alive, but we both stay silent. Raine and I don't do parties, but I begged her to go to this one with me. I wanted one last night to enjoy each other, to not allow the unknown about our future to weigh so heavily on our shoulders, and to soak in these last moments with our graduating class.

I shut my door and jog around my car to open the door for Raine. Before I allow her to move past me, I lean in and give her a kiss. Her breath hitches, and I feel her tighten under my grip.

"Let's forget about the future for a bit and just enjoy our night together, okay?" I practically beg her before we link our hands together and walk toward the crowd.

The graduation party is held at a beachy area by the lake. A large bonfire blazes light around a group of what looks to be about thirty of our classmates. Music is blasting from a speaker that sits next to two kegs and several coolers that I'm sure are packed full of alcohol. How do they expect the cops not to show up tonight?

I find Luke, and he wraps an arm around my shoulders. The scent of alcohol punches me in the face as he shouts, "The party can officially begin, boys!"

"It smells like the party has already started." I wave a hand in front of my face and laugh at my friend as he trips over a log and falls onto his back. I reach a hand out and help him up, and that's when I see it—a shiny black bruise under his right eye.

Raine sees it too. She inhales and reaches up to touch his eye. "Luke, what happened?"

He shoves her off him lightly, and his once chipper mood quickly dissolves into disgust. "It's nothing for you to worry about."

"It's not nothing!" she argues.

"Just leave it, okay? I don't feel like hashing it with you tonight." Hurt washes over her face, and as much as I love my best friend, I could give him a second black eye for treating her so harshly. Raine shakes her head, her eyes finding mine for a second before she mumbles something about finding Olivia and stomps away.

"What's your deal, man?" I hiss and tug him to the side, away from the rowdy group.

"Who do you think?"

Who. I should have known. I cross my arms together and raise a brow, waiting for him to explain. "My dad showed up to my mom's house after the ceremony, and we got into an argument. And because I'm eighteen now and refuse to let him control my life anymore, he made sure I had a souvenir to remind me that I'm wrong."

Luke lifts up his dark-green shirt, revealing another bruise on his ribcage. How could a person be such a monster? I thought my father was bad, but Davis takes the cake. Unlike me, Luke doesn't have a positive male figure to help him heal, like Pops was for me, and it breaks my heart for him. The thought sends hot rage down my spine.

"If my mom didn't need me, I would move away with you and Raine," he confesses, looking toward the crowd and pulling a bottle of beer to his lips.

"I, uh..." I start to say, but my throat feels dry. "We're not—"

"You're not what?" he says, snapping his head to look at me.

"We're not leaving."

I look over the crowd before I find Raine. She's a few feet away, closer to the water line, sitting next to Olivia on a log. Olivia is listening intently to whatever Raine is telling her, and she reaches over to give her a big hug. Raine's back is to me, but Olivia's eyes are searching the crowd, and once she finds me, I don't miss the sharpness in her gaze.

"I can't leave. I'm staying to help Pops out for a while. Raine refuses to leave without me."

The laugh that escapes Luke is wicked. He brings the bottle back to his lips and takes a big swig before tossing the empty bottle onto the ground. "You're so selfish. She can't stay here. If you think my dad treats me bad, you have no idea what he'll do to Raine. Even though she'll be eighteen in a few weeks, that means nothing to him. As long as she's here, he'll make sure she slowly rots."

"But she can live with her grandparents for a while until we—"

"That never stopped him before. He's addicted to control, and you can't save her. Nothing can except distance. He'll find a way to ruin her."

He'll ruin her.

The words ring inside my head and sink deeply into my heart. I'm supposed to protect Raine, not put her in danger. I know Luke is right. Davis will never stop, and I'm going to be the reason she can't get away from him.

Selfishly, I want her to stay, but when you love someone, sometimes you have to choose to let them go. Promise me you'll make sure she gets out of this town.

The promise I had made to her Mamaw sobers me to the reality of our choices. If I choose to go with Raine, I'll be selfish in leaving my family when they need my help. If I let Raine stay, it'll be for my own selfishness. There's only one way to do this right by everyone, and it's for me to deny what I want most.

"I have to break up with her," I admit, and the words taste sour in my mouth.

"What?" Luke slurs, his face contorting.

"If I break up with her, she won't have a reason to stay, and she'll leave." I say it matter-of-factly, shrugging my shoulders before peering off into the distance to where Raine and Olivia are still seated. "I love her enough to let her go."

"That's not what I was trying to say," Luke's voice quivers, and he turns toward me, his eyes brimmed with tears. It's the first time I've seen Luke break down his walls and truly shown how broken he is. Davis did that to him. Luke wipes his cheeks and exhales. "But I don't want him to hurt her."

"I don't want that either," I proclaim, holding up my hands, allowing the truth to settle deep within my gut.

He nods, running a hand through his hair before limping away and leaving me alone with my thoughts. Hatred for Davis lights every nerve in my body on fire until I'm consumed with rage. I have to destroy what Raine and I have because of *him.*

But how do I break up with Raine? I look around, begging for an idea to pop out at me, when I see Luke with a shot of something honey brown in his hand. Raine and Olivia are making their way around the fire toward him. Fury seems to be leading my actions, and without thinking, I stomp my way toward Luke and snatch the small glass from his hands.

Raine's eyes widen as she looks at the shot in my hand and begins shaking her head. I despise how she's looking at me. Disbelief and fear wash over her expression. I look at her, focusing on my hatred for Davis, and toss back the fiery liquid.

"Ryland!" she hisses, her mouth hanging open as if she can't believe I did that. I get it because I can't believe it either.

But the need to get her out of Covewood is what's driving me.

"Why?" She shakes her head again, her eyes trailing me up and down. In order to keep my promise to her Mamaw, I have to break a promise I made to Raine. We always said we would never drink alcohol because we both saw how it ruined the lives of our parents. I knew taking a shot in front of her would make her angry with me and, in turn, help me find a way to break up with her.

Even so, I loathe myself right now.

"You know why," I grumble, my voice sounding foreign. "We both know that no matter what we do, we're over."

She blinks, clearly bewildered at how I'm acting, and I feel myself start to slip and want to say I'm sorry. But the image of Raine with Luke's bruises on her face takes over my thoughts, and it's enough to push me to do what I need to do.

"What are you talking about? Where is this coming from all of a sudden?" she hisses, shaking her head in disbelief.

"If you stay, you'll hate me for it. If I go, I'll hate you for it. No matter what choice we make, we'll end up destroying each other."

"That's not true." I watch as fresh tears drop from her eyes, and my stomach tightens, threatening to spill out the whiskey that is currently splashing inside my gut. Olivia wraps an arm around Raine's waist, her wide eyes studying me in surprise.

"I realize now that we just need to rip the Band-Aid off,

Raine. We're over." I speak so fast I can hardly understand myself, but if I don't hurry and get the words out, I never will.

Her face contorts with hurt. "No."

"Yes. I'm not going to try to pretend like this is going to work out between us. I would rather get this over with now so we can both move on with our lives."

"Move on with our lives? Ryland, you are my life. I love you. I don't want to—" A sob escapes her, and something in my chest breaks. Sometimes, in life, you have to choose between which painful route you need to take. I'm choosing the pain of letting Raine go. She'll thank me for it later. Even if I hate myself for it, even more than I hate Davis.

"I'm about to—" Olivia shouts, her hands balled into tight fists, but Luke slides in beside her and tugs her away from us. "Luke, let me go!" she shouts in the distance.

I feel it now, my walls crumbling down around us, and I hate this. I hate hurting her. Why does it have to be this way? But I love her too much to let her stay in a place where she'll rot away. Maybe this way I can figure out things with Davis. Get him put in jail like he deserves or send him packing far away. I need time to do that. I need her safe. And in order to do that, I need her to go.

"Ry, don't do this," she begs.

"I promised your Mamaw I'd—" I let the words slip, my lips quivering. "It'll be better if you leave." Before I can ruin anything else, I turn and walk away.

Chapter Thirty-One

Now

Raine

He lied so I would be safe.

Those words bounce through my head over and over again as I pace up and down Ryland's porch. I can't hear the crashing sound of the lake water or the wood squeaking underneath each step that I take. All I hear is the memory of Ryland's words: *"It'll be better if you leave."*

He made it clear that he chose to break up with me because he wanted to protect me. In true Ryland fashion, he was putting someone else's needs in front of his own. He broke my heart that night; but Ryland wasn't the reason I chose to run away.

"That night destroyed me," I whisper, allowing the tears to escape. I stop in my tracks to turn and look at Ryland. His face contorts, as if my words physically hurt him. I close my eyes and suck in a breath. "But I didn't leave because you told me to."

I open my eyes and blink away the tears so that I can study Ryland. If only he knew how hard it was for me to accept the fact that he didn't love me as much as he once promised. If only he felt how hard it was for me to move away and start over in a place that never felt like home. Because he *was* my home. However, it is time we both overcome the past.

"Something else happened that night. Something I haven't even told Luke yet." I add.

"What happened?" he says finally, pushing himself up from his rocking chair and taking a step toward me. "What don't I know?"

I don't want to tell him. Because the very thing he was trying to protect me from still happened. I know the truth will crush him, but I also know we won't be able to heal from the past if we continue to ignore it. It needs to all be laid out so we can finally move on.

"That night, when I left the graduation party, I came back here," I start, and my hands beginning to tremble as the memories flood my thoughts.

Ryland stands firm in his place, watching me closely, and I want to reach out and comfort him. But I also want to jump into my car and drive far away from this conversation. Every nerve in my body is telling me to run, but I'm done running.

"I went down to the dock, and I waited for you to come home. But you never did." I learned later that he ended up getting drunk and crashed at Luke's house. I don't know why I assumed he would even think to come home after drinking, because his mother and Pops would have been furious with him. But I hoped anyway that we could fix us. That the one shot was all he had, that he realized his mistake, but that's not what happened.

I can see the regret weighing on his shoulders, but instead of sliding into his arms, I lace my fingers together and squeeze, attempting to get my hands to quit shaking before I continue.

"It was late by the time I left here. I was supposed to be staying the night at Olivia's house, but I didn't want to risk getting her in trouble if I showed up well past midnight. If I went to my grandparents' house, I would have woken them up, and they would have asked questions as to why I was upset, and

I didn't want to deal with that at the time. I didn't want them to be upset with you either, so I ended up going home."

I want to talk about what happened without mentioning how much it hurt. There has to be a way to care for the wounds without reopening them, to name the pain without inviting it back in.

God give me strength to say what needs to be said.

"I figured they'd be asleep at that late hour or at least passed out by then. However, Mom and Davis were awake. They were in the living room together when I entered the house, and I caught Davis and his goons making plans for their next heist or whatever it was that they were planning at the time. I don't remember the details. All I do remember is smarting off to him as I rushed to my bedroom. Before I could shut my door, Davis stood in the way and stomped into my room."

At this point, I've stopped crying, focusing more on getting the words out. Ryland places both hands on the back of his head and is now pacing in front of me. *Come on Raine, get the words out.*

"He, uh—" The words are caught in my throat. Ryland stops pacing and stands still for a brief moment. I stare at the back of his head, studying the way his dark hair curls at the nape of his neck, and fight the urge to rub my fingers through its strands and bring him to me for comfort. "He made sure I knew I wasn't allowed to speak to him like that. Nor was I allowed to say anything about what I saw or heard about his plans."

Ryland twists around, his eyes studying me, and my fingers involuntarily travel up toward the scar above my left eyebrow. His eyes follow the movement, realization hitting him hard, and finally he's had enough and closes the distances between us. He rushes toward me, placing one hand on my lower back and the other on the back of my skull.

"Rainbow, I'm so sorry," he whispers into my hair, kissing the top of my head, and the sob I was holding back finally slips through as I let myself feel this pain. I make a promise to myself that this will be the last time that I'll feel this pain because after I finish telling this story, I'll let it go. It doesn't have permission to be a part of my life anymore.

"And then my mom..." I pause to suck in a breath of air.

Ryland's body tenses under my arms before he pulls away, his hands traveling toward my face, staring down at me until I continue.

"She ran into the room and pushed Davis away from me. She turned around and told me to leave."

"Raine, I need you to run away from here and don't come back. Do you understand me?" Her eyes dance with mine. They're the clearest I've seen in years. She wipes my forehead, revealing fresh blood on her hands as she attempts to clean my wound.

"Shannon, you're gonna—" Davis' words are cut off as my mother shoves him back into the wall before looking back at me.

"Run!" she shouts, and I do exactly as she says. I run.

Trauma has a way of permanently changing a person. That's what happened to me that night, and I never really got over it. Through the years, I tried to find some kind of peace with it. I had came to terms with the fact that there was no going back to who I was before.

"I didn't leave because of you. I ran because of fear. I knew you were scared, and I was ready to forgive you and fight for us, but then, after Davis... I chose to leave behind what we could've had. Everyone told me to leave, and I listened. I told myself the lie that I would only be happy if I moved away, that everyone was better off without me. I hung onto something that wasn't real. And because of that, I was the one who broke me."

Ryland was the first person I showed my heart to. And he was the reason I hid it from everyone else. I came to terms with the fact that he was a piece of me that I could never get back. I never stopped loving him. I just stopped letting it show. I demolished my bridges behind me until there was no choice but to move forward.

"I let ten years waste away when we could have been..."

He runs his thumbs across my cheeks, wiping away the wetness, and shushes me. "Don't say that. It wasn't your fault," he says, his eyes intent on my face. I let the confession press against me, the words ringing in my ears. I hold his gaze and blink as he stares right back. He releases his hold on me with a sigh, his hand finding its way through his hair.

"It wasn't yours either," I reply, and he lets out a disbelieving sound.

"I could have found you. Could have tried to fix things. But I didn't feel worthy."

"You're carrying crosses that you don't need to. For far too long, I've held a death grip on the past, but I need to let this go. We both do."

I reach out and tug Ryland's hand away from his hair. Instead, I place it onto the side of my hip and tug him toward me until our bodies are pressed against each other. It can be hard sometimes to know how to express how much you love someone. I could tell Ryland the words right now, but it would never quite capture the depth of it.

Instead, I choose action because I need him to know that, despite our mistakes, I'm not leaving this time. I wrap my arms around him and place my face against that perfect spot on his chest. As soon as I do, he releases a breath and melts into me, wrapping his arms around me and placing his head on top of mine.

I didn't realize that falling in love with Ryland could be so simple. Or that I could fall in love with him twice. But that's exactly what has happened. It is easy to become completely absorbed in him, as if God has put us together deliberately.

Now that everything has been laid out before us, we can move on from the past, and start living the life we've always wanted. *With each other.*

"I'm staying," I whisper, so softly I'm not sure he hears me, but when he moves to look down at me, I know he did. Even though I've known in my heart for weeks, I made the choice officially after the dinner with my mother. "I mean, I have to return to Rockdale and sort out my lease, and pack my things, and quit my job, but I'm moving back to Covewood."

"You're staying?" he asks, raising one brow, not believing my words.

"Papaw wants me to live at the farmhouse." I bite my bottom lip to try to hide my smile, but it is no use. Saying it out loud is the balm I need on my achy heart. "I—"

He interrupts me with his lips. There has been enough talk, enough hesitation, and definitely enough distance between us. I welcome his mouth on mine. My hands glide down his neck, shoulders, landing on the lower part of his back as I push him closer to me.

"Want to try that whole second-chance thing with me?" I ask, a smirk tugging my lips.

"That's all I've been praying for, Rainbow."

Chapter Thirty-Two

Now

Raine

I didn't realize how little I've accumulated over the years, but it only took a few days to box up my entire apartment. When I arrived back in Rockdale ten days ago, the first few days were spent wallowing in bed, too pathetic to do anything else—similar to how I was when I first moved away from home.

The following Monday, I was back at work and put in my two weeks' notice. My replacement at work has caught on quickly, thankfully, and my boss said if I wanted to return home early, I could. That showed me just how important I was to them. Even the friends I made there have all moved on with their lives and dodged my requests for one last dinner before I leave. The life I built in Rockdale has been completely unaffected by my disappearance. Whereas in Covewood, many are struggling without me.

I run my hands through my hair, tugging it into a messy bun, and walk over to the mirror that hangs in my living room. I stare at my reflection. The skin around my eyes has become sunken and dark from lack of sleep. My lips are pale and dry. I look like a mess.

Being here, in this almost empty apartment, has me feeling claustrophobic while loneliness settles quickly behind my ribcage. How did I think this was what was best for me for so many years? I think the one person who noticed was my Mamaw. It might have been why she started dropping hints here and there that she wanted me to return to Covewood. Maybe she hoped that Ryland and I would end up finding our way back to each other.

I pull my phone out of my back pocket and type out a text message to him.

I miss you. I can't wait to come back home.

I catch the alert saying that he's read my text, and the bubbles begin to do a little dance as he types out a reply.

RYLAND

I can't wait to kiss you.

Miles are between us, and somehow Ryland still knows how to make me blush. Heat creeps up the back of my neck with the image of us kissing. It's washed away with the realization that I won't be able to feel the warmth from his lips for four more days.

Just a few more days.

RYLAND

I don't think I can wait that long.

I start to reply back to him that we've waited ten years, what's a few more days, when a knock on my front door echoes off the bare walls of my apartment. Maybe my so-called friends had a change of heart and want to tell me goodbye after all. I practically skip toward the door, more than ready for someone to distract me from the isolation of this tiny space.

As I swing open the door, my mouth falls open at the sight

of Ryland and Annabelle smiling at me. I blink, not believing my eyes, before I'm convinced that this is not a dream. Annabelle squeals with delight as she jumps from her father's arms into mine.

She wraps me into a tight embrace, bouncing up and down while shouting, "Surprise!"

My hands pat her back, and I stare at Ryland. The look in his eyes is slightly mischievous, with just enough seriousness to cause my heart to palpitate. Never would I have guessed that I would see Ryland here in Rockdale. Ten years ago, I prayed so hard that this would happen. That Ryland would find me and love me again.

Here he is, moving toward me, pushing inside of my apartment, and closing the door behind him with his eyes trained on my mouth. He's really here. Even though we made plans for me to pack up my things and come home as soon as I could, that he would be waiting for me, instead he came to get me.

"We're bringing you home with us." Annabelle says sweetly as she removes herself from my arms and hops up and down. Her face contorts and she squeezes her legs together. "But I have to potty first." She rushes to find the bathroom, leaving Ryland and I sharing a laugh.

Once we hear the door shut, Ryland's lips crash onto mine. His callused hands slide up my neck and grip my hair. He pulls me closer to him to deepen our kiss, and suddenly the room falls away. I become lost within his embrace, and I can't get him close enough to me. I kiss him desperately, the years of missing him catching up to me and pouring out in the form of deep, hungry kisses that leave us panting as we pull away.

But instead of keeping the distance between us, Ryland kisses me again with the same passion as before, his hands clinging to the sides of my face, like he's out of air, and I'm helping to preserve his life. This kiss tells me he has missed me as much as I have missed him.

I let out a soft, involuntary sigh, and his hands move down

my shoulders to land on my hips, giving them a squeeze. He pulls back, just enough to where our noses touch, and our breath hits each other. His eyes search mine, emotions swirling within his honey irises, mirroring my own.

"I told you I couldn't wait," he says, his voice gruff.

I laugh, enjoying the bubble of happiness I feel in my chest. "I had no idea you meant it literally." But I'm so glad that he did. My cheeks hurt from smiling so wide, and my lips are still warm from his kiss. I hop up and wrap my legs around him, hugging him with all four of my limbs.

"You were serious about missing me, huh?" He chuckles into my ear and grunts when I squeeze him tightly.

"I can't believe you're both here!" I admit before pushing back to get a better look at him.

"I couldn't sleep last night. I know you need to collect your things here, but it's been killing me letting you come back here alone. I rearranged my schedule and grabbed Annabelle, and we drove all the way here with every intention of bringing you home with us."

The anticipation we've created the past month evaporates. Tears blur my vision as I'm flooded with relief. He's not going anywhere. Not this time. And neither am I.

"My home is wherever you are."

Epilogue

Thanksgiving - 7 Months Later

Ryland

"I think we might be in over our heads with this whole turkey thing," I hear Raine whisper to Olivia.

Luke chuckles beside me, catching the women's attention and earning us a pair of scowls.

"Don't you dare say a word," Olivia threatens us and points a knife our way. Luke and I shrug in unison, holding our hands up innocently. We share a knowing grin once she returns her attention to the uncooked turkey laid out on top of the kitchen island.

Luke leans in and mutters something before being hit with an uncooked dinner roll, and a bark of laughter comes from Zane as he waltzes to the kitchen table with three Ale-8's, handing two to Luke and me before taking a seat across from us. The three of us snicker at one another before clinking our bottles together as we shout, "Cheers!"

"I'm pretty sure its leg is stuck inside it," Raine proclaims, sending a spew of soda from Zane's mouth before he doubles overs with laughter. Raine gags, and I feel bad for letting her take on this task, knowing how unpleasant an uncooked turkey can be to prep.

I stand up and make my way to her. Placing my arms on either side of her. I press my chest to her back before leaning in, bringing my lips onto the curve of her neck. I leave a trail up her skin until I land next to her ear.

She shivers against me and releases a sigh, as if my mere presence releases some of the pressure she's feeling. I love that I have the same effect on her as she does me. We bring each other a sense of comfort, knowing that, no matter what, we'll always be there for each other and never again have something or someone keeping us apart.

"It'll be fine, I promise," I whisper into her ear, and she leans back against me, placing her head onto my shoulder, looking up at me through her long lashes.

I reach up and move a stray hair away from her forehead before leaning over and giving her a gentle kiss. A kiss that tells her everything she needs to know. She sighs again, this time giving me a small smile that feels like a huge victory, and says softly, "I love you."

"I love you too," I tell her, nuzzling my nose against hers, earning a few playful gagging sounds from Olivia and Zane.

"Get a room!" Zane shouts, giving us an eye roll, his smirk giving away that he doesn't mind. He just enjoys giving us a hard time.

Olivia swats me away. "I'm already feeling queasy, thanks to this naked poultry. I don't need you over here making it worse or distracting my help. Shoo!"

Raine looks over at me with a panicked look in her eyes, and I mouth, "*You got this*," before returning to my seat next to the boys. We watch for a few minutes as Raine and Olivia attempt to get the legs out of the turkey, gagging as they grab the slimy, textured skin, and cheering once the legs are undone.

"Five bucks says that Raine pukes after she gets to the giblets," Zane whispers between us.

"It will be Liv. Make it ten bucks, and you're on," Luke suggests, a mischievous grin tugging his five o'clock shadow.

"You want me to stick my hand in it?" Raine squeals, gaining our attention once again.

"Well, yeah," Olivia says with a chuckle, snorting as she does.

I have to admit, this is more entertaining than the football game that's playing in the background. Annabelle skips into the room, looking for me, and once she sees me, I hold out my arms for her. She smiles brightly and takes off in a jog, moving past me, and jumps into Luke's arms.

"Really?" I say.

"Does this mean I'm better than you?" Luke's deep voice rings as he looks over at me, squeezing my daughter into his arms and then giving her a few tickles.

"You wish." I roll my eyes, acting like it breaks my heart once Annabelle peeks over at me, playing into this game she's created. You can't come between a father and his daughter. I also love that Annabelle has two uncles who are completely smitten with her.

But nothing beats witnessing Raine and Annabelle together. I never knew how much easier life would be with a woman around to help me raise my spunky eight-year-old. Single parenting is not for the weak, and knowing that at the end of the day Raine is there to have my back has been a dream come true.

We tackle parent drop-offs and pickups, meals, playdates, baths, and bedtimes together as if we've been doing this all of Annabelle's life. Lately, Annabelle has been requesting for Raine to tuck her in at night and read her bedtime story. And at the end of the day, I get Raine all to myself. As if I couldn't love Raine any more, witnessing her love my daughter like her own has me head over heels.

Since moving back home, Raine has started her own photography business, and I couldn't be prouder of her for chasing her dreams. She works with small businesses, both local and in the surrounding areas, and she's about to open up her own photography studio next to Potter's Art Studio. She's even dabbled in family photography, saying a certain little girl inspired her. It's been a blessing watching Raine blossom these last seven months.

Down towards the edge of the property we recently started working on building a small cabin in which Earl will move into once it's ready. Raine insisted that he live with her in the farmhouse but he claimed it was his time to let it go. However, she then had me come up with a plan for him to still live on the land in order for her to still keep him close by. It's far enough away that it feels like he has his own privacy but close enough that she can always be there for him. To our surprise, he was thrilled with the idea.

I thank God each day for bringing Raine and me back together. I would go through every ounce of heartache all over again if I knew I would end up happily with Raine in the end.

"Why do people do this? We should've just made spaghetti. Oh my gosh, where is the— This is disgusting!" Olivia shouts as her face begins to pale, and she runs to the trash can.

Raine rushes to Olivia's side, rubbing her back, and moves her hair away from her face as Olivia heaves. Annabelle's lips are pinched together. "Annabelle, why don't you go play outside for a bit so this doesn't scar you for life."

Annabelle nods her head, eyes trained on Olivia, before she replies, "Yeah, it's not fun in here."

Zane takes out his wallet and hands a ten-dollar bill to Luke, who's wearing a smug smile of victory. "I know my Liv."

Olivia stands up, wipes her mouth, and then stomps across the kitchen toward us. We freeze with guilty looks spreading across our faces. Olivia snatches the ten-dollar bill from Luke's grasp and shoves it into her pocket.

"That's mine." She snickers, unties her apron, and tosses it at Luke's face.

He mumbles from under the fabric, "Why?"

"Raine and I are done. You gentlemen can handle the bird."

Raine exhales a sigh of relief and gives me a small smile.

"Raine, do you have a toothbrush I can borrow?" Olivia asks.

"Yeah, come on."

Once the women are gone, the guys and I get to work on the turkey. As I'm prepping the glaze, Luke slides over and nudges me with his elbow. "So, when are you going to do it?"

Zane's head snaps up, watching us closely. I haven't told him I bought the ring yet. The look of betrayal on his face is priceless. "Calm down, hoss cat, I was going to tell you before I proposed. And I was thinking either before or after we eat dinner so that everyone's together. I want everything to be perfect."

"Do it before, with a toast. It might catch her off guard," Zane adds and returns to prepping the bird.

"I'm happy for you both." Luke smiles and turns to the speaker behind us and begins blasting some nineties country music as we get to work.

The weather has worked out for us this evening. It's a little chilly when the wind blows, but otherwise, the weather is tolerable as long as everyone wears a thick sweater. Last month, Earl and I worked together on building two large farm tables to hold at least forty people. Zane surprised us with a miniature one for a kids' table. We rented a huge white tent for the event and strung rows of white Christmas lights.

It took us days to prepare for Thanksgiving, and I have to say, everything looks perfect. I just hope it's everything Raine is hoping for. She carries a tray of buttered rolls to the table, and as she turns around, I snatch her into my arms. She squeals with delight, and I plant kisses on her neck, just as I did in the kitchen. It's hard to keep my hands to myself when she's around.

"What do you think?" I ask, placing my hands into hers.

She looks around, studying the meal laid out on the tables, the groups of people mingling together, and she smiles.

"It's perfect. It's everything I imagined and more." Her tone holds more meaning. I squeeze her hands gently with mine and wait for her to elaborate. Her grayish-blue eyes dance with mine, a certain sparkle shining within them as she continues, "After losing Mamaw and having to face the things I avoided for years, I became the most broken version of myself. But then I came out the other side stronger than ever. God took my broken pieces and made me new again. He led us back together and blessed me with the family I always dreamt of having. Look around us, at our loved ones altogether. What more could I ask for?"

Raine wraps her arms around me, her expression relaxing under the white twinkling lights. It's all the confirmation I need to do something I have dreamt of doing since the day I knew I loved her. I place a hand onto the side of her face, gently leading her closer to me.

"I can think of something," I say, my voice husky.

"Oh yeah? Like what?" Her smile widens, a challenge lacing her words, but she sees something in my face that gives me away.

"Marry me."

She moves back an inch, her eyes wide with shock, only for a split second before they soften with a confirmation of their own. "Now that's all I've ever wanted."

"So, is that a—" She slides a hand into my hair, tipping my head forward before smashing her lips onto mine. For a moment, it's just her and me, until we hear the crowd around us begin to cheer. As she pulls away, our eyes stay locked together. I've been waiting for this moment my entire life.

“Yes. Of course I will.” I can’t contain my smile as I bring her lips back to mine.

“Seven months isn’t too soon?” I ask, my insecurities leaking out, but the look she is giving me erases all of my doubt.

“No, it’s perfect. We’ve waited long enough. I’m ready to keep the promise that we made to each other all those years ago. That we’ll give each other the life we deserve.”

“Together.” I add, remembering the conversation, and bring her in for another kiss before I shout, “She said yes!”

Annabelle runs towards us with a huge smile on her face and I grab both Raine and her into my arms, and spin them around as our close friends and family cheer.

And just like that, together we can finally start living the life we’ve waited and prayed so hard for. A life we didn’t know if we would get back, but God reunited us together and blessed us with a second chance.

Raine looks up at me, a hopeful twinkle in her eyes, the same way she did when we were kids. "We're going to make it this time."

And this time, I know she is right.

Acknowledgments

I'm completely full of joy to have found myself writing *this* page. Because the acknowledgments means I did it! I wrote, edited, re-wrote, edited again and again, and self published my very first novel. And I owe a huge thanks to a lot of people so I apologize in advance at how long this might be. It takes a village to write a book and I'm very thankful for the village God has blessed me with.

So first, I have to start off by thanking God. He prompt me in 2022 to chance my dreams of becoming an author and showed me the book to start my writing career off with. He also helped me to remain faithful to him as I wrote this book, to hopefully shine the light of Jesus through out these pages, and tell the story that He needed me to tell and share with others.

To my husband, I never knew what true love was until I met you. It's because of *you* that I'm a big fan of romance, after all. I love *love* because of how it can redeem someone, much like our own personal story. Thank you Wes, for saving me with your love. For your patiences, your understanding, your listening ear, and your support. Thank you for taking the kids on 'Daddy Dates' so I could stay home and write uninterruptedly. But most of all, thank you for being my biggest cheerleader. I love you so much! More than any cheesy romcom, swoony romance novel, or love song could ever begin to describe.

To my children, Kambryn and Madylin, thank you for letting me chase this dream even though it cut into some of our time together. You were patience with me, always encouraging, and cheered me on through the whole process. I hope that this book will help encourage you both to chase your own dreams and to know that your father and I will always be there for you. You made my life complete when I became your mother. I love you both unconditionally.

To my family, your optimism in me fills my heart with joy. I know without a doubt that each of you will be the first in line to buy this book and knowing that, brings a smile onto my face. It also makes me really nervous for some reason so I hope I wrote a good book! I'm thankful that God chose me to be a part of our family.

To my Papa, yes you get your own little place in this acknowledgment section. After all, Earl's character was formed with you in mind. He is my love letter to *you*. Thank you for everything you've done for me, for loving me like you do, and for being my hero. I sure do love you. *Ps. Does this acknowledgment earn me that spot as your number one granddaughter? (Sorry Ashley, I had to.)*

To my church family, your encouragement has made a huge impact on mine and my family's life. You've been on the side lines cheering for me as I wrote this book. I don't have enough space here to thank each of you, but please know just how truly grateful we are and are so blessed to be a part of The Redemption Church family.

To my friends, so many of you have been supportive from the first day that I announced I had wrote a book and I'm thankful for *each of you*! I love you all so much for your loyalty and kindness and so much more.

Michelle Carstarphen, this book would not be what it is today if it weren't for you! You were the first to read this book at its messiest form and helped me to see that it needed to become a dual timeline. Now, I can't imagine this story told any other way. Thank you for your constant stream of wisdom, listening to me rant about story ideas, and for becoming such a wonderful friend. I'm so thankful to have you in my life and I can't wait for the world to see just how incredible of an author that you are! (*Ps. I hope you liked my little wink towards your character Max in this book.)*

Grayson, Cindy, and Stefanie; to our little writing group that has brought my heart so much joy this year. I would be lost without you ladies! You're always there to answer my questions, lift each other up, and share laughs together. I love you all. Thank you for being in my tribe and for writing amazing stories that I hold close to my heart.

Jamie Russell, You've been a huge part of this book and I couldn't have made it to this page if it weren't for you! How does one even begin to say thank you? Especially since you make sure to give my husband a humbling experience anytime you're around and it brings me so much happiness. You're appreciated and loved my sweet friend. Now can we please have a book and coffee date soon?

Tiffany Dick, since 2010 you've been my writing bestie. It's crazy to think that it's been that long. You got to see Raine and Ryland's story back when I very first developed them in 2015 and helped me through out their many forms. I'm beyond grateful for your wisdom, encouragement, and friendship.

To my Beta Readers, Danielle, Rebecca, Jessee, Mary, Jami, Maggie, Jordon; you took a chance on this book, helped me to catch mistakes, and truly made an impact on this story. I'm forever grateful for each of you.

To my Arcs, who have been my hype squat and who've left honest reviews on social media. Thank you from the bottom of my heart for all that you've done. You are the best and I appreciate everything.

Jenn Lockwood, your editing skills are the best of the best and I appreciate your help in cleaning up this book and getting it ready for the world. Thank you for your flexible schedule, especially since I changed my date a few times. I will be recommending your services to everyone.

Sam with Ink and Laurel, for bringing my book cover

dreams to life. As soon as I made the decision to publish a book, Sam was my first investment. She was patient with my particular vision for this cover and truly out did herself. Sam, your art is incredible.

Melody with Whim and Joy, for creating my character art of young Raine and Ryland. You're one in a million my friend. Melody squeezed me into her schedule, had wonderful communication skills, and finished my art in record time. I am so happy with the art she created for this book and am thankful for the opportunity to work with her. I hope to again someday soon.

To the Bookstagram community and the friends I have made there, thank you for welcoming me with open arms. Each of you have made a point to spread the word of my little book, are always uplifting, and have been extremely kind. I'm grateful to be a part of such a wonderful place on the internet and would love to meet each of you in person one day!

And lastly, to my readers, thank *you*. You took a chance on this book, supported my author dreams, and I wish I could hug each and every one of you. I pray this story touched your heart! I am forever grateful for you.

About the Author

India Tungate is a writer of cozy heartfelt christian romance stories. She is living her own happily ever after in a small town in Kentucky with her husband and two children. She discovered her love for writing at the age of ten and has always dreamed of becoming an author. After the loss of her grandmother in 2020, India finally decided to go for it and publish her debut novel, *Raine, Raine, Run Away.*

India spends her time wearing many hats. Besides writing she also manages her small homestead, homeschooling her children, and running a photography business. When she has time, you can find her making memories with her loved ones, volunteering at her church, reading a sweet romance book, or re-watching *The Office.*

Follow India on Instagram at @indiatungateauthor

Don't forget to leave a honest review on Goodreads and Amazon. Every review and social media share helps tremendously. Thank you for your help!

Printed in Dunstable, United Kingdom

80332391R00201